the fidelity files

the fidelity files

Faithfully yours,

Jessica Brody

Jessica Brody

St. Martin's Griffin New York

This is a work of fiction. All of the characters, organizations, and events portrayed in this novel are either products of the author's imagination or are used fictitiously.

www.stmartins.com

Book design by Spring Hoteling

Interior art design by Chahn Chung

Library of Congress Cataloging-in-Publication Data

Brody, Jessica.
The fidelity files / Jessica Brody — 1st ed.
p. cm.
ISBN-13: 978-0-312-37546-1
ISBN-10: 0-312-37546-8
1. Women private investigators—Fiction. 2. Adultery—Fiction. 3. Man-woman relationships—Fiction. 4. Chick lit. I. Title.
PS3602.R6357F53 2008
813'.6—dc22 2008011567

First Edition: June 2008

10 9 8 7 6 5 4 3 2 1

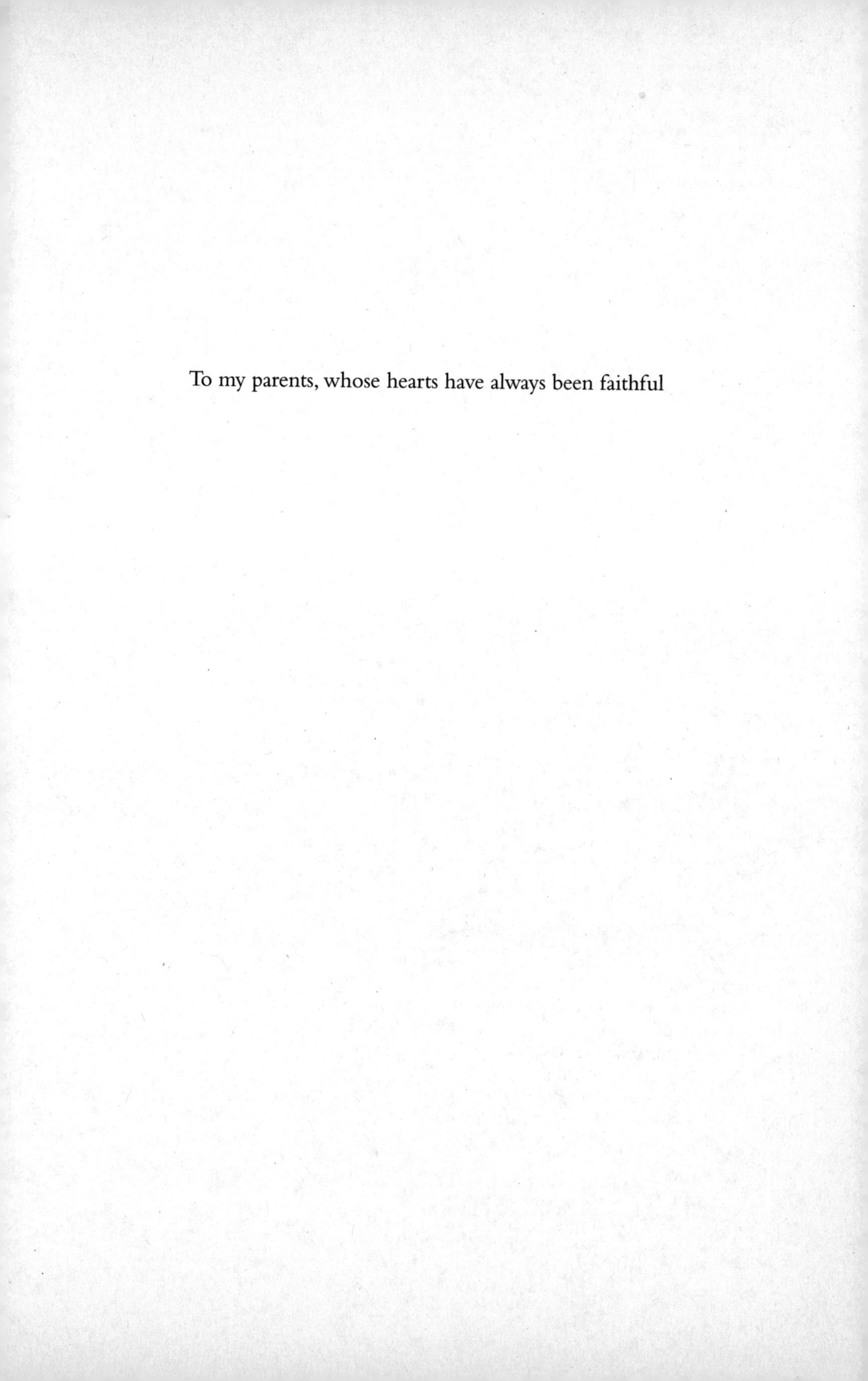

To my parents, whose hearts have always been faithful

the fidelity files

1

changing channels

The man I was looking for was seated comfortably in the back of the hotel bar.

Dark hair, dark suit, tie loosened, top button unbuttoned. He sat alone in a plush, red velvet booth with his left arm casually sprawled out over the top. His fingers gently drummed against the fabric to the beat of the soft lounge music while his other hand methodically brought his nightcap to his mouth for another sip.

I observed him, unseen, from the archway that led into the hotel's lobby.

He was looking for something. Not anything in particular. But something worth distracting him. At least for the night.

I continued to watch as his eyes adeptly found the only other female presence in the bar. He examined her from across the room, and upon taking in her high-rise slacks and unflatteringly conservative turtleneck, looked away, discouraged, and took another sip of his drink.

And that, right there, was my cue.

I brushed a loose strand of hair away from my eyes and walked into the bar, making certain to move slowly enough so that his eyes could catch me. But with the combination of his wandering eye and the observable shortage of customers tonight, it wasn't a difficult task.

Some nights are just easier than others.

They usually start with the legs. Most guys are Leg Men. It's a fact. Two years ago I would have guessed that the male population was *equally* divided into thirds: Leg Men, Butt Men, and Breast Men. Or what I call "the Holy Male Trinity." But now I know the truth: Most men like legs. Although I usually bring three different outfits, just in case. Each complementing one, and only one, of the three features associated with the trinity. But I always start with the legs. It's a safe bet.

Tonight it was a black suit miniskirt with strappy black Manolos . . . no nylons. I call it the "corporate slut" look. It's corporate enough to make them take you seriously and slutty enough for them to know you like being noticed.

For me, it's not about *liking* being noticed. It's my job for them to notice me. And even though some might choose to criticize me on this point, the way I see it, I'm just doing my job.

Whether or not this particular one was a Leg Man became irrelevant as soon as his eyes wandered up from my ankles, over my thighs, and to the elevated hemline of my skirt. Of course, he didn't stop there . . . they rarely do. Only after they reach the hemline, they can no longer rely on their eyes; it's all imagination from there on up.

I passed his booth, acting completely oblivious to his attention, and made my way to the bar, where I slid casually onto one of the high-backed stools.

"Grey Goose vodka gimlet, please."

The bartender, content to finally have something to do on an empty Wednesday night besides shine martini glasses, nodded cordially and placed a cocktail napkin down in front of me before turning to prepare my drink.

With a tired sigh I cupped my chin in the palm of my hand and rested my elbow on the wood-paneled bar. The movement was intended to make me look bored. Long day, long trip, *long,* lonely night ahead of me.

It worked.

As the bartender placed my drink down on the cocktail napkin and I reached for my wallet, out of the corner of my eye I saw a crisp one-hundred-dollar bill slide onto the bar. "Here, let me get that for you," a male voice offered.

I looked up to see the man from the booth standing next to me. I appeared slightly startled by his presence. Why wouldn't I be? It's not like I was *expecting* him to come over.

"That's so nice of you," I said gratefully.

A sly smile appeared across his lips. "My pleasure."

I was here because of a phone call I had received approximately one week earlier. The woman on the other end needed my help.

Everyone who calls that specific number needs my help. That is, after all, why I have the number.

I agreed to meet with her the next morning.

"I'll come to you," I said, offering the same comforting reassurance I give to everyone who calls that number.

I sat in her large, elegantly decorated living room and listened to her story. It was a familiar one; I'd heard it at least two hundred times. Sometimes with slight variations, sometimes nearly word for word.

But always with the same core motivator: fear.

"The maid found this in my husband's pants pocket while she was doing laundry." She reached onto the nearby coffee table and picked up a small, crinkled piece of paper. She looked at it pensively, hoping that maybe if she read it for the hundred and second time it might say something else. Or maybe a new and better explanation would finally come to mind and she could send me home.

No such luck.

She reluctantly handed me the piece of paper with a despondent sigh, and wiped her nose with a crumpled, overused Kleenex. "I'm sorry, I'm such a mess. I just can't believe I'm doing this."

I looked down at the handwritten note and nodded understandingly. "Well, you did the right thing by calling me. It's best to know for sure than to always wonder, right?"

She stared at me with uncertainty. "I guess."

"It is," I assured her. "Trust me."

I had assured many women of the exact same thing. Sometimes, when you're in their shoes, it's not always easy to see. Or better yet, it's not always the way you *want* to see it. The heart and the mind are legendary for disagreeing on subjects like this.

"What do you think it means?" she asked me, nodding toward the small, creased paper in my hand.

I looked down at it again, running my fingertip over the black ink. "It's hard to say," I admitted truthfully. "I've seen a lot of notes like this. Sometimes it turns out to be nothing. But sometimes it turns out to be . . ." I paused, hoping the time lapse would soften the word. "*Something*."

She looked away, fearful tears stinging her eyes. Then, finally, she surrendered a heavy sigh. "My friend who referred me to you said that you do some kind of *test*."

I looked into the eyes of the man standing next to me as we clinked our glasses together and simultaneously took a sip.

"So what brings you to Denver?" I asked, biting my lower lip. The lip-biting technique works brilliantly to suggest that my confidence level is *just* enough to ask the question but not enough to keep from fidgeting while I do it.

Because, despite appearances, I actually knew more about this man than I was letting on. More than he would ever care for me to know. And certainly more than just any other woman in a hotel bar.

For instance, I knew that this particular man liked confidence but not too much. Because with too much, he has no sense of conquest. It comes too easily. If *she* is just a little bit shy, it's more of a challenge. He likes when women make the first move, but only to show an initial interest, then he likes to take over.

I see a lot of men like him.

"My company is acquiring a smaller venture that's headquartered here," he explained.

I nodded my head, intrigued, as if nothing in the world could be more interesting. "And what company would that be?"

The man raised up a finger, motioning for me to wait, and then reached into his jacket pocket and removed a business card. He placed it on the bar in front of me as if to say, *Why waste precious words when the card already says it all?*

I slid the card closer to me and tilted my head to the side as I read aloud with genuine curiosity, as if I were reading the name for the first time: "Kelen Industries."

Then I looked up at him as my expression changed from one of innocent intrigue to one of vague recognition.

"Wait a minute," I said, taking a second look at the card and tapping my finger on it. "I know this company." I paused and pretended to think long and hard, digging way back into my memory.

The man chuckled almost condescendingly. "I highly doubt it. We manufacture—"

"Car engines!" I interrupted with the enthusiasm of a celebrity groupie.

He shot me a look of astonishment. "That's right."

"You guys just released that new 10-cylinder, 5.2-liter engine to compete with the Japanese S8."

He blinked in disbelief and then looked at me with such longing that he could have devoured me right then and there.

"How does a girl like *you,*" he began, giving me another once-over, making sure he didn't accidentally miss a pair of nerdy, taped-up glasses in my breast pocket or a graphing calculator sticking out of my handbag, "know about car engines?"

I blushed, as if he had just found my hidden weak spot. A shameful secret that I kept locked inside, but upon meeting someone of his status could no longer bear to keep concealed. "Just a hobby," I said bashfully.

He smiled and quickly added, "I'm sitting in that booth right over there. Would you like to join me?"

The invite was fast. About as fast as I had calculated. He was an easy code to break; I didn't think I'd have to work at this one. This man was an obvious pro. I definitely wasn't the first woman he'd ever invited to sit down. But luckily, I'm not the jealous type.

It's my job to sit down.

The invite is always necessary, no matter how fast or slow it comes. It's obligatory. I can't invite, I can only accept. It's one of the rules. And since I, myself, invented the rules, it would be silly to break one. For me rules aren't made to be broken. They were made for a reason, and it was usually a pretty good one.

"Well . . ." I hesitated, looking at my watch.

"Just for a little bit," he said persuasively, with an engaging smile.

I considered for a moment. Just long enough to give him the rush of a possible rejection and, as a result, the subsequent rush of a tiny first victory. Men like him live for that victory rush. It's something they don't get at home anymore. And in all honesty, judging by the size of his bank account, something he doesn't get away from home either. A man this rich is rarely turned down. And he knew that.

But the one thing that differentiated me from all the other girls was that I didn't want anything from him in return. I was just there to observe. And, of course, take good notes.

Subconsciously, he wanted the chase. He also wanted the triumph at the end, but working for it made it so much more fun. That's why tonight I had to be somewhat demure. Unsure if I had the time, or the desire, to share a drink with somebody. I couldn't be the type of girl who just sits down with any stranger she meets in a bar. His offer had to seem somehow . . . more intriguing than most.

But then again, that girl is only a design. A fabrication of his perfect woman.

"I guess that would be all right," I said at last.

He smiled and chivalrously picked up both of our glasses, and we walked the few paces back to his plush, red velvet booth, which looked like it could fit five people, six if they liked one another. He waited for me to slide in and then placed my drink down on the table before taking the seat next to me.

"So, where are you from?" he asked, sipping his drink.

"L.A.," I stated matter-of-factly, playfully running my fingers up and down the sides of my glass. "And you?"

It was here in the process that I chose to reach down and adjust the strap on my Manolos . . . while he was digesting my question. Not that it was a difficult question, but at this point there's less and less blood flowing to the brain. So the questions become more difficult. Even the simple ones like these.

But the shoe-strap adjustment is never *just* an adjustment. It's a leisurely slide down the leg, making sure to touch upon all erogenous zones, and a deliberate diversion of my attention. The diversion is always long enough for them, if they so choose, to remove the wedding ring.

And he did.

When I came back up and casually glanced at his left hand out of the corner of my eye, it was gone.

"Orange County," he said, not missing a beat. "Looks like we're neighbors. I have a house in Newport." His casual response said nothing about the fact that he was now minus one very important piece of jewelry. As if the removal of his wedding ring didn't faze him at all. Just as someone would take off their watch at the end of the day, this man evidently takes off his wedding ring when he meets girls in bars.

I smiled delightfully. "Oh, I love it down there! The beaches are amazing. My best friend lives right next door, in Huntington."

"Well then, you'll have to come south for a visit," he offered suggestively. "I have a great pool overlooking the ocean."

I released a perfectly timed nervous giggle. The kind that lets someone know they're making you uncomfortable, but at the same time implies you don't really mind all that much.

"Maybe I will," I replied softly.

Nevertheless, the one thing we *both* knew was that no matter what happened in the next few hours, I wouldn't be making any trips down to Newport Beach in the near future. However, my understanding of that unspoken agreement was just a bit more informed than his.

"It's called a fidelity inspection," I had gently explained to the woman sitting across from me with tears in the corners of her eyes. "And how it works is: You and I will decide on a location where your husband will be in the near future. Preferably somewhere out of town. My research has shown that most infidelity in men happens away from home. I will then travel to that predetermined location and present myself as an 'opportunity.' "

She nodded slowly, taking it all in. One painful detail at a time.

"I will not instigate anything. I will only follow your husband's lead."

"And then what?" she asked, desperately wanting me to come with all the answers neatly wrapped up in a pretty little package. A marriage repair kit in a box. Unfortunately, it didn't quite work that way. With infidelity, there is never a quick fix. But there *is* a solution. And that's why I was there.

"Mrs. Jacobs," I began kindly, "I only offer information. What you choose to do with it afterward is entirely up to you."

She nodded and tried to smile.

The piece of paper in my hand was the first clue. There's always a clue. The question is what you choose to do with it. Will you ignore it and continue living your life, always doubting, always wondering? Or will you do something about it?

This particular clue came in the form of a name and a series of numbers. "Alexis" was spelled out on the page in unmistakably female handwriting, and then underneath was a phone number, followed by the text, "Bathing suit optional!"

Although I didn't want to admit it to the woman sitting across from me, it looked exactly like what I suspected it to be. My friends give out their numbers to guys all the time. And that's what they write. A name and a number. And then sometimes a funny private joke. Something to remind him of the conversation they had had earlier in the evening.

"And you're positive your husband doesn't know anyone by the name of Alexis?" I asked earnestly.

She shook her head. "Not that I know of. Our friends' daughter's name is Alexis, but she's only ten. I doubt she would have written that."

I nodded in agreement and offered a heartwarming smile. "Yes, I doubt it, too." She fidgeted nervously in her seat. She had hoped it wouldn't come to this. She looked down at her lap. Her hands were locked tightly together, and she began to knead them like a loaf of bread.

We sat in silence for a moment, until she finally lifted her head and looked me straight in the eyes. "If you were me, what would you do?" she asked softly.

I looked at her with compassion, ready and willing to help in any way I could. "I would want peace of mind," I said in all honesty.

"What's your name, by the way?" the man in the bar asked me.

"Ashlyn," I answered as I turned toward him and extended my hand.

Of course, it's a code name. I never use my real name. "Ashlyn" doesn't actually exist. She's a hologram. A character in a play. A play I've performed hundreds of times, in a hundred different hotel bars. And yet, they all seem strangely familiar. The same show, over and over again for the past two years.

"What a beautiful name," he remarked, becoming visibly more comfortable in the booth.

I thanked him kindly. It wasn't the first time I'd heard it. Yes, it was a beautiful name. That's, after all, why I chose it. Because if you're going to fight for a cause, you need a good alias to fight under.

"Nice to meet you, Ashlyn. I'm Raymond."

But I already knew his name. That's one of the basics. In fact, I knew a lot more about the man sitting next to me than what was written on his little white business card.

Raymond Jacobs. CEO of Kelen Industries, the second-largest manufacturer of automobile engines in North America. Just shy of thirty-eight years old, he lives in Newport Beach, California, with his wife, Anne, and their three children. His hobbies include sailing, golf, downhill skiing, and wine tasting, although he hardly gets to do any of them because of his hectic work schedule. He likes sushi, but only if it's expensive, the blue fin tuna stuff (he's suspicious of cheap, uncooked fish). He watches hockey and basketball whenever a Texas team is playing, because that's where he grew up. He graduated from the University of Texas with a degree in engineering, a college sweetheart who he proposed to a year later, and a lifetime allegiance to the Sigma Phi Epsilon fraternity.

I always do my research. It makes my job much easier.

"Yes, I know," I said with a faint smile that left my mouth half open so he could see my tongue playfully massaging the back of my teeth.

As soon as he began to stare, however, I quickly shut it and pressed my lips together tightly. Because tonight, with Raymond Jacobs, CEO of Kelen Industries, I am embarrassed at being caught doing anything overly sexual. Especially when people are watching. I practice the tongue-against-the-teeth maneuver in front of the mirror at least twice a week . . . when no one else is around. But when it comes time to actually use it on someone, I am slightly less courageous.

"Raymond Jacobs." I pronounced his name fully and with importance.

"How do you know that?" he asked, suddenly paranoid, as he remembers that he hasn't yet told me his full name.

I coyly pointed to his business card in my hand.

"Right." He laughed at himself, seemingly relieved. Because for the *very* slightest moment, there was just a small flash of panic that I might not be exactly who I say I am.

And the truth is . . . I'm not.

But the mind sees what it wants to see.

"So what are *you* in town for?" Raymond asked quickly, steering the conversation back down its steady path to, well, exactly where he hoped it would go. "Business or *pleasure*?" Raymond's emphasis on the word *pleasure* was far from discreet. He wasn't about to waste a perfectly good opportunity to insinuate.

Ashlyn may have been shy, but she certainly wasn't stupid. I caught his suggestion and laughed nervously at what it implied. He watched my mouth intently, waiting for the laugh to turn from one of uneasiness to one of reciprocated flirtation.

And what do you know?

It did.

"Business," I said with a flitting sigh, as if to suggest the dullness of my trip and the burning desire to make it a bit more interesting.

"What do you do?"

I tucked my hair behind my ear. "I'm a research manager for a law firm."

Ashlyn has had so many jobs. Tonight, however, her job had to be interesting and important. Not overly flashy, but one that required a significant amount of brains. With some subjects, Ashlyn's job is an important component of the mission. But tonight it was becoming increasingly clear that with legs like that, Raymond Jacobs could care less what she did during the rest of the day. As long as her nocturnal activities included a space for him.

"Wow, that must be exciting," he said with an earnest attempt at sincerity.

He wanted this. And he knew what it was going to take to get it: interest and attention. Because from experience, that's what it normally takes to win over girls like Ashlyn.

I flashed the kind of smile that radiates from someone who enjoys her job. "Yes, it's pretty exciting," I began. "Always something different . . . lots of travel. I get to meet new people all the time. And the research I do is usually pretty interesting and informative. The best part is, I learn about things I would never have chosen to learn about on my own."

I laughed to myself as I realized that the whole speech was actually fairly accurate. I did get to travel a lot. I did get to meet new people. Not necessarily the most upstanding kinds of people, but still people. And sometimes the research required for this job can be pretty fascinating. For instance: Over the past two years, I've learned how to speak French, Spanish, Italian, Japanese, German, Russian, and some Arabic. It doesn't really bother me that the only conversations I can have in those languages are all for the purpose of seeing if men will ask me back to their hotel rooms.

But I can't complain.

Grunt work is part of any job. My grunt work is just a bit more . . . literal.

The more I spoke with Raymond Jacobs, the more confident I became that he was what I call a "channel changer." Someone who doesn't feel guilt. These are the ones who keep me awake at night. The ones who go through with it so easily, as if they're just casually changing the TV channel during a commercial break, just to see what else might be on. It's a good test for any man. Can he sit through an entire commercial break without changing the channel? If he can he might have potential. If he can't, toss him out right away. Of course, with the advent of TiVo and DVR, testing capabilities have become somewhat limited.

But the one thing I was fairly confident he *would* feel was remorse. Regret. Although it probably would not come in the form of "How could I do something like this?" but rather as "How could I let myself get caught?" Successful men don't really like getting caught with their pants down . . . so to speak.

Whether or not it will change them is the real human-interest story.

After three drinks and what seemed like hours of pointless conversation, I turned my wrist and looked at my watch. "Oh," I said, seemingly surprised that someone like me could have lost track of time so easily. "It's almost midnight. I should really get some sleep. I have such an early day tomorrow."

I brought my gimlet glass to my lips and slowly tipped my head back, allowing the very last of my drink to slide down my throat. I was also allowing the reality of my parting words to fully infiltrate his mind.

Ashlyn is leaving. And there's no doubt he wants more of her.

It's a guaranteed method for dealing with any man. Married, single, divorced, gay, straight, bisexual. Always leave them wanting more. Never give them enough.

I grabbed my small black handbag and slung it around my shoulder as I slid to the edge of the booth and slowly stood up. I turned to him and paused before speaking again. This gave his eyes time to find their way from eye level, which was now directly between my legs, to my face.

"It was nice meeting you, Raymond."

He cleared his throat. "Do you really have to go?" His disappointment was purposefully transparent. Trying his luck with the "broken heart" card. Because girls like having a heartbreaking effect on men.

I nodded solemnly as I pretended to feel the effects of the alcohol I had just consumed. "Yes, I probably should. But thank you again for the drinks." I giggled. "All three of them." I extended my hand, letting him shake it, feel it, absorb it, long for it. "Good luck with your meetings," I said sweetly, and started to turn away.

"You, too," he said, confused. I could see his mind scrambling for his next chess move. Knowing full well that he still needed to capture the queen, he was not about to let me leave that easily. And that's exactly why I felt comfortable bluffing my exit.

"You know . . ." he started to say, his hand resting contemplatively on the metaphorical bishop of our imaginary chessboard.

I turned back around curiously, as if I had no idea what was coming next. As if I wasn't already five moves ahead of him, just as any good chess player should be.

"I have this great minibar in my room and I haven't even touched it yet. Do you want to come up for another drink?"

Checkmate.

I hesitated slightly. Considering his offer.

I *had* to think about it. To jump at the invite would be out of character. And Ashlyn *never* steps out of character.

I had to be flattered by his invitation, but I also had to bite my lip hesitantly while I thought about it.

So I did.

But the indecision is actually built in for two reasons: (1) the obvious—to allude to the fact that I am unsure about going upstairs with a stranger; and (2) the not-so-obvious—to give him a chance to back out. Yes, it is, in essence, counterproductive to my "mission," but I have to be certain that he really wants it. There's a fine line between testing someone and entrapping them. They are fundamentally two different things, and I don't do the latter. I don't set traps and let men walk right into them. I let them lead the way and observe what they do with a "willing" participant.

Because, in reality, temptation is everywhere.

I'm just a human camera, documenting that reality.

"Yes, I think I would like that," I said, lowering my head half an inch.

He stood up, feeling an extraordinary sense of accomplishment. Letting the rush he longs for every single day to pulse through his veins and fuel his excitement. And together we weaved our way through the bar, around the other tables and into the lobby.

Once in the elevator he pressed the letter *P* for the penthouse, and the doors closed. His lips immediately moved toward mine. His kiss wasn't tender or gentle. It was purposeful. I had agreed to the invitation, and in that simple concurrence, I had knowingly agreed to so much more. It was an unspoken rule. One that Raymond, apparently, was very familiar with.

When he kissed me my mind filled with the same thing it always does: nothingness. It's taken a while to master the art of thinking about nothing. I'd always thought it was nearly impossible, especially for women. Our minds are constantly racing, always analyzing, always planning. But after several meditation classes, numerous books on the art of Zen, and hours of practice, I had finally become a master of nothing. Empty space in my head.

And trust me, it's the only thing you want to be thinking about at a time like this.

Because God knows there are several other options. His wife, his kids, his beautiful mansion in whatever impressive-sounding town he's chosen to live in, the wedding ring once filled with meaning and virtue, now sitting lifelessly in his shirt pocket.

Looking at a man like Raymond Jacobs can be very deceiving. Because to the untrained eye his family, his life, his accomplishments would probably look just like a TV show. The perfect American Dream paradigm. But to an expert like me, it looks quite a bit different.

It's funny. Never as a child growing up watching *Family Ties* or *The Wonder Years* did I picture encountering the husbands and fathers of these shows under these circumstances. But I learned rather quickly that sitcoms never actually reflect real life. They're just an idealistic creation. A utopia in the mind of some producer looking to strike an emotional chord in those of us who live in the real world. A world that, not surprisingly, looks nothing like theirs.

Not yet, anyway. But I have high hopes.

The elevator dinged and the doors opened. He grasped my hand tightly and began to lead me down the hallway toward his room, a playful smile artificially painted on my face.

This is a very crucial time in the process. The game is nearly over, but it's no time to be careless. Any slight mistake, change in character, wrong word could trigger suspicion and, inevitably, an aborted mission. Raymond was far too distracted to be suspicious, but you can never be too sure. No matter how predictable someone is, they can always surprise you. And therefore I can never lose my concentration. My true identity must always be concealed.

Backing out is one thing, but a blown cover is quite another.

He let go of my hand just long enough to fish his hotel key out of his back pocket. I giggled nervously as I watched him fiddle with the electronic lock. Trying it once, getting a red error light, and then trying it again. If only he had stopped long enough to read the red light and respond to its obvious implication.

There are always signs; most just fail to see them.

The green light finally illuminated and he turned the handle and pushed the door open with his back. He reached out his hands and grabbed me around the waist, pulling me in after him.

"There's just one more thing . . ." Mrs. Jacobs had said to me as I was packing up my things to leave.

I tucked the photograph of Raymond Jacobs that she had given me into the pocket of my portfolio and placed it in my bag. Then I looked up at her. "What's that?"

She fidgeted in her seat, the inevitability of her forthcoming question making her visibly uncomfortable. But it was a question that needed to be asked. And she knew she would have to ask it eventually.

I, however, already knew what it would be.

Because it was the same question that always came at this point in the meeting.

The same disturbing image that would perpetually haunt her for the rest of the week, and possibly the rest of her life, unless it was addressed.

"What about sex?" she finally managed to get out. "Do you actually *have* sex with the . . . um . . ." Her voice trailed off. She was unable to even think about it, let alone say it aloud.

"Absolutely not," I said, without even the slightest waver in my voice. This point has always been nonnegotiable, so it was important that I presented it as such.

She breathed a heavy sigh of relief. "Oh, thank God."

I smiled warmly. "Mrs. Jacobs, I assure you, my test is based on an *intention* to cheat only. There is no sex involved."

She shifted again in her seat. "Intention to cheat," she repeated to herself.

"Yes," I confirmed with an emphatic nod of my head.

"So how does that *work* exactly?"

Raymond and I stumbled clumsily through the extravagant, top-floor suite, his lips on my mouth, my neck, my face. Anywhere they could find.

As we fell onto the bed, I made sure that I was on top. It's a much easier escape route when the time comes to escape.

His hands immediately came up and landed on my ass. I moaned with pleasure.

He liked it.

They usually do.

He continued to kiss me as he slid my suit jacket over my shoulders. Then he went for my shirt. Unbuttoning the buttons one by one. I didn't protest. The shirt came off. He took one look at my lavender lace Balconette push-up bra and let out an appreciative sigh. Sure, it was flattering. How could it not be? But tonight, like every other night, the focus wasn't on me. And therefore, I usually took little notice of their "appreciation."

Next off was my skirt, revealing the matching Boyshorts I had on underneath. He touched my hip bones and squeezed. I shivered with believable excitement.

My fingers started unbuttoning his shirt next, stroking his chest and sliding it seductively off his shoulders.

He quivered with anticipation. "Oh my God, I want you so bad."

"Really?" I asked softly, still as demure and unsure as ever.

"Oh, yes," he replied. "You are *so* sexy."

"Good," I whispered.

And with that I rolled off of him, slid to the edge of the bed, and callously started gathering up my items of clothing. Without a word, I quickly located my skirt on the floor, reached down to grab it, and then stood up to put it back on.

"What are you doing?" he asked with more than a hint of annoyance in his voice.

"I'm leaving," I replied blankly, stepping into my skirt and pulling it up around my hips.

He sat up, seemingly too quickly, either because of one too many drinks or a lack of blood flow to the brain . . . possibly both. He put his hand to his head to steady the room. A look of total bewilderment stretched across his face. "Why?"

I knew exactly what he was thinking. That this part was definitely not in the script he had come to memorize. Boy meets girl. Boy buys girl drink. Boy invites girl to hotel room. Girl accepts. But girl certainly does not just change her mind and leave for no reason.

"Because I'm done here," I said matter-of-factly, sliding my arms into the sleeves of my shirt and proceeding to button it up.

And I *was* done.

He shook his head. "I don't understand. Did I do something wrong?"

I shrugged. "I guess you could put it that way."

This threw him off even more. The look on his face was one I'd seen many times. It was an expression of someone tracing steps back in their mind, trying to reassemble a pile of amorphous puzzle pieces that had absolutely no possibility of ever interlocking.

I finished buttoning my shirt and then bent down to help guide my feet into my shoes.

"Wait," he pleaded softly, hoping to sway me once again by his unyielding desperation for me.

But his tactics were useless on me now. I was no longer the same person he had met in the bar.

"Come sit down. Let's just talk. We can discuss car engines if you want," he offered in an artificial display of thoughtfulness.

I smiled without even the hint of feeling. "I'm not who you want me to be, Raymond."

His forehead wrinkled in aggravated confusion. "Huh?"

I was all business now. "I was hired by a Mrs. Anne Jacobs, who suspected that you had unfaithful tendencies, and therefore requested my services as a fidelity inspector."

His eyes grew wide at the mention of her name. "What the fuck?"

And this is where that remorse comes in.

He dropped his head between his knees. His fingers ran through his hair and around to the back of his neck. He pulled his chin up long enough to say, "She *hired* you?"

I stood emotionless and looked him straight in the eye. "Yes." It was my duty now to be completely impassive. No pity, no compassion. Nothing.

He groaned loudly and shut his eyes again. It was time for me to leave. I grabbed my bag and jacket and headed for the door. But not before leaving a small black card on the dresser. The only thing I ever leave behind after an assignment.

I guess you could say it was my calling card. But I don't like to think of it as proof that I was there. More proof that something needs to change.

"Wait," I heard Raymond say again. Out of the corner of my eye I saw him get up and reach down to pick up his slacks, which had been kicked halfway across the room in our semi-authentic heat of the moment. He pulled a black leather wallet from the back pocket and opened it. "What's she paying you, a grand? Fifteen hundred? Look, I'll double it." He reached inside the billfold and started to count out hundred-dollar bills.

I turned around and watched him coldly sift through his pile of money like a miser with his beloved stack of cash. "This is not about money," I responded flatly, before continuing to the door.

"It's always about money," he pressed indignantly. "How much do you want?"

I stopped, contemplated for a moment, and then slowly turned to face him again.

Raymond cracked a triumphant smile at what appeared to be my sudden change of heart.

"I'm sorry," I offered sincerely. "But my loyalty is not for sale."

His smile morphed into a patronizing grin. "Trust me, honey. I have enough money to buy *anyone's* loyalty."

And just then a small, shiny object on the ground caught my eye. I immediately recognized it as Raymond Jacobs's wedding band, having evidently fallen out of his shirt pocket during our earlier disrobing scramble. I bent down to pick it up, and then with the delicacy of a surgeon mending an open heart, I gently placed it on top of the dresser. "Apparently not," I replied.

I never know what happens after that because it's not my job to know. My part is over. The intention has been confirmed. And that's all I'm here to do. To confirm it or deny it.

Now it was time for me to leave.

So I did.

2

a hopeful salvation

In eighth grade I read the story of Pandora's box.

And I've never been the same since.

It spoke to me somehow. Not because I was morbidly obsessed with the fact that one woman alone managed to release all crime, sin, and disease into the human world (which is ironically the same story as Adam and Eve's) but because of the way the story shed a positive light on the subject of human suffering.

Pandora was asked by the gods to watch over a mysterious box that she was instructed never to open. But her relentless curiosity was no match for her waning discipline, and once she lifted the lid, she unwittingly released evil into the world in the form of ugly winged creatures that fluttered out of their prison in a burst of light and air. Upon seeing the hideous beings that had escaped, she panicked and slammed the lid shut again, immediately wondering if opening it had been the wisest decision after all.

But then she heard a tiny voice call from inside the box. *Open, open! Please let me out! I will heal you!* it cried.

She opened the box once again to find that the gods, in a last-minute, compassionate afterthought, had placed one benevolent creature in a box full of demons. That creature was called "hope" and its task was to heal the wounds inflicted by the evil spirits that were now wreaking havoc on our once-perfect paradise.

Upon reading this tale, I felt comforted to know that even thousands and thousands of years ago, when stories like this were written and then passed along from generation to generation, one universal concept held true. Just as it does today.

Hope heals disaster.

My mission has been clear from day one.

Uncover the truth. Set minds at ease. Give women a chance to move on with their lives.

But not everyone sees this job as a worthy cause. And that's why not many people know about it. In fact, that's why *nobody* knows about it.

Not even my best friends.

Not even my family.

To everyone in my life, I am Jennifer Hunter. A hardworking, successful investment banker at Stanley Marshall Bank. And that's exactly who I *used* to be.

The transition was relatively seamless. A new phone number because of a long-awaited promotion and, as a result, a new company cell phone. Long hours and lots of traveling because of high-profile clients and a demanding boss. Nondisclosure on the details of my work because of confidentiality agreements. It really did make a very good cover.

I guess that makes me some kind of "double agent." Leading a double life: the one I know about, and the one that everyone else knows about. I would tell my family and friends what I do, but there's no way they would ever understand. My friend Sophie would call me a home wrecker and my friend Zoë would probably never be able to look at me the same way again.

They just wouldn't be able to see it how I see it.

They'd see me as a woman who knowingly flirts with married men and then breaks up relationships. Ruins families. Tears people apart.

The way everyone would see it.

But to me, that's just the surface. When you dig deeper, there's so much more. But I guess to really understand it the way I do, you'd have to know what I know. You'd have to have seen what I've seen.

And that's why I keep it to myself.

Plus, anonymity is what allows me to do what I do so well.

Some people might wonder how I'm even able to go through with it every single time. How can I be so objective? So far removed?

And how can I not *want* them to pass?

Well, the answer is simple: It's not about what I want.

If you asked anyone on the street if they wanted crime to no longer exist, they would probably say, "Sure, doesn't everybody?" But that still doesn't change the fact that it does.

The same goes for infidelity. It is what it is. It's out there. I can sit around wishing it didn't exist all day long, but that's certainly not going to change anything. Or I can get out there and reveal the fact that it *does* exist. And hopefully make a difference.

The way I see it: I've already changed over two hundred people's lives. And I'm proud of that.

Doubt can wreak havoc in a relationship. Insecurity can torment your life. And in the end, most people just want to know for sure.

More than two hundred women have been offered the truth about their relationships. About the ones they love. And as far as I'm concerned, that's better than living in the dark.

It's better than living in denial.

Because aren't we all just living in denial? Infidelity is all around us. It's the topic of our talk shows, on the covers of our magazines, at the center of our political scandals. But it doesn't seem like anyone's doing anything about it. Except complaining and pointing fingers.

Well, my fingers are getting tired. I'd rather do something about it.

Raymond Jacobs was the kind of assignment that makes me feel good about what I do. Ashlyn definitely wasn't the first girl he'd ever cheated with (or *intended* to cheat with), but now, at least, I could fly back to L.A. knowing that she would probably be the last.

And that's what allows me to sleep at night.

"I'm totally freaking out!" My best friend Sophie's voice came loudly and frantically through my Bluetooth headset as I was driving home from LAX.

"What's wrong?" I asked.

"I'm losing him. I can tell," she said with an exasperated sigh.

Sophie has a tendency to overreact. It's rooted in her insecurities, and as a result, she has a hard time trusting men. She's constantly afraid they'll walk out on her. Probably because all of them have.

"You're not losing him," I reassured her patiently. "What happened?"

"He's not coming," she said simply.

"What do you mean, he's not coming?"

"I mean, he was supposed to fly out this weekend, remember? You were *supposed* to finally meet him. And now he's got some stupid work thing!"

"Well, you can't blame him for that," I told her. "Work is work."

Sophie and Eric had been dating long distance for the past eight months. He was a third-year resident at a hospital in Chicago, and because of his crazy schedule he would usually just pay for Sophie to fly there. The few times he had come to Los Angeles I was away on "business." And even though I had never met him, I could tell by the way she talked about him that he was crazy about her.

Eric was different from all the rest of them. I can't say how I knew that; it was just a feeling I had. And I've learned to trust those instincts without reservation. I just wished I could convince Sophie to do the same. Whenever she falls into one of her panic spirals, I want to sit her down and tell her that I've seen plenty of men who were on the verge of straying, and Eric is definitely not one of them. He didn't exhibit any of the signs of a cheater. And I, of all people, know the signs. But that would probably require a much longer explanation, one I wasn't prepared to give her. So I usually just resorted to more traditional methods of calming her down.

"All I know is once they start canceling dates, that's when it starts to go downhill," she said in a hopeless tone.

"Sophie," I began warningly, "this isn't a 'date.' He lives in Chicago, you talk on the phone at least twice a day, and you've seen him every other weekend for eight months! I think you can safely say that you're past 'dating.' "

"But I really wanted you to meet him . . . finally."

"And I wanted to meet him, too," I assured her. "But I have a feeling this won't be the last opportunity for that to happen."

She paused and reflected. "Well, with your schedule and his . . . you never know."

"Well, I guess I'll just have to meet him at the wedding, then," I jested.

"Shhh!" she urged me. "You'll jinx it! According to *Marie Claire,* the eight-month mark falls right into the beginning of 'prime proposal time' while still lingering in the novelty wear-out phase. It's a dangerous intersection. I have to be very careful of what I say."

I rolled my eyes as I turned my SUV onto Wilshire. "Sorry."

"Are you in town?" she asked.

"Yeah, just flew in from Denver an hour ago. I'll be here until nine tomorrow morning. Why?"

My friends had gotten used to my hectic schedule. Well, they had gotten used to Jennifer the investment banker's hectic schedule. Being in town for mere hours at a time was nothing new to any of them. And as far as they were concerned, I had just as normal a job as any other traveling businessperson. Selling consulting packages, negotiating million-dollar deals, schmoozing with hotshot clients—the usual. I'm sure the image of me dressed up like a sexy corporate bimbo in order to see if some rich woman's husband is capable of committing adultery is the last thing on their minds when they think of me "on the road."

And although this whole thing started out as somewhat of a mini-quest, being a fidelity inspector had actually turned into quite the lucrative career. I worked on a referral basis only. But once word of my services had started to spread, there weren't enough hours in the day to take on all the requested assignments. It had never been about the money . . . but it certainly hadn't made things worse.

"Can we meet up tonight?" Sophie asked. "I could seriously use a 'session.' "

"I'm sorry, hon. I can't," I said regretfully. "I have to work tonight."

Sophie sighed again. It was a phrase she had heard many times. "Okay. But those slave-driver bosses of yours better give you the weekend off. You've worked the last two weekends. Nobody's *that* important."

I laughed. "Yes, I do have the weekend off." Which was actually something I'd been looking forward to all week. "We'll get everyone together. It'll be a *group* session."

"Yeah. For sure," she said, trying to sound upbeat. But I could tell she was disappointed.

"Don't worry," I reassured her again. "Eric's a good guy. I'm sure you're overreacting. A textbook case of long-distance relationship paranoia."

"Okay, thanks," she relented. "I better get back to work. Love you."

"Love you, too."

I clicked off my headset and tugged it out of my ear.

I felt bad that I couldn't be there for Sophie tonight. It wasn't the first time my job had stolen time away from my friends. And it broke my heart every time I had to lie to them. As if it wasn't bad enough that I couldn't be there for them when they needed me, they didn't even know the real reason *why* I couldn't be there.

But I was sure we would analyze Sophie's boyfriend drama quite thoroughly this weekend, when the group was assembled for her "session."

Sophie and I had adopted the term when we were in elementary school. Her dad was a psychologist, and while we were growing up, he saw most of his clients in his home office. He used to come upstairs to Sophie's bedroom in the afternoons and tell us to be quiet because he was "in a session." We always liked the way the phrase sounded: important and confidential. So we decided to make it our own.

After dinner Sophie and I would sneak into her dad's office and take turns sitting in his large, brown leather chair while the other person sprawled out on the couch and came up with ridiculous-sounding problems like "I can't stop making fart noises in class. It's ruining my social life." The "psychologist" would then open up one of the heavy, leather-bound books on the nearby shelf, flip to a random page, and in their best *Masterpiece Theatre* voice say, "Sounds like a textbook case of 'fundamental attribution error.'" Or whatever the longest, most important-sounding term on the page was.

As the years went on, our sessions eventually moved out of Sophie's dad's office, and evolved from silly make-believe problems to real, adolescent issues. But we still always managed to throw in a "textbook case" reference for each and every problem we encountered. It offered a comforting implication. Knowing that all of our problems were documented in some pretentious leather-bound book somewhere made us feel better about the situations we found ourselves in. As if despite all the agony and hardship, there was nothing we could say or do that hadn't already been solved, sorted out, and properly labeled by some hotshot shrink along the way.

In recent years, however, it had mainly been Sophie calling for the sessions. For some reason, drama seemed to have a strange attraction to that girl.

As I turned off of Wilshire Boulevard, I began my usual six-turn routine. As a rule of thumb, I never drive directly home. No matter what. I take five separate side streets before finally turning onto my own street and into the garage of my building. It makes it easier for me to spot anyone who might be following me. Wilshire is a huge street, and someone can tail you easily from a couple of cars back. But the five turns I make before returning home are all on smaller, quieter streets. Anyone making that many unnecessary turns behind me would certainly be noticed. In my line of work I couldn't take any chances. The last thing I needed was some lunatic, enraged husband banging on my door at two A.M.

I waited patiently at a stoplight while the car behind me passed to my left, the driver throwing me a dirty look in the process, and then turned onto my street. I pulled into the parking garage of my complex and parked my Range Rover in its reserved spot. I then quickly gathered up my things and hurried inside. I had only about ten minutes at home before I had to be out the door again to meet with my client, Raymond Jacobs's wife.

I dragged my rolling suitcase behind me, then turned my key in the lock and stepped inside to find the place exactly how I'd left it: immaculately clean.

My work afforded me the luxury of employing a housekeeper, Marta, who comes twice a week. She does an excellent job making my house look and smell new every time I walk through the door. And I know how hard it is to keep a house clean that's decorated entirely in white: white carpets, white walls, white sheets, white comforters, white throw pillows, white countertops.

I remember when my friend Zoë first came over to see my new condo after the interior decorator had artfully transformed it from the washed-up bachelor pad it had been into the chic masterpiece it is now.

"It's very . . . white," she remarked playfully.

"I know. Isn't it great?"

She nodded. "It's amazing. That must have been some raise you got."

Raises and promotions had quickly become my cover of choice as soon as the fidelity inspection business started to take off, and I was suddenly able to afford a lot more than just the basic necessities.

Marta greeted me at the door and took the suitcase from my hand.

"Thank you," I said politely. "I have to change really fast, and then I'm back out." I rushed through the living room toward my bedroom. "Any messages while you were here?"

"No, Miss Hunter," Marta replied cordially in her thick Hispanic accent as she stood and watched me frantically make my way through the house. "I think maybe the phone ring when I vacuum. But I not sure, so I no turn off the vacuum to answer."

I smiled and walked into my bedroom. "That's fine."

"Usual clean?" she asked after me, nodding toward my suitcase in her hand.

I stuck my head out the bedroom door. "Yes, please. Thank you."

Marta nodded and started toward the laundry room as I shut my door to change.

I quickly unbuttoned my jeans and slid my T-shirt over my head. Just as my chin was clear of the neckline, I noticed the blinking message light on my answering machine. I was always curious when people called my home line. Mostly because very few people actually had the number. And most of those people knew to call me on my cell phone. My business cell phone was the third number I had. But that was reserved strictly for clients and new referrals.

I pressed *Play* on the machine as I hurried into my walk-in closet, throwing my clothes into the hamper and sifting through the hangers in the "business casual" section of my closet.

"You have one new message," the electronic voice announced.

"Hi, Jen. It's . . . Dad . . ."

Suddenly, my whole body froze. My hand stopped on a red cashmere sweater, and then dropped numbly to my side, causing the sweater to slip from the hanger and fall to the ground. I stood as still as I could, as if any movement might trigger an emotional minefield, causing the entire room to burst into flames.

I listened intently as my father's voice came through the small speaker. "Look, I know it's been a long time. But I thought maybe we could try talking again." There was a loud muffled sigh and a long pause.

I could feel the anger bubbling up inside my stomach, ready to boil over. I turned my head and looked toward the entrance of my closet, waiting for the next word.

And that's when it came.

"Honey, I'm getting married." He paused again. "She's really great. I want you to meet her. I would really like for you to come to the wedding. It would mean a lot to me. To both of us . . ."

As if released from a witch's evil spell, instantly my body unfroze and I marched into the bedroom. I violently threw myself at the machine. My hand landed with a loud thud on the nightstand, and I managed to locate the delete button. In a zealous rage, I pounded my finger on it at least a dozen times, and then eventually just held it down for what felt like an eternity.

Feeling confident that the message had been thoroughly erased and all remnants of it had been effectively destroyed by the mere force of my finger, I returned to my closet, determined to pick out the perfect outfit for my meeting with Mrs. Jacobs.

My closet, according to an envious and label-obsessed Sophie, was a "fashionista's paradise." Every label was properly represented: Gucci, Dior, Dolce & Gabbana, Marc Jacobs, Fendi, and whomever else *Vogue* or *InStyle* recommended a girl have in her closet.

Because to be honest, I knew very little about fashion. I'd never had a knack for it. And in my line of work, that was always an obstacle.

Most of my outfits required a lot of research and preparation.

I reemerged from my bedroom five minutes later in a conservative green pantsuit with a cream-colored camisole underneath and a colorful scarf tied around my neck. It was a look that *Cosmo* had called "suburban chic" in their August issue, and given that I was about to enter the treacherous waters of chic suburbia (aka Orange County), I figured that outfit was the perfect fit. I slung my gym bag over my shoulder and carried my favorite Hermès Birkin in one hand, and with the other hand I pulled a cheap, black carry-on suitcase I had bought at Target this week, containing my "costume" and other "props" for tonight's assignment.

I stuck my head into the laundry room to see Marta emptying out the contents of the suitcase from last night's trip into the washing machine.

"Thanks, Marta. Have a great weekend."

Her head popped up. "You're welcome, Miss Hunter. You will need your suitcase again tomorrow?"

"Yes, actually I will," I replied. "I'm flying to San Francisco in the morning."

"Okay, I wash it now," Marta said, reaching to the shelf above the washer and dryer and removing a scrub brush and a bottle of industrial-strength disinfectant wash.

"Thank you."

I'm sure she had all sorts of interesting questions about me. Who is this girl? What kind of job keeps her away from home nearly five days a week? How is she able to afford a place this nice at such a young age? (At twenty-eight years old, I was the youngest home owner in the complex.) And most important, why on earth do I have to disinfect her suitcase every time she comes home from a business trip?

But she's never asked me any of these questions. And so I've never felt compelled to make up any stories to answer them. For all I know, she probably thinks that I visit toxic waste sites for a living, or spend my free time roaming the halls of the Centers for Disease Control without a biohazard suit. But that's how I treat everything that could have come in contact with the cheaters I meet . . . like level-4 viruses. Dangerously airborne, extremely deadly, and with no known cure.

I stopped in front of the mirror hanging next to the front door. My long dark hair was pulled away from my face in a loose ponytail.

I scrutinized my reflection.

Something was missing. Did I forget to touch up my mascara?

I leaned in to examine my eyelashes. They looked as black as ever against my green eyes. Maybe I was just tired from the flight this morning. I also hadn't slept very well last night.

I took one last look, painted on a bright smile, and was out the door. But not before a longing glance back at my spotless living room.

As much as I enjoyed the traveling life, it *was* kind of a shame to have such a nice house when I was so rarely in it.

I took Wilshire Boulevard back to the 405 and settled in for the long drive down to Newport Beach. The heart of the O.C. (the show and the county). And Anne Jacobs's home easily could have been featured on any one of the *O.C.* episodes, with its mansionlike appearance and sparkling infinity pool overlooking the ocean in the backyard.

Anne was my third client from Newport Beach in the past month. Word spreads fast in that town, especially when you're a rich housewife lounging at the local spa all day, sharing gossip and, apparently, fidelity inspector phone numbers with other rich housewives.

My normal rate is very high. It's amazing how much people are willing to pay for the truth. To me it has always been priceless. And I guess a lot of people feel that way.

The client also pays for all of my expenses. Flights, hotel rooms, transportation, food, you name it. Anything that will help them get to the information they're seeking. Price is usually not an issue. So it's no surprise that most of my clients have the money to live in houses the size of hotels.

Peace of mind is a hard thing to find these days. And the reality is: Most people will pay for it. That's why I have a job.

I turned onto Anne Jacobs's street, followed it to the end of the cul-de-sac, and then pulled into the long, paved driveway that led up to the house.

There it was, in all its splendor.

I had been there once before, a week earlier when I took on the assignment. The house was still as magnificent as it was then . . . but somehow, it seemed to have lost its sparkle.

Most of the houses I enter are beautiful. But as I've learned, the house is quite often a facade. A mask that would have you believe the inside looks just as beautiful as the outside. And yes, the designer furniture and marble countertops are quite lovely, but the real inside, the inner workings, the relationships are never quite as glamorous. It's a shame, really. We want so much to believe that the insides of these multimillion-dollar homes overlooking the ocean are filled with love, happiness, and trust. But most of the time they just aren't.

My job tends to take off the mask.

"Mrs. Jacobs," I began gently once we were seated in her now-familiar living room. "Are we alone in the house?" I asked.

"Yes," she assured me. "The kids are still at school."

I have a very strict no-children policy when it comes to my job. They are not allowed to be present during any part of this process. Not because I don't like kids. I do. But if there is one circumstance where I'm an advocate for bliss in the form of ignorance, it's during childhood. No exceptions. Kids should never be burdened with the weight of adult relationships, especially those of their own parents. It's hard enough to be a child in today's world. They already see more than they should. I wasn't about to be responsible for irreparably tarnishing the innocence of anyone's child.

"Good," I replied.

She nodded nervously. She was an attractive woman, petite and fairly fit. The lines on her face represented years of PTA meetings, carpooling, and late nights waiting up for her husband to come home from work. I could feel the anxiety radiating off of her like warmth from a space heater. I felt for her. I really did. Being in her shoes was a difficult place to be. But I knew that by hiring me, she had taken the hardest, first step.

The first step down the road to a happier and more honest existence.

I reached out and rested my hand delicately on top of hers. "It's okay. Everything will be fine," I soothed.

She took a deep breath and tried hard to believe me.

I didn't let go of her hand. I kept holding on to it as I inhaled deeply and began speaking. "As we discussed last week when we met . . . "

Mrs. Jacobs turned her hand around and clasped it in mine.

I swallowed hard and flashed another warm smile. This was always the most difficult part. Being the bearer of bad news is never easy. "Per your request, I conducted a fidelity inspection on your husband based on an 'intention to cheat.' Meaning that in order to fail he had to show obvious *intention* to engage in *sexual* infidelity." I paused and took a deep breath. "Unfortunately, your husband did not pass the inspection."

"No," she whimpered, shaking her head slowly.

"I'm sorry."

"No, no," she repeated softly, begging for me to change my answer. To somehow reverse the past.

It's during these challenging moments, when your heart wants to sink away into the darkness, that I have to stay focused. I always keep my mind on the end result. The goal. Why I'm doing this. You can't live in the moment when your purpose is this big. You can't focus on the painful steps that bring you there. Otherwise you'll lose yourself along the way.

I remove the blindfolds that keep people in the dark. And almost everyone has the same initial reaction to the unfamiliar, blinding light. They scorn it. They want to cut the power and go back to their comfortable darkness. But that's the thing about this unique situation. Once you've seen the light, you can't go back. You'll always know it's there. And the most comforting thought for me is knowing that eventually they'll come to appreciate it. That one day, they'll wake up and realize that life's just too short to live in the dark.

"We used to be happy," she whispered.

"I'm sure you were," I said sincerely, as I reached over to the end table next to me, plucked a Kleenex from the box, and handed it to her. She nodded her appreciation as she took it and wiped her nose.

"I always thought we were different. That we weren't *that* couple. I mean, I watched all our friends go through divorces, affairs, therapy . . . you know how it can be in this town. . . . But I just never imagined it would be *us*. Ever."

"You did the right thing by hiring me, Mrs. Jacobs."

She nodded, clearly unconvinced, and stood up to show me to the front door.

"I know it doesn't feel like it now," I continued. "But it will. Trust me."

She dabbed at her eyes with the wrinkled Kleenex and smiled politely, partly believing it, partly questioning it, partly . . . just numb.

I reached into my bag and removed a cashier's check that I had calculated on the plane and picked up from the bank on my way to Anne's house. I placed it on the coffee table in front of her.

"I'm going to leave this check here for you. It's the balance of your retainer. The fees and expenses we discussed have been deducted."

She thanked me, and we walked back toward the entry hall. She reached out and sniffled as she opened the large mahogany door for me. I began to walk through it, but then paused and turned around. Anne stood there, studying me, assuming I would speak.

But I didn't speak. I simply reached out my arms and pulled her into an embrace. At first her body stiffened at my unexpected affection, but it only took a brief moment before I felt her melt into me, and she broke into silent sobs on my shoulder. I stroked her hair as I would that of a little girl who had fallen off her bike and scraped her knee. And in that moment, I'm sure she felt like one.

But like any wise mother, with the experience of a lifetime behind her, I knew something she didn't know. That with time, the scrape *would* heal, the scab *would* disappear, and the Band-Aid *would* eventually come off. And sooner or later . . . she might actually want to go for another ride.

Anne finally pulled away and wiped her eyes again, looking embarrassed and grateful at the same time.

"I'm sorry," she said timidly, laughing at herself.

"Don't be."

As easy as it would be, I never blame myself. There's no reason to. I'm just a messenger. And we all know it doesn't do any good to shoot the messenger.

"You know . . ." I began gently.

She looked into my eyes with anticipation and waited for my next words as if they might be gospel. Something she could take to bed with her at night and wake up with the next morning.

"The human spirit wasn't meant to live in denial. It will always seek the truth."

And just before I turned back to leave, I saw something in her eyes. Something *I* could take to bed with me at night and wake up with the next morning.

It was a tiny speck of hope, struggling to break free and perform its one mission in life. To heal.

For Anne Jacobs it was the hope that maybe I was right. Maybe she did do the right thing.

And there was nothing more in the world I could ask to leave with.

3

father of the bride

Two days earlier my business line had rung while I was in the middle of watching an episode of *Extreme Makeover: Home Edition* on TiVo. It's my favorite show on the air because it always manages to put me in a good mood. Zoë says that's why they call it "feel-good programming." But for me, the reasons are much more deeply rooted than just wanting to feel good.

Because I secretly believed that every client I visited, every house I stepped into and stepped out of, every family I changed was like my own little extreme makeover project. Just with a much less orthodox approach.

"Hello?" I said into the phone.

When answering my business line, I always opted for a standard, informal greeting rather than a typical, "This is Ashlyn," or anything personalized. This approach kept the whole thing more discreet. The caller knows who they're calling. And if it's a call I want to take, I can proceed from there. Otherwise, I can simply tell the caller that they have the wrong number and hang up.

Every so often an angry now-*ex*-husband or *ex*-boyfriend will stumble upon this number and dial it, hoping to get more information about the test they've just failed miserably. And, of course, looking for a scapegoat upon which to release their pent-up anger. Anything to distract themselves from turning inward and facing the real issue.

"May I please speak to Ashlyn?" It was a male voice. Although I have had a few male clients in the past for various reasons, I'm still always wary when a man calls this number.

"What is this regarding?"

"My name is Roger Ireland. I received your number from a close friend, Audrey Robbins. She said you might be able to help me."

I considered, sizing up his voice in an effort to decide whether this would simply be a "wrong number" or a longer conversation. The man on the phone sounded genuine and almost endearingly uncomfortable. This type of phone call was clearly not part of his normal daily routine.

"What kind of help are you looking for?" I asked.

He cleared his throat. "Well, my daughter is getting married in a few months, and I'm not sure I really trust the guy." He paused and then quickly added, "I could be completely wrong, but I just have a bad feeling about the whole thing. I'm worried about her."

"I see."

"I'd rather know now if he's going to break her heart so we don't have to go through with the wedding."

"Well, that's understandable," I said. "Have you mentioned your concern to your daughter?"

"I *tried*. It didn't seem to work. She got really upset and didn't speak to me for a week."

"Right," I responded. It made sense. Young brides-to-be rarely want to hear anything except, "White is a good color on you."

"I love my daughter. I only want her to be happy. But if this guy is no good, I want to prove it to her. To save her from heartache further down the road." He struggled momentarily with his next line. And then finally, "Can you help me?"

I agreed to meet with him so that I could gather some more information. I rarely accept assignments over the phone. I insist on meeting face-to-face first so I can get a better feel for the person who's hiring me and what the assignment would entail.

That phone call was two days ago. So today, after leaving Anne Jacobs's house, I drove back to Los Angeles to meet with Roger Ireland at his office in Century City. I arrived at the twenty-story building on Avenue of the Stars and rode the elevator up to the eleventh floor where a sign read LAW OFFICES OF IRELAND, HAMMERL AND WELCH.

The receptionist smiled cordially upon hearing the name Ashlyn and led me right into his office.

Roger Ireland was a pleasant-looking man, with gray hair and tired eyes, probably in his late fifties or early sixties. His large corner office was filled with a combination of dark wood furniture and brown cardboard boxes. "I'm retiring in a few weeks," he said, after shaking my hand and motioning toward the boxes and random piles of clutter.

I smiled. "Congratulations."

He pointed at a chocolate-colored leather couch by the window, and we sat down. I pulled out my black Louis Vuitton portfolio and flipped it open to an empty page.

"So let me just start by asking you some questions, and then I'll determine whether or not I can take on your case."

Roger nodded, seemingly relieved that I had been the one to initiate the dialogue. I'm sure he was wondering how one would even begin a conversation like this. *"So, you're gonna try to have sex with my future son-in-law?"*

I started by asking him the usual opening questions. The easy stuff. The subject's name, occupation, hobbies, and interests if he knew of any.

The fiancé's name was Parker Colman, a risk management adviser for LDS Securities. He had asked Lauren Ireland to marry him approximately nine months earlier. The elaborate $100,000 wedding was in three weeks, and the bachelor party was scheduled for a week from tomorrow in the land of bachelor parties: Las Vegas, Nevada. I had personally been there at least twenty times since starting this job.

As far as Mr. Ireland knew, Parker liked basketball, poker, BBQs, boozing, and, from what he suspected, women.

"And how does your daughter feel about the bachelor party?" I asked.

"What do you mean?"

"Well, they can be tricky," I explained. "Some women believe that anything goes at the bachelor party. Last final fling type of stuff, just don't tell me about it. Is Lauren like that?"

Roger shook his head. "Oh, no," he replied without reservation. "I know she's been pretty on edge about it. According to my wife, she only agreed to the whole thing because he promised not to go to any strip clubs. And of course, not to . . . you know, *be* with any other girls."

"Okay, then, it sounds like the bachelor party is the best place to conduct the inspection," I stated, jotting down a few details in my portfolio.

Roger agreed with a nod of his head. It's rare for a client to argue with one of my location suggestions. Kind of like how you don't argue with a doctor when he prescribes you medication; you trust that they know what they're doing. A "Yeah, whatever, just do your job so it stops itching" kind of thing.

"Does your daughter play poker?" I asked.

"No," he replied. "Not that I'm aware of. The gambling gene has never really been in the Ireland family."

I made a note and then looked up again. "What about confidence level? Is your daughter the shy type or the confident type?"

Mr. Ireland thought about his response before he spoke. He was taking all of my questions very seriously, and I appreciated his effort. But then again, for the money he was going to be paying me, this wasn't exactly the time to start filling in the multiple-choice bubbles randomly. "Well, she's very confident when it comes to her job. She's the chief technology officer at East Global Tech," he stated with a glowing, fatherly pride. It was obvious how much this girl meant to him. "She graduated cum laude from MIT. Always into the gadgets. When she was little we could never get her to play with dolls or Carebears like all the other girls in her class. All she wanted to do was take things apart. The answering machine, the phone, my brand-new computer." He laughed fondly at this memory, and then more solemnly added, "She's very smart."

"What about when dealing with men? Is she as confident around them?"

Roger shifted in his seat. The question made him visually uncomfortable. He was probably not in the habit of being so involved in his daughter's love life. And I imagined I was the only person in this office who'd ever seen him squirm.

"Not really." He hesitated. "At least I don't think so. I think she's always been a bit reserved when it comes to men . . . meeting them or talking to them. You'd think being in a male-dominated field it would come easy. But then again, she's never really talked to me about those things, so I'm only speculating."

I nodded. "Okay, then. I'll probably start with a chance meeting at the poker table, and then follow it up with another 'coincidental' encounter at whatever club they plan on going to. My experience has shown that when men cheat, it's usually with someone who is a direct opposite of their wife or girlfriend. It's that 'grass is always greener' complex. So I believe the ideal bait for Parker will be someone who's confident in her ability to talk to men and who plays poker . . . *well*."

Mr. Ireland raised his eyebrows. "Do you? Play poker well?"

I flashed a confident smile. "No . . . but I will."

Roger laughed and leaned back in his seat, amused by my confidence, yet clearly never doubting it for a second.

That was one of the fun parts of my job . . . becoming an expert at almost anything in a very short period of time. There are not many occupations that pay you to do that.

I continued. "Bachelor parties are usually tamer on Friday nights, and then Saturday is when they really go all out with the drinking and partying . . . that's when the 'mistakes' tend to be made. So I'll conduct the test on Saturday."

Roger scratched the back of his head. I could tell he was starting to have second thoughts about this whole process. It was now my job to reassure him.

"I think it's a good thing that you called me," I began in a comforting tone. "It's best to test them *before* they get married. If all my clients had done so, then maybe I wouldn't see half of the things that I've seen."

And it was true. I *did* wish my assignments were all bachelor parties and suspicious fiancées. They were so much cleaner. No kids. No law-binding commitments. No homes to be broken and made over. If only everyone would think to hire me *before* the wedding. But as they say, hindsight is twenty-twenty. Foresight is . . . twenty–five billion.

"You're right. I'm sorry. This is just difficult. I don't want to see her get hurt."

"I understand. And hopefully it won't come to that," I said with sympathy.

It was really a win-win situation for everyone. It always is. The first win was obvious. He doesn't cheat . . . congratulations, you found a good one. But the second win . . . that's the one that's not so evident at first. It comes with time.

And it was also a no-lose situation for me. If Parker Colman failed next weekend, it was just one less deceitful marriage I might be asked to expose one day in the future.

"How many of them actually fail this . . . test?" Roger asked with uncertainty. Probably not sure whether or not he really wanted to know the answer.

"It's about half and half," I said convincingly. It was the same lie I told every client. They all wanted to know, but I didn't see the point in telling them the real statistic; it would only freak them out, and the next few days of waiting would be hard enough without all the odds stacked against them, threatening to topple over. Fifty-fifty was an efficient lie. It wasn't enough to give anyone significant hope or doubt, and if the subject failed, it wouldn't seem completely out of the norm.

"Oh, that's not too bad," Roger conceded. "I kind of thought it would be worse." Then he chuckled lightly to himself. "I guess I'm just cynical."

I stifled a reaction. "So if you're ready to proceed with this, we can discuss my fees and some other important details."

He nodded. "Yes, I'm ready. Let's do it."

I continued to explain to Roger Ireland the basics of a fidelity inspection, including the fees associated with the assignment and the retainer that I required for all expenses. He nodded his agreement, more than willing to pay whatever the price to get exactly what he had called me for.

As with most of my clients, money was not an issue.

And finally, I explained what testing for an "intention to cheat" really meant. To my clients it meant everything but sex. It meant that there was no doubt in my mind that had I not stopped things when I did, the subject would have had sex with me.

But to me the concept was much more defined. Much more controlled. It *had* to be. For my own comfort level . . . and sanity. To put it simply, I refused to engage in anything you wouldn't see on network television. (Well, "viewer discretion advised" network television, obviously.) If you wouldn't see it happening on one of NBC's weekly prime-time slots, then you wouldn't see me doing it either. It may sound overly simplistic, but it kept everything safe, legal, and consistent.

After getting back into my car, I placed Roger Ireland's check in my wallet and the photograph of Parker he had given me in my portfolio. From my bag I pulled out my Treo smartphone, which multifunctions as my business phone, my day planner, my address book, and my e-mail in-box. It's helpful when I'm traveling all the time, since I'm able to get my e-mails, phone calls, and text messages all in the same device. And I have my entire life schedule programmed into it, as well. In other words, if I ever lost the thing, I'd be fucked . . . royally.

I removed the metal stylus and marked out all of next Saturday and half of Sunday for my trip to Vegas. Then I checked the clock on my dashboard. I was right on schedule. Just enough time to make a quick stop at the gym for an abbreviated workout, a rinse in the locker-room shower, and then off to my next assignment.

I stuck my Bluetooth headset into my ear and clicked it on. After a series of quick beeps I clearly pronounced the name of my travel agent into the mouthpiece.

I waited as my phone dialed.

"Hi, Lenore. I need to book a flight to Vegas," I said pleasantly as I turned left out of the parking garage and onto Avenue of the Stars.

"Hi, Miss Hunter. No problem."

I heard typing through my earpiece. "Weren't you just in Vegas?" she asked, making small talk as she searched for an available flight.

I laughed my normal "I'm so busy" laugh and replied, "Yes, lots of clients send me to Vegas. It seems to be a popular place to do business lately."

"That it is," she agreed. "All that investing to be done in those huge hotels!"

"Exactly."

As I was probably one of her bigger clients, Lenore was always good at remembering the details of my job. Well, my fake job, rather. "Okay, what time do you need to arrive?"

After a quick calculation in my head I told her seven, giving myself a generous time cushion to account for delays, traffic, costume malfunctions, etc.

More typing and then: "Okay, I have a first-class seat on a flight that leaves LAX at five forty-five P.M., getting you into Las Vegas at six-fifty. Will that work?"

"Perfect. Let's book it."

"And will you be staying at the Wynn again this time?"

I thought back to my conversation with Mr. Ireland. "No, my client will be staying at the Bellagio. I'd like to stay there as well."

"No problem. I'll take care of it and e-mail you the itinerary by end of day today."

"Thanks, Lenore."

"With all these trips lately, you've probably racked up more frequent-flyer miles than Superman," she remarked, amused.

I laughed into the phone. "You're probably right."

I clicked off my headset and turned onto the entrance of the freeway, preparing to sit in bumper-to-bumper traffic for at least the next forty-five minutes.

In all honesty, sometimes I did feel kind of like a little, mini-Superman. Dressed in my kick-ass, body-accentuating costumes, flying from city to city to fight against the evils of infidelity. I even had my very own secret identity. All I was missing was the ability to see through walls . . . and, apparently, drive through traffic.

I leaned my head back against the headrest and reached up to massage my forehead with the back side of my hand. I was starting to feel the effects of my long day. In this job, the days were never short. And I was exhausted most of the time. But I refused to complain.

After all, it was entirely by choice.

And I've never heard of Superman whining about *his* long-ass days.

4

fantasy football

At six P.M. the gym was packed. Hordes of people trying to work off their guilty pleasures of the day. Older men attempting to lose inches off their waistline, younger men attempting to add inches to the circumference of their upper arms, and forty-year-old housewives with thousands of dollars of plastic surgery trying desperately to compete with the slim and perky twenty-year-olds who have managed to master the art of working up just enough of a sweat on the elliptical machines to make their bronzed midriffs glisten, but not enough to wash off the layers of natural-*looking* makeup on their faces.

I slipped my iPod into its case and secured it onto the waistband of my shorts. As I pushed the locker-room door open, I braced myself for the awaiting crowd of people. I bowed my head and attempted to lose myself in the music blaring out of my headphones as I weaved through the theme-park-worthy line of people waiting to use the elliptical cross trainers and made my way to the row of treadmills.

My weekly exercise routine consisted of two days of thirty-minute cardio and two days of Pilates at a studio in Santa Monica. I would probably only be able to fit in a twenty-minute run today if I wanted to get to my next destination on time.

As I warmed up with a slow jog, I could feel eyes on me. I knew that to everyone else I looked like just another L.A. twenty-something gym goer, starving myself to fit an unobtainable mold so I could attract a rich husband, and then, in five years or so, an even richer one.

But I wasn't anything like them. In fact, I was quite their opposite.

I was just as fit as them. And my naturally olive-colored skin glistened just as much when I sweat. But my motives were so far removed from their world.

Yes, I also worked out so I could attract men.

But not to find a rich husband. To expose an unfaithful one.

In fact, I *had* to look like all of those other girls. Because most of the time that's who these husbands will cheat with if given the opportunity.

I reached down and skipped through my iPod playlist until I found an upbeat song, and then increased the speed on my treadmill. I ran to the beat of the music, and after two short minutes I could feel the beads of sweat forming on my forehead.

The release felt amazing. Like a rush of energy and power racing through my entire body. After I had run flat-out for twenty minutes, I pressed the *Cool Down* button, and slowed to a brisk walk. I pulled my towel from the handlebar and wiped down my face.

As the preprogrammed cool-down feature of the treadmill gradually decreased my speed, I reached back and tightened the rubber band holding my ponytail in place.

It was then that I noticed the man walking beside me, on the next treadmill over. I turned my head and looked at him. He was already looking in my direction, and when our eyes met, he smiled at me.

I smiled back politely.

He was attractive. Probably in his mid-twenties, with light brown hair, gentle eyes, and a toned body.

Just as I was about to turn my attention back to the floor-to-ceiling windows in front of me, I saw his mouth move. He was saying something to me, but all I could hear was the blasting of incomprehensible punk rock lyrics in my ears.

For a moment I considered just ignoring him, chalking it up to the fact that I was wearing headphones and therefore granted immunity from having to make any type of gym small talk. But, I reasoned, it would probably be rude to turn my head and pretend I didn't see him try to speak.

So I pulled out the ear buds and said, "Sorry, what?"

He chuckled. "Oh, I just said I've never seen anyone run with such passion before. It almost looked like you were running from the bogeyman or something."

I laughed and brushed a strand of damp hair behind my ear. "Yeah, never a big fan of the bogeyman."

"Are you training for something?"

"Yes . . . life," I replied sardonically.

"That's a good one. I'll have to remember that one."

I smiled.

"I've never seen you in here before."

I picked up my water bottle from the plastic holder on the treadmill's dashboard and took a sip. "I don't usually come to this location. It just happened to be near work."

My treadmill slowly came to a stop, and I watched as his slowed as well, almost as if they had been perfectly timed to stop one after the other.

He looked at me and grinned at the unspoken coincidence as we both stepped back onto stationary ground.

"You work around here? What do you do?" he asked.

I shrugged. "I'm an investment banker. I'm valuing a firm that's located a few blocks from here."

"Wow, an investment banker. That's pretty big time. So you're smart *and* cute. A deadly combination."

I blushed and fidgeted with my iPod. "Thank you. What do *you* do?" I asked immediately, anxious to get off the subject of me and my fake job.

"I'm a video game designer."

"Really? Any I might have heard of?"

He shook his head sadly. "Probably not. I work for a pretty small design company. We haven't really had any huge releases yet. We just completed a game called Powerless. It's kind of like a political Sim City."

I nodded. "Sim City. I've heard of that."

He laughed. "Well, I guess that's a start."

"Actually, I'm still waiting for Carmen Sandiego and Oregon Trail to make their comeback."

He laughed. "Oh my God. You remember Oregon Trail?

"How could I forget? We used to play that every day during recess in the fourth grade. 'Becky has cholera.' " I impersonated the detached bluntness of the game's memorable on-screen updates.

"Becky has died." He followed suit in an equally mundane voice.

We both cracked up.

"Hey," he began with charming timidity. "Can I treat you to a smoothie downstairs?"

I wiped the back of my neck with my towel. "Um . . ." I stammered awkwardly.

"Maybe a PowerBar?"

"I actually have plans tonight," I said with regret. "I should really get showered and go."

He nodded, and then covered his less than obscure disappointment with another smile. "Okay. Maybe another time then?"

"Sure," I said politely. "Another time." I smiled at him and then started off toward the locker room. I heard his pace quicken as he strode up next to me.

"But if you don't normally come to this location," he said, stepping in line with me. "I might not see you next time."

I laughed at his persistence and then stopped and turned to face him, crossing my arms in mock defiance. "So what exactly are you suggesting?"

He fidgeted slightly with his feet and looked down at the ground. "I'm just saying that you should probably give me your number. Just in case I *don't* see you next time."

His approach wasn't exactly smooth, but it was somewhat endearing. I don't normally give out my phone number. Especially to a guy I had just met on a treadmill. But the man standing in front of me wasn't like most of the guys who normally ask me out. He stood apart.

And that was why I said, "Okay, sure. Why not?" And then recited my prestigious Westside 310 number as he eagerly removed his phone from his backpack pocket and punched in the corresponding digits.

He looked up at me and grinned. "I'm Clayton, by the way. So you'll know who it is when I call."

"Nice to meet you."

After a thorough rinse in the locker-room shower, I toweled myself off and checked my phone. I had three new e-mails. I quickly browsed the in-box. One was from my mother, something about an online test to determine your overall botany knowledge. Another from Sophie thanking me for putting up with her drama earlier in the day (a very common e-mail to come to my phone). And the third was the itinerary for my Vegas trip, as promised, from my travel agent.

I quickly threw on a casual change of clothing, slung my gym bag over my shoulder, and made a beeline for the front door.

Enough of these flirtatious trips down elementary-school memory lane. It was time to get serious again. There was work to be done.

I started my car and entered my next destination into the navigation system. Per the GPS lady's suggestion, I turned left out of the parking lot, and in 0.7 miles, merged onto Century Boulevard.

Tonight a man named Andrew Thompson was scheduled to meet his dream girl.

He just didn't know it yet.

According to his wife, Andrew has always had a thing for flight attendants. Flight attendants and football.

"It started out as a joke between us," she had explained to me last week during our initial meeting. "He'd see one on TV or in the terminal and whisper something to me like, 'Honey, we *need* to get you one of those outfits.' It used to be cute." She somberly shook her head. "A lot of things used to be cute . . . including me."

So tonight I had invented what I believed to be Andrew Thompson's ideal woman. A football-obsessed flight attendant. Prim and proper in the air but down and dirty when she's drinking beer and watching her favorite team play on ESPN. The truth is, most men who are going to cheat are probably going to cheat regardless of what you're wearing or what kind of sports statistics you manage to casually toss into the conversation. But that's not always the case. Some guys will cheat with anyone, while others are more specific. More particular. I have to be prepared for both. That's why fulfilling a fantasy is always the safest bet.

But in the end it was really all the same to me. Cheating is cheating. It doesn't matter how selective you are when you do it.

A big part of my job is research. Preparation. I like to gather as much information as I can before going out on an assignment, because the more I know going in, the faster I can count on getting out. Creating someone's fantasy girl, however, isn't just about knowing in advance that they have a thing for flight attendants or poker players. Just as being a successful door-to-door vacuum salesman isn't only about being able to recite the sucking power ratio of the latest Hoover model. In the time it takes for that house door to swing open, you have to be able to come up with an instant analysis about the person standing behind it. You have to immediately "know" exactly what he/she wants to hear about vacuum cleaners. Otherwise you'll just end up with a door slammed in your face.

I guess if I *were* some kind of female superhero, this would be considered my identifying "superpower." Although I'd have to say that it's really just more of a knack. It's taken me a few years to perfect, but now it comes fairly naturally.

You know those mathematical geniuses who can break any high-profile, top-secret code in a matter of seconds?

Well, I can't do that.

But, what I *can* do is much more difficult. I can decipher any man you put in front of me . . . in less than thirty seconds.

That's right. Like an open book.

I don't know where it came from. I suppose I was just born with it. My friends call it a "gift from God." I wouldn't exactly go that far. If only they knew what it was really used for.

But, I must admit, being able to decipher men as fast as a cryptologist breaks top-secret codes can definitely come in handy when you're expected to encounter a different man every night as his supposed dream girl.

Andrew Thompson lived in San Francisco with his wife, but tonight he was in Los Angeles for business, staying at the Westin by the airport. I asked the valet at the hotel to escort me quietly to the back entrance of the building, discreetly slipping him a large bill to encourage compliance. He gladly accepted it and walked me around the side to a small, unadorned glass door that he respectfully held open for me. Pulling my black suitcase behind me, I located an empty public restroom on the ground floor and made my way into the handicap stall at the end of the row. I quickly shed my clothes and pulled out my flight attendant's uniform from the suitcase.

It actually belonged to a friend of mine who really *was* a flight attendant for Continental Airlines. I had explained to her that I was going to a fantasy-themed party where you were supposed to come dressed as a popular sexual fantasy. I told her that I wanted to dress up as an active member of the "mile-high club" and hoped that the flight attendant garb would properly communicate that.

She giggled at the idea and readily agreed to let me borrow it.

I zipped up the navy-colored skirt around my waist and pulled the matching jacket over my shoulders, adjusting the gold wings that were pinned to the lapel. I then slipped my Birkin into the suitcase and replaced it with a simpler black shoulder bag. Much more representative of a flight attendant's salary.

I fixed my hair and touched up my makeup in the bathroom mirror and then took a deep breath before opening the door.

Andrew Thompson was believed to be at the hotel bar, watching the college football game. Because, according to his wife, "he never misses it."

USC versus Michigan. Andrew's alma mater, and, coincidentally, tonight . . . Ashlyn's as well.

I didn't have the luxury of being able to scope out the bar and locate the subject before entering. I had to make a grand entrance. It was all part of tonight's charade. And therefore I had to trust that Emily Thompson's knowledge of her husband's evening, after-work activities would be accurate. Otherwise, my charade would be wasted on a bunch of semidrunk, overweight college-football fans.

As I approached the lobby I could see the entrance of the hotel bar about one hundred feet in front of me. I picked up the pace, jogging frantically through the relatively busy lobby, pulling my suitcase behind me and attempting to dodge other hotel patrons as I desperately made my way toward the faint sounds of cheering.

I burst into the bar breathlessly, slowing my pace and wiping my brow with the back side of my hand. "What'd I miss? What's the score?" I took a deep, much-needed breath.

There were five guys sitting around the bar, staring up at the TV screen. All five of them turned to look at me. The grand entrance was a success.

I spotted Andrew Thompson at the far end with, thankfully, an empty bar stool next to him. I immediately made my way over, careful to keep my eyes attentively glued to the screen. I casually slid in next to Andrew, resting my suitcase off to the side and my purse on top of the bar.

I stared obliviously straight ahead as Andrew subtly gave me a once-over. I turned briefly to him and smiled. "Hi," I said aloofly, and then returned my attention to the game.

It took him a minute to come out of his trance, and then he finally replied, "Thirteen-nothing, USC."

"Damn it!" I cursed, shaking my head in disapproval. "Smith's been underestimating his injury. I knew they should have played Wilde."

Out of the corner of my eye I saw Andrew momentarily ignore the game completely and look at me in utter astonishment, trying to digest the words coming out of my mouth. Because he knew as well I did that they made perfect sense.

God bless the Internet.

He slowly turned his attention back to the TV screen, the look of bewilderment never leaving his face. It was as if he couldn't even believe women like this actually exist, let alone sit next to him in a bar. Only in his wildest fantasies.

I continued to concentrate solely on the game, managing to successfully order a beer from the bartender without ever altering the direction of my eye line.

The timer on my cell phone went off at 7:15 P.M. Exactly when I had scheduled it. And to anyone else, namely Andrew Thompson, the tone I had programmed as the alarm would sound exactly like a phone ring. Without turning my head away from the TV, I fumbled in my purse, pulled it out, and brought it to my ear. "Yeah, I saw it," I said informally, as if I didn't even have to look at the caller ID to know exactly who was calling me at this moment in time.

This is what happens when there's a Michigan football game on. I watch it, and whoever this person is calls to commentate.

I listened to the silent earpiece. "I fucking told you Grady was incapable of making plays like that." I paused to listen again, keeping my eyes straight ahead. "No, no, no," I argued with the phantom caller. "He's a fucking freshman. What did you expect? Four hundred sixty-six yards in one season is nothing to brag about."

I heard a small chuckle come from Andrew's direction. I glanced at him out of the corner of my eye and flashed a knowing smile, as if we were sharing a mutual annoyance with anyone who has faith in a player like Grady (whoever the hell he was).

He smiled back, and I knew that my research was paying off.

"Look, I'll call you tomorrow, okay?" I waited for a response and then quickly added, "Yeah, whatever, bye." And hung up the phone.

I let out a frustrated sigh and tossed the phone onto the bar. "Fucking loser," I mumbled under my breath.

A commercial break came on, and I suddenly noticed the beer sitting in front of me. I picked it up gratefully and took a long, refreshing gulp. "God, what a day."

"So you had to have gone to Michigan," Andrew said, watching me intently.

I turned and grinned. "Hell, yeah!"

"Class of '85," he said proudly.

" 'Ninety-nine," I shot back competitively.

"Ouch! Do I feel old?"

I looked him up and down in a mock assessment and then shrugged. "You don't look it," I said matter-of-factly.

"Thanks. So you're a flight attendant?"

I eyed him skeptically. "No, I just like to wear this outfit to pick up guys in bars."

He laughed.

Tonight I was a hard-ass and according to Andrew, quite an intriguing one at that. So far my "analysis" was right on course.

I chugged down the rest of my beer, and he rushed to order me another one. "A girl who likes football and knows how to drink beer. I can certainly appreciate that."

"If every woman had to be sweet and cheerful to the assholes I deal with on a daily basis, they'd chug beer, too."

He laughed again. "That bad, huh?"

"It's like fucking sugar and spice up there. Makes my teeth hurt."

The bartender brought my beer and we clinked glasses, offering a hopeful toast to the doomed fate of our beloved Michigan Wolverines, just in time to turn our attention back to the screen as the commercial break ended.

Two hours and seven beers later, Andrew and I were wasted. Well, actually, Andrew and *Ashlyn* were wasted. I was fine. I never allow myself to get drunk on an assignment. I've spent the last two years building up my level of tolerance to alcohol for specifically that reason. Alcohol makes you lose focus, makes you do stupid things. Case in point: seventy-five percent of the men who have failed my inspection were under the influence of at least *some* amount of alcohol, if not a very large amount. Some people might try to argue the legitimacy of the inspection because of this factor. My public, professional opinion: The legitimacy decision is entirely up to the client. But my own private, personal, would-never-dare-share-with-anyone opinion: They can shove their legitimacy issues up their asses. Alcohol is an everyday part of life. If you can't drink it and still manage to stay faithful to your wife at home, then you either shouldn't be drinking it or you shouldn't have a wife at home.

But that's just one of my own humble opinions. I keep those to myself.

Andrew and I had moved from the bar to a table in the corner, where we commiserated together and washed away the pain of a bitter loss to USC.

"I guess it's better that we lose to an undefeated than a nobody," I said, holding my head in what could only be interpreted as drunkenness mixed with wallowing in despair.

Andrew finished off his beer in one definitive gulp, slammed the empty glass down on the table, and then leaned across and looked me straight in the eye. "Has anyone ever told you how *hot* you are?" His eyes were starting to glaze over.

"Okay, no more beer for this one!" I called out to the now-empty bar, raising my hand up in the air and pointing at the top of his head.

He reached up and pulled my hand down, holding it in his own. "I'm serious. You have no idea, do you?"

I stayed in character, waving away his comment as if it was ludicrous. "Stop. You sound like a fucking lame ass right now."

He pulled my hand closer to him, and I immediately felt the wedding ring on his fourth finger. He hadn't even bothered to take it off. Or rather, he hadn't remembered. It made me believe that he was probably a first-timer. Not a professional like Raymond Jacobs, whose wedding ring slides on and off like a pair of flip-flops.

But it doesn't really matter. First-timers, old-timers, seasoned pros—they all blend together in my mind once it's over.

And anyway, it's not my place to judge. If a wife or girlfriend or fiancée chooses to forgive him on the grounds that it was his "first time" and he more than likely learned his lesson, then that's their choice. I only deliver the information that was requested of me. I don't tell them how to use it. And I don't make recommendations.

"Would it be weird if I asked to kiss you?" he asked, his expression suddenly turning serious.

I considered this for a moment, placing my fingertip thoughtfully on my chin, in an effort to continue my act of silly intoxication. "Um, no . . . but it might be weird if you asked to *smell* me."

He laughed. "Oh, I already smelled you at the bar. And you smell good."

"Hmm. Like airplane food?" I asked, struggling to maintain a serious expression, and then eventually bursting into uncontrollable drunken laughter.

Andrew laughed with me. "Do you want to get out of here?"

"Good idea."

"My room?"

I nodded vigorously, as if it was the best idea I'd heard in years, and how come it had taken him so long to suggest it.

His body shot up from his seat like a rocket, and with his hand still tightly grasped around mine, he pulled me behind him.

In the end Andrew Thompson never actually *asked* to kiss me. Once we were behind closed doors, he just went for it. He kissed me like a drunk boy at a frat party. Sloppy and horny. It was almost as if the football game had brought him back to his youth, and now he was reliving his carefree party days as a student at the University of Michigan. And to top it all off . . . with a flight attendant.

As he continued to kiss me, slowly peeling off the layers of his fantasy ensemble, he silently marveled to himself that it was just as amazing as he'd always imagined it would be.

Andrew never did take off his ring. It was almost as if he simply forgot it was there. Like it had become a part of him and his everyday life, but somewhere along the way its symbolic meaning had evaporated into the air of a monotonous marriage.

I didn't forget about it, though. I felt it every time his hand brushed over my skin. The cold, hard metal interrupting every inch of his touch like a constant reminder of exactly what I was doing. And, more important, exactly what *he* was doing.

But I didn't object. I let his lips explore and his hands wander, wedding ring and all.

Because it's my job to *not* object.

Always the willing participant.

No matter how much it disgusted me. No matter how much it repulsed me.

That's why I always removed myself from the situation. I was never Jennifer Hunter at that moment. Kissing a stranger. Letting his hands explore my body. I was always Ashlyn.

Because Ashlyn never came home with me.

Ashlyn never changed into my white cotton pajamas that smelled like fabric softener from Marta's diligent laundering. Ashlyn never snuggled in-between my white satin sheets, with the stuffed elephant I'd slept with for years. And Ashlyn never woke up and saw her reflection in my bathroom mirror the next morning.

That was Jennifer. And so therefore it was important to keep them as separate as possible. Because as soon as those lines are blurred, that's when everything starts to fall apart. That's when it becomes personal.

And in this business, nothing can be personal. It's like drenching your emotions in lighter fluid and then standing dangerously close to an open flame. And as much as I wished my arms and legs and heart were made of steel, I was still human. I was no robot.

Ashlyn, however, was my shield.

"I've always wanted to sleep with a flight attendant." His voice was muffled as his lips buried into my neck.

"I guess it's your lucky day, then."

"It most certainly is," he cooed.

And that's when I brought Andrew Thompson's lifelong fantasy to a crashing halt.

Maybe he would never fully understand the words that came out of my mouth when I told him who I really was. And maybe he would never fully appreciate the light I shed on the current state of his marriage. But there was one thing I knew for sure: He would never look at a flight attendant the same way again.

5

the origin of the species (part 1)

When I stepped back inside my condo at the end of the night, the contrast with the dark hotel room I had just left was overwhelming. It felt like I had exited a whole different world and entered this one. The other world was dark, full of distrust and lies. This world was beautiful, spacious, sparkling, and white. Like a commercial for all-purpose cleaner.

It was a place I could be myself.

Not anybody else.

This week alone Ashlyn had been a lawyer, a grad student, a sorority girl, a research manager, and a flight attendant. It was nice to just be me again. Jennifer Hunter.

There was only one problem.

As I stared at myself in the mirror after stripping away all the mascara that covered my eyes and all the foundation that transformed my face, I couldn't help but feel like the girl staring back at me was becoming a stranger.

Less and less familiar every day.

And that was hard to ignore.

I exhaled loudly and shut off the light, extinguishing the unfamiliar face with the darkness.

I climbed into bed and snuggled under my white sheets. They felt soft on my skin. Like flower petals. I looked longingly at the pillow on the other side of the bed. Except for Marta's soft hands, it had remained untouched for more than two years. I reached under it and pulled out my tattered, stuffed purple elephant. The one I've slept with every night since I was twelve years old.

And I remembered that first night like it was yesterday.

Snuffles the elephant had never been my favorite stuffed animal. He had been sitting on the window seat of my room since the day I was born, but I had never taken a particular liking to him.

I inadvertently named him Snuffles when I was two, because I would see him in my bedroom after watching *Sesame Street* and would shrewdly remark that he looked a lot like Mr. Snuffleupagus. Except I couldn't pronounce the entire name of Snuffleupagus, so I would simply point to the purple elephant and say, "Snuffle." Which later was changed to Snuffles.

But I had always favored other toys. Leo the Bear, Floppsy the Rabbit, Frank the Fish. Each night rotating them out, enjoying the variety and excitement of a new bed companion as I fell asleep.

Snuffles never really made it into the mix.

When my mom would tuck me in at night we would always go through the same selection routine, "the bedtime game," as we liked to call it.

I would happily climb into bed and nestle under the covers of my Rainbow Brite comforter or My Little Pony sheets (depending on the age), and she would walk to the windowsill and stand purposefully in front of each toy like a drill sergeant making a daily bunk inspection. Her hand would linger approximately six inches above the head of each animal, and she would wait patiently through my series of resolute head shakes until my eyes would finally light up and my head would fall into an eager nod as she approached the chosen one.

My mom would then pick up the toy privileged enough to be selected for cuddle duty and carefully deliver it into my outstretched arms.

"How come you never pick Snuffles?" she would ask me every once in a while, as I consistently, night after night, allowed her hand to graze past the purple elephant, as it never received my legendary nod of approval.

To which I would shrug and say, "I don't know. I just like the other ones better."

And then from time to time she would pick up the lonely, neglected purple elephant and hold it close to her face, breathing in the smell of his soft fur. "You're making him feel lonely, though."

I would simply roll my eyes and say, "Oh, Mom. He'll get over it."

And then my mom and I would share a laugh as she brought over my friend of choice and lovingly tuck him in next to me before kissing me good night. As the years passed I became less and less interested in stuffed animals. And by the time I was twelve my mother couldn't pay me to sleep next to one.

"Mom," I would say in a warning tone when every once in a while she would ask me if I wanted to play our beloved nighttime selection game again . . . just for old time's sake. "If word ever got out that I sleep with a stuffed fish named Frank, my reputation would be ruined."

My mom would then shake her head and laugh. "I'll bet every single girl at your school has a secret animal that she sleeps with." But I never believed her. There was no way I was ever going to fit in with the popular eighth-graders at school next year if I was still acting like a five-year-old at home.

But then one night, everything changed. Everything became different.

And everything would *remain* different from that night on.

My mom had gone away to visit my grandmother in Chicago, who I was told was having an operation on her knee.

"Her knee is getting too old for her to use, so they have to give her a new one," my mom had explained to me as we drove her to the airport.

"A *new* one?" I asked in a snotty voice, trying to maintain my usual "I could care less about anything my parents say" attitude.

"Yes, they're going to take her knee out and replace it with a metal one."

"They can do that?" I blurted out in amazement, and then quickly regained my cool. "I mean . . . that's kind of weird."

"Fortunately for Grandma, they can," my mom said, reaching back and gently patting my own healthy knee.

"Well, why can't I come?" I asked, folding my arms defiantly across my chest. As much as I wanted to be the cool preteen girl who didn't care where her mom traveled to or how long she would be gone, I still didn't like the thought of being away from her.

"Because Daddy needs you to stay here and keep him company."

I rolled my eyes and groaned loudly enough for both of them to hear. I so wished my parents would start talking to me like an adult and not a twelve-year-old. But deep down, my mother's comment made me feel needed. And I liked that. Without saying another word, I settled into the decision that maybe I should stick around and serve my civic duty as "only child."

My dad had been married once before. A long time ago. He had a daughter with his first wife. But I rarely ever saw my half-sister Julia, except at large family gatherings. I didn't really mind our infrequent contact, though. I always got the feeling that she didn't really care for me all that much. Which was probably true. She was ten years older than me, and looking back on it now that I'm almost thirty, I can understand how the new baby from the new wife could be a bit of a downer.

So as far as I was concerned, it was just Mom, Dad, and me. And I had absolutely no complaints about that. I enjoyed being an only child. Most only children beg for siblings, but after seeing how much Julia resented me, I was content not having any.

But as it turned out, my dad didn't really need me there to keep him company. He had to go to a business dinner that same night, and instead I was stuck with the babysitter, a twenty-year-old college student named Elizabeth who my mother had recruited from my summer camp two years earlier. She had been a counselor there and, as my mom explained to me after a lengthy discussion with the camp director one day, was "very responsible and trustworthy."

"Why do I have to have a babysitter?" I argued with my dad.

"We've been through this, Jenny," he warned. "You can stay home alone when you're thirteen, but not twelve."

"I'll be thirteen in nine months!" I shouted back. "I don't really see how nine months can make all that much of a difference."

But there was usually no arguing with my father. And I would have called my mom and let her argue for me, but I knew that she wouldn't have taken my side on this one. Thirteen had always been the magic year to look forward to in my life. It was when I was promised to have my own phone line, my own TV, and the ability to stay home without a dreaded babysitter there to tell me what to do.

For the most part, Elizabeth was perfectly nice and pleasant to be around. And I always admired her good looks and sense of style, hoping that one day I would grow up to look and dress similarly, but at this stage of my life she represented another chain that locked me to my youth while all my friends were being allowed to grow up.

And to make matters worse, Elizabeth would send me to bed at ten o'clock. She never let me stay up late. You would think that being not so far removed from the awkward preteen years herself she would be empathetic to my struggle and understand the pure exhilaration you experience when you're allowed to stay up past your normal bedtime. It was like every five minutes of forbidden awakeness was equivalent to five extra years tacked onto your age.

But she would simply wait by the door as I got into bed, switch off the light, and then hurry back downstairs, eager to return to whatever show was blaring from the TV, and, of course, whomever she was blabbing to on the phone.

After she left I would usually sulk in my bed for about five minutes before drifting off to sleep to the faint sounds of her laughter and gossip mixed with late-night infomercials.

The night my mother went to Chicago started out like any other night Elizabeth was hired to watch me. She stood in the doorway, waiting as I climbed into bed and pulled the covers up to my chin.

"Five more minutes," I tried to negotiate for the tenth time.

"Good night, Jenny," she said vacantly, and then turned off the light and closed the door behind her.

I lay awake, staring at the ceiling, my arms crossed, my whole world on the verge of collapsing, and, in truth, missing my mom terribly. I knew she wasn't coming home for another three days, and it saddened me to think about that.

I exhaled my frustration loudly, and then reluctantly turned onto my side, tucked my hands underneath my pillow, and tried to fall asleep.

I must have dozed off for nearly two hours, because when I was awoken by distant voices and muffled giggles, the clock on my nightstand said it was midnight.

I turned my ear toward the door and listened as the sounds became more and more intrusive. I rolled my eyes and groaned softly. Another late-night Elizabeth gabfest.

Most of the time, I was able to drift back to sleep despite the noise, but tonight was different. Tonight it seemed incessant. And unusually irritating. So I climbed out of bed, quietly opened my door, and tiptoed down the stairs, determined to put a stop to this annoying interference. But as I grew closer to the living room I heard something I had never heard before. I stopped and listened. It was the distinct sound of a male voice, coming from the next room.

I smiled mischievously as I continued to tiptoe my way down the hallway, hoping to catch my so-called "responsible and trustworthy" babysitter with an uninvited male visitor in the middle of my parents' living room.

I felt a surge of sinful exhilaration flow through my body, knowing full well that once I caught her in the middle of doing something inappropriate while I was under her care, it would be the end of her. That would certainly teach my parents to leave me alone with a lovesick college student.

Maybe they'd finally decide to loosen their death grip on that stupid "not until you're thirteen" rule, and next time I would finally be able to stay home by myself.

I placed my palms flat against the hallway wall and stealthily stuck my head around the corner of the living room, ready to jump out and scare them enough to send the unwanted guest packing.

But what I saw in that room sent me into a spiral of shock. It was a cold-blooded numbness like nothing I'd ever experienced before, not even when my friend Sophie and I found that videotape in her dad's closet. The one with naked men and women doing what we only assumed to be things that were done on TV and no place else.

But unlike the videotape we had found, which neither one of us was able to bring ourself to shut off, I had no trouble tearing my eyes from the sight that lay in front of me.

With a rush of sheer panic I spun my head back around the corner and shot up the stairs, careful to tread lightly so that the sound of my bare feet on the wooden steps wouldn't draw attention.

The last thing I wanted was to be discovered, seeing what I had seen.

The stairs seemed to go on forever. As though there were ten times as many as there had been when I came down less than a minute ago. When I finally reached the top I crept into my bedroom and silently closed the door behind me. The room was quiet. And I managed to drown out the whispered voices and muffled moans coming through my door by focusing on the sound of my heart thumping loudly in my chest.

I felt tears of fear and disbelief well up in my eyes as I allowed my body to crumple to the ground, trying desperately to make sense of what I had just witnessed. Trying to figure out what it meant and what it *would* mean for the future.

In the darkness of my bedroom the same image repeated in my mind. Like a scene from a movie, being rewound and played over and over again, without any signs of stopping.

It was Elizabeth, on the couch, her head tilted back on one of the throw pillows, her trendy top casually thrown onto the nearby coffee table. Her bra was red and black, like the kind I used to see in the Victoria's Secret catalogs that I would steal from the trash compactor after my mom had taken them from the mailbox and thrown them away. And the hand that was gratifyingly caressing up and down her bare stomach and ravenously around the sides of her slender waist . . . was my father's.

He was kissing her in a way I had never seen him kiss my mother. Like he was devouring her. But yet, her satisfied moans were agonizingly similar to the ones Sophie and I had heard on the videotape, and it made me believe that she didn't exactly mind being devoured.

When my parents kissed, it was tender and sweet. A gentle brushing of the lips that lasted maybe a second or two, three if they were saying good-bye before one of my dad's business trips.

But there was nothing tender and sweet about what my father was doing downstairs. His lips weren't even closed. They were open, and so were hers. It was almost like the way the eighth-graders kissed in front of their lockers, but much more adept.

Sophie had found out a few years before that it was called "French kissing." And I remembered asking my mom about it when I was nine years old. She laughed and explained, "Some people just like to kiss with their mouths open."

"Why?" I asked, clearly not understanding why anyone on earth would want to do that. At age nine the inside of a mouth was merely the place where chewed-up food lingered before it was swallowed. Far from an "erogenous" zone.

My mom shrugged, amused by my curiosity. "I don't know. Maybe because for some people it feels good."

Now, suddenly the thought of my babysitter, Elizabeth, making my dad feel good with her open-mouthed kiss made me bolt up to my feet and grasp desperately for the light switch on the wall.

The bright glow was a welcome salvation. It chased away all the lingering images and brought focus to the happy and joyful landmarks that were scattered about my room. The posters on my wall illuminating the envied influences of Paula Abdul, Janet Jackson, and The Party. The Madame Alexander doll collection my mom and I had started three years ago after she had given me my first one for Christmas. My pink boom box with the latest Debbie Gibson tape inside . . . exactly where I had left it after Sophie and I had choreographed a dance routine to the song "Electric Youth."

Then my eyes found their way to my nightstand, with the framed photograph of my mom propped up on top of it. It was a picture my dad had taken while she was pregnant with me. She was sitting in the backyard of our first house, lounging on one of the chairs. Our dog, Casey, who was then only a puppy, was making her laugh by determinedly attempting to climb onto her lap. It wasn't a particularly special picture. But I had found it in my mom's photo box a few years before and asked if I could frame it and put it in my room.

I picked up the frame and held it in my hands.

That night I felt an emotion for my mother that I'd never felt before: pity. She had always been the wise one, the one who knew everything about the world and all the things in it that she needed to protect me from.

And tonight, as I stared at the picture, it was clear to me that our roles had suddenly been reversed.

She was now the one who would need protection. And I was the only one who could give that to her.

I grew up that night.

In one accidental glance that revealed a side of my parents' life I never knew existed, in that one glimpse at the complexities of an adult relationship, I knew I had taken a giant step closer to becoming an adult myself. A step I always naively assumed came with a private phone line and a later curfew.

I placed the picture down and climbed back into bed. Not daring to shut the light off again, I tried desperately to ignore the distant sounds that continued to find their way from the shadowy living room, up the long staircase, and through the small crack under my closed door.

Three nights later my mom came into my room to kiss me good night for the first time since she had left. "Sweet dreams," she said, walking toward the door and resting her hand on the light switch.

I suddenly sat upright in bed. "Mom?"

"Yeah?"

"Play the game," I requested softly.

She cocked her head to the side and smiled at me. "The bedtime game?"

I nodded.

"But I thought you were too old for that," she teased, moving toward the windowsill.

I looked down at my lap and fidgeted with the edge of my comforter. Then, with a rush of unexpected strength, I picked up my head and looked her straight in the eye. "I'm not," I said confidently.

The smile on her face brightened up the entire room as she took her usual place in front of the first contestant. It was exactly as I had remembered it. My mom played the game with the same flawless delivery as she always had. It was like we hadn't missed one single night in all those years.

She started in front of Leo the Bear. I obstinately shook my head. She raised her eyebrows curiously, and with one step to the left, moved on to the next contender.

Frank the Fish?

I shook my head.

Floppsy the Rabbit? Always a popular choice.

I shook my head again.

I knew exactly whose turn it was. And he had waited long enough.

When she reached Snuffles the Elephant, I nodded triumphantly and reached my arms out for him to be brought to me.

"Well, isn't that an interesting change of heart?" my mom said with genuine surprise, as she carried him over and placed him tenderly in my awaiting arms.

I held him close and buried my face in his soft purple fur. He smelled new and fresh and . . . untainted.

I lay back down under the covers and tucked him into the once highly coveted spot in the crook of my elbow. My mom kissed me again on the forehead and then leaned over and kissed Snuffles as well. When she stood up she looked at me, her eyes filled with questions.

Questions that I knew I would never be able to answer.

Not because I didn't know, but because I would choose not to.

"Are you okay?" she asked.

I nodded, swallowing back tears that threatened to flow without end.

"So why Snuffles? Why now?"

I took a deep breath and pulled him in closer to me. "I just wanted to make sure he wouldn't be lonely."

6

full circle

Saturday morning I awoke at nine-thirty A.M. to the ring of my home phone. It was my first day off in what felt like months. I pulled the extra pillow over my head and tried to drown out the sound until eventually, after five rings, it stopped. I searched under the tangled sea of sheets and blankets for Snuffles and finally found him lying on the floor next to my bed, looking outcast and rejected.

I reached down and pulled him back into bed, tucking him under my arm again and cooing gentle apologies in his ear before drifting back to sleep.

The phone rang again thirty seconds later.

I groaned loudly and looked at the caller ID. It was Zoë. "What?" I said groggily into the phone.

"What the fuck do you think you're doing, asshole?!" Her voice came screaming over the line.

Yep, it was Zoë, all right. She had a habit of driving while she was talking on the phone. Which didn't always make for the best conversations, as she also had a habit of engaging in serious road rage. I pulled the phone away from my ear until she had finished yelling at whatever idiot had been daring enough to cut her off.

"Sorry." Her voice returned to its normal, snappy tone. "I'm on Sunset. Apparently they don't teach you how to merge in West Hollywood."

"Is there a reason you're waking me up on a Saturday?"

"Oh, right. Brunch in one hour."

I rubbed my eyes and looked at the clock. "What?"

"Hey, don't take it out on me. Sophie called it. Apparently it's an '*emergency.*'" Zoë clearly was not excited about being dragged to brunch either. Especially since we all know what it means when Sophie uses the word "emergency." It normally consists of a group session in which Sophie panics and makes a big deal about nothing and we all attempt to console her. And as much as I liked being able to console my best friend in her times of need, this happened to be the first morning I was able to sleep late in over two weeks. So needless to say, I wasn't exactly thrilled about it being interrupted for an emergency brunch.

"Did she say what it was about?"

"No. She wouldn't tell me. She said it was IPO."

"Initial public offering?" The investment banker in me ventured a guess at Zoë's latest use of instant-message speak.

"In-person only. But it's not like she has to tell us what this is about. You know it's going to be about— Loser! Are you blind? That's not a fucking turn lane!"

I waited for the elongated honking sounds to subside before asking where this emergency brunch would take place.

"Café Montana."

I groaned and threw the covers off of my body. "Fine. I'll be there."

"You better. I don't want to be the one to tell Sophie you're not coming."

Zoë and I had both learned a long time ago that you can't argue with Sophie when she has her mind set on something. She can make you feel like the lowest, most unsupportive friend in the world if you dare say no to one of her urgent requests.

I yawned and pulled myself up to a sitting position. "I can't promise to be joyful."

"Good. I'm on my way to pick up John. See you in a bit."

And before I could even respond she had hung up the phone. I set it down next to me and lingered on the edge of my bed for a minute, attempting to rally enough energy to stand.

I felt utterly exhausted. My post-assignment meeting with Andrew Thompson's wife yesterday morning in San Francisco had been draining. Most meetings only take about an hour. The women usually want the news, and if it's bad, they usually want me out of their sight. And I don't blame them. I assume their appreciation for my services comes much later, and by that time I'm far removed from their lives. But I don't mind that. It's something I've come to terms with over the years. I've accepted the fact that this just isn't the type of job where you can expect flowers and a thank-you card as a token of gratitude.

But Emily Thompson clung to me like a cotton shirt that had been dried without fabric softener. I was there for over three hours, and as a result missed my flight home and had to go standby on the next flight back to L.A.

By the time I left she had taken me through three family photo albums, over an hour of home videos of Andrew and the kids acting out favorite scenes from Disney movies, and countless stories of their child-free college days, when everything had been about fun, partying, booze, and sex.

Times like these are, by far, the most challenging part of my job. Because when I walk into these people's homes I can feel the critical stares coming from the family portraits hanging on the walls. And when you're in my shoes, you don't just look at these pictures. The pictures look back at you. And they don't just watch you enter their house, they judge you for being there.

Without even bothering to take a shower or wash my face, I dragged myself toward the casual section of my walk-in closet and lethargically pulled on a pair of jeans and a hooded purple sweatshirt. I'm sure Sophie will criticize my informal ensemble in a place like Café Montana, but at this point I could care less. She was stealing my only sleep-in day in weeks; she would have to suffer through my sweatshirt and ripped jeans. And so would Café Montana.

Plus, this is L.A. Dressing casually in a nice place doesn't make you look like a scrub; it makes you look like a celebrity.

I brushed my hair back into a loose ponytail at the base of my neck and pulled a Lakers cap over my head. I grabbed my two cell phones and my keys, shoved them in my new Fendi Spy Bag, and was out the door.

I keep two cell phones with me at all times. A Treo for my business line and a pink Razr for my personal line. The business phone, according to my friends, is the "mind-controlling device that keeps me chained to the evil empire of my overly demanding investment bank." But in actuality, it's linked to the unlisted phone number that is passed around among affluent housewives, mothers, girlfriends, and anyone else who might be in need of my help. The secret network of suspicious women of the world. If they had their own yellow pages I'd be listed under "crucial services."

The number is not published anywhere. I simply will not allow it. My services are offered by referral only. Grassroots, word-of-mouth . . . call it whatever marketing mumbo jumbo you want, that's just the way I work. The minute you start advertising your number on a local bus stop bench is the minute right before you lose your credibility, your confidentiality, and your certain air of mystery. All three very important aspects of this job.

On my way to the restaurant my personal cell phone rang. And just as I was about to shut the damn thing off and ignore the world for a few hours, I saw my niece Hannah's name on the caller ID. My mood instantly changed. Like magic.

"Hi, honey!" I said into the phone.

"You're still coming next Friday, right?"

Hannah was turning twelve next weekend. Her mom (my half sister, Julia) had planned a family dinner with some of Hannah's closest friends on Friday night, and she couldn't have been more excited about it.

"Of course, I'm coming!" My voice was light and animated. It was partially a result of Hannah's uplifting effect on me and partially a creation designed especially to camouflage the nature and harsh reality of my real life. If there was a way I could shield her eyes from everything I've seen in the world, I would. In a heartbeat.

But I knew it was impossible. She was going to come face-to-face with it sooner or later. Even if I never slept, never ate, never watched another minute of TiVo and simply devoted every waking hour of my life to taking down the bad guys, there was still no way I could change the world in time for her to grow up.

"Good," she said with satisfaction. "'Cause I told my best friends that you're coming and that you have like the awesomest clothes in the world."

I looked down at my current ensemble of ripped jeans and a sweatshirt and could immediately picture Hannah's disapproving expression. "Well, I can't wait to meet them. But, actually, I gotta run. I'm on my way to brunch with some friends."

"You're so lucky. I want to come to brunch with you and your friends."

I laughed at her eagerness. It reminded me of myself when I was her age. Well . . . before the night everything changed, anyway.

"I promise, you'd be bored out of your mind," I assured her.

"Nah-uh." She was determined. "I bet you guys talk about totally cool stuff."

I imagined what our "cool" conversation would be like today. Sophie going on and on about every single tiny detail of her so-called "drama" with Eric the night before, and then me trying desperately to convince her of all the reasons why he *wouldn't* want to leave her, while Zoë tries to keep her composure and John tries to change the subject so we can all talk about him.

"You'd be surprised," I told her.

I arrived at the restaurant to find Sophie sitting alone at a table in the back. She waved me over and I maneuvered my way through the closely laid-out tables and took the chair next to her.

"Okay, so what's the big drama? Textbook case of dysfunctional relationship between man and phone? Or nocturnal activity selection dispute?"

"Not until everyone's here," she insisted.

I tilted my head and studied her face. There was something there I wasn't expecting to see. I had counted on wading into a sea of Kleenexes, tears, and uncertainty, followed by a long sob story about Eric and how things were suddenly completely different between them, and she wasn't sure how their relationship would ever recover.

But that's not what I saw in her eyes as I watched her. She looked . . . dare I say it? Happy. Almost blissful.

I was about to open my mouth and comment on her unusual air when I was interrupted by a loud, nasally sound coming from the front of the restaurant.

"There they are," John practically yelled to Zoë as they pushed their way to the back.

John was the only guy we ever allowed to infiltrate our close-knit girl circle. Of course, it *did* help that he was gay and could therefore join in on all conversations and offer very valuable advice relating to men, fashion, celebrity gossip, and blow jobs. (Of course, not necessarily in that order.) But personally, I think he prefers hanging out with us. Mostly because he just doesn't like other gay men . . . except the ones he's sleeping with.

"I'm so hungry, I could eat my own head," he said dramatically as he pulled out his chair and plopped down into it.

"That's ridiculous," Zoë said, visibly irritated. "What would you chew it with?"

John shot her a look and she sneered back. The two of them were almost always in the middle of some type of mock competition over who could be the most clever and the most annoying at the same time. Sometimes it was amusing to watch, but most of the time it just got old . . . fast.

"There have to be a zillion restaurants in L.A. and we always come here." Zoë opened her menu, completely oblivious to Sophie's unmistakable glow.

"I like it here," Sophie defended herself timidly, her hands tucked under the tabletop, like a shy child eating for the first time at the grown-ups' table.

"Did you know that it would take four-point-five lifetimes to eat at every single restaurant in the city of Los Angeles without ever duplicating," Zoë stated expertly, keeping her eyes locked on her menu. "And *that's* if you start at age five!"

"Did you have a date with the heir to the Zagat fortune last night?" John asked.

Zoë shrugged. "I read it somewhere."

"Yeah, but you'd *need* four-point-five lifetimes because of all the crap you'd be eating. You'd probably only live to be, like, fifty," he retorted. "I mean, places like Roscoe's Chicken and Waffles ain't exactly gonna help keep you alive."

"You guys!" Sophie pleaded loudly, causing Zoë to eye her suspiciously from behind her menu. "Aren't you forgetting something?"

Zoë and John exchanged mutually oblivious glances.

"Well, I don't know what *you're* referring to," John began smugly, "but guess who hooked up with the second runner-up from *So You Think You Can Dance* season three last night?" His face beamed with pride, as if he had just announced his acceptance into a secret society of celebrity groupies.

"*Second* runner-up?" Zoë raised her eyebrows.

"Hey, honey, it's better than your lame-ass excuse for a celebrity hookup."

She rolled her eyes. "I didn't hook up with him because he was on the *Real World,*" she argued defensively. "I hooked up with him because I thought we had a very deep connection."

"Anyway!" Sophie interjected again, redirecting the attention of the group back to the issue at hand. "I didn't summon you guys here to talk about John's drunken conquests."

"You didn't?" John feigned confusion.

"Did you all forget that I had something I wanted to talk about?"

Zoë shrugged and took a sip of her water. "No, I didn't forget. You just don't look upset so I assumed you'd gotten over it by the time we got here."

Then she reached around the back of my chair and affectionately patted Sophie on the shoulder. "Like you always do."

Sophie nodded in agreement. "I know, I know. I tend to overreact."

John looked away and fake coughed the word "understatement."

"Actually," Sophie started, luring our attention in. "I asked you here today because I have *good* news."

We all looked at her questioningly. My first thought was a promotion. She'd been waiting for one at work for over a year, and it was always being held up because of . . .

"Eric and I are engaged!"

My thoughts suddenly came to a crashing halt as her words collided with me like a Peterbilt truck. I couldn't compute them, nor comprehend their implication. I stared at her in disbelief, wondering if maybe I had misunderstood. No, actually . . . *certain* I had.

Then I heard John and Zoë scream, and at least five other tables turned to see if someone had either been murdered or spotted a celebrity. Because in an L.A. restaurant, nothing else is worth interrupting brunch for.

I continued to gape at her, my mouth hanging open, my head a blur. I tried to figure out what the hell she was talking about. I thought I had heard the word "engaged" but that couldn't have been right. My friends didn't get *engaged*.

Maybe she said en*raged*. That would certainly make more sense given Sophie's propensity for drama. Yes, actually, now that I think about it, I'm positive that's what she said. She and Eric are *enraged* about something.

But then Sophie pulled her left hand out from underneath the table, where she apparently had been hiding it since we walked in the door, and held it up so we could all see the enormous diamond that radiated almost as brightly as her face.

Zoë immediately leaped into action, leaning over me to get a closer look at the ring, pushing my body against the back of my chair in the process. I sat motionless, leaning as far back from the table as I could to avoid getting whipped in the face by Zoë's long, dangling, blond hair. But, more important, to avoid the large, menacing rock that seemed to be drawing closer with every threatening move of Sophie's hand.

I watched the whole spectacle unfold in front of me like an old silent black-and-white movie. Pictures without sounds. Quiet, muted faces mouthing words of congratulations and joy. But somehow, completely unable to participate.

"Jen," I heard Sophie's voice come through a long wind tunnel, and suddenly all the humming and buzzing in my ears vanished.

I blinked. "Yeah?"

"What's wrong?"

I looked up to see Zoë's and Sophie's faces staring at me from behind the giant diamond. Zoë was now hovering over the back of Sophie's chair to get a closer look.

"I . . . um, I thought you weren't able to see him this weekend," I said weakly.

Sophie's face glowed brighter. "I know! But it was all a ploy to catch me off guard. He showed up last night and surprised me!"

"OMG," Zoë gushed in her typical IM speak. She usually resorted to it when she wanted to be extra dramatic and express something either truly grotesque or truly mind-blowing. Or occasionally just to save time. "How'd he do it?"

Sophie's beaming face never dimmed for a moment. "Well, I was sitting at home alone, pissed off because he wasn't answering his cell phone. It was turned off. And I assumed he had shut it off because he was out drinking with his stupid friends from the hospital."

Zoë and John nodded eagerly, hungry for more, as if stranded on a deserted island and marriage proposal details were their only hope of survival.

"And then the doorbell rang. I had absolutely no idea who it could be. No one ever rings my doorbell, except my landlord when she's delivering a package." Her voice was fast and animated. And with every word her eyes lit up like sparkling firecrackers. "And I almost didn't open it because when I looked out the peephole there was no one there."

"This is good," Zoë confirmed, egging her on.

Sophie grinned and continued. "But I thought, what the hell, maybe it's a package she forgot to drop off earlier. So I opened the door."

"And he was there!" Zoë interjected, considerably proud of her supersleuth, Encyclopedia Brown–esque ability to conclude the story before it was fully revealed to the audience.

"Yes!" Sophie exclaimed. "He was there! On one knee, holding out the ring!"

John and Zoë exchanged a sentimental glance worthy of a true Hollywood romance.

"And that's why I couldn't see anyone through the peephole," Sophie explained.

"Because he was down on one knee!" Zoë stated the obvious in an overly sappy tone that I rarely ever heard from her unless she was mocking a soap opera, a reality show, or a colleague she disliked for being "too girly."

"Exactly," Sophie replied, in the same tone.

The three of them simultaneously let out an emotional sigh, and then upon becoming aware of my lack of participation, turned and stared at me. The same unnerving, inquisitive expression spread across each of their faces. It was as if they were a group of scientists examining a newly discovered alien species from another planet. A planet where, evidently, the word "engagement" didn't exist in the local language or telepathic form of communication.

I stared blankly at the closed menu in front of me.

"Jen?" Sophie implored. "What's the *matter*?"

I looked up at her, dazed. "Huh? Nothing."

"What do you mean 'nothing'? I'm getting *married* and you haven't reacted at all!"

The truth was, I didn't know how to react. I didn't know how to think. Up until now the only marriages and engagements in my life were the ones I exposed as fraudulent. Not the ones being planned for my best friend.

But in regards to the present conversation, that certainly wasn't a viable explanation for my strange behavior. "I'm sorry," I said, trying to shake myself from my daze. "I guess I'm just in shock. Congratulations!"

Sophie's confused frown slowly turned into another beaming smile as I leaned over to hug her.

"Fabulous, honey. Well done. Way to latch on the ol' ball and chain," John commended her.

"Thanks," Sophie said, turning to each one of us, her silly lovesick grin as prominent as ever.

I admit it was wonderful to see her so happy. But something wouldn't allow me to be happy *for* her. And it ate me up inside. I wanted to jump up and down and squeal with delight the way Zoë had . . . and even John. After all, I was her best friend. We'd been best friends since the third grade. If anyone should have been involved in some type of celebratory jumping ritual, it was me. But it felt like there were weights in my shoes and bricks on my shoulders cementing me down to the ground. Forcing me to resort to a time-perfected, skillful performance of forged emotions. Just like every other day of my life. Playing the role of the flight attendant, the lonely businesswoman, the raging sorority girl, the irresistible computer geek, the merciless temptress. And now, apparently . . . the overjoyed, congratulatory best friend as well.

But the problem was, that was something I never thought I'd ever have to fake.

Even though my friends didn't know what I really did on all those business trips, I still felt like I could be myself around them. I still felt like they were the only ones who really knew *me.*

A few lies here and there. A handful of harmless cover-ups to explain why my housekeeper cleans out my suitcase with disinfectant, or why I can never talk on my business cell phone when they're around. But I've never had to act like someone else.

I've never had to fake it with them.

The server soon approached the table, and as I watched Sophie place her usual eggs Benedict order, I realized that something had changed.

In all of us. Our group would never be the same again.

Sophie was engaged. She was going to get married. And she had the ring to prove it. Everything would change from here on out. She would move in with him. They would buy a house together. And suddenly it would be "we" want you to come over for a BBQ; "we'd" love it if you could meet us for drinks; "we" haven't agreed on a day-care for the baby yet.

But as much as I wanted to believe it, I knew that a fear of change wasn't the real reason I couldn't be happy for her. It was something else. Something much darker. And I certainly wasn't about to let that show through and cast a shadow on everyone's joyful brunch.

So as soon as the server disappeared, I painted a happy, best-friend smile on my face, and with anticipation in my voice I successfully helped Zoë cover all the required, post–engagement announcement questions.

An hour later I said good-bye to Zoë and John as the valet attendants drove up to the curb in Zoë's car, and then watched as she handed over her parking stub and tip before driving away. Sophie and I stood silently, waiting for our turn to repeat the familiar Los Angeles parking routine.

I stared down at my feet, trying desperately to avoid acknowledging the silence that had, for the first time in twenty years, turned awkward. I reached into my bag and pulled out a five-dollar bill, ready to tip the valet as soon as he appeared with my Range Rover.

And when I couldn't take the silence any longer, I decided to break the ice. "So when do I finally get to meet this nice Jewish boy of yours?" I said in a rich New York accent, mimicking Sophie's overbearing grandmother just as we'd been doing since elementary school.

Normally that's when Sophie would either laugh hysterically at what she calls my "goya Jewish accent" or break into a well-practiced grandmother imitation of her own.

But not today. Instead she blurted out anxiously, "I need to talk to you."

And there it was. The urgency. The paranoia. The neurotic Sophie I knew and loved had finally returned after a brief, brunch-long vacation on the island of worry-free, post-engagement bliss.

"What is it?"

She tugged me a few steps farther away from the curb. Her eyes darted back and forth as if checking our earshot radius for spies and hidden bugs. "It's a bit, well . . . unconventional," she began warily. "And when I tell you, I don't want you freaking out. I've been thinking about it for a while now and ever since the engagement last night. I've made a decision, and I'm going to go through with it."

I wrinkled my forehead and looked at her quizzically. "What the hell are you talking about? Are you joining the CIA?"

Sophie looked around suspiciously again. "No. It's just that you know how paranoid I am . . . about Eric and everything."

I sighed. "Yes. But he proposed to you last night. You said he was going to move out here after he finished his residency. I think his intentions should be pretty clear by now."

The words were coming out of my mouth, perfectly rehearsed with flawless enunciation and indisputable sincerity, and yet . . . for the first time, I found myself having a very hard time believing them.

"Which only makes it even more critical," she urged.

"Soph, you're talking in code. I don't understand what you're getting at."

She lowered her eyes, almost in shame, and then slowly reached into her bag and pulled out a small, folded-up piece of white paper.

"There's this girl at work," she began reluctantly. "I was talking to her one day at lunch . . . about Eric."

I nodded.

"And she told me a story . . ." She paused and began to unfold the paper in her hand. "About a close friend of hers who hired someone. Like a . . . a specialist."

I felt the blood in my veins turn to ice. Every inch of my skin was instantly covered in tiny goose bumps. I was suddenly very thankful for my big and bulky clothing selection. It was the only thing hiding the sudden horror that washed over me.

"What . . . *kind* of specialist?" I asked faintly. Even though I had a sneaking suspicion I knew exactly what kind she was referring to.

It was a kind I knew well. Very well.

All too well.

Sophie took a deep breath and looked up at me with remorseful eyes. As if she was apologizing in advance for my inevitable disappointment in her. Like she had finally cracked under the pressures of her insecurities . . . and she knew it. "Well, she called her a 'fidelity inspector.' "

I closed my eyes and nodded painfully. The familiar title suddenly feeling . . . well, not so familiar. Foreign even.

And cold. Very, very cold.

When I opened my eyes again Sophie had finished unfolding the piece of paper in her hand. I hardly noticed the valet standing in front of my Range Rover, waving his hand in the air, trying to get my attention, because I was completely spellbound by the letters and numbers that seemed to jump right off the paper in front of me, attacking the very core of my nervous system.

It was almost funny. I'd never actually seen it with my own eyes before. Even though I knew pieces of paper like this existed all over the city. All over the country, even. But ironically, I was seeing one for the very first time.

Ashlyn
310-555-2120

7

intervention

"Jen!" Sophie's voice awoke me from what I could only pray was a dream.

I blinked and looked down at the piece of paper in my hand for the third time. It was no dream. There was my name . . . my secret identity, written clear as day. And right below it was the number to my business line. It had come back to haunt me. My by-referral-only business had not come close to home, it had come *to* my home. To my best friend. My life. It was all too surreal for me to even attempt to make sense of it.

There was only one thing I knew for sure had to be done.

"Are you crazy? You're not actually thinking of calling this person, are you?" I demanded, my voice strained and distressed.

"You don't even know what she does. My friend said her services are invaluable."

I snorted. "I can only imagine what she *does*." As soon as the words left my mouth, I felt guilty for betraying myself.

Sophie took the paper from my hands and studied it.

"It's some sort of undercover test."

I watched her slip into a meditative state as she ran her fingers over the letters on the paper. " 'Ashlyn,' " she read aloud. "It's a pretty name."

Hearing that name come from Sophie's lips sent shivers up my spine.

She looked up at me. "Supposedly she's very good at—"

I immediately snatched the paper back from her and crumpled it up. "This is insane!"

"Hey!" she said, reaching unsuccessfully for the note. I felt like we were two five-year-olds fighting over the last piece of good chocolate from Grandma's candy jar. "What are you doing?" From the confusion in Sophie's eyes I could tell she was thinking that *I* was the insane one. And the truth was, at that moment she was probably right.

My heart was racing and I could feel my body start to slip into panic mode. My eyes darted toward the valet stand, where I saw a small black trash can. I took one giant stride and tossed the paper in the trash. "I'm saving you from doing something you'll regret."

Sophie put her hands on her hips and glared at me. "Something I'll regret? You don't think I'll regret marrying someone who might one day cheat on me?"

Her words once again turned the blood in my body ice cold, and I felt like someone had stuck me inside a meat locker and bolted the door shut. It was exactly the reason I did what I did. To *avoid* regret. To offer answers to those who wanted them . . . those who needed them. Women just like Sophie.

But those women *weren't* Sophie. That was the thing. They were nameless, practically faceless. They were easily forgettable.

Well . . . almost.

I couldn't let my best friend suffer through what I had seen so many women suffer through. Not a chance. Besides, Eric wasn't even the cheating type. I was almost positive about that. True, I had never met him, but I had a sixth sense about these kinds of things . . . even from a distance.

I had a superpower, damn it!

Although, the more I tried to ignore the fact, the more it haunted me: the real reason I had thrown away that number. And it was a very selfish reason.

Sophie couldn't know.

She couldn't find out.

I had to keep the secret. And tossing that thing into the nearest trash can was the only way I knew how.

"Miss." A voice came from my left. I looked up to see one of the valets in his red jacket motioning toward my awaiting car. "Your car is here." His tone hinged on aggravation.

"One second!" I snapped back, causing him to cower slightly and step away.

Sophie tossed me a concerned look. "Jen, what's gotten into you?"

I bit my lip and tried to smile. "What do you mean?" But who was I kidding? I knew damn well that I wasn't fooling anyone.

"First you don't react to my engagement announcement, then you freak out when I tell you I want to hire someone to make sure Eric is a trustworthy guy before I marry him, and now you're yelling at some poor, innocent valet for no apparent reason. This is definitely not you."

She was right. It *wasn't* me. I wasn't sure who the hell it was. I took a deep breath. "I'm sorry. I've been under a lot of stress at work," I lied quickly. Ah, yes. The legendary work scapegoat saves the day again. "Look, let's talk about this some more later. It's a lot of information to take in all at once. I just need time to digest it."

"Okay . . ." Her voice trailed off with uncertainty.

"Just promise me you won't do anything or call anyone until we've talked this through."

Sophie lowered her head and fidgeted with her valet stub.

"Promise me!"

"Fine, I promise," she finally conceded.

There was a moment of awkward silence between us as I attempted to collect myself. "Hey, I know! Let's get together for drinks tonight and celebrate your engagement!

The mention of her engagement immediately brightened her face again, and she smiled. "Totally! I'm in!"

"Great!" I exclaimed, forcing every ounce of excitement I could muster into my voice. "You can bring Eric! I'll finally get to meet . . ."

Her face sank again as she shook her head. "Eric left this morning. He really *did* have to work this weekend."

"Oh."

"But he's flying me out next weekend," she added hopefully.

I placed my hand on her shoulder. "Well, that's good news."

She nodded. "But *we* can still go out."

"Definitely. I'll call Zoë and John on my way home and we'll all meet up."

But I didn't call them on my way home. My mind was turning faster than a tornado and my thoughts seemed just as destructive. A major crisis had been averted . . . at least temporarily.

How on earth would I convince Sophie not to go through with this? Or should I even try?

My meeting with Roger Ireland only a few days ago was repeating over and over again in my head. I heard my own voice playing on an endless loop: *"It's best to test them* before *they get married. If all my clients had done so then maybe I wouldn't see half of the things that I've seen."*

Sophie was doing exactly what I would have advised her to do had she been . . . well, anyone else but her.

I thought about my options.

The first one was to just tell her the truth. *This is what I do. That's my phone number on that piece of paper and I've been leading a double life: my own and some imaginary girl's named "Ashlyn."* It would certainly solve the problem of having to watch my friend go through with something as stressful as a fidelity inspection. There was no way she would want *me* testing her fiancé. That was a given.

But was I really prepared for her to know? Would she even understand? Would she forgive me for keeping it a secret for more than two years? And would I have to tell the others as well? Zoë? John?

Just the thought of that made me feel sick to my stomach.

I moved on to option two: Convince her not to go through with it. *Eric is a trustworthy guy; he'd never cheat on you. This is a ridiculous idea!*

That seemed like the more viable option. But it would require more lying. And not just small "little white lies" like "I'm in Boston because a company is in the middle of a billion-dollar acquisition and their investors just backed out." Oh, no. These would be much bigger lies. Because they went against everything I believed in. Everything I stood for.

And even if I did try to persuade her to just let it go, what's to say she would even listen? No one knows as well as I do that trust isn't something anyone can convince you to have. It's something you have to find within yourself. And in the end, most people just hire someone like me.

Of course, I could always go with option three. But I suppose that would require me to actually come *up* with an option three. And so far I was drawing a blank. So there went that idea.

By the time I arrived home I had made a decision. That destructive little piece of paper was in the trash, but that meant nothing. She had gotten the number once; if she wanted to, she could easily get it again.

I just had to get to her first. Explain myself and hope to God she understands.

And tonight was the perfect time to do it.

I called up Zoë and John and told them to meet us at our favorite bar at 10:00. Then I called Sophie and told her to meet me at 9:00. One hour should be enough time to work my magic. Hey, if I could convince a forty-year-old CEO of a reputable auto engine manufacturer that I knew how a spark plug worked, I should be able to convince my best friend of what I was about to tell her.

Should being the operative word, of course.

Sophie and I found a quiet booth at the back of Jayes Martini Lounge, an upscale Brentwood bar that had recently replaced our former local hangout after Zoë insisted that it had become overrun with "HDFBs" (horny drunk frat boys). Plus, Jayes offered us a much larger selection of fun, froo-froo, girly martinis that would surely make James Bond cringe.

Sophie slid into the booth and looked disconcertedly toward the front door. She checked her watch. "I wonder why they're not here yet."

"Actually," I said, sliding in across from her, "I told them to come later. There's something I want to talk to you about."

Sophie placed her small, lime-green handbag down next to her, then set her drink on the table and arranged it perfectly so that it sat centered between her shoulder blades. Finally she looked up at me, ready for whatever was coming . . . or at least she thought so.

"What's up?"

"It's about before," I began. "The name and the number you showed me."

She nodded. "The one you threw in the trash."

I smiled. "Yeah, that one."

"What about it?"

"Well . . ." I swallowed hard. Here goes nothing. "There's something you don't know about me."

Sophie laughed loudly, and it came out more like a snort. "Jen, I've known you since we were eight. I know *everything* about you."

I nearly cringed. Her words stung, and it made what I was about to do that much harder.

"Well, you don't know this," I said sincerely.

The seriousness in my voice immediately got her attention and held it. She leaned in closer and waited.

"You know that . . . well, *skill* I have?"

"Men reading?" Sophie said promptly. That's what she and Zoë had endearingly nicknamed it a long time ago, when we first discovered I was blessed with it. Although tonight it seemed more like a curse.

"Yes . . . that." I took a deep breath. "Well, recently it's been . . . let's just say 'enhanced.' And now it's more than just a . . . you know, party trick. It's . . . well, it's pretty damn accurate."

I could feel a groan building up in my throat. I sounded like one of those crazy psychics on Venice Beach, trying to convince some gullible tourist to buy into my mind-reading abilities. It was pathetic.

Sophie crinkled her forehead. "What do you mean?"

I stammered, searching for the right words, but they wouldn't come. It was as if they didn't even exist. The English language just wasn't designed to explain something like this to your best friend. "Fuck it!" I finally said. "I know for sure that Eric's not the cheating type, and that's all there is to it."

I released a heavy sigh and then watched Sophie's reaction carefully, waiting for any indication of conviction. She looked down and touched the frothy top of her Orange-Dream Martini with her fingertip.

Her lack of words made me feel obliged to add more of my own. Lots more. "Just trust me on this one. Like I said, I'm hardly wrong about men . . . you know that! You don't need to go through with this fidelity-whatever crap. It's totally useless." I was starting to ramble. "He'll pass this so-called 'undercover test' with flying colors, and then you'll forever have to hide the fact that you sent out some professional to *spy* on him because you didn't trust him! You don't want to start this marriage out on the wrong foot, do you?"

"You've never even met him. How can you be so sure?"

I hesitated, scanning the room for help, any kind of help. "I . . . I . . . I've never met . . . *that* guy," I said, quickly pointing to a man at the bar who was attempting to chat up a tall, attractive Asian girl, and unsuccessfully at that. "And I bet I can read him."

Sophie looked over at the man at the bar, then turned back and skeptically crossed her arms over her chest. "Okay, fine."

I twisted in my seat and watched the subject in the dark pants and starched gray button-up shirt. I studied him exactly as I would study a client's husband or boyfriend. I looked for tiny details . . . small, unnoticeable mannerisms. There was usually no method to the madness; the answers just *came* to me somehow . . . almost magically.

"Well, for starters, he likes Asian women."

Sophie rolled her eyes. "C'mon . . . that's a little obvious. *I* could have told you that . . . and I know *nothing* about men."

I held up my hand. "Yes, but would you be able to tell me that he's never dated one before?"

Sophie's doubtful expression slowly morphed into masked intrigue, and I knew I had to keep talking. "This is a relatively new obsession for him. He's always liked classic-looking white girls. Blond hair, blue eyes, the usual. In fact, he'd never even given Asian girls a second glance. But he probably recently saw *Memoirs of a Geisha* or some other movie that had a beautiful Asian woman in it, and then suddenly he wondered why he'd never noticed them before.

"So, very soon after, he decided he would start trying his luck with Asian women. Partly because he now saw how beautiful they were, but mostly because he just hadn't had any success with the blondes. He comes to bars at least twice a week to try to meet girls, but for the most part, it's a fruitless effort. Because he doesn't know how to talk to them. In attempting to impress women he ends up sounding either too anxious or too arrogant, because those are the only strategies he knows."

I took a deep breath and sat back in my seat. I knew I was right. I only hoped that Sophie knew it too.

She stared at me, her mouth gaping. "Have you been practicing or something?" She spoke slowly and cautiously, as if I were a crazy, volatile witch who had been known to chop people up and bake them into pies when aggravated.

I took a sip of my chocolate mint martini and avoided eye contact. "No . . . it's just something that has progressed with age, I guess. Like balding."

Sophie continued to stare at the man, who was now standing alone at the bar after the Asian woman had promptly rejected him and moved on to work the next room. "But how do I even know that you're right?"

And with that I was immediately out of my seat, with nothing to lose—except possibly my best friend if this plan didn't work out. "I'll prove it to you."

Sophie skeptically observed from the booth as I walked over to the man, tapped him on the shoulder, introduced myself, and politely invited him back to the table with an unassuming smile. He followed me willingly, and I stood next to him in front of the booth.

"Sophie, this is Brad. Brad, this is my friend Sophie."

They shook hands, and Sophie shot me a look implying her lack of confidence in my sanity.

"Brad," I began playfully, "Sophie and I were wondering if we might be able to ask you a question. You know, to get a guy's opinion."

The man looked apprehensively from me to Sophie, unsure of what this was all about but relatively certain he didn't want to walk away from two attractive women who had, for some reason, handpicked him from the crowd to help appease their curiosity.

"Sure," he responded warily.

"Great!" I said, giving his upper arm a flirtatious squeeze. "Well, we saw you chatting with that *beautiful* Asian woman just a few minutes ago, and we started talking about guys who have a thing for Asian women. We were just wondering what that was all about. Is it because they're exotic looking, or because . . ." I trailed off, knowing full well that he would interrupt me.

And he did.

"Actually . . ." he started.

"Mmm-hmm?"

"I'm probably not the best person to ask. I've just recently developed a 'thing' for Asians, and judging by the way that one blew me off, I'm not sure how long it will last." He chuckled, trying to mask his feeling of rejection.

I looked at Sophie with an "I told you so" expression and then returned my attention to my unassuming guinea pig. "Really? Why's that?"

The man shifted his drink from one hand to the other. "Well, the truth is . . . I just rented *House of Flying Daggers* and . . ."

I gasped and grabbed Brad's arm. "Isn't Ziyi Zhang breathtaking?"

Sophie looked at me suspiciously, and then Brad let out an orgasmic sigh. "Yes! She's . . . amazing. In fact, don't tell anyone, but I just added *Memoirs of a Geisha* to my Netflix queue today."

Sophie's mouth dropped open again, and she shook her head at me in disbelief.

Brad continued talking. "It's not really the kind of movie I'd usually watch, but . . ."

"Well, that's about all we wanted to know." I gave him a brusque pat on the back and slipped into the booth across from Sophie. "Thank you so much for your time."

Brad watched us, certain he had missed something. He opened his mouth to speak but then on second thought decided he probably just didn't want to know . . . and he *definitely* wouldn't understand. In his mind he would chalk it up to "Women are from Venus" and that would be the end of it.

He nodded. "Glad I could help," he said, slightly annoyed, and then headed back to the bar for another round of rejection.

"So?" I said to Sophie after Brad was out of earshot.

Sophie closed her eyes and surrendered a laugh. "Wow, Jen. All I can say is 'Wow!' "

"So now you'll believe me when I tell you that Eric is trustworthy and you should reconsider this ridiculous test thing?"

"What test thing?" Just then Zoë's voice came sailing over the top of the booth. I looked up to see her standing mere centimeters from where Brad the Bewildered had stood only moments ago.

I checked my watch. Damn, she was early. "Nothing," I said quickly. "I thought we weren't meeting until ten."

Zoë scooted in beside Sophie. "I'm sorry," she said, sounding insulted. "I didn't realize this conversation was IO." (Invite Only.)

I sighed and glanced at Sophie. "It wasn't. Sophie and I just got here."

Zoë smiled at us, completely oblivious to anything that might have gone on before she arrived. She craned her neck around and scoured the bar. "Where's the server? I'm gonna order a drink."

I tossed a pleading glance at Sophie.

"I'll think about it," she said quietly.

Zoë turned back around and immediately demanded to see Sophie's ring again, as if it might have somehow changed color or shape since she left it this morning.

I knew that our private chat time was officially over. It was all in Sophie's hands now. I only hoped that I'd made an impact.

One big enough to keep the secret.

John arrived slightly past ten o'clock and after Sophie's overexaggerated account of my "remarkable" men-reading story, the rest of the evening was spent pointing out random people in the bar and urging me to reluctantly recite their life history. I felt like some sort of sideshow act at the circus freak show.

"She did it again!" Zoë exclaimed, after returning from the bar where she had been sent by John and Sophie to either confirm or deny my most recent analysis, of the tall and sexy bartender.

"He's a grad student?" Sophie asked eagerly.

Zoë nodded. "Getting his master's in psychology at UCLA."

They turned and stared at me in awe. "How did you know it was UCLA?" Sophie asked in amazement.

I suddenly wondered if sharing my improved "superpower" with Sophie had been such a good idea. I had intended it to be simply a persuasive tool to convince her not to hire . . . well, *me* to test her fiancé, but now it was getting out of hand. I was starting to worry that my friends knew too much and might start to get suspicious.

"And how did you know he's not just an actor?" John quickly followed. "I thought all bartenders in L.A. were actors?"

I exhaled loudly and started in on another explanation. My fourth for the evening. "Just look at him. He's definitely not an actor. Watch the way he carries himself. He's not here just for show. He's here with purpose. He has much more to offer the world than a nice face and the ability to take off his shirt for the camera. Bartending is *also* the perfect gig for students because it allows them to work at night. And he's too old to be an undergrad. That leaves grad school."

In unison, all three of my friends turned and watched the bartender as he poured a drink for a male patron.

"And the fact that he works here," I continued, "in Brentwood as opposed to downtown or Hollywood, means he's probably not studying at USC. Too far of a commute if he wants to make it to work by six P.M. That leaves UCLA."

They all turned back and looked at me again.

I attempted to downplay it. "It's just a basic process of elimination, really."

"WTF, mate?" Zoë shook her head in disbelief.

Sophie looked to me for a translation.

"What the fuck," Zoë clarified with an impatient raise of her eyebrows. She hated having to speak in complete phrases; it wasted too much precious time. Acronyms were much more efficient. Well, assuming that everyone *else* knew what they stood for.

"I mean, I always knew you had a knack, but this is really something," Zoë continued, her eyes wide and wild with inspiration.

I shrugged and tried to think of a clever way to change the subject. But judging by the dumbfounded expressions on my friends' faces, I knew it wasn't going to be easy. "Something I just picked up, I guess." I tipped my head back and poured the rest of my martini down my throat.

"If only there was a way you could make money doing that," Zoë remarked, the wheels in her head turning.

I laughed weakly. "Yeah . . . if only."

"Or at least find a date once in a while." John sipped his Bahama-Mama Martini and winked at me.

"Ha! Like I have time to date."

Sophie reached across the booth and placed her hand gently on top of mine. It felt warm against my cold and clammy fingers. "He's right though, Jen. We're actually starting to get worried."

The mood of the conversation suddenly took a very somber turn as I looked up to see each of my friends nodding their heads in agreement. I had a sneaking suspicion that an ambush was coming my way. "What do you mean, *worried*?"

Even Zoë's voice lowered to a tender lull. "We mean, you never date. As in never *ever,* and we know it's not for lack of opportunity. I've seen the way guys look at you." She motioned to the rest of the group. "We *all* have. And we're starting to wonder if it has to do with something more than just not having the time."

I immediately turned defensive. "Like what?"

Sophie shrugged innocently. "That's what we've been trying to figure out."

I could feel anger boiling up inside my stomach. I was beginning to think I knew exactly how George Washington felt when it was discovered that Benedict Arnold was working for the British. "So what, you guys just sit around discussing why I don't date? And then toss out ideas like a goddamn team of sitcom writers? Don't you have anything better to do with your time than analyze my lack of a dating life?"

Sophie eyed Zoë, indicating she had suspected I might react like this.

"I have a very busy schedule . . . as you all should know," I defended. "And my work is very important to me. Dating is, by far, the last thing on my mind."

"Jen, darling, we're only looking out for you because we care." John jumped in with his soothing, gay-man-in-a-straight-woman's-world act. "And it's our job to make sure you don't end up an old maid."

Zoë stifled a giggle as I sighed in frustration and rolled my eyes.

"Seriously," Sophie urged me. "You haven't been on one date since . . . since . . . well I don't even remember."

I lowered my eyes and stared at the soggy cocktail napkin under my glass.

"Did you ever think that your lack of dates might have to do with something else?" Sophie asked.

I cupped my chin in my hand. "Like . . . ?"

She looked to Zoë, who gave her an encouraging nod. Sophie took a deep breath. "Like your parents."

A lump formed almost instantly in the back of my throat. I could feel the tears well up in my eyes. I quickly looked away, blinking them back. She had hit the sore spot. The core. And she didn't even know it. She didn't even know what it really meant. If I was going to win this argument I would have to steer them clear of all things relating to the truth. To that fateful day when my normal, preteen life morphed into something else. Something I had never even dreamed of.

I heard the faint sound of my cell phone ringing, and I immediately dug into my bag to silence it, annoyed by the rude interruption. I could feel my hands start to shake. I reached up and held tightly to my empty glass to steady them. "This has nothing to do with my parents," I said softly but sternly.

We all knew it was a lie. A transparent, unmistakable diversion from the real story. But only I knew how far the lie really went.

"Just think about it, Jen," Sophie began. "Three years ago your mom sits you down and tells you your dad cheated on her and they're getting a divorce. And suddenly you have no time for dating. It's a textbook case of—"

"I'm telling you, this has nothing to do with them," I interrupted her, my voice hardening.

Sophie reached out and grabbed my hand again. "Jen, not all men cheat."

"This is coming from *you*?" I exploded, pulling my hand away.

"Well, at least I dated!" she shot back, the amplified level of her voice taking me by surprise. "At least I got out there and opened myself up to the possibility of being vulnerable to someone."

"Yeah, you're vulnerable, all right. So vulnerable that you have to hire someone to prove to yourself just how freaking vulnerable you really are!"

Zoë and John had officially been kicked out of the conversation. Out of the corner of my eye I could see their heads bob back and forth like spectators at a tennis match. They were no longer oblivious; they had *definitely* missed something important. But now it was pretty obvious that neither one of them really wanted to know. You'd have to be an idiot to want to get in the middle of whatever this was.

"What about you?" Sophie yelled back. "You haven't even *kissed* a guy in . . . I don't know how long!"

I groaned and bit my tongue. To my displeasure I was still able to taste the traces of Andrew Thompson from only a few nights ago.

Sophie lowered her tone. "Jen, what are you so afraid of?"

"Apparently, not as much as *you're* afraid of," I mumbled, slightly under my breath.

"Well, whatever it is, I think it's keeping you from being truly happy."

I could feel the anger and resentment and frustration continue to well up inside of me, and the worst part was, I knew I couldn't even utter one tenth of what I really wanted to say. "How do *you* know what makes me happy?" I growled, thankful for the humming background noise of the bar to soften my seemingly unwarranted outburst. "Just because I don't *live* for a rock on my finger like you did doesn't mean I'm not happy!"

Sophie bowed her head and stared down at the table. I worried that maybe I had gone too far . . . said too much. And just as I was about to open my mouth to mumble some sort of apology, she whispered, "Jen, you don't even speak to your own father . . ."

"This conversation is over!" I stood up and squeezed my way past John until I was clear of the booth. My three friends stared up at me in bewilderment, as if they hardly recognized me. But I didn't care. I had a much bigger problem on my mind: I hardly recognized myself.

"For the last time. This has nothing to do with my parents."

And with that I stormed out of the bar.

I sat in the parking lot in my Range Rover, wondering if I should go back in and apologize for my outburst. Apologize for what I said to Sophie.

After all, they were only looking out for me, right? They couldn't possibly know what was really going on, because I didn't tell them.

I watched the front door through my spotted windshield, waiting for a familiar face to exit, race across the street to the empty parking lot, and hop into my car, demanding an explanation. Demanding the truth.

And I had a sneaking suspicion that at that moment I would give it to them.

But no one came.

A group of drunk girls stumbled out, followed by the newest member of the Ziyi Zhang fan club, and then nothing. No one.

I guess there *was* an option three, after all: Scream at Sophie in front of everyone, accuse her of being overly vulnerable and afraid, and then hope that somehow the tough love approach would get through to her and she would change her mind about wanting to seek outside "help."

I sighed and reached down to put my car in gear. It was then I noticed a blinking red light coming from inside my bag. My cell phone. I had a voice mail.

With my foot planted firmly on the brake, I fished out my phone and dialed into my message box. A vaguely familiar voice came through the earpiece. "Hi, it's Clayton. I hope you remember me. We met at the gym a few days ago. You know . . . when you were running from the bogeyman. Anyway, I'd still love to take you out for that smoothie . . . or PowerBar . . . or maybe even a whole meal, if you're up for it. Give me a call back when you get a chance. My number is . . ."

I ended the call and laughed aloud at the irony of it all. Fate definitely had a funny way of reminding you of what needed to be fixed in your life. Although tonight it seemed more like a nagging than a gentle reminding.

Well, what do you know? I thought as I pulled out of the parking lot. *It appears I have a date, after all.*

8

pour some splenda on me

I couldn't sleep that night.

Sophie's voice was echoing in my mind. I turned on my bedside lamp and stared at my phone. Should I call her? It's not like it was the first time we'd had a fight in our twenty years of friendship. But this one was different. It stood out among all the squabbles about borrowing skirts and forgetting to return phone calls and breaking plans to hang out with boys.

She had touched upon something. And for the life of me, I couldn't manage to let it go.

I checked the clock on my cell phone. It was too late to call her, anyway. Besides, why should I be the one to call? She was being unreasonable and insensitive, too. She should be the one to apologize first.

Right?

As I lay my head back against my pillow and stared at the white stucco ceiling of my three-bedroom condo, paid for with my own, hard-earned money, decorated with my own burning desire to live in a world of whiteness and clarity, the confusion slowly began to unravel. And the walls started to close in.

I attempted to distract myself by trying to outline shapes in the seemingly random arrangements of white cement that covered my ceiling, just as I had done so many times as a young girl, sleeping with the lights on, searching for anything that might appear recognizable and therefore meaningful. But after a few short minutes I knew that wasn't working.

And I also knew the only thing that would.

I had to take another look inside the box.

I rolled onto my side and pulled open the bottom drawer of my nightstand. The drawer that served one purpose, and one purpose only: to hold the locked container that waited inside.

I reached into the drawer and drew the small, wooden box close to me.

It used to be my mother's. And before that, it was her grandmother's. She had kept it on a shelf, in a small alcove at the back of my parents' walk-in closet. I always loved the look, feel, and even the smell of it. The distinct cedar aroma that escaped every time I lifted the lid. It was old and worn and smooth to the touch. I would sneak into my parents' closet when I was little, carefully turn the tiny, brass key that my mom kept in the lock, and open it, reveling in its contents.

My mother never kept anything particularly special or secret worthy in the box. A few pieces of old jewelry, a picture of my great-grandmother, and an old coin whose significance was never fully explained to me. But I liked the sensation I got when I snuck into the closet to look inside the box. Like I was uncovering something I wasn't supposed to see. I would pretend that I was an archaeologist, stumbling across some great, long-lost artifact that, if revealed to the world, would provide a solution to years of unanswered questions and unsolved mysteries.

One time my mom found me looking in it. And in staying true to my shadowy fantasy, I was sure that I would be in some kind of trouble. Caught red-handed. Something about how I was too young to know such truths. Too innocent to be exposed to such stories that the box surely contained. But she simply laughed adoringly at me and asked, "What's your obsession with that old box, anyway?"

I quickly shut the lid and shrugged, feeling foolish and childish for making it into something that it clearly was not. "Dunno. I just like it" was my timid response.

My mom later gave the box to me as a gift, when I graduated from college. "It's always seemed to mean more to you than it has to me," she said.

When I accepted the gift with a grateful smile, the simple touch of it brought back all the memories and sensations that it had evoked when I was younger. A feeling of sacredness. A treasure chest for secrets.

And five years later I had found just the thing to keep inside it.

It had become my own Pandora's box. Nearly empty, except for that last tiny ounce of hope.

I no longer kept the key in the lock, the way my mother used to. I hid it underneath a thin layer of velvet fabric that lined the insides of the nightstand drawer. I had carefully peeled back the edge of the cloth and placed the key inside, locking the secret away.

I now removed the cherished, brass key from beneath the fabric and placed it in the lock. And as I turned the key and opened the lid, the warm sensations ran through my fingertips.

They were different sensations now that I was older and had my own secrets to keep. I no longer felt the thrill of a childhood make-believe game, saving the world with the discovery of a magical relic. But the thrill that ran through me as I peered inside and viewed the contents of the beloved treasure chest was just as exhilarating. And the soothing feeling of accomplishment that came over me as I closed the lid and placed it back inside the bottom drawer was just as satisfying.

And like magic, two minutes later I was fast asleep.

The next day, while lounging on my bed, I decided it was a good time to call back my new friend from the gym.

"Hello, Clayton?" I said into the phone.

"Yes."

"Hi, I'm just returning your call from last night. We met at the gym the other day. My name is . . ."

"Yes, hi! How are you?"

I smiled. "Fine. A bit stressed with work, but good."

"Yeah, tell me about it. What is it you do again?"

I cleared my throat and tucked a strand of hair behind my ear. If anyone bothered to study me carefully, it wouldn't take them long to realize that this was my "tell," the unquestionable sign that what I was about to say was a bluff . . . a lie. But fortunately for me, no one ever had any reason to suspect that I might lie. "Investment banking," I replied.

"Oh, right."

I rolled onto my side and propped my head up with my hand. "So, how have you been? How's the gaming world?"

He sighed. "Busy. Although, I did pitch your idea for an *Oregon Trail* revival to my bosses."

I laughed. "And? Did they go for it?"

"Unfortunately, no. I was brutally rejected."

I snapped my fingers. "Aw, that's too bad. But I suppose I'll live."

Clayton laughed. "Good. In that case, do you have plans for Wednesday night?"

As it turned out, I didn't have plans. And I had a strong feeling that getting out of the house would be a good idea.

By Wednesday night, Sophie and I still hadn't spoken. Which I was still convinced was *her* fault for not picking up the phone to speak to me. Of course, I could just call her, but I wasn't quite ready to admit defeat yet. So instead I busied myself with finding the perfect outfit for my first date with Clayton that night.

After spending nearly a half hour in my closet, sifting through hangers and cursing the architect who had had the nerve to design a closet this large, and therefore capable of holding far too many outfit selections for the human mind to possibly choose from, I finally decided to go with a pair of New Religion jeans that, according to my niece Hannah, were totally in style right now, and an off-the-shoulder brown sweater. My hair was pulled into a low ponytail that sat slightly to the left side of my neck. According to *Cosmopolitan* magazine, this updo was supposed to make your hair *look* somewhat messy and thrown together in a hurry. Which, after spending too much time in my closet, wasn't far from the truth.

"I must admit," Clayton said sheepishly, as we sat in a quiet Italian café in Santa Monica. "It's been a long time since I've asked a girl out . . . I was very relieved when you said yes."

I took a sip of my Chianti. "Well, then, I have to admit, I almost didn't."

He smirked. "Why's that?"

I placed my wineglass down and nervously picked at the edge of my cocktail napkin. "I don't really date a lot."

"I guess, neither do I," he said awkwardly, looking down at his lap.

"My friends are always giving me a hard time about it. So this time I thought, What the hell?"

He lifted his wineglass in the air. "Well, then here's to taking your friends' advice."

We clinked glasses and I silently remarked on just how good Clayton looked in the soft candlelight.

He wore a pair of dark blue jeans and a red button-up shirt that complemented his beach-blond hair perfectly. I immediately speculated that he was from the Midwest. Los Angeles is inundated with Midwestern transplants, filling our streets with their pretty-boy faces and strong, corn-fed bodies. Although most of them are actors, all hoping to become the next Chris Klein or Ashton Kutcher.

Zoë liked to call them "FOPTs" (fresh off the potato truck). But given their irresistible appearance, even *she* couldn't complain about them. Because there was absolutely nothing *to* complain about. They were, in a sense, flawless. They had charming good looks, sweet dispositions, and extremely good manners. That is, until the superficial values and egotistical claws of Hollywood had had their time to sink in.

Clayton, however, with his knack for designing futuristic worlds and simulated cities, was thankfully not one of the aspiring actors, and therefore could probably be counted on to keep both his good looks *and* his charming personality.

The night carried on as we shared childhood memories, high school horror stories, favorite TV shows, favorite movies, Quiznos versus Subway, tea versus coffee, Diet Coke versus regular. All the essential get-to-know-each-other topics.

I was very pleased to learn that I had correctly identified his FOPT-ness when he told me that he had grown up in Iowa. And *he* was very pleased to learn that we both shared a love of karaoke.

"I guess we know where this date is going next, don't we?"

I grinned. "There's a bar across the street that does karaoke until two A.M."

"The poor neighbors."

We laughed and stood up from our table. Clayton threw a few bills down on the check presenter and then reached down and took my hand as we walked out of the restaurant and ran like giddy schoolchildren across the street toward a dark bar with one fluorescent red light illuminating the entrance.

The bar was a complete dive. I had been there once before with Sophie and Zoë when we, on a whim, felt the need to sing the hits of Britney Spears in front of complete strangers. A whim that, thankfully for the complete strangers, hadn't resurfaced since.

We entered to the sound of a strained voice singing "I Love Rock N' Roll" and found a seat near the stage. Clayton flipped open the book of song choices and eagerly started skimming the titles with his fingertips. "Actually, I think you should pick our first song," he said, pushing the book across the table.

"Ah, so this is going to be a duet?"

Clayton raised his eyebrows. "Unless you want to go up there alone."

I quickly opened the book. "You know, I've always been a fan of duets."

He laughed again. "Good. Then choose."

Out of the corner of my eye I could see him watching me as my fingertips skimmed the song list. "Okay, I got it," I said, arriving at a title and silently thanking the karaoke gods that it was available.

"What?"

I turned the book around so he could read my selection.

" 'Pour Some Sugar on Me'?"

I crinkled my forehead. "No good?"

"Are you serious?"

I pulled the book back, possessively. "Okay, okay. I'll pick something else."

He yanked it out from under me. "No! I love that song! It's my karaoke classic!"

I giggled and stood up. "Good then. I'll put in the request."

Two hours later I had discovered the secret to a successful first date: Def Leppard. The crowd finally booed us off the stage after *three* Def Leppard tributes (although, I'm sure the actual members of the band would question the use of the word "tribute"), insisting that we move on and broaden our horizons.

"So have you had enough Def Leppard for one night?" he asked, after we returned to our table.

I eagerly reached for the songbook. "Yes. Let's move on to Bon Jovi!"

Clayton laughed. "I don't know. I think I'm pretty spent."

I looked at my watch. It was 11:45 P.M. My expression turned to disappointment. "Already? But it's so early."

"We could go back to my place and watch some TV." He shrugged his shoulders, as if trying to imply that my response to his invitation was completely irrelevant.

Although we both knew that it wasn't.

I shrugged back. "Sure, why not. Got any *Family Guy*?"

He smiled contently. "All five seasons on DVD. I knew I liked you."

I nodded approvingly. I probably could have already told you he had all five seasons of *Family Guy* on DVD. In fact, he probably had the *Family Guy* movie as well. But I imagined first dates were more fun when you weren't able to read the other person like an open book. And as much as Sophie or Zoë would kill for that kind of skill on some of *their* dates, the novelty for me had worn off some time ago. And most of the time I wished I could just be more like my friends. So I could walk in the door of a restaurant and not instinctively point out all the men inside who were cheating on their wives—or capable of doing so. So I could order from a waiter and not be able to tell you his life story just by the way he says "Anything to drink for you?" No men-reading skills, no jaded opinions. Just . . . normal.

But that was obviously a relative term.

And for tonight I would just have to keep on pretending.

Clayton and I made it through approximately fifteen minutes of our mutually favorite *Family Guy* episode before he leaned in to kiss me. I didn't resist.

He was a gentle kisser. More passion than impatience. His tongue playfully teased my bottom lip, and after a few short seconds, I was able to adapt *my* end of the kiss to match up perfectly with his, another useful skill I'd picked up along the way.

Kissing is a power game. Just like dancing. The men will *usually* lead, but in some cases they like following. I can normally tell five to ten seconds into the kiss if he wants to be in control . . . and just how much control that includes. Because it's not just black or white. You lead, I follow. I think of it in percentages. Most guys kiss in an 80-20 ratio, 80 percent of the kiss being controlled and dictated by him, 20 percent left to your discretion. Which means you get to throw in a tongue thrust or a lip nibble every once in a while, but for the most part, they're in the driver's seat.

I can imagine that's why some first kisses are so awkward, both parties trying to dictate the ratio at the same time. He wants 80-20 but she's only used to giving 60-40. It's chaos. I'm all for equal rights, women's liberty, etc., but over the years I've learned a thing or two about Mars and the men who live there. When it comes to kissing, it's like doing the tango: You just follow.

Which is probably why tonight our kiss was far from awkward. It was damn near perfect. If I had to guess . . . a 55-45. But there was no time for guessing, not when his lips felt the way they did. It was the kind of kiss a woman can feel in her thighs. The kind of kiss that makes you grateful that you're sitting down. Because had you been standing up, your knees might have buckled underneath you.

The soft moans escaping from my lips as they gently melded with his told him what kind of kiss it was. It also told him that I wanted more.

He moaned back and pressed his tongue slightly deeper into my mouth. I reached my hand around to the back of his head and pulled him closer to me. Then his hands went for my sweater and lingered hesitantly along the bottom hemline. I threw my arms straight in the air, indicating that I wanted it off just as badly as he did. The sweater came flying over my head. My purposefully sloppy side ponytail was yanked upward and then fell back into place, now extremely more disheveled looking than the magazine had originally suggested.

The off-the-shoulder sweater (now officially an off-the-body sweater) was tossed to the side, and I watched Clayton react to my red strapless push-up bra. Of course, this was exactly the way the wardrobe selection had been designed. To garner a reaction.

Because in my life, the truth is . . . nothing happens by chance.

Everything is premeditated.

It keeps me in control at all times.

If I can predict it, I can manage it. If I can calculate it, I can manipulate it. After all, Clayton was just a man, like any other man. And men are my specialty. No matter where or when I apply the knowledge.

I knew we would end up back here. I knew he would take off my sweater. And I knew that in the next five minutes he would attempt to unbutton my jeans and lower the zipper. I also knew that in those five minutes I would let him.

Because I was a girl who never dated.

And therefore I was a girl who hadn't had sex in a long time.

And *therefore* I was a girl who wouldn't say no to it.

Until I heard the sound of a key in a lock. It was faint. Almost silent. Clayton was too busy pressing his fingertips against my stomach to even notice. But I noticed. I notice everything. Another occupational hazard, I guess.

I glanced toward the front door in time to see the handle turn slowly and the door creak open.

Clayton replaced his fingertips with his mouth as he kissed my stomach and stopped at my jeans, playfully brushing across the fabric with his lips.

He was oblivious to the mysterious visitor. That is, until she made her presence known, in a very loud way.

"*What the fuck are you doing?*" I heard a loud shriek come from the front door as it slammed closed.

Clayton's head shot up like a rocket launch. "Rani?" His eyes glazed over with fear. "I . . . I thought you were in Cabo with the girls."

"I knew it!" she screamed, tears welling up in her eyes. "I knew you would do this! You piece of shit!" Suddenly, a small purse came flying through the air. I successfully dodged it, allowing it to hit Clayton squarely between the eyes.

That was my less-than-subtle cue to leave. I pulled myself to my feet and tried hard to tune out the sound of their voices as I picked my sweater up off the floor and slid it over my head.

Clayton quickly stood up and reached out toward the petite, Indian girl standing motionless (and purseless) in the middle of the living room. "Rani, I just wanted to—"

"Don't touch me. Don't you *fucking* touch me!" She stepped back and batted his hand away.

"Baby, I'm sorry. I'm so sorry," Clayton pleaded.

"I'm just gonna . . ." My voice intentionally drifted off as I grabbed my bag and quietly made my way toward the door, keeping my head down to avoid eye contact.

Clayton ignored me. It figured. I was of little importance now. Now that she had unexpectedly showed up. But I suppose I was used to that . . . falling from grace in a matter of seconds. In a normal week, I went from being the sexiest woman alive, to being, well, pretty much the devil in a blink of an eye at least three times. I've learned not to take it personally.

I've learned not to take a lot of things personally.

I watched as the argument escalated and moved into the kitchen, Rani storming through the dining room with Clayton following closely after her like a puppy begging for forgiveness for chewing on her favorite pair of shoes. I could hear their voices. Hers was loud and full of anger. His was soft and saturated with apologies.

As I placed my hand on the doorknob, I immediately heard the sound of footsteps getting closer. Coming back *from* the kitchen. I turned my head to see one angry woman stomping toward me. Fury in her eyes, and vengeance in her step.

I glanced anxiously toward the safety the front door promised to provide once I was on the other side of it. I turned the handle and pulled it toward me. But an inch was all I got. Her hand landed on top of mine, and in one swift motion and a very loud thud, the door was shut again. I froze and looked up at her. My face blank. My mind restless.

"Ashlyn," she said gently, her face softening for a moment.

I smiled back, unassumingly. "Yes?"

Her hand slid off mine, and I was suddenly free. "Thank you," she said with a painful sigh.

I let go of the door, now moist with the sweat of my hand, and patted her tenderly on the shoulder. "You're very welcome."

She wiped her tearstained face and sniffled. "I was right." Her voice was filled with paradoxical questions. Questions like: "Would I have felt better if I were wrong?" Trying to answer them was like setting your mind on fire and watching it burn.

I took a deep breath. "Unfortunately, you usually are."

She nodded and choked back a quiet sob. "Then I did the right thing?"

I craned my neck to glance past her into the kitchen. Clayton had taken a seat at the table, his head between his knees, his hands running through his hair. His regret seeping through every pore of his skin.

Then I looked back at Rani, her dark eyelashes damp with tears and her breathtakingly exotic features filled with uncertainty. She looked like a princess. The kind you read about in fairy tales of far-off lands and unfamiliar cultures. But tonight, here, unfortunately, the princess would feel the pain of a real world. The agony of a real life. And the bitterness of an unhappy ending.

Hers was a question I was used to answering. A comfort I was used to giving. And the response would be the same as it always is.

"Yes, Rani. You did the right thing by hiring me."

9

the art of bluffing

Okay, so I had a little help.

Rani had told me that Clayton liked karaoke. She even mentioned Def Leppard. And *Family Guy.* And all the other things that we were supposed to have in common. All the things she suspected would be true about the girl he would cheat with, the final detail being that she was white.

Rani didn't want the normal ending. The black card on the dresser. The cold, hard truth being explained as I pull my sweater over my head and leave him with one, drawn-out, pitiful glance.

It wasn't enough for her. She wanted to see it. She wanted to catch him. She wanted to look him in the face during the moment of his betrayal . . . and during the moment of his realization. She wanted him to know that she knew, and would always know.

It's not how I typically conclude my assignments. But then again, Rani wasn't a typical client.

I had met her in the self-help section of the Barnes & Noble on the Third Street Promenade. She seemed to share my thirst for knowledge. But her thirst on that day turned out to be quite different from my own.

As I browsed through titles on the far wall of the small alcove, filled floor to ceiling with books that promised to cure all of your innermost fears, I saw her out of the corner of my eye. She looked lost. Pulling books off the shelf, thumbing through a few pages, and then, visibly discouraged, placing them back with a despondent sigh. Although she was dressed simply in a pair of sweatpants, Ugg boots, and a hooded sweater, her exotic beauty radiated throughout the tiny room.

I inconspicuously inched my way closer to her, pretending to skim the authors that I passed along the way.

As I drew nearer I was able to make out some of the titles she was examining. *Is He Cheating On You? 829 Ways to Tell; How to Catch a Cheater; 28 Telltale Signs of a Cheating Spouse.*

I could see the longing in her eyes as she searched through the titles. It was a longing for something these books just wouldn't give her. I knew that, and deep down, she knew that too. But this was the only thing she could think of.

No wonder she looked so lost.

My heart went out to her. Her flawless face was lined with sleepless nights spent staring at the one she loved, watching him breathe, asking questions in her mind that she prayed would be answered in the morning . . . or the day after, or the day after that. Anything that would allow her to sleep again.

"Can I make a suggestion?" I asked gently, nodding toward the current book in her hand.

She looked up, at first ashamed, as if she'd been caught looking at porn in her grandmother's house. But then her expression clouded over with misplaced appreciation. "No good?" she asked, her voice craving assistance. An expert in this area was something she'd been yearning for, but she doubted the squirrelly guy with the mismatched belt and shoes working at the info counter of the bookstore would quite fit the bill.

I shook my head regretfully. "I wouldn't know. I haven't read it."

She quickly reached for another book from the shelf and showed it to me. "What about this one?"

I shook my head again. "Actually, I haven't read any of them."

She studied me with confusion. I certainly *looked* perfectly normal, but maybe I was just another nutcase wandering the streets of Santa Monica, doling out random relationship advice. "Then what's your suggestion?"

Rani was one of my "pro bono" clients. I didn't charge her a dime, mostly because she didn't have one. She was working night shifts at Starbucks to put herself through law school.

"We've been together since high school back in Iowa," she explained as we sat at one of the cafés on the promenade and sipped lemonade. "I've never been with anyone else. And neither has he."

"You don't look like you came from the Midwest," I joked.

She smiled and watched a pedestrian pass by on the sidewalk. "My family moved there from India when I was fourteen. My dad got a job running the local office of his technology firm, and it was the perfect opportunity for us to 'start a better life.' At least that's how it was explained to me." She paused and reflected. "I was popular in India. I was well liked. I had lots of friends. I never wanted to leave. The kids in Iowa were mean. Really mean. They constantly mocked my accent and the way I looked. I was surrounded by blond hair and blue eyes. *That* was what was pretty. That was what was considered beautiful. That was what got you friends and a boyfriend . . . I guess.

"Nobody would let me sit with them at lunch, so I used to read in the library. Normally you weren't allowed to bring food in there, but the librarian made an exception for me." She chuckled to herself. "I think she felt sorry for me."

I nodded and took a sip of my lemonade, waiting for her to continue.

"Then one day, Clayton came in. I had seen him before. He was on the soccer team. And he was so beautiful. I thought he had come into the library to find a book, but his eyes found me instead, and he walked straight toward my table and sat down across from me. He said he knew I came in there every day and he wanted to see what all the fuss was about. Why the library was the new hot spot, or something like that."

"That's sweet," I said.

She nodded. "He was always sweet. He came and ate lunch with me every day. He never asked why I was there or why I refused to eat lunch in the cafeteria with everyone else. I don't think he needed to ask."

I was thoroughly engrossed in her story. "And then?"

"And then everything. We've been together ever since."

"So why the books? Why the doubt?"

She sighed and smoothed her ponytail with her hand. "*Because* we've been together ever since. I think he wants more . . . I think he's curious about what he's missing. I think he wants a white girl."

I nearly spit out my lemonade. "What? Are you serious? You're beautiful!

Stunning! And he picked you out of a *sea* of white girls . . . *because* you were different. Why all of a sudden would he change his mind?"

She shrugged and shook her head helplessly. "I don't know. It's just a feeling. I see him looking sometimes. I just don't know if I grew up to be the girl he's supposed to be with. After ten years, how do you even know? How can anyone choose a soul mate at age fifteen?"

I pressed my lips together and looked away. "You can't," I conceded.

"He's not going to cheat with a one-night stand from a bar. I'm sure of that. He's not the type. If anything, he'll want to meet someone, go on a date, see what other genuine options are out there."

I nodded and reached out to touch her hand. "Let me help you."

She cocked her head to the side. "How are you going to do that?"

"I offer a very special service. For women like you. It's not something you can find in any book."

I could tell by the look on Rani's face that she was intrigued. So I continued to tell her exactly what I do and have done for the past two years.

Her reaction was interesting. I'm not used to having to explain this situation to someone who has no idea what's about to be presented to them. Most of my clients are usually at least somewhat prepared for what I'm about to tell them. After all, they did call *me.* And I half expected Rani to jump up out of her seat in disgust and storm off onto the Promenade, leaving me with the bill and lemonade dripping down my face. But she didn't. She simply looked at me the way a religious zealot might look upon a newly found ancient relic. At first, with disbelief . . . doubt that it was really authentic. And then finally with an awestruck numbness that changed everything she's ever believed in.

"But I don't have any money to . . ."

"I just want to help," I assured her.

I could see her eyes welling up with tears. Tears of thankfulness, tears of fear, and tears of relief that she would finally be getting the answer she'd been looking for.

And that she wouldn't have to rely on a book.

I stood outside the door of Clayton and Rani's apartment. I could still faintly hear the voices inside, arguing. That would last awhile, I imagined.

Rani was right. You can't pick your soul mate at age fifteen. But a small part of me wanted to root for them. Wanted them to work it out, to be able to see this incident as a breaking point and a place to move forward from. A hurdle that must be leaped and cleared before the road can ever be smooth again.

But I make it a rule not to root for anyone. And I also make it a rule not to make exceptions. So before I walked away, I let my hand softly touch the wooden door as I said good-bye to Princess Rani.

The next day was my third and final poker lesson before my assignment in Las Vegas on Saturday. I had found a poker tutor on Craigslist last week after I met with Roger Ireland concerning his daughter and her fiancé. And given the recent poker craze that had hit the country, it wasn't a difficult thing to find.

When I first made the call to the tutor, I told him that I wanted a poker mastery crash course. I needed to be able to impress a client during an upcoming business trip to Vegas, which was true enough. And my tutor, Ethan (or "the Cowboy," as he preferred to be called), didn't seem to care what my purpose was for learning the game, as long as my check cleared so he could deposit it into his online-poker account.

"So, during our last two lessons," he began, adeptly shuffling a deck of cards in front of him, "we focused on the rules of the game, the rounds of play, the strategies for calculating your odds based on how much money is in the pot, and of course, how to determine the hands of the other players." I sat in Ethan's basement, where he had set up a mini poker shrine. Photos of famous players decorated the walls, three professional poker tables dominated the center of the room, and the carpet looked identical to the noisy, colorful carpets you find inside any of the casinos on the Strip.

I picked up four of the chips in front of me and began practicing my chip twirls. Ethan had demonstrated them briefly during our last lesson, and I'd been watching the players on ESPN gracefully spin chips around their fingers while contemplating their next action. I realized after watching it on TV that the chip tricks were almost as important in appearing to know what you're doing as playing the game itself. And as much as I knew I needed to play the game well, I also knew that Saturday night would be *all* about appearances.

"But today we're going to add the final step of this process . . ." the Cowboy continued.

"Chip flipping?" I asked hopefully.

"Bluffing," he stated seriously, clearly enjoying the suspenseful spotlight.

"Ah."

"It's the hardest part of poker to master. But once you do, the rest of the game is easy."

"Lying?" I confirmed.

"*Fooling* the other players into believing you have something when you don't . . . or that you don't have something when you do," he replied self-importantly.

"So, lying," I repeated again.

Ethan took a deep breath, seemingly frustrated at my simplification of his big suspenseful moment. "Yes, I suppose you could call it lying. But bluffing is so much more than just telling a little white lie. White lies are easy. They're simple and believable because people have no reason *not* to believe you. Bluffing in poker is a different skill altogether. It's an art. You have to make someone believe you when they have every reason in the world *not* to."

I nodded and smiled to myself. "I honestly don't think that will be a problem."

Ethan considered my confidence and then tapped the deck of cards against the table and began to deal. "Okay, hotshot. Let's see what you've got."

Friday evening rolled around, and I, of course, was running late . . . as usual. This time, however, it wasn't to an assignment but to my niece Hannah's birthday dinner in Westlake Village. I quickly slid into Hannah's favorite pair of jeans and a Baby Phat tank top and dabbed my eyelashes with mascara.

I drove to the entrance of the 405 and merged into what can only be described as a "parking lot," given the mobility of the cars around me. Hannah's parents and my mother lived in Thousand Oaks, which is about thirty miles north of here. But in Southern California, nothing is ever measured in miles. It's measured in estimated driving time, which is calculated by taking into account several different variables. The most important being: time of day and day of the week.

For example: If someone asks the question "How far do you live from Thousand Oaks?" I immediately respond with two additional questions: "At what time? And on what day?" Because at eleven o'clock in the morning on a Tuesday, I live approximately one hour from Thousand Oaks. But at five o'clock in the evening on a Friday (like today), I live closer to two and a half hours from Thousand Oaks. And, lastly, at two o'clock in the morning on a Saturday, I live twenty-five minutes from Thousand Oaks (driving at a reckless ninety miles per hour).

In fact, most people in Los Angeles don't even understand the concept of distance measured in miles. If you say, "It's about five miles east of here," to a Los Angeles native, they'll most likely look at you like you're from a foreign country, and then ask, "Well, if I leave at four-thirty, how long will it take?"

Most people think the world is split into two measurement standards: the metric system that nearly everyone in the world uses and the pain-in-the-ass, inconsistent American system that even *we* can't seem to master. But in actuality, the world is split into *three* standards: the metric system, the pain-in-the-ass American system, and the SoCal system. Or what I like to call "the space/time incontinuum."

And it appeared that the SoCal system was accurate again. I exited the freeway approximately two hours later and sped down the suburban parkway toward the restaurant. I glanced at my dashboard clock. I was officially late. My half sister, Julia, would certainly have something to say about it. I pushed down farther on the accelerator. Just as I prepared to slow down and turn onto the correct street, I saw flashing lights in my rearview mirror. I looked up and groaned. Just what I needed right now, to have to deal with suburbia police officers who have nothing better to do than write tickets to people driving two miles above the speed limit. Although, I admit, I was doing more like twenty over.

I pulled my car to the side of the road and began to formulate an escape route. Not the kind where you jump from the car, run for the bushes, and wind up on the six o'clock news. The psychological escape route. It's much more effective.

I watched in my side-view mirror and silently thanked God when I saw that the officer was a man. That made my life a hell of a lot easier. I rolled down the window, switched on the overhead dome light, and sat up straighter in my seat.

"Good evening, ma'am," he said, stepping over to my open window.

"Miss," I corrected him in a tone that was not so much annoyed by his wrongful prefix but more like granting him permission to use the right one.

"*Miss,*" he emphasized, with no break in his unforgiving front.

"Bluffing is half about putting forth something that is untrue and half about reading your opponent."

Tonight my opponent was married. His wedding band glimmered in the light of my overhead dome lamp. I handed him my driver's license and proof of insurance and he studied them. The trick now was to figure out what *kind* of married man he was. The kind that was undyingly faithful to his wife or the kind that I normally deal with. The fact that he was wearing his wedding ring on the job is evidence of the former. But it wasn't enough.

And that's when I noticed the small, white stain on the shirt pocket of his uniform. It was faded and appeared as if someone had tried to wipe it away in a hurry with a wet cloth, but there just hadn't been enough time to remove it all.

"Once you've read the opponent, then you're set. You can design your play."

Officer Kendall, as I read off his name tag, was happily married. Or at least for now. Which meant I would have to put the seductress card back in the deck tonight. He would have none of it.

Most married couples with a young baby—at least one young enough to still spit up on Daddy's uniform right before he leaves for work—are in a state of renewed marital bliss. Their relationship, as well as their existence as human beings, has reached a new level. They've brought life into the world. And combined with the proud sporting of the wedding band, Officer Kendall wasn't going to let some sexy girl in an overpriced SUV stand in the way of that bliss.

Which meant I would have to come up with another angle.

He pinned my license onto his clipboard and shined the flashlight into my open window. "The reason I pulled you over tonight, Miss Hunter, is because . . ."

I squinted into the light. "I know, I know. I was speeding. I'm very sorry." My voice was apologetic. Genuine and free of all traces of mocking.

"You were going pretty fast," he pointed out, flipping open his ticket book.

I subtly cocked my head to the side in order to get a glance at the pen he was pulling out from his shirt pocket.

Bingo.

My angle.

I lightened the tone of my voice considerably. "You know, you look really familiar. Have I seen you before?"

He was highly unamused. "No." He began to copy down the information from my license.

I pretended to rack my brain, all the while watching his pen fly across the page out of the corner of my eye. "Yes! You're trying to change careers, aren't you? My colleague is handling your file at Lex Harrison."

His face lit up. "You work with Mona Pietrik?"

"Sure do. I remember seeing you in there the other day." I giggled girlishly. "You're the one with the new baby, right?"

I could see his whole exterior soften, and I knew I was on the right track. Nearly home free. Or restaurant free, rather. The pieces were all fitting together: new baby, new lifestyle, new, safer career that would assure he was home in time for dinner every night . . . and without a bullet wound in his head.

"Yes, that was me."

I smiled like I was greeting an old friend. "I had no idea you were a policeman."

He sighed. "Hopefully not for long. Writing speeding tickets is definitely not something I want to do forever."

I groaned. "I know what you mean. Before I started working in the career counseling office I had this awful job collecting used towels at the gym. I came home every day smelling like other people's BO!"

He laughed aloud. "That's horrible!"

"Tell me about it." I paused. "Well, Mona is excellent at her job. I'm sure she'll find you something perfect!"

"Thanks," he said, ripping the half-written ticket from his booklet and crumpling it up in his hands. "Will you tell her I said hi?"

"Of course I will!"

He handed me back my driver's license and insurance card and closed his ticket book with a friendly wink. "Have a good night . . . and slow down out there."

Ten minutes later I pulled into the parking lot of a cheesy Italian chain restaurant in Westlake Village. I was the last one to arrive. Hannah yelled out my name and came running halfway across the restaurant to greet me. I hugged her thin frame close to me and stroked her curly blond hair as she buried her head against my collarbone.

"Hi, honey! Happy birthday!"

"Thanks!" Hannah said, giving me a squeeze before prancing back to the table and reclaiming her seat at the far end. As I followed after her, I saw my mom seated at the opposite end. I paused for a moment, pretending to take in the lively walls of the restaurant, which were covered in photographs of people I didn't know but somehow thought that I should.

In all actuality I was mustering up the courage to talk to her. I wasn't sure how much she knew about my dad's engagement, and frankly, it placed me in quite a bit of a catch-22 . . . again. I certainly wasn't going to be the one to tell her, because I could care less about what my dad did these days. But I also didn't want to be the recipient of any more details than I already knew. He was getting married. That was plenty. But my mother wasn't the kind of person to store away her emotions. And ever since the divorce two and a half years ago, with my dad bitterly cut out of the picture, I'd been the involuntary beneficiary of the manifestations of those emotions.

And I wasn't sure I could handle another eruption tonight. Not with everything going on in my own life. Not when I had to store away so many emotions of my own.

Just as I'd done for the past sixteen years.

To protect her.

I pointed at a framed black-and-white photograph of a heavyset woman holding two watermelons in front of where her breasts would be and offered a small laugh. "That's cute," I said as I walked over to my mom and pecked her on the cheek. "Hi, Mom."

She reached her arms over her head and hugged me awkwardly around the neck. "Hi, Jenny. Did you get my last e-mail with the botany IQ test?"

"Yes, I got it on my phone. Sorry, I've been busy. Haven't had time to take it yet." Ever since my mother discovered the Internet a few months ago, she's basically turned into a fifteen-year-old Web junkie, spending the majority of her time doing online personality tests, downloading music and TV shows, sharing photographs, talking in chat rooms until the wee hours of the night. I think she even mentioned something about instant messaging a few weeks ago. Just the thought of my mother online talking to strangers around the country about her favorite lasagna recipe was too far-fetched for me to even process.

I pulled out the chair next to her.

"No, here!" I heard Hannah shout from the other side of the table. "I saved you a seat over here!"

I turned to my mom and flashed her a look that not only expressed my apologies but also said, "What can you do? She's twelve." She smiled back and nodded her acceptance.

As I scooted in-between Hannah and one of her friends, I couldn't help but feel a small wave of relief. Followed quickly by guilt. I should *want* to sit by my mother. I should *want* to hear every tiny, painstaking detail of what she's going through. Because she's my mother, and she's been through a lot. Too much. But as I settled in to hear stories of makeup and annoying homeroom teachers and girls that clearly stuffed their bras because their boobs are totally uneven—and lumpy—I was reprehensibly grateful for my involuntary seating assignment.

I apologized for being late, intentionally leaving out the part about my near speeding ticket. My mother would reprimand me for driving too fast and putting my life in danger. And the rest of the table would want to know how I managed to talk my way out of it. I didn't really feel like explaining it. Plus, it would arouse suspicion. Jennifer Hunter doesn't talk her way out of speeding tickets. Or if she does, then why hasn't she managed to talk her way *into* a marriage proposal?

"We weren't sure when you would finally show up, so I went ahead and ordered for the table," Julia said in an accusatory tone that grated on my nerves.

I bit my lip and restrained myself from making a snide comeback, deciding to save my energy for later, when the questions start coming and I'm forced to remember all my cover stories flawlessly. Because one tiny, erroneous detail is almost always caught by someone. And then I find myself having to invent stories to cover up for the fact that I don't remember my original stories. And once you change the original stories it's like breaking the valve on a water spigot: The questions start flowing uncontrollably and with no end in sight.

I still failed to understand why Julia insisted on hanging out with my mom's side of the family anyway. She was my dad's daughter from his *first* marriage. I knew his first wife, Julia's mother, lived in some far-off state like Connecticut and Hannah only saw her about once a year. But why on earth wasn't she having family dinner with our father and his *new* fiancé? Why did she always want to hang out with my mother? When I was growing up she always seemed to hate her . . . and me for that matter. And after she got married we hardly ever saw her. It wasn't until recently that she mysteriously moved three streets away from my mom and suddenly became her new best friend.

Hannah immediately took command of the conversation and introduced me to the two girls sitting to my left, Olivia and Rachel. I said my polite hellos and waited patiently for the inquisition to begin. And less than five minutes after I sat down, like clockwork, it started. The questions began right on schedule.

"So, Jen. What's the latest with the dating scene?"

At that moment it was as if everyone at the table stopped what they were doing. Conversations fizzled out. Fidgeting came to a halt. All eyes were on me. Even Olivia's and Rachel's. And they didn't even know me.

"Always bluff believably. Use the cards already on the table to come up with a credible story."

"Well," I began. "I went on a date with this one guy I met at the gym. Clayton . . ."

I watched the faces around the table light up one by one, like staggered Christmas lights. Julia, her husband, my mom, Hannah, her two teenybopper friends. They were all waiting. Could this be the one? Could he be it? I like the name Clayton. Maybe he'll be my new uncle/brother-in-law/son-in-law. Maybe he'll save Jen from the looming perils of eternal singlehood. After all, she *is* almost thirty.

"But it turned out he had a girlfriend," I completed the brief story.

The woes of disappointment filled the air. I tried not to laugh. Because to me it was somewhat comical. How predictable they all were. How one mention of a new man's name left them all salivating at the mouth.

"What a slimeball!" Hannah exclaimed.

I patted her hand gently, thanking her for her reassuring insight.

"Oh well," my mother said. "Better luck next time."

"Yep," I agreed, and then for good measure threw in, "He's out there somewhere," hoping to put a definitive end to the conversation. The ultimate silencer. *She's optimistic. I guess that's all we can ask for at this point. Let's move on, shall we?*

"Well then, how's your job?" Julia's husband asked.

I shrugged. "Fine, you know. The usual."

"The bank keeping you busy?" asked my mom.

I nodded and took a sip of my ice water. "Superbusy. Just got back from Denver last week and I'm off to Vegas tomorrow."

"Wow, Jen. Your life is so cool. I'm so superjealous!" Hannah said.

I forced out a humble smile as I reached for a piece of bread and shoved it in my mouth. Anything to keep me from starting to chew on my bottom lip. Tonight I was going to try my hardest to make sure *this* family reunion didn't end as most of them did . . . with the taste of my own blood in my mouth.

Halfway through the meal I could tell that Hannah and her friends were starting to get antsy. They had been picking at their plates of pasta for the last ten minutes while Julia talked incessantly to my mom about her most recent living room redecorating project. So I leaned in and suggested to Hannah that she and her friends come to the bathroom with me for some girl talk.

The three girls perked up immediately, eagerly pushing their chairs back.

As soon as we entered the ladies' room, I produced a small wrapped box from my bag and handed it to Hannah. "Don't tell your mom you got it from me," I said with a wink.

She wasted no time tearing off the wrapping and revealing the tube of Trish McEvoy designer lip gloss that I had bought her for her birthday. "Yes!" she exclaimed, opening up the box and removing the contents. "This is exactly what I wanted!"

Hannah turned to the mirror and applied a thin layer of the gloss, and then handed the tube to Olivia, who eagerly applied the next forbidden coat.

"Nick is going to flip when he sees you in this," Rachel said to Hannah, admiring the color.

I suddenly felt my stomach flip slightly. "Nick? Who's Nick?" I tried to sound casual and curious, as any girl talk participant would.

Hannah turned to me, her eyes immediately lighting up. "This boy at school that I like but barely even knows who I am."

"She doesn't just like him. She's *obsessed* with him!" Olivia clarified, and then passed the lip gloss to Rachel. "His third-period class is right next to her locker, so she always takes an *extra*-long time to get her books for that period."

I looked to Hannah for a sign of admission. She bowed her head shamefully in acknowledgment of the truth. "I think he might be the *one*."

I nearly choked on my own saliva. "The *what*?"

"You know, the one perfect person I'm meant to spend my life with."

"Like Big and Carrie on *Sex and the City,*" Rachel explained, as if the concept of "the one" was a new idea that had yet to hit the masses.

"You *watch Sex and the City*?" My voice was starting to rise. I could feel a lump forming in my throat. Hannah nodded, looking at me strangely. As if to insinuate "What's gotten into you? You're starting to sound like my mother."

"Rachel's parents have all the seasons on DVD," Olivia informed me. "We watch them in her room when her mom's at work."

I suddenly found a deeper appreciation for my parents' "No TV in your room until you're thirteen" rule.

"Oh," I said quietly. But my mind was far from quiet. It was rapidly indexing every single sex scene in that entire series, and then my stomach felt the corresponding lurch that came with the thought of my innocent little niece watching any one of them.

But I found myself trapped. Trapped between being the cool aunt, who buys illegal lip gloss, and the jaded, bitter, fidelity inspector aunt, who wants to somehow, somewhere along the way, convince her niece to "get thee to a nunnery" and never trust any man in the world except for God. And even *that's* negotiable.

"Anyway," Hannah continued, "Nick is my Mr. Big. He's tall and cute and—"

"And probably an asshole?" I burst out suddenly. "Like every other man on this planet. Trust me on this one, Hannah. One day they're promising you the world and the next day, it's 'Oh, I'm sorry. I just don't think I'm the monogamous type.' "

I heard a small clank as the tube of designer lip gloss rolled out of Rachel's hands and hit the hard tile floor of the bathroom. And then . . . silence. They all stared at me in disbelief. Jaws hanging open, eyes wide. Then Olivia and Rachel looked at Hannah accusingly. *I thought you said she was cool.*

Hannah's eyes pleaded with me. *I thought you* were *cool.*

Olivia leaned over to Rachel and whispered, "What does monogamous mean?" To which Rachel just subtly shook her head, either in an effort to say "I don't know" or "Don't do this now, the woman's crazy!"

I quickly tucked a strand of hair behind my ear, cleared my throat, and painted a smile across my face. Then I let out a laugh that I prayed sounded like a mocking insult. As if I couldn't believe these girls had actually fallen for my pathetically talentless performance.

"I'm just kidding, you guys! C'mon, lighten up." I reached down to pick up the lip gloss and then nonchalantly applied an extra-thick coat, hoping that the sticky liquid from the tube might actually cover up what had just burst forth from my mouth.

Their uneasiness hesitantly turned into smiles, but they still eyed me with caution. Ready and waiting for me to explode again. Hannah gave me a confused look, so I patted her reassuringly on the shoulder and whipped out my best slumber party advice. "The best thing you can do is play it cool. Don't let him know that you like him too much. Men are funny like that. The minute they know you have feelings, they lose interest. So pretend that you *don't* like him and you'll drive him crazy!"

"Really?" Rachel looked at me in bewilderment, as if I had just revealed an eleventh commandment. A new rule that had never even existed in her world until now. It was the one that came right after "Thou shall not take *American Idol*'s name in vain."

I couldn't stop my niece from dating. And I definitely couldn't stop her from loving. So I figured the best thing I could do was at least make sure she was armored before sending her out to fight the emotional Crusades.

"Really," I confirmed decisively, relieved that I had managed to steer their focus away from the fact that I had just totally lost it . . . for the *second* time in one week.

"Now," I said, pulling a wad of paper towels from the nearby dispenser and handing one to each of the girls. "Wipe off the lip gloss so your mother doesn't see it."

As I watched Hannah and her two friends file out of the restroom ahead of me, I wondered how I would be able to continue to prepare her for the real world. Obviously my previous impromptu tactic hadn't gone over so well. Today it was just glossy pink makeup and a middle-school crush. But what about tomorrow? And the next day? What would those days bring? She was so eager to grow up. Just as I had been.

I only prayed it wouldn't happen as fast for her as it had for me.

"Jen." I heard my mother's voice calling me as we returned to the table. "Jenny, I need to talk to you." She patted the empty chair next to her and I numbly walked around to her side of the table and sat down. Here it comes. The family drama.

She put her hand gently on my leg. "Have you heard about your father?"

I wanted to close my eyes and disappear. The last thing I needed right now was to get into a discussion about my mother and father. But I knew that even if I did close my eyes, when I opened them again she would still be there. And the question mark would still be spray-painted across her face.

"Yes, I did. He left a message on my machine." I cringed slightly, waiting for the outburst, the flood of tears and aggression, and of course, the guilt that would never be spoken.

But it didn't come. Not this time.

Instead, my mother simply squeezed my hand in hers and said, "How are you handling it? Are you okay?"

I gave her an odd look. This was highly unusual. I had grown accustomed to packing my purse with extra Kleenex every time I knew I was going to see my mom, because it almost always ended in a discussion about my dad, which almost always ended in tears gushing down her face and me attempting to console her.

I blinked in disbelief. "Yes, I'm okay. I just don't think about it."

My mom frowned. "I'm not sure that's the healthiest way to deal with this, Jenny."

"Mom, I'm fine. Really. You don't need to worry about me."

She sighed and removed her hand from my leg. "But I *do* worry about you, honey. I really do. This dating thing is starting to concern me."

I crinkled my forehead. "What 'dating' thing?"

My mom fidgeted with her napkin and lowered her voice. She leaned forward. "Well, you know, you're getting older now, and I just worry that maybe the fact that you're still single has something to do with—"

"Oh, not you too!" I groaned.

"What do you mean, me *too*?"

"Never mind," I said quickly. "Look, Mom, I honestly don't want to talk about this. And I can assure you: The only reason I'm not in a relationship is because I don't have time for one. My work keeps me very busy. Love can come later."

It was something my mom was used to hearing because my love life was a topic she was known to bring up . . . often. Although the fact that she had just now paired up my father's love life with my lack of one was somewhat unnerving.

The obvious disappointment on her face was hard to miss. "Well, you know, women don't have the luxury that men do of putting love on the back burner. We have biological clocks to adhere to. And the longer you wait, the more likely that front burner is going to run out of gas."

I put my hand up. "Mom, I refuse to have the same conversation with you every time. When the right man comes along, that's when it will happen. And until then I'm not going to date just for the sake of my biological clock."

There was so much more I wanted to tell her. About Sophie and Eric, and Andrew Thompson's flight attendant fantasy, and Raymond Jacobs's wedding ring, and the real reason my date the other night was a complete disaster.

But I couldn't.

My mom wouldn't be able to know that side of my frustration, because she didn't know anything about that side of my life. A side I had kept secret from everyone for more than two years.

My family knew nothing of Ashlyn, what she represented, or what she hoped to accomplish. But the ironic part was . . . she was born out of a family affair.

10

origin of the species (part 2)

When I was twelve years old, my dad became a stranger to me.

It only took one night, one moment, one look in the wrong direction for my feelings about him to change completely.

At that age I couldn't fully understand *what* I had seen or what exactly it meant. And at that very moment of seeing my father with my twenty-year-old babysitter, I didn't exactly make any conscious decision to feel differently about him. But when I finally drifted off to sleep several hours later, and woke up in the morning with the image still as fresh in my memory as if I were watching it happen all over again, something changed in me.

My dad and I drove to pick up my mother from the airport, and I didn't speak to him the entire way. Not because I was choosing to be angry; that kind of premeditated emotion was far too complex for me to understand, let alone produce. It was because I had no idea *what* to say to him. I feared that anything that came out of my mouth, anything at all, would end with an involuntary recounting of the truth, followed by tears, many, many tears.

"Is something wrong?" my dad asked as we veered off toward the Arrivals area of LAX airport.

I shook my head, staring intently out the window at the passing cars and world travelers.

To this day I can still see the airport signs above, meticulously sorting out those who were coming from those who were going. I distinctly remember sitting in that front seat, focusing all of my attention on the other side of that window, and utterly dreading the arrival of my mother and all that would come with it. All of the choices I didn't know how to make. All of the responsibilities I didn't know if I could handle. I desperately wished I could escape. Flee to the land of glorious "Departures." Fly away to Hong Kong, or Tahiti, or some other far-off place and never come back.

"You're awfully quiet," my dad remarked at my silence.

I simply shrugged.

He pulled the car up to the curb, and his eyes quickly scanned the passenger pickup area for a familiar face. "We're a little early," he said, checking his watch.

I continued to stare out the window, afraid to acknowledge his existence.

"You know," my dad began after a moment of silence. "Sometimes there are things we want to tell somebody but it's difficult to do so."

I didn't respond. I could feel tears stinging the back sides of my eyelids. I quickly blinked them away.

So my dad kept talking. "And then sometimes there are things we want to tell people but probably shouldn't."

I suddenly spun around to face him, my face filled with questions that would never be answered. Did he know? Had he seen me? As I replayed that dreadful night over and over again in my head I could have sworn I had escaped up the stairway unseen. I had made sure of it. But is it possible he could have *heard* me?

"What do you mean?" I asked, trying to hide the curiosity in my voice and cling to a more casual, aloof tone.

My dad seemed to be thinking carefully about his next words, weighing all the options like a mental thesaurus search. "What I mean is, sometimes there are things that are better left unsaid."

"Why?" I shot back, almost defensively.

He reached out to gently touch my face, but I instinctively flinched. My dad tried to play it off with a lighthearted chuckle as he removed his hand and rested it on the gearshift. "Different reasons," he said with a half shrug, as if he didn't really care one way or the other if I was listening. "Mostly if you know that the truth will hurt someone."

I reached up and gently tugged at my bottom lip, trying to digest everything he was telling me, but at the same time trying to figure out if there was a hidden motive behind it. And to be honest, it was far too much for my twelve-year-old brain to compute.

Then my dad turned his entire body toward me and looked me directly in the eye. "Especially if it's someone you love," he added in a critical tone.

I quickly looked away, wanting desperately to read his mind, dissect his thoughts, search through his memories like a card catalog index. But there was no time. I looked up to see my mother exiting the terminal and hurrying over to the car. Without another word I immediately unbuckled my seat belt and climbed into the backseat.

My dad faced forward again, as if nothing had happened. As if we had merely been discussing last night's episode of *Doogie Howser, M.D.* and now that conversation was over.

But that conversation was far from over in my head. In fact, it was repeating incessantly. Trying to locate clues, key words, anything that stuck out as unusual. But unfortunately, nothing did. And I couldn't help but think that it all just seemed like a random piece of fatherly advice arriving at a very inopportune time.

The backdoor of our minivan slid open and my mother's round and cheerful face leaned in and kissed me on the cheek. Then she opened the front door and settled into the passenger seat, reaching back and resting her hand affectionately on my knee.

"So? How was everything while I was gone?" she asked brightly. Blissfully. Innocently. Completely unsuspecting. And it was like a knife in my chest.

I smiled back. "Fine."

At that moment, the confusion faded away. Everything that had just come out of my father's mouth suddenly made perfect sense to me. Why would I purposely hurt someone I loved? Or more important, someone who loved me . . . unconditionally?

The answer was: I wouldn't.

That's when I made the choice. That I would never utter a word of this to anyone. Not to my mom, not to my dad, not to Julia . . . not even to Sophie, my best friend. And in fact, the more I never spoke of it, the easier it was to effectively convince myself that it hadn't actually happened. And the more I convinced myself, the easier it was to never truly deal with it. Never have to process it. Never have to give it that second thought my mind was begging to give it. This way I could go on with my life. Talk about boys with Sophie, complain about not having a phone in my room, feel delightfully naughty in putting on lipstick and eye shadow when I knew my mom would disapprove.

But what I didn't realize as I made that conscious decision to lock the secret away in a vault that had no combination was that my life wouldn't go on like that. It wouldn't be as naively simple as I had hoped.

Sure, I could talk about boys and makeup and phones in my room. But I would never *feel* the words that were coming out of my mouth. I would never *relish* in the innocence of being a child-turned-teenager. And when I would grow up and turn fifteen, and sixteen and seventeen, I would date boys, I would kiss boys, I would even share my body with them. But I would never love them. I would never be vulnerable to them. At least not the way I wanted to love them and be vulnerable to them. Not the way Sophie did.

And thus began my life of make-believe.

When my mom got home from Chicago after visiting my grandparents, I was able to use her as a shield. As long as she was around I would never have to be alone in a room with my father. I would never have to sit in silence with him while fighting the temptation to ask the burning question that wouldn't leave me alone. *Why?*

Why would you kiss another woman when you have Mom? Why would you wait until she was out of town to do it? Why don't you love her the way you're supposed to?

All these questions would eventually boil down to one essential, unsolvable puzzle: *Why do people cheat?*

The divorce came when I was twenty-five. My mom discovered that my dad had been cheating on her for several months with a woman from his office.

Exactly *how* she found out, I don't know. I never asked. It was a detail I wasn't sure I could handle. Funny, you would think that after the burden I'd been carrying around for all those years, one tiny little additional piece of information would be an easy enough thing for me to digest. But it was exactly the other way around. If I had to internalize one more element of my parents' failing relationship, I would certainly lose it. That whole camel back–breaking straw phenomenon.

But whatever the reason, however the method, she found out about this one. And she left him.

To say I was relieved would be like saying, "I'm thirsty" in the middle of a desert. It's an understatement beyond all understatements. And it doesn't even begin to do justice to my true feelings.

"Jennifer," my mom had said tearfully after sitting me down in the tiny, one-bedroom apartment I was renting at the time. "I need to talk to you about something."

I took a seat next to her and gave her my full attention. "Yeah, Mom?" It was rare for her to come over to my apartment by herself, let alone with the introduction of "I need to talk to you about something." So I was immediately concerned.

"Your father and I have decided that our marriage just isn't working the way that it used to, and we think it's best if we split up and get a divorce."

The reaction was easy to fake. The tears were genuine. But according to my mom, they were the painful, heartbreaking tears of a child who had just lost the only family she's ever known. But in all actuality, they were tears of joy, relief, and most of all, liberation from the dysfunctional household that had imprisoned me for far too long.

I felt like someone had opened a door that I had been leaning and pressing and pushing against for years. A door that had kept me trapped inside a dark room full of secrets, and I was afraid of the dark. But it was all over now. Everything would be fine. I could come clean. I could tell her what I'd been keeping locked up all this time. Because it would no longer matter. She had seen the light and she was moving on. The past would be in the past and I could finally release the demons that had been haunting me throughout most of my life.

"Why?" I asked, my tone filled with curiosity but my head filled with expectation. Because I already knew the answer.

She sniffled slightly and reached out to touch my face. I saw the struggle in her eyes. Her fight to stay strong for a daughter who couldn't possibly understand the complications of an adulterous marriage. "Honestly, honey. Your dad was not faithful to me." She swallowed hard and attempted to regain her courage and composure. "And when I confronted him about it, he admitted that he hadn't been faithful for a while."

I swallowed hard before managing to ask, "How long a while?" Even though I was pretty sure I already knew. But I needed to know what *she* knew. I needed to know just how much honesty he had given her.

"More than ten years," she said softly, bowing her head.

More tears fell. My mom reached out and held me close to her. She stroked my hair like I was a child. And, ironically, I felt just like one. It was exactly the kind of comfort I needed . . . thirteen years too late.

I knew this was it. This was the time to say it. All it would take was a simple "I know" and my whole world would change. My life could start over. I could even attempt to find some of the childhood that I had lost to sleepless nights and merciless anxiety. I opened my mouth to speak the words that promised to heal me.

But instead I heard my mother say, "I just wish I would've known earlier."

"What?" I asked, panic filling my eyes. I couldn't even begin to fathom the logic behind her statement. At age twelve the only thing that had made sense was protecting her from the truth. What you don't know can't hurt you. "Some things are better left unsaid," as my dad had so poignantly put it. And that rationale had followed me into my adult life. I'd never even allowed myself to reassess it.

She smiled tenderly at me and took my hand in hers. "You know, so I could have moved on with my life. So I wouldn't have wasted all those years, being married to a man who wasn't loyal."

And those were the magic words.

Not only because they made perfect sense, but because they were the exact opposite of the words that had led me so far down this stray path. And the fact that they made perfect sense was the reason I had to shut the door again. I couldn't let my mom know that I had been responsible for her lost happiness. My immature, naive choices had taken years off her life . . . literally.

And the whole time I thought I was protecting her, I was actually protecting *him*. The very person I had grown to loathe and look down upon had actually benefited from my silence.

How can anyone even begin to forgive something like that?

So the secret remained locked inside there . . . to this day.

After that I stopped talking to my father. There was no reason for me to pretend anymore. I had been told the truth and now I had every right to hate him. All the anger and hostility I had been building up for years could finally be released . . . justifiably.

I no longer had to find clever ways to disguise my pent-up resentment toward him. No more picking fights over trivial things like channel changing and junk food and homework just to keep myself from boiling over inside at the very thought of how he had disrespected my mom. He had made a mockery of my family, of life as I knew it, and for so many years, I had to force myself to even look him in the eye. But now, fortunately, I would no longer have to try.

For the next three years my dad tried to restore communication between us. I didn't answer e-mails, or return phone calls, and I had in the darkness of my living room pretending not to be home whenever he tried to "stop by for a visit."

I wanted nothing to do with him.

And now, at least, there was no question why.

11

a heart flush

I recognized Parker from his picture right away. As I scanned the tables at the Bellagio Poker Room I assumed the other early-thirty-something guys scattered around the room were friends of his, judging by the way they were all dressed: ready to hit the clubs once poker was deemed no longer entertaining.

I gave my name to the poker room manager standing at the front podium, along with one of the several hundred-dollar bills I had stuffed into my small white leather Versace clutch.

"Table number 13, please," I said quietly, motioning ever so slightly toward the table where my subject was seated.

He nodded his understanding and discretion as he slyly relieved me of my large bill.

I followed him through the poker room and was offered a seat directly across from Parker. I felt his eyes watching me as I approached the table and lowered my body into the seat. The low-cut top coupled with my cleavage-maximizing bra was clearly a good choice. I could tell right away that it was working.

A Breast Man.

After hearing Mr. Ireland's depiction of him I'd had a sneaking suspicion he would be. I suppose that's what you get from two years of experience in this game—sneaking suspicions.

I made specific eye contact with him, leaving no doubt in his mind that my first impression of this perfect stranger was a good one.

A delicate smile inched its way across my lips.

He reciprocated quickly before being drawn back into the game as the cards were dealt.

I played my hands carefully. Folding most of them immediately. Waiting for good cards to come my way, just as Ethan, my poker tutor, had instructed me during my lessons. I used the waiting period in between hands to advance my *other* game, the one that consisted of purposeful, across-the-table flirting: glances, smirks, visual appreciations of his poker skills and resulting winnings.

Tonight I was a player. And not just at poker.

Because this was, in fact, his bachelor party. If Parker was going to cheat tonight, it was clearly going to be with a one-night stand . . . a fling. Someone who knows how to have fun and knows it will mean nothing in the morning. A girl who doesn't necessarily do this with *everyone* she meets, but when she meets someone intriguing enough, there's no telling what she might do with him, or *to* him.

So that's exactly the girl I was.

Twenty minutes after sitting down I was dealt an ace, queen of hearts and I decided to slow play it. Meaning I didn't raise the bet right away. I simply called all bets before me and pretended I had a mediocre hand and was patiently waiting for a card to fall that might improve it. The slow play was a strategy that Ethan thought he had taught me during our lessons. But in all actuality I had been using it regularly for the past two years.

Two more hearts came on the flop, along with the king of diamonds. I now had four cards to a flush. I needed one more heart to complete the hand.

Parker bet, and I assumed he must have had at least a pair of kings, if not three of them. He had been betting aggressively since before the flop, meaning he probably had something good in his hand.

The seven of hearts came on the river, and I now had the flush. I withdrew from my flirting game for a moment to recall my poker lessons. I studied the cards on the table, and it only took me a few seconds to confirm that I had the highest possible hand—which, Ethan had informed me, is also known as "the nuts." And it wasn't until this very moment that I fully understood the meaning behind the nickname, as it seemed to be exactly where I had a hold of Parker.

He bet twenty dollars.

Everyone after him folded and the action was on me. It was just the two of us now.

I felt his eyes watching me with every move I made. He wanted to see if I was as good at poker as I was at tossing seductive glances to relative strangers. It would say a lot about how well I would "perform" later on in the evening, should it come to that.

And by now I was growing fairly confident that it would.

I can usually tell within ten minutes of interacting with a subject whether or not he will fail. It's all part of that men-reading superpower, I guess. Parker was as good as done. And he hadn't even been drinking yet. It was looking like Mr. Ireland's fatherly intuition was dead-on.

Even though I knew I held the highest hand in the game, I pretended to contemplate my decision to call his bet. I pressed my lips together tightly, took another peek at my cards, and fidgeted with my chips.

He watched me intently. Half hoping I would fold so he could feel some sense of conquest over me and half hoping I would call so he could continue to feel the exhilaration of playing these two simultaneous games at once. Although we both knew they had practically merged into one.

I carefully measured out a perfect doubling of his bet and pushed it toward the center of the table.

"I raise," I said, looking up and locking eyes with him. My stare had two meanings: (1) I'm not afraid of you, and (2) I'm not afraid of you.

"Raise, make it forty," the dealer confirmed.

Parker arched his eyebrows, studying me, taking me in, using this unique moment to stare me up and down as if he were only contemplating my bold poker move.

We both knew he was not.

He took his eyes off me long enough to check his two cards and then briefly scan the five cards laid out on the table. Then it was back to studying me.

"Either you made a flush on the river or you've been holding out on me," he said.

I ran my fingers along the side of my chip stack. "I've definitely been holding out," I confirmed with a raw honesty in my tone. "But I'm tired of waiting."

The seven other players observed us. Eyes darting back and forth from Parker to me, then back to Parker. They could sense the sexual tension in the air, feeding off of a mutual love of the game and a mutual thrill of the hunt.

Tonight I was the perfect match for Parker Colman.

He looked down at his chips. "Well, you're not the only one," he said, pushing another twenty dollars out in front of him. "I re-raise."

"Re-raise, make it sixty," the dealer announced.

It was like having our own personal referee of the game, the dealer's only purpose being to make sure we each knew the rules, we each knew the stakes, and neither one of us got hurt in the process . . . well, at least not physically.

Little did the dealer know he was chaperoning the exchange of much higher stakes than just sixty dollars.

Parker's move was exactly what I had anticipated. He read my earlier hesitation and interpreted it as fear. Fear that my hand might not be good enough. This was, of course, exactly how I wanted him to interpret it.

Now, without any hesitation, I immediately pushed all my chips into the center of the table. "All in," I declared.

"Re-raise. Make it three hundred," the dealer broadcasted after counting my chips.

Re-raise, make it your fiancé, I thought.

Parker scrutinized me. As did the rest of the table. Who *was* this girl? She sits down looking relatively clueless in her tight jeans and revealing top, and in only twenty minutes she's managed to get a pot up to nearly six hundred dollars.

I kept a straight face, only revealing a very small, select portion of my intentions. Just enough to keep things interesting.

By this time two of Parker's buddies had appeared from a nearby table and were standing behind him, observing the action.

I was sure he had the three kings. If not, he would have folded. Especially with the flush possibility on the board. Which means he'd had me beat until the last card fell.

Three kings is a very difficult hand to fold, but it doesn't mean you shouldn't. And I was certain that by the end of the night he would wish he had.

Parker called my raise and pushed a large stack of chips into the middle. The dealer instructed us to flip over our cards. The look on his face was one of pure horror. The only hand that could have beaten him was staring back from my side of the table. I couldn't help but silently observe the interesting foreshadowing of the situation.

"She pulled the heart on the fucking river!" he groaned to one of his friends.

I smiled as the dealer pushed me the large pile of chips. "Sorry, that's just the nature of the game," I replied, half sympathetically, half gloating. It was exactly the combination he would respond to.

He sucked up his manly pride, and in a sincere voice and a very sportsmanlike manner, offered up a courteous, "Good hand."

"Thanks," I replied, as I attempted to stack up all my newly earned chips.

I pretended not to notice as Parker and his friends made a joint decision to call it a night at the poker tables and move on to a club. I strained my ears to hear where they were planning to go, but unfortunately, I wasn't able to catch a location.

"Well, it's been nice playing with you," he said in the general direction of the table, but more specifically to me.

There were a few murmurs from the other players, reciprocating the sentiment, and I looked up and said, "Yes, a definite pleasure."

Before leaving, he turned back around, as if he were going to say something else, but all that came out was, "Maybe I'll see you around."

I smiled. "Maybe you will."

And he would.

As soon as the boys were out of sight, I scrambled to throw my chips into a rack, grab my stuff, and make my way to the cashier.

I cashed out with exactly $650 more than I had started with.

As I stuffed the bills into my bag and headed toward the front entrance of the casino, I made a mental note to start taking on more assignments where I got to make an extra 650 bucks on the side. Not a bad arrangement at all.

I hid myself from view as I watched Parker and his ten or so friends hop into a consecutive series of taxis in front of the hotel. I would have to find out their destination before I went upstairs and changed into my "clubbing" uniform.

After the last cab pulled away from the curb, I walked outside and approached the taxi attendant. "Can you tell me where those guys went?" I asked, slipping a hundred out of my bag and into his hand.

He looked down at it, his reaction implying that this kind of request was not uncommon around here. "The Palms," he replied calmly and resourcefully, as if I had only asked him where the nearest ATM was.

"And what's the name of the club there?"

He looked down at my bag, the very direction from which his hundred-dollar bill had just emerged.

I groaned. "I don't think so," I said, turning on my heels and heading back toward the front door. I was quite certain the concierge would be happy to tell me the name of the club inside the Palms Hotel . . . for free.

"The nightclub Rain is there," he called after me.

I turned back around. "Thank you for your help."

"I get off at midnight. Can I look for you there later?" he asked with a flirtatious raise of his eyebrows.

"I don't think so," I said again, before returning to the casino.

An hour later I reemerged into the cool desert-night air in a slinky turquoise dress, a pair of "intention to fuck" heels, and an eye makeup job worthy of a *Vogue* photo shoot. (Mostly because I copied it from one.)

"Palms Casino?" the taxi attendant asked me with a smart-ass inflection and a sly smirk.

"Yes, thank you," I said flippantly, as if our previous encounter had never taken place.

He put me into the next cab and I was off, ready to accidentally bump into Parker Colman for the second time this evening.

Tonight, as Ashlyn, I was supposedly partying with some friends at Club Rain in the Palms Casino. The rest of my party had already decided to hit the dance floor, but I was much more in the mood for a drink.

So I proceeded to squeeze by a group of thirty-something guys on my quest to reach the bar. Among them was a tall brown-haired man, masculine, good looking, obviously there to celebrate his bachelor party because he was wearing several Mardi Gras beads around his neck and a giant leopard-skin pimp hat on his head.

As I pushed myself past the group, a sense of recognition flashed over the man's face.

"Hey, I know you," he said.

He had obviously been drinking. I could smell the alcohol on his breath. For some reason, this seemed to make me smile.

The recognition transferred across the small space between us and onto my face as well.

"Yes, you do. What a coincidence. Twice in one night. Lucky me."

"No, lucky *me,*" he insisted. He turned to his buddies. "Look, it's the girl who took all my money."

A few of his friends recognized me immediately and whispered something inaudible into the bachelor's ear.

"I'm Parker." He extended his hand.

I shook it firmly, then allowed my palm to slide seductively away from his as I retracted it. "Ashlyn."

"Pretty name. Can I buy you a drink?" he offered.

"I don't know. *Can* you, after I took all your money?"

He laughed. "Well, technically you should be buying *me* a drink. But that would be so un-chivalrous of me. So I guess I'm going to have to manage."

"Jack and Coke," I replied with a smile, clearly intrigued by his good looks and gentlemanly manners. And I made no effort to hide it.

"Hey, that's what I'm drinking!" he said, holding up his half-empty glass. It certainly hadn't been his first.

"You have good taste," I remarked.

"Evidently, so do you."

He was good at this. I was impressed.

The bartender poured me a drink and I held my glass up next to his. "To Vegas?" I suggested.

"To things happening *in* Vegas . . ." he insisted.

". . . and staying there."

We toasted and I took a long gulp from my glass. The bachelor looked on, once again impressed by this mysterious and very attractive woman standing in front of him, practically oozing sex. But then again, this was Vegas. Everything oozes sex in Vegas.

"Do you want to dance?" he asked me.

There was the invite. That obligatory, necessary, all-powerful invitation.

He had initiated. And now I could follow.

Without saying a word, I slid my stylishly polished finger through one of his Mardi Gras beads and began to pull him toward the dance floor.

As the groom-to-be followed closely behind me, he could feel his pulse escalating. His hand wanted to slide down my back and caress the shape of my hips. His mouth wanted to fall helplessly along the length of my neck, push my hair aside, and feel my skin under his lips. He could hear the voices of his friends growing distant, cheering him on as if he were leaving to go into battle. He could feel himself getting hard with anticipation . . .

And then his body jerked upright. Something snapped his attention back to the room, the music, the lights. The memory of something waiting for him back at home. Some*one* counting on him to keep his word.

He bargained with his inner voice.

It's just a dance, he told himself. *And this* is *my bachelor party.*

If a subject has been drinking, it makes my job easier. Not only in the obvious way, in which alcohol makes people less inhibited, more sexual, more willing to stray, but also in the unobvious way, in which I can be less cautious. Men under the influence of alcohol are less suspicious by nature. They don't notice coincidences. They don't hear slipups. They simply enjoy their state of inhibition.

Although Ashlyn's personality tonight was still very well defined and premeditated, I felt myself relax on the dance floor. I knew I had little to worry about. There was no doubt that this night would end up in Parker Colman's hotel room. The inspection was as good as failed.

The music was loud and sensual. The pressure of his hands on my body intensified as the song continued. His touch started off soft, a faint exploration of my exterior silhouette, and then little by little, it pressed into me. Harder, more forceful, like he was massaging sexual tension right into my muscles. His fingers wrapped around my waist and pulled me toward him. His body thrust against mine and I could feel his chest muscles. His pecs were strong and defined. As if separate from my body, I watched my hands reach up and grab them. Knead them.

The music began to pulse through my veins. Louder and louder, until I felt like it had become a part of me. Controlling my movements, steering my every step.

His powerful hands spun me around and landed just above my stomach. He pressed my back into him. His fingers ran up and down the sides of my waist, just barely escaping the curves of my breasts and lingering just long enough on my hipbones to know that the underwear I was wearing didn't cover much.

As he brushed my hair away and began to tenderly kiss the back of my neck I felt something I hadn't felt in a very long time . . . something I *never* felt on an assignment. A tingling between my legs.

I closed my eyes, letting the touch of his lips send shivers up and down my back and through my entire body.

He aggressively turned me around again to face him and his lips went straight for mine.

I didn't fight it. Not that I ever did. But this time something was different. I didn't *want* to fight it. That natural reaction to push him away that I have to fight with every single assignment was nowhere to be felt.

His kiss was strong, masculine, tasting of whiskey and Coke. It made my knees want to buckle.

What the hell is wrong with me? I thought. *Could it be the alcohol?*

That was ridiculous. On past assignments I had drunk three times as much as I had tonight and could have passed a roadside sobriety test with flying colors. No. There was something else happening here. Something inexplicable. And definitely terrifying.

There's certainly no rulebook for this job. At least not a published one. But if there were this would be on page one as the biggest misdemeanor of them all. The Golden Rule of fidelity inspections. As far as he's concerned you can't get enough of him and all the scandalous things he's doing to you. As far as *you're* concerned . . . you might as well be numb from the forehead down. You don't feel, you don't get involved, and you certainly don't enjoy.

But there was something about Parker's hands and his mouth. They were intoxicating. My tolerance level was supposed to be off the charts, for alcohol *and* this kind of thing. But tonight I felt like an absolute lightweight. Getting drunk off of one dance. One touch. One amazing kiss.

"Let's get out of here," he whispered in my ear.

I nodded. I didn't even have to say anything. And I was afraid that if I did, it would be something I would regret. And possibly something that might get me fired and my reputation as an honest professional destroyed.

Don't lead, just follow, I reminded myself. But one question kept repeating in my mind: *If I enjoy it, does it still count?*

He pulled me in front of him and walked close behind me, his arms wrapped around my body, his legs walking in unison with mine, his lips still continuing to send shivers down my back and into my toes.

I tried desperately to stay in character. Ashlyn is a pro at this. Ashlyn is not a stranger to leaving bars with random men. Ashlyn would giggle at his advances.

So I did.

"You smell incredible," he said, stopping his lips long enough to inhale my neck.

"What about your friends?" I asked, glancing in the direction of the bar where we had begun this runaway evening.

"They'll be fine," he assured me. "It's my bachelor party."

And it was those words that finally sobered me up. Instantly. Not because I was reminded that he was engaged to someone else and I was definitely crossing the line for being even remotely turned on by his touch, but because of what the words implied. "It's my bachelor party." *My friends expect this of me. I would have cheated with anyone. You just happened to be there . . . twice.*

"Are you okay with that?" he asked, most likely feeling my shoulders suddenly stiffen.

I immediately relaxed my body and slipped right back into character. I could slowly feel Ashlyn once again slide into the driver's seat. I ran one finger over his cheek and down the underside of his chin. "Of course. You're not married *yet,* are you?"

The numbness returned to my legs, then my hips, followed by my stomach, my arms, and my breasts. As we exited the front of the Palms Hotel, he turned me toward him and kissed my lips. Yep, those were numb again, too.

Everything was back to normal. Or so I hoped.

Parker playfully tossed me down onto the bed and practically fell on top of me. I moaned with pleasure as his hands massaged my thighs from the outside of my dress.

I braced myself for what was coming next. More kissing, more touching, more fake moans coming from my lips. But it didn't come. None of it. Without warning, his hands suddenly fell limp alongside my legs, and then eventually withdrew.

I wasn't sure what had happened. I searched his face for a clue. He was quiet, pensive, contemplative. He looked me in the eye, preparing to say something. Something important.

"Wait a minute," he began.

My first thought was that he was having doubts. That he might actually turn me down. The alcohol had worn off, something reminded him of his fiancée, whatever the reason . . . this unlikely candidate looked poised and ready to be one of the select few who passed the inspection.

I fought the smile that was attempting to penetrate my facade. The thought of someone passing was always exhilarating. Yes, it would mean my initial read on him was wrong, but this was hardly the job in which to be proud. Most of the time I practically *prayed* I was wrong.

"What's the matter?" I asked, naively.

"Something's not right," he replied.

My heart started to pound. This was it. It was really going to happen.

"Really?" The tone of my voice bordered on clueless.

"You've changed," he said, matter-of-factly.

My small glimmer of hope slowly started to melt into a very large pool of confusion. "What are you talking about?"

"You were all about this on the dance floor, and then as soon as we left the club it was like you just shut off."

My stomach lurched as I began to realize what his hesitation was really about. It was about me. I had fucked up. I had lost control . . . just for a second. And now I was about to sabotage an assignment because of it.

"I, um, I don't know what you're talking about."

He sat up. "It feels like you're just going through the motions or something. Like you're on autopilot but your mind is somewhere else."

Oh, dear Lord.

I started to panic. It just goes to show: *No* good can ever come from losing focus in this job. You can never let your guard down, even for a minute.

My thoughts were a blur. Was he really questioning my motivations or was this just an excuse? That tiny ray of hope was ironically clouding my view of reality. I couldn't seem to let go of the thought that maybe he was having second thoughts after all, and that my abnormal behavior tonight was just a convenient way out. A magical solution to dissolve the glue that held him captive in this sticky situation.

"That's crazy," I replied defensively.

"Is it?"

It suddenly occurred to me: *If he turns me down now, I'll never know the real reason why.* Will it be because he really wanted to be faithful to his fiancée, or will it be because I screwed up? The implication of confusing these two very different scenarios was severe. I, of course, would assume the latter.

How would I ever report back to Roger Ireland if I wasn't 100 percent sure about the results? *"Um, he passed . . . well, sort of. It's complicated, see . . ."*

No way. That would never fly. I had to know for certain before I left this room.

"Parker." I sat up and faced him, trying to look serious and provocative at the same time. "I'm not going through any motions. I want what you want. I think you just have to decide *what* you want."

There. I put the ball right back in his court. It wasn't the ultimate fix, but it would hopefully give him something to chew on for a while.

Then I had another thought. One far more sobering than any of my others. What if he had been tipped off about me? Intercepted by someone in the course of the night. Giving away my true intentions. Revealing everything.

If that were the case, it would mean Parker was just *playing along,* going through the motions, setting *me* up to fail. Slow playing *me!*

There was an awkward silence between us.

He looked over at me, obviously wondering what was going through my head. Funny, I was wondering the same thing about him. I wasn't sure which one of us was more desperate for a mind-reading device right about now. Especially when my internal one was failing me so miserably.

My superpowers had never been so out-of-tune in my life. Like Parker Colman, of all people in the world, was my kryptonite. Everything felt chaotic. As if someone had placed a magnet next to my compass and the needle was spinning in crazy circles.

Because, for the first time tonight, I had absolutely no idea what he was holding in his hand. The cards on the table were meaningless to me now. It wasn't as easy as having the nut flush when you're pretty sure your opponent is holding three kings. And when you don't have a clue what the person across from you is playing with, there's no way you can know how much to bet.

I tried to mask my anxiety as he continued to study my face. As if trying to map out his next play based on what I could possibly be hiding.

Trying to figure out if I still had those two hearts in my back pocket.

And then realization and relief washed over his face.

"Wait a minute," he said with a knowing smile. "Okay, how much are my friends paying you?"

I smothered a gasp. "*Excuse* me?"

"You're an escort, right? My friends paid for you. But they were sure I wouldn't sleep with you if I knew who you really were, so they told you to pretend you were all into me and shit, right?"

My eyes widened. And just as I was about to throw the whole thing out the window, fold my hand, leave the table, and for the first time abandon the job half finished out of pure pride, something in me clicked.

Parker had just made the ultimate poker faux pas: He had showed me his hand before the game was over. And suddenly I had the edge I was looking for. I knew *exactly* how to play.

I violently pulled myself off the bed and started huffing and puffing around the room in search of my shoes.

I made sure that every aggravated, insulted, emotionally wounded bone in my body was perfectly visible *and* audible.

"Oh my God! I have never been so insulted in my entire life!"

Parker's face immediately turned bright red, realizing his utterly horrendous mistake. He panicked and jumped up from the bed, reaching out to grab me and pull me close to him. "Wait, don't leave. I'm sorry. I don't know why I said that."

I shoved him away. "You think I'm a *hooker*?"

He stammered. "I'm sorry. I just sensed a change in you. I didn't know what it was. I overreacted. I got paranoid. It was the alcohol talking . . . not me. Please don't leave! I really want to spend more time with you."

I placed my hands on my hips and glared at him, seemingly deciding whether I had it in my heart to forgive him. Seemingly deciding just how much I wanted to have sex tonight. And then my voice softened slightly, to an almost vulnerable murmur. "Do I *look* like a hooker?" I asked, with hope of reconciliation in my eyes.

"Of course not! You are so beautiful and sexy and . . . classy! God, I want you so bad, it's driving me crazy." He put his arms back around me. This time gently, affectionately, with a forced adoration he prayed would be convincing enough to keep me from walking out the door. To keep me in his rented bed.

It worked.

Somehow I knew it would.

The pout on my lips slowly eased into a forgiving smile, and he once again placed his lips on mine. I didn't fight it.

His kiss was tender at first. It had to be. And he knew that. But he wasted no time bringing it back to the intensity it had been only half an hour ago. And I wasted no time reciprocating.

After all, I was tired. And ready to go to sleep. It had been a long night.

My performance from then on didn't matter. He believed me. He had no other choice.

Roger Ireland and his daughter would at least have a clear answer when I got back to L.A. Even if it was a heartbreaking one. Because when Parker crossed that point of no return, I knew for sure why he had failed. And it certainly wasn't because I had.

But this time, in this game, when I finally revealed *these* two hearts in my pocket, he didn't offer me any polite, "good hand"–type of gesture. I guess he wasn't in a very sportsmanlike mood anymore.

But I didn't mind.

That's just the nature of the game.

12

letter labels

As I closed the hotel room door behind me, I knew it would only be a matter of time before Parker Colman found the black business card I had left on the dresser. A small reminder of the events that had come to pass. A souvenir, if you will.

No doubt he would see it from his place across the room, exactly where I had left him. Sitting on the edge of the bed, his head hung low between his knees, his guilt palpable, and for the first time in his life . . . feeling vulnerable. He would lift his head momentarily and the shiny black surface of the card would catch his eye. He certainly hadn't remembered it being there before.

After a few moments his curiosity would get the better of him and he would muster the energy to pull himself off the bed and approach the mysterious foreign object.

He would frown with bewilderment as he looked down upon my little souvenir. Not quite sure what to make of it. On the topside of the card he would simply see the letter "A" printed in an ornate, crimson font. Almost calligraphic. He would then reach down and pick up the card, feeling the raised surface of the elegant lettering against his fingertips.

And it wouldn't be until he turned the card over, dialed the toll-free number printed on the back, and listened carefully to the recorded message that he would finally understand.

The remorse would wash over him again . . . this time, unbelievably, ten times stronger, causing him to stagger back toward the bed, slowly lowering his body onto the comforter, using his hand to steady his shaky form.

The black telephone receiver would hang lifelessly off the edge of the nightstand, the automated female voice playing on its continuous loop still faintly audible from his new position only a few feet away.

The 866 number is the fourth and final listing in my repertoire of phone numbers. Although this one never rang through to any home line or cell phone. This one never connected the caller to any type of voice-mail service. And this one was, by far, the most untraceable number I owned.

The female voice on the other line wasn't my own. It was a computer program that generated voices just human enough to make people feel comfortable, but at the same time, just digital enough to inform the caller that this message was not recorded by an actual person, and therefore there was no use in trying to match it with any voiceprint database in the world.

And until Parker Colman found the energy to stand up and physically hang up the receiver, the continuous loop would play on forever: *"The card you've just received indicates your involvement in an undercover fidelity inspection."*

I often wonder if any of them actually keep the card. Although, I somehow doubt it. It's not exactly the kind of souvenir you hang on to and store in your top drawer for memory's sake. But I've always been especially proud of my little black calling cards.

The procedure with the card all depends upon my mood. Sometimes I tell them exactly who I am and why I'm there, then I hand them the card. Double whammy. And sometimes I just walk out and leave the card for them to find . . . on top of the TV, the nightstand, or slid underneath the door.

I considered the routine fairly lenient. After all, I *could* just sew the letter

right onto the front of their shirts before I leave. But I think that ritual might be just a tad bit outdated.

With Parker I chose to tell him to his face. Mostly because tonight I wasn't given any convenient opportunities to sneak out the door. So I simply stopped his hand as it began to wander up my dress, pushed myself off the bed, stood in front of him, and while staring him straight in the eye, confessed the truth: that tonight was a setup. An inspection. And his results were "unfavorable."

Then I picked up my bag and walked out the door. I don't even think he noticed me place the card down on top of the dresser. But one thing's for sure: This was certainly the worst card he'd been dealt in a long while.

I walked down the hotel hallway, hypnotizing myself with the brightly colored carpeting that seemed to go on forever. I reached the elevator and pushed the call button. I took a deep breath and exhaled loudly.

Thank God, that's over, I thought to myself as I checked my watch. It was 2:15 in the morning. Early night for Vegas, I would imagine.

The doors opened and I stepped inside, quickly scanning the daunting selection of numbers until I found the one marked with the number 24. I pressed it and then leaned against the back of the elevator as the doors slowly closed. I thought about the suite on the twenty-fourth floor that was waiting for me. The white cotton sheets, the soft, fluffy pillows, the . . .

Suddenly a hand reached between the closing doors, barely avoiding an amputation. I jolted to an upright position, somewhat irritated by the unexpected company on what had promised to be a very peaceful elevator ride. Most likely at this time of night it was a group of drunk twenty-somethings who could barely stand up and would probably start pressing all the buttons like a Ritalin-deprived ADD child . . . or worse yet, another bachelor party.

But when the doors opened there was only one person standing on the other side. And he was now sober as hell.

It was Parker.

And he definitely did not look happy.

I swallowed hard and eyed the doorway, wondering if I would be safer out there or in here. Spatial logic told me a wide-open hallway with an endless supply of doors to bang on was a much better bet than an eight-by-eight-foot elevator with an emergency stop button glowing in red.

"We need to talk," he said matter-of-factly, his hand still holding the door open.

I struggled to keep my composure, staring him straight in the eye, just as I had done only a few hours before at the poker table. *I'm not afraid of you,* my glare said. But the truth was probably far less heroic.

I said nothing, letting the silence speak for itself.

"I love Lauren. We're getting married in three weeks. And I'm not going to let you and your stupid little fidelity—whatever the fuck it is—get in the way of that."

"Probably should have thought of that before you attempted to put your hand in my crotch," I shot back, and then immediately regretted it. The best way to deal with an outraged husband or, in this case, fiancé, is to say nothing. Keep calm and add nothing to the conversation that might fuel his rage.

"It's my bachelor party!" he shouted back, as if this was supposed to convince me to walk away and forget the whole thing.

"Unfortunately, I don't think my client sees it the way that you do," I replied coolly and evenly.

Parker groaned. "Lauren would never do this. She would never hire someone to set me up. It had to be her father. He was the one who hired you, wasn't he?"

I didn't respond.

"Roger Ireland is a stuck-up old man who will never find anyone good enough for his precious daughter."

I stood strong in front of him, my stance confident, my eyes unyielding. "If you'll kindly remove your hand from the door, I'd like to leave now."

Out of the corner of my eye I could see the number 24 still lit up like a beacon guiding everyone and anyone right to my hotel room. I prayed he wouldn't step into the elevator and notice the illuminated button. He couldn't know that I was staying in this hotel, or worse, what floor I was staying on. He had to think what all the men think, that I mysteriously disappear into the night like a figment of his imagination, never to be seen or heard from again.

Parker's once-reserved irritation suddenly erupted into full-blown rage. "Okay, this is ridiculous." His voice level rose at least three decibels. "I'm not going to just let you walk out of this hotel and run home to tell my fiancée and that freak of a father of hers that I 'almost' had sex with you." His mocking intonation on the word "almost" left no question of his sentiment regarding this procedure.

Thankfully during his mini-rampage he had thrown his arms violently in the air, releasing the doors in the process.

I took a step backward into the center of the elevator car and pressed down hard on the *Close Door* button. "With all due respect, Mr. Colman. You don't really have a choice."

The doors began to close on cue, and just when I thought I was in the clear, his hand came through the crack again and pushed them back open, stepping menacingly into the elevator with me, now even more pissed-off than before.

That's when my heart rate started to speed up. I had dealt with angry men in the past. It was an obvious part of the job. It's not like a husband who has just failed his inspection is going to say something like "Oh well, my bad. Thanks for helping me realize what's really wrong with my marriage." Most of the time they get angry, so it normally doesn't come as a surprise when they do.

But this guy was taking it too far. And I wasn't about to be in a confined space with him in this condition. Plus, he had been drinking all night. Excessive alcohol plus knowing your fiancée is probably going to call off your wedding in a matter of days, plus, well, let's face it, blue balls . . . is not a happy combination.

Parker stepped right next to me and clamped his large hand around the upper part of my left arm. His grasp was tight and filled with warning. It felt like I was getting my blood pressure taken at the doctor's office and the new nurse on staff had no idea when to stop pumping air into the armband.

"I don't think you understand what I'm saying." He spoke softly but ominously.

I knew my next move had to be fast in order to catch him off guard.

He turned his head slightly and I immediately sprung into action. I reached up with my right hand, grabbed the wrist he was using to hold on to my arm, and twisted it swiftly and forcefully opposite the way it was intended to bend. His grasp immediately loosened as his body fell forward. As soon as my other arm was free I rammed it upward, making full contact with his nose. He toppled over in pain and, most of all, shock.

"What the hell . . . ?" he yelled, reaching for his bleeding nose and struggling to stand upright. But the impact with his nose was not helping his balance. He stumbled toward me. I knew that with him at six foot two and approximately two hundred pounds and me at five foot six, and barely passing the 110 mark, I was no match for him physically. So I had to use my present position to my advantage.

My knee popped up, hitting him squarely between the legs. He staggered backward out of the elevator from the blow and slammed into the wall behind him, doubled over in excruciating pain. I could see the cloud of rage and humiliation slowly begin to cast a shadow over his face. But by the time the room stopped spinning and he could even comprehend what had just happened to him, the elevator doors were closing again.

And this time his hand wasn't fast enough to stop them.

The next morning I awoke to the sound of my wake-up call. I was still wrapped in the Bellagio cotton robe I had put on after my twenty-minute cleansing shower the night before. A thorough attempt to remove Parker Colman from my mind and any part of my body. After all the standard post-assignment scrubbing, I doubted there were any skin cells left on my body that had come into contact with him; however, the washcloth hadn't seemed to do much to cleanse me of the memory. But then again, it never does.

I checked out of my room at the front desk, where I could pay my bill in cash. Most hotels require a credit card to secure the room, but a one-hundred-dollar-per-day cash deposit usually does the trick. This also allows me to check in under a different name. Credit cards can get you in trouble. Especially if someone like Parker Colman manages to find a male hotel employee with a sympathetic ear, and then suddenly my cover is blown.

Once seated in my American Airlines first-class window seat, I pulled my headphones out of my bag, slid them over my head, and closed my eyes. The Las Vegas assignments are always nice. It's just a short, forty-five-minute plane ride home. The New York assignments are the worst. Six torturous hours on a plane after a long night of dealing with corrupt businessmen (and I'm not talking about tax evasion).

I usually wear headphones on the plane. Whether or not I actually have music playing through them varies according to my mood. I hate airplane small talk. It's a waste of time. The plane rides are my time to relax, think about nothing, read my favorite gossip magazines. It's my down time. I've learned over the years that people on airplanes will still attempt to chitchat with you, *even* if you obviously appear to be reading something. But they'll pretty much leave you alone once they realize you can't hear them. Which is why I made sure to purchase those extra large, noise-canceling headphones. No chitchat from random strangers was getting through *these* suckers. In fact, they should be called "meaningless-small-talk-canceling" headphones.

It's not as though I'm not a sociable person. It's just that I have enough friends. I'm not looking for any more. And to a stranger, my life is always a big fat lie anyway, so what's the point in bringing another victim into my web of fabrication?

I used to enjoy talking to people on airplanes. Back when Jennifer Hunter was just Jennifer Hunter, and therefore I could be anyone I wanted to be. Ironic how I used to love to make up stories about who I was, where I was going, what I did, who I had just fallen in love with. But now that my life was just one big made-up story, it wasn't quite so amusing anymore.

I must have drifted off to sleep to the sound of Joss Stone playing in my ear, because when I awoke, we were in the air. I was somewhat surprised that the flight attendant hadn't woken me up to remind me to shut off my "portable electronic device." Maybe she could tell I had just been through a rough night and decided to cut me some slack.

I could feel the presence of someone in the seat next to me, but I didn't acknowledge them. It was easier to pretend that they weren't even there. I stared out the window as the large buildings that made up the Las Vegas Strip grew smaller and smaller in the distance, giant structures resembling the monuments of Paris, New York, ancient Egypt, and even medieval kingdoms.

The idea of Las Vegas always made me laugh. Can you imagine what archaeologists millions of years from now will think when they unexpectedly discover the city of Las Vegas? They'll be as confused as hell. Digging away, looking for any clues that might help them understand that ancient, mysterious species they call "human beings" who were wiped out by a devastating tragedy of their own making. And then suddenly . . . what's this? It looks like one of their cities. But wait a minute. Didn't we just see that same artifact when were digging in what was then referred to as the country of "France"? And what about this one? We found something *remarkably* similar in what was previously known as "New York."

And the human species would continue to remain a mystery for all of time, with a new underlying question to ponder: Why would a species choose to build identical monuments in two very different places? Talk about a world wonder.

I suddenly felt a tap on my shoulder. I was jolted from my thoughts as I looked up to see the flight attendant taking drink orders.

I slid off my headphones long enough to order a Diet Coke, and just as I was about to slide them back on . . .

"So did you win?"

I turned to my neighbor, who I now noticed was a man in what appeared to be his mid-thirties, attractive, with gentle eyes that revealed a lifetime of experiences. Some good. Some bad.

"I'm sorry?"

"Did you win?" he repeated. "Or I guess, what I should ask first is . . . did you gamble?"

I dropped my headphones in my lap and stifled a groan. Here we go. Let the airplane small talk begin. You take your chitchat-canceling headphones off for two seconds and bam, you're cornered.

I smiled politely. "Yes, I played some poker."

"And . . . did you win?"

Initial reading: wealthy, single but not against marriage or family. In Vegas for business and, refreshingly enough, probably not the cheating type.

Meeting one of the few faithful ones left in the world is always a pleasant surprise. It's almost like spotting an endangered species while hiking in the wild. You immediately want to whip out your camera to document the sighting. Otherwise, how will people know to believe you?

I flashed a warm smile. "I won a few hands here and there."

The flight attendant placed our drinks in front of us. My good-looking, non-cheating neighbor had ordered a tomato juice. An honest drink. I'm always wary of airplane passengers who order hard alcohol at eleven in the morning.

"Good for you. A girl who plays poker . . . that's rare."

I guess we were *two* endangered species sitting right next to each other on the same flight leaving Las Vegas. What are the odds?

"Yeah, well, what can I say? I'm a fan of any method of making money that doesn't require you to report it to the IRS."

He laughed. "And what do you do when you're not hustling people out of their paychecks?"

And here come the lies. "I'm an investment banker. . . . What about you?"

"I work for the IRS," he said in an apologetic tone, lowering his head.

A slight wave of panic washed over me, along with an entire ocean of awkwardness. I took a sip of my Diet Coke. "Um . . . I was just kidding about the . . ."

"I'm afraid I'm going to have to arrest you for years of back taxes on unreported gambling earnings."

The smile on his face allowed me to release a loud gush of air and, of course, a laugh of relief. "Good one."

"Hmm, a poker player who can't see an obvious bluff. I'm not too confident in your abilities all of a sudden."

I stammered. "Well, to be fair, it wasn't exactly an *obvious* bluff."

"Please. I got a D-minus in eighth-grade drama class! I couldn't act my way out of a cardboard box."

"Well, I'm not exactly sure, but I think placing children in cardboard boxes might be bordering on child abuse." I pretended to ponder the thought.

"Yes, well, that was twenty-five years ago . . . back then, it was more of a gray area."

"And that would make you thirty- . . ."

"Ah, so she's also a human calculator."

"And you're a D student, it would seem," I shot back.

He shook his head as he took a sip of his juice. "I said I got a D in a drama class. It doesn't make me a D student, just a D actor."

As he set down his drink, I instinctively looked to his left hand. No ring. Just as I suspected. Single. My reading was, as usual, right on the money.

"So what *do* you do when you're not pretending to be an undercover IRS agent?"

If I were to guess, I would have said marketing or advertising. He was too clever to be an accountant. And not suave enough to be a salesman. So it came as no surprise when he said:

"I'm a marketing consultant. Harrah's Casinos is one of our clients."

Right again. It was almost too easy.

Our conversation continued for another twenty minutes, and just as I was about to have second thoughts on my general aversion to airplane small talk, the pilot's voice came over the intercom. "Good morning, ladies and gentlemen. I've just received word from the tower in LAX that there are some pretty bad thunderstorms hovering over the Los Angeles area. We're going to have to land in Palm Springs and wait for the storms to pass over. I apologize for any inconvenience this may cause you, but we want to make sure it's safe to land before we bring you into L.A."

I looked over at my neighbor, and we groaned simultaneously.

"I thought it never rains in L.A.," I complained.

"It doesn't," he confirmed, "but I made some calls."

"So you're something of a miracle worker?"

He turned toward me and held out his hand. "I'm Jamie Richards."

I shook it. "Jennifer."

"Just Jennifer? Like Cher or Madonna?"

"I prefer to be compared to the likes of Michelangelo, if you don't mind."

Jamie laughed. It felt good to have someone genuinely laugh at one of my jokes. Someone who didn't have a wife at home. Someone whose laugh wasn't overflowing with ulterior motives.

And honestly, it felt good to laugh back . . . ulterior motive–free.

"All right. I'll play along with the first-name-only thing. But just a suggestion: You might want to pick something more unique than 'Jennifer' if you're going to walk around last name–less."

"You're right. Fine. It's Jennifer . . . H.," I said coyly.

He looked impressed. "Wow. First name, last initial. We're making progress. Do you feel okay? Is this conversation moving too fast for you? Do you want to take a short break and get back to me?"

I looked out the window at the approaching Palm Springs runway. "Well, it doesn't look like we'll be going anywhere anytime soon."

"So, you decided to reveal a letter? Do I get one every hour?"

I smirked. "If Jennifer H. was enough to distinguish me all the way through high school, it should get you through the next few hours . . . at least until we get back to L.A."

"Fair enough, Jennifer H."

"Hey, consider yourself lucky. That's one letter more than most strangers on airplanes get. Or any strangers, for that matter."

"Oh, I do."

I looked at him questioningly.

"Consider myself lucky," he clarified.

I blushed and turned my head toward the window, suddenly very interested in watching our landing.

After a grueling forty-five-minute-turned-four-hour flight, I stepped off the plane in Los Angeles to the sound of my personal cell phone ringing.

"Sophie's very upset. You should call her." Zoë's breathless voice came roaring through my earpiece.

"What are you doing? You sound like you're running a marathon."

"I'm trying to turn left on San Vicente and there's no turn arrow. Apparently, the drivers in Santa Monica all got their licenses from a vending machine."

I exited the terminal, my rollaway suitcase in tow, and walked toward the valet parking attendant. "If Sophie's so upset, why doesn't she just call me?"

"Oh, c'mon! Get a clue, you selfish bitch!"

I stopped in my tracks. "Huh?"

Then I heard the infamous honking sounds and I continued walking.

"Sorry. This woman apparently needs a phone book so she can see over the steering wheel. You know how it goes. Look, it's been a week. Don't you think you're overreacting a bit?"

I handed my ticket to the valet. "I can't really talk about this right now. I'm just getting my car at LAX and I'm totally exhausted. Why don't I call you tomorrow?"

"Fine." Zoë gasped for air.

"Are you sure you're all right?"

"I told you, I'm trying to turn left at an intersection with no arrow. Of course I'm not all right. Call me tomorrow!"

I hung up the phone and slid the Bluetooth out of my ear.

"Well, you certainly got off that plane fast."

The voice startled me and I dropped my Bluetooth headset on the ground. As I reached down to pick it up, I turned around to see Jamie standing behind me, his own valet ticket in hand. I quickly popped back up to a standing position, nearly losing my balance in the process. I grabbed onto a nearby railing to steady myself.

I forced out a laugh. "Yeah. I guess I've just had my fill of airplanes for the day."

He eyed me with an amused smirk and I immediately felt self-conscious. I was used to getting smirks from men, just not ones qualified by "amused." And definitely not ones that came right after I just nearly did a face plant on the airport sidewalk. I tried to compensate by leaning casually against the rail and crossing one ankle over the other, convinced that this was a much more attractive side of me.

Not that I cared what this random guy thought.

"You didn't even say good-bye. I feel so used."

I laughed. "For what? Airplane small talk?"

"Yes, exactly. For a quick and easy distraction during a four-hour flight."

I lowered my head. "Guilty as charged. So you're a valet guy, too, huh?" I said, motioning toward his ticket.

He nodded. "So worth the extra few dollars. Plus, my company pays for it."

"Right," I stated. "Mine, too." And it was true. Somebody *always* paid for it.

"Well, I'm glad I bumped into you again, because I wanted to ask you a question. But you ran off so quickly and you didn't leave behind any glass slippers or something that might prove useful in finding you later."

"How realistic is a shoe that only fits *one* girl in an entire kingdom of people? I never understood that."

"Well, she had very tiny feet," he explained, looking down at mine. "Yeah, yours look pretty normal. I would have a hard time even *with* the slipper."

I laughed, and an awkward silence fell between us. Awkward because I usually know exactly what to say to people . . . especially men. But standing there with Jamie, I felt uncomfortable, almost tongue-tied. As if I didn't do this kind of thing for a living nearly every single night of my life. But right now all that Ashlyn confidence that had made me so successful at what I do was nowhere to be found. It was just me. And I had never been very good at this sort of thing. Plus, the fact that Jamie seemed to get better looking with every passing minute didn't help much either.

"So what I was going to ask you was if you'd like to have dinner with me tomorrow night."

The statement took me by surprise. I definitely hadn't seen it coming. Men like Jamie didn't ask out girls like Jen. He seemed so worldly, so mature, so far away from anything I was. Ashlyn attracted guys like Jamie all the time . . . well, the married, unfaithful versions of him. But not me. Not like this. Not when there was no one around to pay me after I was done.

I shifted my weight anxiously, still unable to respond. Like suddenly the words were stuck in my mouth and refused to come out.

"Wow, I didn't realize it was that difficult a question. Maybe I should have phrased it more simply."

I let out a nervous giggle. "No, Jamie. It's not that. I just don't think that would be a very good idea."

He nodded understandingly. "As in, not a good idea because you have a boyfriend or not a good idea because you have an infectious disease?"

I saw the valet approaching in my car and I bit my bottom lip. "No. No boyfriend."

"Damn. Had to be the disease. What is it? Cholera? Ebola? The plague?"

I laughed and shook my head. "No. It's just kind of complicated."

"Well, that's good to hear. Because I *love* complication. Give me something simple and I'll just fall asleep."

I smiled. He was sweet. Almost too sweet. So much of me wanted to just accept the date. A *real* date. With no distrusting girlfriends waiting outside to break down the door. No scarlet letters. No page-long list of things to say, movies to like, karaoke songs to sing. But the other part of me screamed, *No! Don't do it!* Because I felt this overwhelming sensation that I knew where it would go. How it would turn out. Why read the book when you already know how it ends?

"I'm sorry," I said, stepping off the curb and making my way to the awaiting valet. "It was really nice meeting you, though."

And then suddenly a profound sadness fell over me. The kind of sadness that comes from already knowing how the book ends. From knowing that you'll never have that same rush of adventure and excitement and suspense that normal people feel when they pick up the latest bestselling, happy-ending, till-death-do-us-part novel and can't wait to start devouring its pages.

"Well, if you ever change your mind, or just feel the need to call someone up and confess the *second* letter of your last name . . ." Jamie reached into his jacket pocket and pulled out a business card. "I think it's my last one. I've been saving it for you." He flipped it over and examined the back. "Look, it's even got some of my random scribbles on the back from when I ran out of scratch paper."

He extended the card to me and I took it. I placed it in the back pocket of my jeans as I removed a twenty-dollar bill and handed it to the valet. "Thanks," I said to both of them.

"Well, I guess we'll always have Palm Springs," Jamie said in a pathetic Humphrey Bogart imitation.

I rolled my eyes and said, "*Now* I understand why you got a D in drama."

He laughed, and then with a sincere voice and a smile that nearly made my heart melt, he said, "It was nice meeting you, Jennifer H."

But I wasn't quite sure if my heart was melting from adoration . . . or from fear.

The fear that I may have just made a mistake.

As I got into my car and drove away, my everyday world re-engulfed me like an old familiar blanket. The steering wheel, the radio, the navigation system. And most of all, Roger Ireland's client file just barely visible from the inside of my bag. Tomorrow morning I would tell him what had happened during my fateful trip to Vegas, then he would tell his daughter, and yet another wedding would be called off. Another happy, make-believe ending thwarted by the harsh reality of the real world.

Maybe I just wasn't meant to read books.

13

questionable intentions

"Marta!" I called from my bedroom. "Have you seen my off-white Dolce and Gabbana blouse?" I ventured into my closet for the third time on Monday morning and sifted, yet again, through the hanging shirts. As if by magic, in the time it had taken me to dump the entire contents of my hamper onto the floor, the missing article of clothing might have materialized out of thin air and hung itself up neatly in its proper place.

But it hadn't.

Marta, on the other hand, *had* managed to seemingly materialize out of thin air. She stood in the doorway of my bedroom, a clever smile painted across her lips and the freshly ironed shirt hanging daintily from her outstretched finger.

I let out a sigh of relief. "Oh! Thank you, thank you, thank you! You are the best!"

I took the shirt from her hand and pulled it on over my nude-color bra. I was running approximately ten minutes late for my ten o'clock follow-up meeting with Roger Ireland, and I had been very grateful when Marta showed up thirty minutes ago and started her normal cleaning routine. It always made me feel more at ease knowing she was there. And I still couldn't figure out if it was because of how clean I knew the place would look and feel when she was done, or if maybe it was just her.

"You're welcome, Miss Hunter. *Muy bonita.* Working today?"

I smiled and pulled my hair out from underneath the collar. "Always."

She smiled back and then quickly spun around to return to her work.

I checked my makeup in the bathroom mirror, did a quick touch-up on the loose waves in my hair, and emerged into the kitchen. Marta was busy scrubbing the inside of the oven. She was bent over at a ninety-degree angle with her entire upper body hidden inside of it. All I could see were her legs keeping her balanced on the wooden floor as her ample backside swayed back and forth in the air while she cleaned.

"I'm leaving your check here," I said to her as I ripped a page out of my checkbook and placed it on the counter. Then I proceeded to fill my Gucci tote with all the appropriate "tools" I would need for the day: wallet, two cell phones, breath mints, and sunglasses. I closed the bag, slung it over my shoulder, and snatched up my keys.

"Car people call while you in the shower!" Marta called from inside the oven.

I stopped and turned around. "What did they say?"

"They say you have recall."

I sighed. Just what I wanted right now. Another part of my life in need of repair. If only you could perform recalls on other aspects of your life. One quick trip to the mechanic and suddenly everything that seems to be malfunctioning in your life is magically repaired.

"A recall? On what?"

"I no know," her voice reverberated. "They give me appointment for eleven o'clock."

"Today?" I panicked, instinctively pulling out my Treo and checking my schedule.

"No." Her head reappeared from inside the oven and she brushed a sweaty hair from her forehead. "They say Wednesday."

I clicked to Wednesday. Thankfully the morning appeared empty; I typed in the appointment. "Okay. I'll take the car in. Thank you, Marta."

AS I quietly rode the empty elevator up to Roger Ireland's office, my mind was filled with all sorts of noise. I stared at myself in the mirrored elevator doors. Into my own tired, hardened eyes. Despite my best attempts to utilize the magic of makeup, my reflection was pale, worn out, visibly troubled. When did it all get to be so complicated? My best friend and I weren't on speaking terms, I had practically exploded at my naive, twelve-year-old niece, and Parker Colman had almost taken me down in an elevator.

I don't think Revlon makes a concealer for that.

And still, as hard as I tried, I couldn't find a way to erase the image of Jamie's face from my convoluted, highly compartmentalized mind. Something I had *always* managed to do before.

I couldn't wait for this meeting to be over so I could finally concentrate on sorting out my life. God knows it needed some serious sorting.

The doors opened and I straightened my posture, smoothed my hair and blouse, and pulled open one of the large, double-glass doors that led into Roger Ireland's law firm.

"Let's make this quick," I mumbled to myself.

I felt fairly certain that Roger Ireland was a reasonable man. Concise and to the point. And since he wasn't a wife or a girlfriend, this should probably be an easy "post."

The receptionist showed me in immediately.

"Good morning, Ashlyn," she began, leading me down the main hallway. "Mr. Ireland and Miss Ireland are waiting for you in his office."

"Thank you," I started to say, and then stopped suddenly in my tracks. "Wait, did you say *Miss* Ireland?"

The receptionist smiled naively. "Yes, his daughter. Lauren?"

Suddenly my feet felt as if they were trapped in mud. What the hell was *she* doing in there? Mr. Ireland said he was going to tell her himself. Much later. Meaning, after I had left the building and all surrounding areas. I had not mentally prepared myself to deal with a bridezilla two weeks before her wedding. Especially one who was about to find out that her fiancé isn't quite the guy she thought he was.

I tried to keep the look of pure dread from spreading across my face as I continued to follow the receptionist down the hallway and into Mr. Ireland's office, although I couldn't help but feel like I was walking to my own execution.

She swung the door open for me and I prepared myself for the worst.

"Ashlyn!" Roger greeted me pleasantly and stepped forward to shake my hand as I hesitantly entered the room. "Good to see you again."

I looked around the office and noticed an attractive brunette sitting at Mr. Ireland's desk typing frantically into a keyboard. "Dad, your directories are all messed up. That's why you can't find the source of this data stream."

Roger smiled at me. "This is my daughter, Lauren."

Lauren took one last hopeless look at her father's computer monitor and then stood up. She smiled brightly as she walked over and offered me her hand. "Pleased to meet you, Ashlyn. Thanks for coming by. Won't you sit down?" She motioned to the couch and took a seat in the nearby armchair.

I eyed her strangely. She was certainly pretty upbeat about this whole process. Was she in denial? Well, she certainly wouldn't be the first bride I'd dealt with who was.

I studied Mr. Ireland's only daughter as I took the safer seat *across* from her. She was definitely prettier than I thought she'd be. Not that I'm normally one to stereotype, but after Roger Ireland's lengthy explanation of his daughter's extensive computer skills, I kind of pictured someone a little less, well, elegant.

She was tall and slender with long, dark hair that she had pulled back into a very businesslike ponytail. Her clothes were a bit on the boring side: brown pants with a matching jacket. And her beige turtleneck underneath left no skin showing.

I glanced down at my current outfit selection. A gray pencil skirt that was slightly on the tighter side and the off-white blouse that Marta had supplied me with earlier. The blouse was unbuttoned just enough to *suggest* the existence of cleavage. I suddenly wished that I could turn around and button up the last button. I wondered what she must have been thinking about *my* ensemble. Not that it mattered, but I assumed she had to be forming at least some kind of an opinion about a girl who seduces betrothed men as an occupation.

Roger looked extremely nervous. I could have sworn I even saw small beads of sweat appearing on his forehead. But Lauren was the exact opposite: calm, composed, and extremely pleasant. I was thoroughly impressed. Most women in her position were pacing the hallways, wringing their hands together, biting off their beautifully manicured fingernails. But not Lauren. I started to doubt Mr. Ireland's initial evaluation of his daughter. He was pretty confident that she was the jealous type, somewhat insecure about men. That was not who was being represented in this office today. I had pictured a girl not unlike Sophie: suspicious, uneasy, and above all else, distrusting.

I felt myself relax somewhat. Maybe this wouldn't be as bad as I thought.

"So my dad told me I simply *had* to come down here today and see these floral centerpieces for myself." She then eyed my empty hands. "Did you bring pictures of them?"

My sudden comprehension of the situation hit me like a shock wave. I nearly doubled over in my seat.

Lauren looked questioningly from my unfamiliar face to her dad's, now fully aware that something was not adding up.

"Dad?"

Mr. Ireland slowly wiped his forehead with the back of his hand and came over to the couch to sit next to his daughter. He put his arm around her shoulders. "Lauren, honey, Ashlyn is not here to talk about flowers for the wedding."

She sat up straighter in her seat and turned her eyes toward me, suddenly a new sense of distrust forming in her eyes. "What *is* she here about, then?"

He cleared his throat and looked to me for help. I stood motionless. I had no idea what to say. Demure housewives, hopeful fiancées, bitchy businesswomen . . . I had confronted them all. But a bride-to-be tricked into attending a meeting of this nature? That was a first for me.

He looked me in the eye with an apologetic frown. "I thought it would be best if she heard the outcome directly from you. I wasn't sure if she would believe me."

Lauren's face filled with panic. "What outcome? What are you talking about?"

I tried to smile just as pleasantly as she had when I walked in the door. But I was surely unsuccessful.

And then something occurred to me. Roger Ireland was highly confident that Parker had failed this test. Otherwise he would have never decided to bring Lauren into the picture. Because if Parker *had* passed, he probably wouldn't want her to know anything about this whole thing. Despite the inflated fifty-fifty odds I had given him in our initial meeting, Mr. Ireland seemed to be betting on a much more certain outcome.

He shifted his body so that he could face his daughter, whose eyes were pleading for answers. She was uncomfortable, not only in being out of the loop, but also because of the growing suspicion that the loop had something to do with her.

"Sweetie, Ashlyn is a professional fidelity inspector."

She scrunched up her face in what I could only describe as horrified confusion. "A what?"

"She tests men . . . like Parker . . . for unfaithful tendencies."

Lauren shot right up from her seat.

"You hired this woman to test Parker?"

I was now the uncomfortable one. And the nauseating emphasis she placed on the words "this woman" definitely hadn't helped. Not only was I going to have to relay these disappointing results to Roger *and* his daughter, but I was apparently going to have to sit through her delayed acceptance of the process as well.

"I can't believe you would do that!" Lauren shouted at her father, stepping away from the couch and pacing in front of his desk.

Her body language was now starting to more resemble the typical behavior of a "fiancée in waiting."

I should have known she was in the dark. What fiancée greets an incoming fidelity inspector like a flower specialist coming to talk about wedding arrangements? I've always said women are harder to read than men.

"Lauren, I only did this because I love you and I care about you. And I was worried that Parker wasn't going to treat you the way you deserve to be treated."

"You never liked him, Dad! *Never!* Come to think of it, you've never liked *anyone* I've dated!"

And there I was, caught right in the middle of the father/daughter argument I would most likely never have.

"That's not true! Honey, please sit down and just listen to what she has to say."

"No! I won't sit down and listen to *her.*"

And just like that I had gone from a welcomed guest to a *her.* It wasn't a title I was unfamiliar with. But it also wasn't a title I really wanted to deal with right now. Especially when I had come to this meeting fully expecting *not* to have to deal with it.

"Honey, please . . ."

Lauren continued to pace. "Where do you even *find* someone like that? What, does she advertise in the yellow pages under 'Slut Services'?"

"Lauren Marie Ireland! That was completely uncalled for!" Roger shouted in a stern, fatherly voice. "Ashlyn is a professional and I received her name from a close friend."

I started to stand up. "Maybe I should go and come back when you've had some more time to discuss this."

He lowered his tone and spoke gently to me. "No, wait. Please stay. She didn't mean that. She's angry at *me* not you." Then firmly to Lauren: "Honey, sit down right now. Ashlyn is going to tell us the outcome of this test, and then she's going to leave. After that you can hate me all you want."

Lauren glared at me and crossed her arms. "I'll stand, thanks."

I nodded sympathetically and sat back down. "However you're comfortable," I managed to get out in a half-cheerful tone.

Mr. Ireland took a deep breath and leaned forward in his seat, waiting for my next words with great anticipation.

I forced a smile as I started my usual spiel. "Okay, here's how this part of the process works: I will tell you the outcome of the inspection and then you can decide how much detail about the night you want to hear. I'm happy to recount as little or as much as you want. That part is entirely up to you."

Lauren groaned audibly and rolled her eyes. Her father shot her a warning glance as I tried to ignore both.

I looked to Roger. "As you requested during our initial meeting, I conducted a fidelity inspection on Parker Colman." I glanced at Lauren and spoke carefully. "Meaning that in order to fail he had to show a clear intention to engage in . . . sexual infidelity."

"Oh my God!" Lauren growled in disgust.

Roger ignored her and offered me a nod of encouragement.

I paused and took a deep breath, looking from Lauren to Roger and then back at Lauren again. "Your fiancé, Parker Colman, unfortunately did not pass the inspection."

Roger collapsed against the back of his chair, seemingly in relief. And I wasn't sure if the relief was directed more toward the fact that now (or at least eventually) he would be off the hook with his daughter, or toward the fact that thankfully there would be no chance he would have to let this asshole into his family.

Lauren stood frozen in shock. Trying to absorb this whole unexpected chain of events and the highly disconcerting news that had come along with them. She looked at me, puzzled and confused, before leaning against the desk behind her for support.

Roger immediately stood up and rushed over, hugging her thin frame close to him. She pushed him away. "Don't touch me."

"Lauren, I know you must be upset at me right now, and I don't blame you. But I hope someday you'll thank me for this."

"This is ridiculous!" Lauren exclaimed, stepping away from her father.

"How do we even know this woman is telling the truth? I mean, who is she to tell me that Parker is a cheater. She doesn't even *know* Parker."

I've dealt with many women in denial before, and I've learned that the best way to fight an accusation of fraudulence is *not* to fight it.

"Lauren," I began calmly and gently, "it's not my job to convince you of anything. My job is to tell you exactly what happened with your fiancé when he was given the opportunity to be unfaithful to you. That's all."

"So what *did* happen?" she asked in a sarcastic tone. As if anything I said from here on out would be considered complete bullshit. But I knew she wouldn't have asked if she wasn't curious.

"Well, we met at the Bellagio Poker Room, and then later in the evening at the nightclub Rain in the Palms Casino."

I saw her eyes widen slightly at the mention of the very familiar locations. Recognizable stops on the weekend itinerary that had been safely pinned to a bulletin board or taped to a refrigerator for quick reference.

"He bought me a drink at the club . . . several actually, asked me if I wanted to dance, and then invited me back to his hotel room."

"*He* invited *you*?" she clarified.

This is why I always insist on following, not leading. Leading can easily get you into trouble.

"Yes," I confirmed.

"Honey, I tried to tell you. He's a player," Roger explained gently. "He's not the right guy for you. I did this so you could see it for yourself. So you wouldn't make a huge mistake by marrying him."

Lauren continued to glare at me, ignoring her father's speech. "And then what? Then you guys had sex?" Her tone was not only accusing . . . it was soaked with repulsion.

I closed my eyes and re-gathered my strength. "No, that's not what I do. I test for *intention* to cheat only."

"What the hell does that mean?" Lauren shot back in a snotty tone.

I was having a hard time remaining in my seat. For the first time in my life I felt like strangling someone. And I wasn't sure if it was because Lauren Ireland was annoying the hell out of me or if it was because she was the closest and seemingly most deserving target on which to take out all my pent-up anger and frustration.

Fortunately, Roger interrupted. "It means that Ashlyn has proven that

Parker has cheating tendencies. That given the opportunity to have sex with someone else, he would."

"How does she know for sure if she didn't *actually* have sex with him?"

Roger sighed loudly, obviously running out of steam—and fast.

This time, I helped *him* out. "Lauren, I stop the sex from happening at the last possible moment. But I am more than confident that Parker would have engaged in intercourse if I hadn't interrupted."

Roger looked to Lauren eagerly. Watching her expression. Wondering if she was finally going to come around.

She sat on the edge of his desk and re-crossed her arms against her chest. "Well that doesn't say *anything*. You have no idea if he would have gone through with it. Knowing Parker, he would have realized that what he was doing was wrong just in time and stopped it himself."

I wanted to jump out of my chair, put my hands on her shoulders, and shake her. Shake her violently. All the while yelling, "Wake up and smell the scum bag, you idiot! He kissed me, he fondled me, his hands were all over me. He wanted me so badly he probably would have paid me for it! If you are too stupid to see what kind of loser you're wasting your time defending, then maybe you don't deserve to know."

But instead I calmly stood up, grabbed my bag, and quietly made my way toward the door. I wasn't sure how much longer I would be able to just *sit* there and do or say nothing. "My work is done here."

I opened my bag and removed a small envelope and handed it to Mr. Ireland. "This is the remainder of your retainer. If you have any additional questions about the assignment, please feel free to call me."

I walked straight past Lauren, feeling her angry stare burning an imaginary hole through my blouse. She looked me up and down, sizing me up, trying to find something to hate about me. Something she could use as an excuse to forgive her cheating fiancé.

I stopped just short of the door and turned around. In the most compassionate voice I could possibly manage to force out of myself, I said, "I know this is hard. And it's not my place to judge or tell you what to do. Whatever you choose to do with the information I have just relayed is entirely up to you. But just know this . . ." I lowered my head and prepared myself for something I had never said to a client before. But this time, somehow I knew, it needed to be said.

Lauren Ireland faced me, waiting for me to speak. The look on her face said, *I could care less what you're about to say,* but the look in her eyes said, *Please, tell me. I'm so lost right now.*

"Parker Colman *is* the cheating type," I began. "I knew it the moment I saw him. And trust me, whatever you believe he did or did not do with me . . . he'll do with someone else. I've seen so many marriages fall apart because of cheating husbands and women who choose to stay blind to the truth for far too long. What I've given you today is a glimpse. A glimpse into what could be and what you can change. Believe me when I tell you . . . it's a gift."

I placed my hand on the doorknob and started to turn it, looking back once more before walking out the door. "Life's too short to live in the dark," I said to Lauren, and maybe somehow, some way . . . to myself as well.

14

fwd: fw: fw:

I awoke the next morning to the sound of very loud knocking.

With every second I tried to drown out the noise it became more difficult to do so. Then came the melodic tones of my doorbell. I checked the clock on my nightstand. It read 7:42 A.M. I groaned loudly.

People have got *to stop waking me up in the morning.*

I pulled myself out of bed and treaded slowly to the door. Judging by the urgency of whoever was on the other side, opening that door was apparently the only thing that would stop the incessant knocking and ringing. The mellow chimes I had chosen for my doorbell in hopes they would be soothing to the ear certainly weren't serving their comforting purpose at this moment.

I peered through the peephole and immediately let out an aggravated sigh. I should have known. Who else would be so persistent?

"I can see your eye in the peephole!" John's voice came loudly through the thick wood.

"I'm opening it!" I called back as I unbolted the top lock, followed by the second lock, and then swung the door open.

John was already halfway inside my living room by the time the door was fully open. "It's about time. I was standing out there for five minutes."

"I know," I stated, annoyed. "I heard you."

"Look, Miss Huffy, I don't know what got into you last weekend, and truth be told, I don't really care. We have bigger fish to fry this morning."

"Since when do we *ever* fry fish in the morning?" I asked, weary and still half asleep.

John clearly wasn't amused. "What I *mean* is, we have a problem."

"I know, I know," I said with a yawn, and closed the door. "Zoë already called me. Look, she's just as much to blame for this as I am. I don't know why I have to be the one to—"

"What are you talking about?" John called back at me as he began searching my house for some unknown object like a bloodhound on a missing person's trail.

"I'm talking about Sophie," I replied, fairly certain he was referring to my current nonspeaking terms with my best friend.

"What about her?" John stuck his head in the corner behind my dining room table, and then seemingly unsatisfied, moved into the kitchen.

I cocked my head to the side. "Isn't this about . . . ?" My voice trailed off. Clearly it wasn't. So then what was it about?

I watched John open the cabinet above my kitchen's built-in desk. "Do you have a search warrant? What are you looking for?"

John left the kitchen and headed down the hallway toward the bedrooms. "Your laptop."

I hurried after him, not exactly thrilled at the idea of him snooping through my stuff. "Why?"

He turned and faced me, his hands on his hips. "You have some explaining to do."

I shook my head. "What are *you* talking about?" Then I paused and thought about what time it was. "Wait a minute, aren't you supposed to be at work?"

John was the assistant to a big-time Hollywood talent agent who insisted that John arrive no later than seven every morning so that he could sort through his boss's morning e-mails, search the industry trade magazines for articles appropriate to his line of work, and most important, get his office organized from the night before and his coffee prepared to perfection.

John turned into my office, and upon spotting my open laptop sitting on my desk, sprinted toward it and started maneuvering the mouse. "I *was* at work but I told them I had to leave for a doctor's appointment."

I stood behind him and ran my fingers through my dirty, uncombed hair. "Why would you do that? You *never* leave work."

"You'll see . . ." he said with dire suspense, typing an address into a fresh Web browser.

I sighed. John was being overly dramatic. Exaggerating like he always does. Making everything into a mini–soap opera episode. Sometimes it was amusing to watch, but at 7:45 in the morning it was just plain annoying. And, for the life of me, I couldn't understand what could possibly be important enough for him to leave work.

That is . . . until I saw what was now on my computer screen.

And suddenly I understood.

I let out a loud, pained gasp. My eyes widened as far as my half-awake eyelids would allow them. I simply couldn't believe what I was seeing.

John watched me, his eyes, his hands, every part of his body asking for an explanation . . . no, *demanding* one.

I ignored him, staring blankly at the screen. Studying it. My whole body seemed to go into shock. "Where did you find this?" My voice was shaking.

"What does it matter *where* I found it, Jen? What the fuck does it mean?"

I scratched my head as my natural instinct kicked in. Find the lie. Find the diversion. Think of a simple explanation and then build a story around it.

But my mind was blank. There was no explanation. There was no lie. And that was all there was to it.

John studied me as I continued to stare at the screen, completely speechless.

Staring back at me . . . was me.

There were at least half a dozen pictures of me, all taken in random places around my neighborhood. There was one of me picking up dry cleaning, putting gas in my car, driving, eating lunch, coming home from a Pilates class. There was even one of me walking down the street, sipping a latte from Coffee Bean. And the one thing that all of them had in common: They were all taken without my knowledge and, more important, without my consent. Which is pretty obvious from the fact that I'm not even looking into the camera. They almost reminded me of those candid pictures you see in *Us Weekly* magazine. The kind the paparazzi are paid thousands of dollars for. There's always a caption underneath saying something about how celebrities are just like normal people because they pick up their own dry cleaning or because they drink coffee while they walk . . . obviously implying that the American public thinks celebrities incapable of walking and drinking at the same time.

But that wasn't the caption for any of these pictures. The Web site wasn't focused on the fact that I was skillfully walking *and* consuming a hot beverage simultaneously. In fact, it wasn't focused on anything I was doing while the pictures were being taken. But clearly something I had done *before* the pictures were taken.

Think this woman is hot? Beware!
She goes by the name of Ashlyn, and if she tries to seduce you,
she was probably hired by your wife.
Don't let what happened to me happen to you!

Panic-filled questions raced through my mind. The most imminent being: How did they find me? How did they know where I would be?

The chance that a former assignment had just *happened* to be there when I was getting coffee *and* filling up my car with gas *and* eating lunch *and* coming home from Pilates, and then just *happened* to have, from the looks of it, a very professional camera on him every single time seemed ludicrous and out of the question.

No. This person clearly knew where I lived. They had followed me . . . on more than one occasion. But how? I was always so careful to cover my tracks to diminish the chances of this *very* thing ever happening. If they had followed me home one day, I would have noticed. Especially with the insanely indirect route I made a habit of taking.

Unless a client gave me up, in a moment of weakness. A desperate attempt at last-minute reconciliation, perhaps. But even *they* didn't know where I lived. Or my real name to use to track down my address.

Was it possible that I had slipped up somewhere? Used a credit card where I should have paid cash? Drove directly home instead of making my usual six turns? Signed my real name on a hotel room receipt?

I took a deep breath and looked at John. "Listen," I said sternly, "I *need* to know where you found this."

He could sense the urgency in my voice. He looked from me to the screen and the familiar face in the pictures that was suddenly no longer familiar to him. "The link came in an e-mail forward from a friend."

My eyes widened again, certain I had misheard him. "An e-mail *forward*?"

John nodded solemnly.

"Because your friend knew that you knew me?"

He shook his head. "No. . . ." He hesitated. "Because he thought it was amusing."

Amusing. The word stung me. My professional career—amusing. My life's work. My mission. My only quest and purpose on this planet was considered . . . amusing.

"So like, one of those forwards that you pass along to your friends and somehow it manages to circle the globe in a matter of days?"

He nodded again and I felt the room start to spin. I steadied myself on the desk.

"How did anyone even get those pictures?"

"Oh, they have people you can hire for that sort of thing, darling," John explained. "Spy photographers or some shit like that."

My arm gave out from underneath me and I fell helplessly back into my leather desk chair. I held my head in my hands. John knelt down on the floor beside my feet and stroked my head. He still didn't know what to make of any of this. But he did know one thing: It certainly wasn't amusing to me.

"But these pictures were almost all taken on different days. I remember each and every one of these outfits I'm wearing. For instance," I said, pointing at the screen to the picture of me filling up my gas tank at the 76 station down the street in a pair of jeans, a pink-and-cream-colored camisole and a dark gray sweater. "I wore that to a poker lesson I had last Thursday. That means that the photographer has been following me for the last week! It's creepy!"

John nodded sympathetically.

"How would he even know where to find me?" I asked, not really expecting an answer.

John remained silent as he waited patiently for the initial shock to wear off. "Is it true?" he finally asked.

I lifted my head and looked into his eyes. They were soft and focused. But the most comforting sight of all was that there wasn't even the slightest trace of judgment.

I nodded.

John nodded back, quietly taking in the truth. I watched him react, seeing the wheels turning in his head. The puzzle pieces were all falling into place. The mysteriously empty spaces that were once breezed over and quickly forgotten about were suddenly filling with meaning and explanations that made perfect sense.

"They *hire* you?" John asked in a soft, inquisitive tone.

I nodded again.

"To test their husbands?"

I sighed. "I call it a 'fidelity inspection.' I've been doing it for the past two years. I wanted to tell you guys, I swear. But I was sure you'd all judge me. Especially Sophie."

John laughed and stood up, looking down on me. "Judge you? Honey, I *idolize* you!"

"Huh?"

"You're bringing 'em down. Taking on the cheaters. Freeing the world of evil. That's some serious shit."

I suddenly found myself laughing as well. "Well, I think that's taking it a little far, but . . ."

"Fuck that!" John said triumphantly. "I'm all for it. In fact, I think it's brilliant. You're practically Wonder Woman." He placed his hand on his chin and waxed pensive. "Hmm . . . maybe I should get myself into this business. I bet you get a lot of ass that way . . ."

"John!" I exploded, standing up and slapping his hand away from his chin. "I don't *sleep* with any of them!"

"*You* don't . . . but *I* would." He continued his deep contemplation charade. "Yes, I can see the advertisements now. 'John's Cheater-Buster Business.' It'll be a huge hit."

I rolled my eyes and sat back down in my chair, pulling it up toward the desk. "Isn't 'gay cheating' an oxymoron? Go back to the office. I have work to do."

John leaned over my shoulder, suddenly extremely interested in whatever I was doing on my computer. "What kind of secretive, cool spy stuff do you have to do? Steamy IM conversations with adulterous husbands? Elicit correspondence with desperate housewives?"

"No," I stated firmly, pushing his face away and typing wildly on the keyboard.

"C'mon, I *need* more details. Do you dress up in kinky outfits? Do you speak with cute accents? Do you—"

"John," I interrupted him, narrowing my eyes.

He stamped his foot on the ground like a petulant child refusing to eat his vegetables. I simply shook my head, trying not to crack a smile. John had a unique way of making me laugh no matter what was happening in my life. And I don't think he even realized it.

"I need to do some research on this Web site." I squinted at the screen and read the site's Web address aloud: www.dontfallforthetrap.com. I grunted. "Wow. Well, aren't they clever," I said sarcastically. "I don't even set traps. I follow, not lead. The guy who put this site up is probably some fucking loser who can't even take responsibility for his own stupid actions."

John, still not giving up on his pursuit of details, grabbed hold of my T-shirt and started yanking on it. "Jennnnnn, pleeease. I neeeed something!" he whined.

I relinquished a sigh and turned my chair to face him. "Fine," I began indignantly. "Yes, once I had to do a British accent because a client said her husband was a sucker for girls with accents."

John nodded, half satisfied. "And . . ." he prompted.

I let out an incredulous laugh. "And just the other day, I dressed up as a flight attendant."

"Now, *that's* what I'm talking about!"

I shook my head in wonderment as I turned back toward the screen. I scrolled up and down the page, searching for information. Clues that might help me solve this nauseating mystery. I frowned. "There's absolutely nothing on here that could even hint at who was behind this."

John shrugged his shoulders. "You can always look it up on one of those Internet registrars. Like whois.com or something."

I turned and eyed him curiously. "What?"

"They have databases online that hold all the public records for Web site domain purchases."

"How do you know this?"

"I stalked a boy at work once."

"Ah." I nodded, and turned back to the computer. "How'd that turn out for ya?"

He shrugged again. "We dated for a week."

I opened another Web browser and navigated to the registrar John had mentioned. I typed in the name of the Web site that was blasting my, until now, well-kept secret to the world and hit *Search*.

Another window popped up filled with several lines of incomprehensible gibberish. I scanned the text for a recognizable name or company or something.

But the only thing that made even the slightest bit of sense was the constant repetition of the word *anonymous.*

"What the hell does all this mean? Anonymous?"

John leaned over my shoulder and read the screen. "Yeah, that's what happened to me. It means whoever put that Web site up chose not to make their identity known to the stalker world. It's really a travesty, in my opinion. I mean, taking away every man's right to harmlessly stalk, what happened to the First Amendment?"

"John, I'm not a stalker."

He walked over and plopped down on my office couch. "Tomato, to-*ma*-to."

With a frustrated sigh I closed my laptop and turned my chair to face him. "This is horrible."

"Look on the bright side. You're the next *Star Wars* kid."

"Huh?"

John crossed his legs and leaned back, soaking in the spotlight of my attention. "Remember that kid who filmed himself having a lightsaber fight in his garage? And someone got ahold of the video and blasted it all over the Internet?"

"Vaguely."

"It's called viral marketing. Entertainment companies use it all the time for publicity. It's when something noteworthy gets put up on the Internet and it spreads like wildfire by word of mouth alone. Usually through e-mail forwards. Such as the case of yourself."

"Great." I sulked. "So I'm the new face of viral marketing."

"That's the spirit!"

I rubbed my forehead with my fingertips and moaned loudly. "What a morning."

"Can I make a suggestion?" John asked in all seriousness.

"I'm not doing any accents."

John stood up, walked over, and put his hand on my shoulder. "Narrow down your search."

I bit my lip. "I know . . . but I don't even know where to start."

"I have to get back to work. But you should *start* by thinking about who would possibly *want* to put up a Web site like that."

"Um, John . . . that could be over two hundred people. It's not like any of those men were exactly *pleased* after I left. I mean just the other day I . . ."

I suddenly stopped, my mouth hanging open, my mind racing.

"What?"

"Parker Colman!" I shouted out, completely disgusted. "I tested him in Vegas the other day, and when he failed he practically attacked me on the elevator."

"So you think it was him?" John asked purposefully.

"It has to be. He came after me like a psychopath!"

"And he can afford a scheme like this?"

John's question confused me. All of my clients were wealthy. When I discussed my fees and expenses, I never heard anyone complain or question the cost. Sure, sometimes I took on a few pro bono assignments, as favors to women who were desperately in need of some sort of guidance but just couldn't afford to pay for it, like in the case of Rani and Clayton. But for the most part my clients always seemed more than willing to pay whatever price to get the answers and peace of mind they were looking for. Money was never an issue.

The truth was priceless.

That's the way I'd always seen it.

"What do you mean?" I asked.

"I mean," John began, "spy photographers? Anonymous Web sites? Mass e-mail circulation? This kind of scheme takes some backing. Think about it. This isn't an amateur move. This is like national exposure. Someone definitely means business, and they've got to have a hell of a lot of extra cash lying around to make sure it gets done. But I guess anyone who can afford to hire you . . ."

I shook my head. "No, he didn't. I mean, his fiancée didn't hire me. Her father did. I'm not sure if Parker has any money at all. I think that was one of the reasons her dad suspected him in the first place. That he was just after the family trust fund."

John nodded. "Hmmm."

And the more I thought about it, I realized that some of these pictures were taken *before* Parker Colman's assignment. Like the one of me filling up my gas tank on the way to my poker lesson. That poker lesson was in preparation for Parker's assignment in Vegas. So it couldn't possibly have been him.

"So back to square one?" John asked as I walked him to the front door.

I sighed. "Yeah, I guess."

He gave me a long hug and squeezed me just the slightest bit tighter than he normally did. "Just think," he offered sympathetically. "This guy has got something to lose. Something big. Probably more than most."

"Yeah," I agreed. "But you have to swear you won't tell anyone," I urged him before I closed the door. "Especially not Sophie or Zoë. Somehow I don't think they would see it the way you do."

"I won't," John promised.

"You're sworn to absolute secrecy now."

He nodded. "Taking it to the grave, my dear."

"Good."

As I closed the door I immediately starting racking my brain. My mental database of names that seemed to go on forever. Every one containing a different story. A different motivation. A different interpretation of the word *love*.

And yet, they all blended together in my mind.

"National exposure," I said aloud.

What a nightmare.

In my quest to reveal the truth at any cost, I had blindly failed to consider an entirely different truth, one that now seemed more obvious than ever: Revenge is apparently priceless as well.

15

universal surrender

Later that night, I sat staring at my computer screen, waiting for some brilliant idea to come to me so I could figure out how to identify the still-anonymous owner of that very annoying Web site, when I heard the front door unlock and open.

I sat very still in my seat. The pictures of me on the screen stared back at me. Mocking me. Laughing at my misfortune.

And now whoever had taken them not only knew where I lived and where I got coffee, he also had a key to my front door!

But how? How would he have a key?

I heard footsteps walking through the living room, echoing on the hardwood floors and approaching the hallway. I began to panic. I had pepper spray and a stun gun, but it was in my bedroom. Where I always assumed I would be during a situation like this. After all, isn't that where the attacks always take place in the horror films? When the victim is lying in bed? So naturally I would keep them in my nightstand. A hell of a lot of good they did me now.

I could hear the intruder coming down the hallway. I reached for the cordless landline phone on my desk but the cradle was empty.

Damn! I must have left it on the coffee table.

I was trapped. If I tried to make a dash to the bedroom to grab the stun gun, I would surely come face-to-face with him. And if he had a weapon (which he most definitely would) he would be able to get to me first.

I eyed the window in front of me. I was on the top floor of the building. Four floors stood between me and the ground. I would never survive a jump.

More footsteps.

Then I remembered a fire escape. It was actually outside of the *bedroom* window. Only a few short, cliff-hanger steps away. I could grab on to the drainpipe hanging from the roof and shimmy my way to the bedroom window. Then, once on the fire escape, I could climb safely to the ground.

I could hear the footsteps getting closer. If they were looking for me, they would check the guest room first before coming into the office. I had approximately ten seconds . . . twelve if they made a stop at the hallway closet.

I quietly stood up from my chair and reached out in front of me, pulling the window open. I knocked the edge of the screen with the palm of my hand and it willingly popped out of place. I watched it float slowly to the ground, and then heard the small clank of it hitting the sidewalk. I swallowed hard, confident that I would make a much bigger "clank" should I follow it to the ground. The space the open window provided me was small at best. It would be a tight squeeze. I stuck the top half of my body out, looking for something to step onto.

That's when I heard the footsteps behind me, entering the office.

I froze.

"You never called me back yesterday, bi-atch!" I heard Zoë's shrill voice call from across the room and reverberate through the open window.

I let out an audible sigh of relief and quickly pulled myself back inside, dusting the dirt from the windowsill off my hands.

"What are you doing?" she asked, eyeing my current state.

I looked uneasily back toward the window. "I thought I heard a dying bird," I replied blankly.

"And you were going to give it mouth-to-mouth?"

I let out a nervous laugh and quickly reached over to shut my laptop, hiding the photographic evidence of my job from Zoë's view. "I forgot I gave you a key," I said, immediately regretting the day I readily offered free entrance to my home to both Zoë and Sophie.

She shrugged and exited the office, making her way down the hallway and into the kitchen. I followed after her. She picked up a can of Coke Zero that she had placed on the counter and took a sip. Then she grabbed a sealed Pop-Tart from inside her purse. "Mind if I toast this?"

I plopped down on the couch and flipped on the TV. "Fine," I said, still trying to calm my nerves from my near near-death experience.

"I bet you haven't called Sophie yet, either, huh?"

I reluctantly told her that I hadn't.

It wasn't that I didn't want to call Sophie. I just hadn't had a chance to think about my personal life ever since my secretive professional life had been plastered on the Internet for anyone and everyone to see.

Zoë threw her frosted Pop-Tart into the toaster oven and leaned her elbows on the kitchen counter. "You know, you really hurt her feelings. She was just trying to help."

I glared at her. "Since when do you take sides?"

"I'm not taking sides. I'm just trying to smooth things over so I don't have to be in the middle of this. Plus, you're usually the one she calls with all her neuroses, and now I've become your involuntary replacement. And honestly, I don't think I can handle the job much longer."

It was true. Sophie did usually call me first when she had a problem or a breakdown or just to vent. And suddenly I really missed getting those late-night phone calls. And what I wouldn't give to be able to tell Sophie everything that had happened to me over the past few days: that beautiful man I met on the plane; that god-awful Web site; my elevator attack. Or even if I *couldn't* tell her the real versions of all those stories, at least I'd have someone to tell *something* to. Suddenly my life felt incomplete without Sophie in it, neuroses and all.

"She hurt my feelings too, you know."

The toaster dinged. Zoë removed her Pop-Tart, placed it on a paper towel, and came and sat down next to me on the couch. "I know. Everyone hurt everyone's feelings. But can't we all just forget about it and move on with our lives like adults?" She took a bite.

I watched her. "This is coming from someone who's eating a fruit-filled toaster pastry with blue frosting."

"It's their newest flavor," Zoë defended. "And I didn't have time to eat dinner."

"Mmmm. Nutritious."

"C'mon," she pleaded. "Be the bigger person. You know how sensitive Sophie gets."

I crossed my arms and stared at the blank TV screen. "I'm always the bigger person. For once I'd like *her* to apologize."

"She had a point," Zoë said softly.

My head darted around to face her so fast I swore I heard a small pop in my neck. "What?"

"This prolonged dating drought of yours, Jen? You're obviously afraid of something."

"My work keeps me very—"

"Busy, we know." Zoë took another bite and then offered it to me.

I shook my head.

"But I'm sorry. No one's *that* busy. There has to be another reason."

The lies started swirling around in my head. Just like they always did. A slot machine of excuses. Which jackpot winner will it be this time? No time for men? No interest in men? A desire to focus on my career? Maybe even a casual joke about after listening to all of my friends' scary dating stories the whole thing seemed pretty pointless anyway.

But the wheels kept spinning. The lies kept whooshing by faster than I could reach out and grab one. It was as if suddenly, after a lifetime full of easy bluffs and effortless stories, it wasn't so easy anymore.

I opened my mouth to speak but nothing came out.

"Well?" Zoë demanded, tossing the last of her Pop-Tart into her mouth. She scrunched up the paper towel, stood up, and walked into the kitchen to throw it in the trash compactor.

I remained silent, hoping my lack of response might throw her off and cause her to lose focus. Then maybe she'd change the subject.

"What's this?" she asked, examining a small white card on the kitchen counter.

I guess it worked.

I sat up straighter and craned my neck to see over the top of the couch. "What?"

"Jamie Richards," Zoë read aloud from the card.

I slumped back down. "Oh, just some guy I met on the plane. Marta must have found the card in my jeans pocket when she was doing laundry."

Zoë raced back to the couch and jumped into the seat next to me. "A guy? Do tell."

I shrugged. "Nothing to tell. We met, we talked, we landed. That was about it."

"But you're gonna call him?"

I shook my head decisively. "No. Why would I?"

"Was he cute?"

As soon as the question left her mouth, a tiny smirk snuck across my lips. In fact, I hadn't even realized it had appeared until I heard Zoë exclaim, "Oh! He is! You can see it all over your face!"

I quickly erased the smirk. "What are you talking about? He was funny. That's all."

"Cute *and* funny. Now you *have* to call him."

I shot her a skeptical look. "Why?"

Zoë instantly turned intellectual. It's the expression she gets right before she's about to impart some long-lost wisdom to you that she's convinced will change your life forever and for that you should be both eternally grateful and desperately trying to figure out how you ever survived this far without it. "Because you just don't pass up fucking awesome guys, that's why! It's bad karma."

"Bad karma?" I challenged.

"Yes. The universe has sent you a gift. A hot, available man. And when the universe sends you a gift like that, you take it. Trust me, you do *not* want to piss off the universe. Because when you fuck with the universe, the universe fucks back."

"Well, if I don't want him, can't I just *re*-gift him like all other gifts I don't want? Maybe I'll give him to you."

Zoë shot me a warning look. I took that as a no. "Don't fuck with the universe, Jen. Don't even *joke* about fucking with the universe. You'll never win that game." Then she stood up, grabbed her Coke Zero from the coffee table, and took a long last gulp.

I smiled politely. "Whatever you say, Zo."

"Okay, well, if you're not dreadfully afraid of the unforgiving, vengeful god of hot men, then at least be afraid of me. If you don't call him I'm going to hunt you down and stuff you in my trunk. Don't forget: I know where you live *and* I have your key!"

I wiped the blue Pop-Tart crumbs from her seat onto the floor as I tried to hide the small shiver that crept up my spine. "Yes, how could I forget?"

Zoë opened the front door wide enough to fit an entire elephant parade through. She paused for effect, looked me directly in the eyes as if she were about to finally divulge the secret ingredient in Coca-Cola to a room full of inquiring minds, and then said, "And call Sophie!" before slamming the door dramatically behind her. Zoë had always been a fan of grand entrances, and as it would seem, exits as well.

On any normal day her dramatic departure would have left me introspectively reprimanding myself for waiting so long to call my best friend after a stupid fight in a bar, and then finally reaching for the phone, dialing Sophie's number, and humbly commencing the lengthy exchange of mutual apologies and the incessant back-and-forth battle of blame ownership.

But this wasn't a normal day.

And come to think of it: What is a normal day for me, anyway?

I rationalized that I would be in a much better mental and emotional place to effectively resolve everything with Sophie after I had successfully resolved everything else in my life . . . namely, capturing my unknown, evil Web site avenger.

And while Zoë had been going on and on, waxing poetic about the laws of the universe with respect to relationships, I had been having a revelation.

Okay, "revelation" is a very strong word. Let's just call it an idea. An idea that for the first time since I saw my own face on that computer screen gave me a tiny ounce of hope.

I returned to my office and flipped open my laptop again. On the screen was the same useless page of information that I had been staring at for a full hour.

This Web site belongs to . . . "None of your damn business" is what it should have said. Because that's practically what it implied.

But now, as I looked at it again, with my new mini-revelation fresh in my mind, it suddenly didn't seem so useless anymore. I scrolled down to the bottom of the who-is page that John had directed me to and found a line item that read "Name Server," followed by a name: "NS2.Fiztech.net." Now, I had certainly never been a computer genius, and ever since the invention of the Internet I've felt as if the people around me had suddenly been upgraded with a foreign language memory chip that I had somehow failed to receive in the mail.

But fortunately for me now, a little over three months ago, I had received an assignment that forced me to sit down and learn about some of this stuff: a chief technology officer from Silicone Valley who had married the first woman he fell in love with because he had been convinced she was the only woman who *would* marry him. And at the time, because he was a lowly, fairly unattractive network administrator for an office supplies distribution company, she probably was. But then time passed, he got slightly better looking, and more important, his bank account and business card title got slightly more impressive, and suddenly, girls he had never even dreamed of talking to, let alone marrying, were very interested in learning all about the exciting field of information technology. Girls like Ashlyn: a motivated, techno-savvy systems analyst trying to survive a harsh, male-dominated field.

Who knew that my knowledge of information technology would ever come in handy again?

In fact, thanks to my previous research, I had more than just an inkling about what a name server was. And, as opposed to what I might have thought four months ago, it wasn't asking me to assign a name to the person who brings me chicken wings at Applebee's. It was the name of the company where the Web site was hosted.

In other words, it was the company that had sold cyberspace to whomever was terrorizing me on the Internet. A digital self-storage rental house, if you will.

I quickly typed the company name into a new Google search. The results were definitely in my favor. It was exactly what I was hoping for. The small Web hosting company of Fiztech.net was owned by one lonely, solitary person.

And thankfully, that person was a man.

A man who would soon be getting a very unexpected visit.

But before I could pay my unexpected visit to Jason Trotting of Fiztech.net, I had to take care of *my* unexpected visit to the Range Rover dealership for the recall on some malfunctioning part in my car.

On Wednesday morning, I pulled into the service line at the far end of the dealership and stepped out onto the pavement. A man dressed in a black polo shirt tucked into khaki slacks approached me with a clipboard.

"Good morning," he said. "Do you have an appointment?'

"Yes," I said, leaning into the car and pulling out my purse. "Eleven A.M. Jennifer Hunter."

He scanned his clipboard. "I'm sorry, I don't have you down on my list. Are you sure it was today?"

I frowned and craned my neck to glance at his list. "Fairly sure." I was almost certain Marta said today at eleven A.M.

He shook his head. "Hmm. I don't know why you wouldn't be on here then."

I muffled an aggravated groan. "Great, so I have to come back another time?"

He smiled and shook his head. "Of course not. Let's just bring you inside and take a look at the computer. We can take care of it today."

I thanked him and then followed him through the sliding glass door that led into the service department.

"What are you coming in for? Oil change?" He took a seat behind a tall desk with a computer terminal stationed on top of it.

I sat down across from him. "No. Um, a recall on something. I'm not sure what exactly; my housekeeper took the call."

He nodded and began typing on the keyboard. "And you have a 2008?"

I nodded back.

He looked strangely at his screen. "That's odd. Someone contacted you for a recall?"

"Yes."

"Well, I'm afraid we have another misunderstanding. There are no recalls on your model at this time."

"Huh?"

"I don't see any recalls in the system. Someone must have called you by mistake. People get on the wrong call lists all the time. I'm very sorry for the inconvenience."

I shrugged and picked up my purse and sunglasses from the desk. "All right. Well, since I'm here, I might as well get my oil changed. I think I'm due in a few hundred miles anyway."

He typed again. "Okay. And how about we'll get you a complimentary rental car to compensate for bringing you down here. That way you can just come back tomorrow to pick up your vehicle."

I smiled. "Perfect."

As I crawled on all fours around the backseat of my car, scrounging for any last-minute items I would need to have in the rental, I heard the service guy's voice call from outside. "Jennifer?"

"Yeah!" My voice strained as I carefully attempted to back out through the open door, a stack of loose papers in hand, and step onto the ground. But unfortunately, I wasn't able to avoid an inadvertent and very painful bump on the top of my head.

I massaged the throbbing spot with my hand as I looked around for the source of the voice.

And that's when I saw him.

And he was the furthest person from the Range Rover service guy who I ever expected to see, let alone call my name while I was playing crouching tiger, hidden dragon in the backseat of my SUV.

"Hi," I said awkwardly, smoothing out the hair that I had most certainly mangled into oblivion while attempting to soothe my growing, tumor-size bump.

Jamie Richards stepped out of the blinding sunlight and into the comforting shadow of the service department overhang. "Is your head okay? That looked pretty bad."

"What? No, fine. It was nothing. Happens all the time."

It happens all the time?

What the hell was he doing here? And why the hell was I saying stupid things like that?

"Jamie," he reminded me, touching his hand to his chest.

I attempted a giggle; it came out more like a gargle. "Yeah. No, I remember."

"Well, there goes my self-esteem," he said playfully. "See, I had convinced myself that you had forgotten my name and that my business card went through the washing machine and dryer—twice—and was left unreadable. It made me feel better about the fact that you didn't call."

I laughed. "Right. Sorry. That's actually *exactly* what happened. Except it was the wash cycle with extra bleach."

He nodded. "Thank you. I feel much better."

"I didn't know you drove a Range Rover."

"I don't." He pointed to the sign on the overhang. It read, "Range Rover/Jaguar Exclusive Dealership."

"A Jag, huh?"

"Guilty as charged. Twenty-five-thousand-mile checkup time."

"Now, do you actually pronounce it like the British girl in the commercial, '*Jag-yoo-ar*'?" I asked with my best elitist-mocking accent.

He laughed. "No. I pronounce it the dumb-ass American way. '*Jag-wire.*' And all the guys at work make fun of me and tell me I'm not allowed to own a car I can't pronounce."

"They're right. You should have gotten a BMW."

"Should we trade, then? You can drive my car home and I'll take yours. I can say 'Range Rover.' "

I shook my head. "Absolutely not. I love my car. *And* the seventy-five dollars it costs to fill it up every week."

"Seventy-five dollars!"

"I know," I said, shaking my head. "I should have just gone for the hybrid. I thought this car would make me look 'cool.' Until I realized that smog and pollution aren't really all that cool."

"Well, you don't know what you're missing. The Jag is pretty damn 'cool.' "

"You got me there," I admitted. "I've never been in one."

"That's why you're having dinner with me this week. Strictly for the sake of our negotiation. You have to actually sit in a *Jag-yoo-ar* to fully appreciate it."

And there it was again. That pang. That longing to say yes to him. This was my chance to prove to Sophie that she was wrong. That I wasn't afraid of anything. See, I can say yes to a date. I can let a guy take me out. I can even think he's cute. Really cute. There's nothing *wrong* with me.

"You can't turn down a perfectly good trade unless you have all the facts," Jamie continued. "As an investment banker, you of all people should know that."

And then, there *that* was again. The lie. The truth that I would have to keep hidden throughout the entire date. The stories I would have to regurgitate with enthusiasm. What kind of pillow talk consists of a fabricated existence? How was I supposed to bond with any man who didn't even know about the most important aspect of my life? It seemed so terribly impossible, not to mention . . . depressing.

"So what do you say? Dinner? Tomorrow?"

"Yes," I immediately blurted out. Before my heart could continue to pang and before my head could continue to rationalize. And as much as I hated to admit it, Zoë's universal theory seemed to be right on. Here was the universe, putting the same guy in front of me, *twice* in one week. Repetition is usually the sign of some kind of insistence. And who am I to argue with an insistent universe?

At first Jamie looked almost surprised, but then he smiled and said, "Great. What time should I pick you up?"

I pulled my Treo out of my bag and skipped ahead one day to Thursday. "How about eight?"

"You're not actually consulting a Palm Pilot, are you?" he asked, appalled.

I smirked. "It's better than consulting a psychic, isn't it?"

"Good point. But I'm sorry, I'm afraid I'm going to have to retract my invitation. I could never have dinner with a girl who keeps a Palm Pilot."

"Hey, I'm a busy girl. Do you want to have dinner or not?"

He paused and patted his shirt pocket. "Hold on, I think I might have to consult *my* Palm Pilot on the issue." He removed a similar phone/calendar device from his pocket and began histrionically tapping the keys, like a child who had just gotten ahold of his father's PDA and was playing "important businessman."

I laughed and playfully folded my arms across my chest.

"Okay," Jamie finally said. "*My* Palm Pilot and I have discussed the matter, and we have decided that we *would* enjoy the pleasure of your company Thursday evening for dinner."

"Really? So this will be a party of three, then?"

"Oh, I don't do anything without him."

I was just giving Jamie my phone number so he could call me for directions to my house when a female voice summoned me from inside the service department. "Miss Hunter?"

I turned around. "Yes?"

"Your rental car is ready. Would you mind coming inside and signing a few papers for us?"

"Not at all." I turned back to Jamie. "So I'll see you at eight?"

"Ah, the mysterious letter H is finally revealed!"

I laughed. "So now you know. The secret is out."

Not all the secrets, the voice in my head annoyingly reminded me. I chose to ignore it, decisively silencing every persistent premonition that this whole thing was a big mistake.

"Now, does the last name Hunter symbolize any sort of characteristic personality trait in you?" Jamie asked. "Like how the Native Americans used to name their people by what they liked to do? Sitting Bull, Dances with Wolves, Swimming Naked . . . Man Hunter?"

I laughed again, this time in an attempt to mask my uneasiness. "Well, I guess you'll just have to find out, won't you?"

"I'm rooting for the Swimming Naked one."

"Don't press your luck," I warned. But I couldn't help remarking that he was probably more on target with the Man Hunter suggestion. Although I much preferred the qualified version of *Evil* Man Hunter.

I waved good-bye to Jamie, wished him luck with his "Jag-wire," and followed after the woman who would be providing me with my rental "Batmobile" for the day.

My stand-in, superhero vehicle was not nearly as nice as my usual mode of transportation but, nonetheless, it managed to successfully get me to my destination in one piece.

Although I had to admit: Tonight's superhero-esque activities were not exactly "all in a day's work." Tonight's agenda consisted of a much different kind of endeavor. Yes, it essentially utilized the same skills and costumes. But the end result would be of a much different nature. I rationalized, however, that it fell in the realm of the same quest and, therefore, was allowed.

Besides, I'm sure sometimes Superman has to thwart off evil in a more roundabout way. As much as he'd like to, sometimes he can't just go straight after the bad guy; he has to go after the source that's aiding the bad guy. His bank account. His accomplices. The mad scientist who stays up nights in his laboratory manufacturing whatever magic goo-like substance gives the bad guy his superhuman strength.

Or, in my case, the guy who's hosting the bad guy's Web site.

I had e-mailed Jason Trotting the night before, posing as a very wealthy Armenian Internet entrepreneur who, if he managed to land as a hosting client, would surely secure his financial future for the rest of his life—and the lives of all of his next of kin.

He, of course, agreed to meet me (or "Vartan," as I had introduced myself) tonight at an upscale hotel bar in Westwood.

Needless to say, Vartan would never show up.

The Internet, unfortunately, was not kind enough to supply me with an identifying photograph of Jason Trotting. So I would have to test my luck and look for, hopefully, the only guy sitting alone in the bar waiting for someone.

And as luck would have it . . . there were three.

Fuck! I silently cursed as I walked inside and surveyed the sparse crowd. One table of business associates, chatting about marketing plans. Another table with an adoring couple who would surely be booking one of the five-hundred-dollar suites upstairs by the end of the night, if they hadn't already. Two typical Los Angeles twenty-something girls sitting at the bar, dressed to the nines—just in case Jerry Bruckheimer happened to walk in looking for his next Hollywood starlet, or maybe even just some arm candy to take to his next premiere. And three men, each occupying their own table on different sides of the room.

Sporting a surprisingly realistic-looking blond wig and overly dramatic, dark eye makeup, I maneuvered myself over to a partly hidden corner where I could start taking inventory. Knowing that this guy, of all people, had probably seen the pictures of me on the Internet more than once, I had had to take proper precautions. The blond wig had been a very expensive costume accessory that I'd purchased about nine months earlier, when I met with a woman who was convinced that her husband was one of those gentlemen who preferred blondes. The blonde part was true enough . . . the gentleman part? Debatable.

I subtly adjusted my wig and began my reconnaissance.

Okay, Lonely Man #1: mid-fifties, no wedding ring, drinking Scotch, and not-so-inconspicuously checking out the two wannabe arm candies at the bar.

Ninety-five percent chance that it's not him. Jason would probably be in his late twenties to mid-thirties, given the line of work he's chosen. And he definitely wouldn't risk blowing this multimillion-dollar business opportunity to check out women. He would be watching the door.

Lonely Man #2 and Lonely Man #3 both fit those criteria.

Both were in their early thirties, style-challenged, and intently keeping both eyes glued to the entrance of the bar.

I studied them a little longer. Carefully observing how they reacted to each new customer who walked in. Knowing that the man I was looking for would essentially be waiting for an Armenian man named Vartan, I only hoped that deductive reasoning would kick in when the other one responded to an incoming female.

No good. They were virtually indecipherable. Even with my superpower.

So I would have to take a chance.

I waited until it was exactly thirty minutes after Vartan's scheduled arrival time, and then I approached Lonely Man #2.

"Hi," I said sheepishly. "Are you waiting for someone?"

He looked up and flashed me a flirtatious smile. "All my life. And it looks like I found her."

I struggled to stay in character and fought the urge to roll my eyes. I laughed playfully, as if this were the most flattering comment I'd ever received in my life. "No, I mean, someone in particular."

He nodded. "Yes, actually. A business associate."

I smiled. This was probably him, but I had to play it wisely.

I frowned. "Oh, okay."

Out of the corner of my eye, I saw Lonely Guy #3 get out his wallet and place a twenty-dollar bill on the table next to the check. He was getting ready to leave. I had to move fast and figure out if the man sitting in front of me was Jason Trotting or just some random guy with bad pick-up lines.

"Are *you* waiting for someone?" he asked me.

I started to turn back to answer his question when a flashy white object caught my eye from across the room. Lonely Man #3 had picked up a glossy white folder and was tucking it under his arm as he stood up. I tilted my head and squinted my eyes to get a glimpse of the logo on the front.

Fiztech.net.

Bingo.

Flustered, my eyes darted back and forth between Lonely Guy #3 and the door. I had about twenty paces to stop him from walking out.

"Yes. And I think that's him," I said to the man in front of me, and then quickly darted to the other side of the room.

Keeping the flustered look on my face, I stepped directly in front of the man with the white folder who was now pulling a computer bag over his shoulder. "Hi, sorry I'm late! You must be Charlie."

He looked at me, completely confused. Had he missed something? Was Vartan really a woman? Or had he simply sent this woman to do business in his place? But why did she think his name was Charlie?

"No, I'm Jason," he clarified, half hoping the woman would slap herself on the forehead and say, "Oh, right. Sorry. My mistake."

But I didn't.

Instead, my shoulders dropped and my face fell into a disappointed frown. "Oh," I began. "Damn. You're cute, too."

This made him nervous. And clearly even more confused. "Excuse me?"

I giggled. "Sorry. I'm supposed to be meeting a blind date. And I don't know what he looks like. I was kind of hoping it was you. But it appears I got stood up." I twisted my mouth to the side, expressing not only my disappointment but now also my crushed ego.

His eyes were sympathetic. "Well, if it makes you feel any better, I got stood up, too."

"Blind date?"

He shook his head. "No. Blind business meeting. Potentially *huge* client. Looks like I'll be eating at Carl's Jr. for another eight months."

I laughed. "Good one. So how about a drink to nurse our shattered egos?"

I figured that since this wasn't a normal assignment and Jason wasn't anyone's husband, boyfriend, or fiancé—from what I could tell—there was no harm in me initiating the action for once. And this was a subject I simply couldn't afford to let walk out that door. Not when he held such valuable information in that vault of a brain of his.

By our second drink I finally felt ready to go for the kill. Jason had told me all about his Web-hosting company and how it barely paid the bills, and if he didn't land a client like Vartan sometime soon, he'd have to go back to working in a tiny cubicle writing code sixty hours a week.

"C'mon," I attempted to cheer him up. "You have to have at least *one* big client that keeps you afloat."

He shrugged and took a sip of his beer. "Yeah, I guess," he said nonchalantly. "I just signed a pretty big account. Some local hotshot who rented out a few hundred gigs of space. Although I don't think he's going to keep his contract for very long. He didn't sound like he needed anything permanent when we spoke on the phone."

This *had* to be it. Local, recent, short-term. How could it not be?

"Well, that sounds promising," I encouraged. "What's his story?"

He shrugged again. "Not sure really. He refused to give me his name.

Some type of top-secret operation, I guess. So what about you? What's *your* story?"

"He didn't tell you anything about himself?" I blurted back, desperation seeping into my voice. I quickly covered it with a flirty smile. "I mean, that just seems really weird."

Jason looked at me somewhat strangely. "Yeah," he began warily. "I guess I could've looked it up from the name of his company, but it didn't really matter to me." He attempted to change the subject again. "So you were waiting for a blind date, huh? I guess that means you're single?"

I laughed and took a sip of my drink. "Yeah. Single. Gotta love the single life."

"Well, I'd love to get your number and maybe take you out sometime. I hope you like Carl's Jr."

I laughed again . . . on the outside. But inside I was screaming. "Maybe I know him," I suggested casually.

"Maybe you know who?" he asked.

"The guy . . . your client. If you tell me the company's name, I might be able to tell you the guy who owns it. I'm in PR. I work with a lot of companies."

Jason shot me another strange look. I'm sure he was beginning to have second thoughts about his invitation to eat fast food. But at this point I didn't care what he thought. He obviously hadn't recognized me through my disguise, or maybe he just never even bothered to look at the Web site his client put up. But I knew one thing: I wasn't leaving without a name.

"Um, Kelen Industries, I think," Jason finally surrendered.

The hand that was vainly running through my artificial hair froze in its place and then slowly dropped down to my side. As I let his words sink in, I couldn't for the life of me think of any of my own. Did he just say what I think he said?

"So, do you know him?" Jason practically patronized me.

I nodded slowly, somewhat in a trance.

"Really?" He raised his eyebrows. "Impressive."

Of course, there was no reason why I *shouldn't* know him. I had read at least twenty news articles about all the wonderful changes his company was making in the world of car engines. I had seen the inside of his suite in a random hotel in Denver. I had stroked his wife's hair as she cried on my shoulder. He even attempted to bribe me into staying quiet. Oh, yes. I certainly *knew* him.

I marveled at how right on the money John had been from the very beginning. I now realized that if I had to make a mental list of all the men who would attempt something like this, this man would most definitely be at the top.

I took a deep breath as the lost sensation slowly returned to my tongue, and I was finally able to speak. "His name is Raymond Jacobs."

16

support line

After thanking Jason Trotting for the drinks and leaving him with a fake phone number, I disappeared into the night with just the information I had come for.

I don't know why, but I guess I somehow thought that once I knew who was responsible for the Web site, I would suddenly feel better, that all the anxiety would simply melt away. I guess I failed to realize that once I knew the identity of my evil nemesis, I would actually have to come up with a plan to stop him. And unfortunately, I hadn't thought that far ahead.

Of all people. Why'd it have to be him?

Raymond Jacobs. The vodka gimlet drinker who, two weeks ago, had gobbled up my impressive knowledge of car engines without even a single reservation. I had to hand it to him, though; he'd definitely pulled this stunt together fast. My trip to Denver felt like two days ago. And standing in Anne Jacobs's entry hall, hugging her, telling her she'd done the right thing, felt like yesterday. Suddenly I found myself wondering if *I'd* done the right thing by even taking on the assignment. Raymond Jacobs was clearly not the kind of man to get run over by a truck and then wait in the road to die. Oh, no. He got right back up and ran out to buy an even bigger truck.

As I drove home the feeling of anxiety started to consume me. I wanted to crawl into bed, pull the covers over my head, and never come out.

I wearily dragged myself up the stairs of my building and through my front door. I collapsed onto the bed like a ton of bricks. The walls felt like they were closing in on me. And the only person I really wanted to talk to was still not talking to me.

It was always times like these when I would call Sophie, make up some bogus story about something that upset me at work, and she would calm me down. She would soothe me with her words and her comforting voice. It was the voice of someone who's known me forever and has been there for me through everything . . . well, almost everything. Because even though the solutions she came up with only applied to a make-believe problem, and the words she used usually had nothing to do with what was really going on in my life, it didn't matter. It was the fact that she was there for me. To listen and to respond.

And I knew that I had to call her.

I knew that I couldn't continue to *not* have her in my life. She was too important to me.

"Don't it always seem to go that you don't know what you've got till it's gone?"

I reached over to my nightstand and grabbed the phone off its charger. I started dialing.

But before I hit the last number I was stopped by the sound of a different phone ringing. It was my business line. I hung up my home phone, picked up my bag from the edge of the bed, and fished out the ringing cell phone. "No Caller ID" was plastered on the screen of my Treo. Nothing new. Most people block this kind of call. Hell, most people block this whole section of their life.

I pressed the green *Talk* button and held the phone up to my ear. "Hello?"

There was a muffled voice on the other end, and I couldn't make out a single word the person was saying.

"Hello?" I repeated into the phone.

More static.

"Hello? I can't hear you. Can you hear me?" I paused and waited. Still nothing. "Bad connection. I think you should call back."

And just as I was about to hang up, the static cleared, and a soft and very confused voice came through the line. "Jen?"

I sat very still on my white cotton comforter. And then, convinced that I had simply picked up the wrong cell phone, I pulled the phone away from my ear and held it in front of my face, double-checking that this *was* in fact my business line.

The word *Treo* was blatantly plastered on the top of the phone. My personal cell phone was the pink Razr. I suppose the simple night and day difference in weight would have been sufficient enough to distinguish the two, but I had to see it for myself. With my own eyes.

"Jen, is that you?"

I knew the voice. I'd known the voice for years.

There was no more interference. The connection was crystal clear and the voice . . . was unmistakable. The irony was thicker than liquid chocolate and not nearly as sweet. It was the very same voice I had been hoping to hear on the other end of the phone for over a week now.

But what do you know? It was coming through the wrong fucking phone.

"Hello?" The voice demanded an acknowledgment. And before long, it would undoubtedly be demanding an explanation as well.

I cleared my throat and attempted to impersonate an eighty-year-old woman who had fought a lifetime, losing battle with Virginia Slims. "Yes? How can I help you?"

I should have just hung up. Right then and there. I should have just put down the phone, not answered for the rest of the night, or the rest of my life perhaps, and just left it at that.

I should have done a lot of things.

But I didn't. And now the voice knew.

"Jen, is that you?" it repeated, slightly more aggravated and a lot more insistent.

I sighed and surrendered to it. "Yes, Sophie. It's me."

There was a long silence, followed by a short but very distinct *click*.

I pulled the phone away from my ear and looked at the screen. "Call Ended," it informed me.

The phone slowly slipped from my sweaty fingers and I watched it disappear into a sea of white cotton and down. I held my forehead in the palm of my hand and closed my eyes. Because I knew. I knew for sure. The call wasn't the only thing that had just ended.

I bit my lip and waited. Waited for the inevitable callback.

If I knew Sophie at all, she needed that extra moment for everything to sink in. For the information to process and the world to start making sense again. She was like a slow desktop computer, one of those older models that required just the slightest bit more time to perform the simpler tasks, like opening up a Word document or transferring between applications. I could almost see the frustratingly slow hourglass icon hovering above her head.

But this time the task wasn't simple. And this time, after the extra moment had passed, and even the extra few after that, the world still wouldn't make sense. The program still wouldn't run. And the hard drive would inevitably crash.

My house had never felt so silent in the entire eighteen months that I'd lived there.

And then the phone rang. Not my business cell phone, not my personal cell phone. But my landline. My *home* phone. And it felt all too appropriate.

The number was no longer blocked. The caller was definitely ID'ed.

"Hi," I said softly into the cordless receiver.

There was more silence. She had dialed my number before she had finished processing. There would be silence. And I would wait.

"Hi," she finally said back.

I could almost hear her gears turning. The questions were popping up faster than she could sort through and prioritize them. The looming "illegal operations" were threatening to shut down the whole system if the answers didn't start coming—and fast.

And then somehow, remarkably, Sophie managed to sort through all of the streaming data and effectively generate one simple question that summed up every query struggling to run at once.

"It's you?" she asked faintly.

I nodded, knowing full well that she couldn't see me. But also somewhat thankful for it at the same time. I wasn't ready for her to know. I wasn't ready to stop coming up with bogus stories about work and having her console me on them.

And I certainly wasn't prepared for her to find out like this.

So much for my successful skills of dissuasion. Sophie had gone right back to that woman at her office and asked for the phone number again. *My* phone number. I should have known. Me of all people should have been the first one to remind myself that a woman on a quest for knowledge is as unstoppable as a man on a quest for sex.

"Yes, it's me," I confirmed, shamefully. I knew the reaction I was going to get. I knew the judgment I was going to have to endure. And so I took a deep breath and prepared myself for the blow.

"You're . . . Ashlyn?" She was still waiting for me to break out into laughter and tell her it was a huge joke. That I had told her colleague to give out my number so that I could teach her a lesson. That there never even *was* an Ashlyn. That I made it all up. Surprise! You've been punk'd!

And I suppose I certainly could have. But instead, all I said was, "Yes."

"How could that be? You work for an investment bank!"

"Work*ed* for a bank," I explained. "I haven't worked at Stanley Marshall for about two years."

More silence. More careful computations.

"Remember that promotion I got? A little over two years ago? A bigger office? A new cell phone?"

The deciphering key was finally starting to take shape, and it was suddenly no longer just illegible lines of code. It was an entire story. An entire life that she knew nothing about, but now suddenly couldn't believe that she had missed.

"Yah . . ." she said hesitantly.

"Well, it wasn't a promotion."

"But how many? And why didn't you tell me? And—"

"I couldn't tell you!" I insisted. "I couldn't tell anyone. Nobody knows. It was just a decision I made on my own. Something I had to do for me. Plus, I didn't think you'd approve."

"Of course I wouldn't have approved! Married men, Jen! *Married!* And you kiss them?"

I bowed my head. "Uh-huh."

"And let them touch you?"

I could hear the disgust hanging between the syllables of her words. The images in her head were projecting onto the empty white walls of my bedroom, like a giant movie screen.

And at that moment . . . we were one. One mind. One thought. One vision.

I saw me as she saw me.

And I didn't like it.

"Uh-huh," I managed to get out, blinking back tears.

"I . . . I don't even know what to say."

I closed my eyes. "Sophie. Why don't I come over? We'll open a bottle of wine and we'll talk about this. I'll tell you everything. I'll start from the beginning and I won't stop until you understand where I'm coming from. All my motivations. All my reasons. They're in there, I promise. And they're good. I can prove it to you."

"I can't see you right now." Her words were fast and her tone was distant. Sophie may have only lived five minutes away from me by car, at almost any time of the day, but tonight she was a million miles from here.

And that was finally a distance *this* Southern Californian could understand.

"Okay," I said softly, the first tear successfully fighting its way from beneath my tightly shut eyelid and triumphantly making its slow victory parade down my cheek.

"I feel like I don't even know you."

I opened my eyes and several more tears followed closely behind. "But it's still me, Soph! I'm still the same person. I didn't change over the past two years; I shouldn't have to change over the past two minutes!"

"But you *did* change!" she fought back. "You're not even who you say you are. You're an entirely different person. With an entirely different name even!"

I sniffled. "It's just a stage name," I offered hopefully. "Like a character in a play. Or a TV show. Ellen Pompeo plays Meredith on *Grey's Anatomy*. Evangeline Lilly plays Kate on *Lost*. I play Ashlyn . . . in a weekly TV show about a girl whose job it is to expose cheating men to the women who love them!"

But Sophie wasn't convinced. "Those are TV shows! They're not real. This is real, Jen! These are real people! It's not pretend. It's not like when we were little, playing with my dad's psychology books or playing house." She paused. "Although I never thought you'd grow up to play the home wrecker."

"You wanted to hire me!" I shot back, wiping my running nose with the back of my hand. "You were going to call that home wrecker and hire her to wreck *your* home!"

"That's when it wasn't you!"

"What difference does it make whether it's me or the girl next door or Marilyn Fucking Monroe? You wanted the same thing that all my clients want. You wanted something that *I* give. Peace of mind." My voice softened and I stroked the white duvet cover underneath my knee. "And now you're going to hate me for giving it to other people?"

Sophie didn't respond right away. I could hear her breathing. Her breaths always got shorter and louder when she was upset. "I just need some time to think."

"Okay," I murmured. Because who was I to argue? There was nothing more I could say to convince her not to hate me. And there was definitely nothing I could add to convince her to accept me. Or accept what I did.

But as I hung up the phone I felt a small ounce of comfort in knowing that despite everything else, at least I could finally be certain that I had convinced her not to go through with it. She would never again even think about hiring anyone to seduce her fiancé. And it took the longest, bumpiest, most un-traveled road to get there. But I was finally there. In the clear. Sophie knew. There would be no more secrets. No more excuses. No more lies.

And even though I'd never felt such an unsettling hollowness in all my life, somewhere deep inside, beneath the frustration, beneath the horrific fear of losing my best friend, I felt my very first taste of serenity.

Until thirty minutes later, when I heard a knock at my door.

I peered through the peephole at Sophie's un-brushed hair, un-made-up face, and unadorned pink sweatpants. I attempted to paint a courageous smile on my face as I swung the door open wide.

She stood on my doormat, completely still, her mind clearly not made up yet as to whether or not she was actually going to come inside. As if MapQuest would only take her this far. What came next, she still wasn't sure.

So I rested my head against the side of the door and looked at her with pleading eyes. Not pleading for forgiveness, but pleading for understanding. Support. Unconditional friendship.

But what I didn't know at that very moment was that what she came here to say was ultimately not going to be a testament of her friendship . . . but a testament of mine.

Thinking back, I had underestimated her ability to adapt. Her ability to upgrade to a faster processing speed. And ultimately, her ability to not only accept the information she was provided, but to allow it to completely corrupt every ounce of logic in her entire system. Like a virus.

She stood up straight and looked me directly in the eye. Her voice never faltered as she recited the same line she must have rehearsed over and over again in the five-minute drive to my condo. "I still want you to test Eric."

17

the origin of the species (part 3)

I guess you could say I stumbled into my current job as a fidelity inspector. It's not like I planned it. It's not like I woke up one morning with the brilliant idea that I wanted to spend the rest of my life seducing married men.

The first one was, for all intents and purposes, an accident.

It was a work happy hour. The crowd had finally dwindled down to just me and a few young female coworkers from my investment bank. After a few too many Rolling Rocks, we began what started out as a very innocent but amusing game of Truth or Dare. Which eventually morphed into just "dare." It was all very harmless. "I dare you to pretend you knew the bartender in high school, and then act offended when he doesn't remember you." Or "I dare you to walk up to that table and ask them how they're enjoying their meal." But after a few more beers it started to take a more scandalous turn, when dares to casually say "Nice balls" to the people playing pool and dares to flash pieces of covered skin to passersby seemed to become more amusing and popular than the less risqué versions that had entertained us earlier in the evening.

The hot seat had passed several times around the circle, and at approximately 11:30 P.M., it landed on me for the last time.

"Okay, Jen." My colleague Rebecca pointed a long polished finger in my direction.

I smiled and brushed a strand of hair behind my ear. "Yes," I replied confidently and fearlessly. I had successfully fulfilled my last dare with flying colors when I walked into the men's room, motioned confusedly to the urinal, and said, "What a strange-looking sink" to the man inside. The girls had watched from the restroom hallway, laughing hysterically and high-fiving one another like frat boys at a porn convention.

Rebecca eyed her two neighbors knowingly, and they all exchanged smiles.

"What?" I asked, wanting to be a part of the secret.

Her eyes drifted off to a man at the end of the bar, who was dressed in a smart business suit and mingling with a group of other well-dressed professionals. "See that guy over there?"

I surreptitiously glanced to my right. "The one holding the glass of whiskey?"

Rebecca's face showed her clear distaste for his choice of alcohol as she nodded. "Yes."

"Okay," I confirmed.

She exchanged another verifying glance with Hilary and Tina on either side of her. "Well, you have to go over there, talk to him, and without ever suggesting anything, get him to ask you back to his place."

I burst out laughing. "Yeah, right."

But when I looked up, expecting to see three faces laughing right along with me, I was greeted with nothing but deadpan expressions. "You're kidding, right?"

Rebecca shook her head. "No. C'mon, the stakes are getting higher, step up to the plate."

I looked over at the man again. "No! I can't do that."

"If anyone can, it's you," Hilary piped in.

"What does that mean?" I asked.

"It means," Tina began, "that you're by far the best looking of any of us, and *we* have this little theory that no matter what the place or the time or even the outfit you're wearing, any man would jump at the chance to take you home."

I snorted. "That's ridiculous!"

"I don't think so," Hilary replied matter-of-factly.

"What? Did you guys plan this? Before we even got here?"

Hilary looked to Rebecca. It was obvious they had.

"Not exactly," Rebecca clarified. "It's just come up a few times . . . like at lunch or whatever. I mean, we see how all the guys at the office look at you."

I scrunched up my face. "No!" I insisted. "That's not true."

"Prove it," Rebecca challenged.

"But he's married," I protested, noticing his ring.

"That won't stop him," said Rebecca cynically. "He's still a guy."

I looked desperately to Hilary and Tina, hoping for a counteroffer. I received none. Apparently this was a spectacle to which *everyone* wanted to bear witness.

To this day I don't know if it was the ambush or the Anheuser-Busch, but after a long, hesitant look at all three of them, I silently pulled myself out of my seat, slung my bag over my shoulder, and slowly strolled the three paces to my very first subject.

The rest of the story went pretty much the same as all my subsequent stories. Flirty glances, coy smiles, witty banter. A slight exaggeration of my level of intoxication. And as it turned out, Rebecca, Tina, and Hilary were right. I didn't exactly get an invite to his house, but it didn't take long for him to ask me if I wanted to go someplace less crowded, and according to my panel of judges, that was good enough.

When I said the whole thing was an "accident," technically I was referring to the day after. When I found out what these "lunchtime conversations" behind my back were really about.

The next morning at work Miranda Keyton, a vice president of mergers and acquisitions, pulled me into her office for an impromptu meeting.

I found it somewhat odd that she would be requesting to meet with me alone. As I was only an analyst at the firm, requests were usually streamlined from her through many levels of bureaucracy, and then finally reached my lowly level after they'd been picked apart, analyzed, and altered by several echelons of the corporate food chain.

So I could only assume that getting a direct request from Miranda was either really, really bad news, like "Pack your bags, you've been laid off," or really, really good news like, "Pack your bags, you're moving to an office. You've been promoted."

As I stepped timidly into her corner office Miranda looked up from her computer screen, pushed her glasses onto the top of her head, and offered me a pleasant but reserved smile.

I smiled back.

"Close the door please, Jennifer."

Definitely not good news.

I closed the door behind me and took a seat in one of the chairs across from her.

"Thanks for coming in," she said as she leaned back in her black leather executive chair and studied me from across the desk.

"Sure."

"Well," she began, folding her hands in her lap. "I just wanted to call you in here to thank you personally for what you did."

I nodded, mentally rummaging through all the e-mails I had sent out in the past twenty-four hours that would have somehow ended up in Miranda's in-box. "You mean the, um . . . the, uh, DVD market analysis thing?" I ventured.

Miranda smiled, *almost* endearingly, but not quite. "No, Jennifer. I mean the 'my husband analysis' thing."

I frowned in confusion. I certainly didn't remember any requests relating to her husband. Had one of those recent data inquiries been initiated by him for some reason? Had he been using the bank's internal resources for some research of his own?

"I'm sorry," I said, trying not to sound completely clueless, but rather as if that *specific* analysis had merely slipped my mind momentarily, and a simple keyword would surely trigger the correct memory center of my brain and put me right on track with the conversation. "Which request was that?"

"The one from last night," she stated candidly.

This completely threw me off. And now I most definitely appeared even more out of the loop than before. I hadn't even been in the office last night. I was at a bar with a bunch of people *from* the office. Investment bankers were notorious for working late nights, even *all* night. In fact, last night we were out celebrating the first pre-seven P.M. departure in what had felt like months.

"I'm sorry," I began again, now convinced that I sounded like a complete moron, but at this point not really caring that much. I just wanted to know what the hell she was talking about and kindly let her know that she was obviously confusing me with someone else. "I wasn't working last night."

"Well, not in your normal capacity, anyway," she joked to herself. "But you definitely helped me out."

I sat in silence, waiting for an explanation. I wasn't about to continue to look at her dumbfounded, saying inept things like "Huh?" or "What?" or "I'm sorry" over and over again like an incompetent idiot.

"You hit on my husband last night . . . at the bar."

My mouth dropped. I blinked nearly two dozen times, completely flabbergasted. I could feel my face getting hot. Twenty straight hours in the blazing afternoon sun would have been no match to the deep red color my skin was now exhibiting for all to see. I didn't know what to say. And if I had been afraid of sounding like an idiot just a few seconds ago, it was surely nothing compared to the babbling sounds that were involuntarily coming out of my mouth at this moment.

"Uh . . . um . . . but . . . the thing is . . . I . . . um . . . I didn't know he was your . . ."

"Of course you didn't!" she exclaimed, as if it were the most obvious thing in the world. "If you did, there was no way you would have *ever* gone through with it!" She chuckled lightly, somewhat amused by the whole thing. In my mind she was starting to look a lot like Dr. Evil from *Austin Powers,* sadistically plotting the destruction of the planet unless someone agreed to pay her one hundred billion dollars.

"You mean . . . ?"

She nodded her head sadly. "I'm afraid so. I'm very sorry to have brought you into this whole mess. I know it's not any of your business. And certainly not your problem. But I had to confirm my suspicions."

I felt like I had just been knocked in the head with a sledgehammer but miraculously lived to tell about it. I just couldn't believe that the entire thing had been a setup, which would mean that Hilary and Tina had been in on it from the beginning. And that whole Truth or Dare game had just been a ruse to get me to that final challenge, the one that apparently had been Miranda's idea all along. Although, honestly, it didn't surprise me that Hilary and Tina had gone behind my back in order to satisfy one of Miranda's requests. Analysts will do just about anything to kiss up to high-level VPs.

I didn't know how to respond or what to say to her. What kind of response do you even begin to formulate in a situation like this? It's not like there's a section about this kind of thing in any proper social etiquette handbook, and my college class in business relationships certainly hadn't covered it.

And if I was speechless then, you can imagine my reaction when I got a phone call a few weeks later from a woman who introduced herself as "a close friend of Miranda Keyton's," asking if she could pay me to provide her with the same invaluable service I had afforded Miranda.

"I need to know the truth," she explained to my stunned silence on the other end of the phone. "I need to confirm my suspicions so I can stop wondering and move on." Her words poked at a deep wound inside of me. One that I never thought could ever be fully healed. But for the first time in months, after seeing my mother mourn the loss of so many years of happiness due to a lifetime of blissful innocence, I felt a twinge of restitution.

I couldn't turn back time and erase the choice that had deprived my mother of her right to know. But maybe I could at least help this woman uncover hers.

And the next woman.

And the next.

Until I found myself right here. Right now. Staring at another woman's quest for enlightenment. Only this time the woman was my best friend.

The girl who used to drive me around in her parents' minivan. The girl who was first to get her period, kiss a boy, get her driver's license, lose her virginity, and still find time to share it all with me. The girl who came to me with every problem, every question, every dilemma, every freak-out, every fear, and every decision. And I was always there for her. I've always been her rock. Her solution, her answer, her voice of reason, her equilibrium, her pacification . . . and her friend.

And now she was coming to me for this.

Even if it hadn't started out that way, that's what it was now.

And who was I to deny her? Especially when I'd devoted my life to eliminating denial.

"All right," I said to Sophie's pleading eyes. "I'll do it."

And the moment I said it, I knew I had made a huge mistake.

18

passengers and "drivers"

As if completely unphased by the concept that I, her best friend, would soon be attempting to seduce her fiancé, Sophie pushed her way through the door, plopped down on the couch, and immediately launched into all of the preparatory details.

"Okay, great," she began, reaching into her purse and pulling out her black day planner. "Eric comes into town in a week. He said he wants to catch up with some old college friends. So they'll be out at a bar, drinking, acting stupid . . . you know, guy stuff. I think *that* would be the perfect time to do it." She made a small note in her planner.

I watched her in complete shock. If I didn't know any better, I would have thought she were planning her boyfriend's surprise birthday party—not his fidelity inspection. She certainly was the most ambitious and organized client I'd ever taken on.

"Okay," I said cautiously.

She began furiously jotting down notes on a blank note page. I leaned over to try to read what she was scribbling. No luck.

And then, in one fluid motion, she ripped the once-blank page from her notebook and handed it over to me.

I reluctantly sat down next to her. "What's this?" I asked, squinting at the messy handwriting.

"A list of things that Eric likes. His hobbies, favorite foods, movies, et cetera. I figured it might come in handy."

I stared at the list, absolutely speechless. Part of me wanted to laugh, but I knew it wouldn't be appropriate. She was basically doing my job for me. These were all the exact details I had to practically squeeze out of the women who hired me. But not Sophie. She was as diligent about this process as a new car buyer walking into a dealership armed with a stack of industry reports, pricing models, and cash-back-incentive newspaper ads. Not that I was complaining. Anything to lessen the burden of what I had just agreed to do.

"So that day works for you?" Sophie asked me, pulling my attention away from the words "White Castle," which had been scribbled furiously underneath the heading of "Favorite Fast Food."

"Uh-huh," I confirmed vacantly.

"Jen!" Sophie practically shrieked.

I grimaced at the sound.

"Shouldn't you be entering all this in that stupid Palm Pilot phone you take everywhere?" And then under her breath added for good measure, "And now I know *why*."

I pulled myself off of the couch. "Right. Doing it now."

Sophie eyed me with trepidation. "You know, I kind of thought you'd be a little bit more on the ball about this stuff. You seem very blasé about the whole thing. Are you this unprofessional with all your clients?"

I grabbed my Treo from my bag and headed back to the couch. "Well, honestly, Soph," I began. "You're not really a typical client, now, are you?"

Sophie twisted up her mouth as she contemplated my question. "Well, no. I know that. But listen, for this particular purpose, I want you to treat me like any other client. I don't want any special treatment or considerations. Do exactly what you do with every other guy you flirt with."

"Oh, so now suddenly you're okay with my flirting with married men?"

She shrugged and closed her day planner, sticking it awkwardly back in her bag. "Why not? You're serving a purpose, right?"

"A purpose that happens to serve you as well?"

Sophie rolled her eyes. "Whatever."

I laughed at her. "You know what this means now, don't you?"

She turned toward me. "What?"

I leaned back against the couch and pressed my hands anxiously against my thighs. "It means I'm going to have to tell Zoë."

"Why?"

"Because John knows, and now you know, and it was fairly easy for *me* to keep it a secret from all of you, but what are the chances that both of you are going to be able to successfully keep it from her?"

"John knows?" Sophie asked, surprised, and honestly, appearing a little hurt. "Why does John know?"

"Trust me, it wasn't me who told him."

She eyed me with curiosity and I proceeded to tell her the very abbreviated version of my little Internet celebrity status, all the way up to the point where just tonight I had found out that Raymond Jacobs was the culprit behind all of it.

"So what are you going to do?" Sophie asked after I finished.

I shrugged my shoulders and released a pained sigh. "I don't know yet. Try to talk to him, I guess?"

"You think that'll work?" she asked with about the same amount of doubt as I was feeling inside.

I tucked my feet underneath me and fidgeted with the fraying cuff of my jeans. "Not sure. I suppose it's worth a try."

"Well, I'm glad that Zoë's going to find out," Sophie proclaimed after a short but loaded silence.

I smiled. "Why's that?"

She sat up proudly. "Because now at least she'll know for sure that I was right."

I crinkled my forehead. "About what?"

"About you!" she exclaimed. "You know how long it took to convince her that your little lack-of-dating problem really was a problem? She insisted that it was just work-related. But I *knew* it was something more, and it turns out . . ." Her voice trailed off as her thought process came full circle.

"That it *was* work-related?" I maintained with an amused smirk.

Sophie waved my comment away. "You know what I mean."

The doorbell rang as I was stepping out of the shower on Thursday evening. A brief panic hit me as I did a double take at the clock. It was only six-thirty. Jamie wasn't supposed to pick me up for our date until eight o'clock. I immediately worried that I might possibly have marked down the wrong time.

I peered through the peephole in the door to find Sophie and Zoë standing anxiously on the other side. I reluctantly opened the door.

"What are you guys doing here?" I asked, somewhat aggravated by their surprise visit.

"Well, nice to see you, too, bi-atch!" Zoë feigned offense.

"Yeah, not much of a welcome committee, are ya?" Sophie added.

I held my towel around me with one hand and rested the other on the door handle. "Sorry."

"So what's this big secret that everybody knows about but me?"

I glared at Sophie.

"Sorry!" she said. "I thought you would have told her by now!"

"It's only been a day!"

Zoë looked impatiently back and forth between me and Sophie. "Well?" she demanded. "Here I am. So tell me, already!"

I opened the door wider and motioned for them to come in. They stepped around me, and without any hesitation seated themselves on the couch, like guests on a talk show waiting for their personal interviews to begin. I closed the door and started to make my way to the bedroom. "Let me just put on some clothes."

"No!" Zoë insisted. "Nothing I haven't seen under there. You'll tell me *now*."

I rolled my eyes and tucked the edge of my towel under my armpit. I sat down next to Sophie. "Okay, so what did you already tell her?"

"Nothing!" she cried defensively. "I just asked what she thought about your news and she looked at me like I was crazy. Then I realized that you hadn't said anything and I insisted that you tell her yourself."

Zoë tapped her stiletto heel against the hardwood floor. "I'm waiting."

I let out a loud sigh. "I didn't really want to tell you like this. I was waiting for the right time to sit you down and explain everything to you."

Zoë motioned to the couch. "Well, we're definitely not standing."

I ran my hand over my wet hair. "Okay. To put it simply, I'm not exactly an investment banker."

Zoë's face remained expressionless as she waited for me to continue.

"In fact, I'm not an investment banker at all. For the past two years I've been doing a very different kind of job."

Still no reaction. So I kept going.

"I . . . um . . . women hire me to 'test' their husbands and boyfriends for, let's just call it, 'unfaithful tendencies.' "

Zoë's tongue ran over the front of her teeth as she earnestly contemplated my last sentence. However, if she had reached any sort of opinion about it, her face still refused to show it, almost as if I had simply informed her of my decision to switch dry cleaners. Although, knowing Zoë, she would probably have had an opinion about that, too.

Maybe she just hadn't been given enough time to fully absorb it. "You see, Zo"—I decided to try another approach—"I go out and flirt with these men . . . pretend to be interested in them to see if they'll try to have sex with me."

There . . . that should do it. It doesn't get more blunt and visual than that.

But the look on her face was still nothing more than someone trying to remember where they had last seen their missing keys. She was completely unresponsive to anything coming out of my mouth.

Sophie watched her intently and then turned to me, her eyes searching for answers, but unfortunately, my eyes were asking the same exact questions. We were both at a total loss.

Zoë finally looked at Sophie, then at me, and with a slight shrug asked, "Is that all?"

Sophie stared in utter disbelief. "What do you mean, *is that all?* Don't you find that just a tad bit shocking, Zoë?"

She contemplated this as well, and then with another shrug and a simple shake of her head, replied, "No, not really. I mean, it was pretty obvious that Jen hasn't been an investment banker for a while now."

"It was?" I spit out, stupefied.

Zoë laughed affectionately at me. "Um, yeah, Jen. Sorry, you're not that good of a liar."

"So you've known all along?" Sophie asked.

Zoë leaned back against the couch. "Well," she admitted, "I didn't know *exactly* what she'd been up to, but I knew something was different. She hasn't been the same for a few years."

I sat staring at my friend in complete astonishment. All this time I thought I was fooling everyone. And I almost was. Everyone except Zoë, that is.

"Plus," she continued, "I ran into that guy Nate Evans last year at the movie theater. Remember the guy from Stanley Marshall who you tried to set me up with a few years back? Well, anyway, he told me that you quit, like, months ago."

"But . . ." I couldn't even begin to make sense of what she was saying. Here I was thinking I would have to go through one more round of relentless questions from another close friend, but in all actuality it was the other way around. "Why didn't you ask me about it? Why didn't you confront me when you knew I didn't work there anymore?"

Zoë took a deep breath. "I don't know. I figured you were doing your own thing. And when you wanted to talk about it, you would come to us. So I just let you be."

"Wow." Sophie was bemused, looking just the slightest bit jealous that Zoë had so easily broken part of the code when she had been in the dark this whole time.

"But good for you, though," Zoë offered. "I must admit, it's kind of nice not having to speculate on what you might be up to anymore. For a while I convinced myself you were stripping at that club down the street from here. But honestly, I stopped trying to figure it out about six months ago."

"So you think it's a good thing?" I verified.

She nodded. "Sure. I mean, I don't blame you for wanting to do it. After what happened with your parents."

My shoulders slouched and I nodded softly. "Right."

Sensing my discomfort, Zoë quickly changed the subject. "So what are you getting ready for now?" she asked, gesturing toward the wet towel clinging to my body. "Another night of flirting with the unsuspecting?"

I stood up and hiked the towel higher around my chest. "No," I said quietly. "I'm . . . well, I'm going on a date, actually."

Both of my friends simultaneously jumped off the couch with more uniformity than an Olympic synchronized-swimming team. "What?" Sophie screeched.

"It's that guy from the plane, isn't it?" Zoë speculated with exhilaration.

Sophie turned to her. "What guy from the plane?"

"Jen met this cute guy on the plane back from Vegas and they totally hit it off, and she told me that she wasn't going to call him, but I knew she would."

"Well, you just know everything these days, don't you?" I asked, walking toward my bedroom.

The girls followed shortly after, like two dogs persistently pursuing a toddler snacking on crumbling pretzels.

"I know you, Jen," Zoë stated proudly. "You think no one knows you. But you are so wrong. You're more readable than you'd like to admit."

"Not to the men she seduces," Sophie shrewdly pointed out, wanting so much to compete in what she now perceived as a "Who knows Jen better?" competition.

"That doesn't count," Zoë replied. "They have so much testosterone running through their bloodstreams, I doubt they would notice if she wrote, 'This is a setup' across her forehead in red lipstick. Fooling an idiot male with a hard-on who's had sex with the same woman for the past twenty years isn't exactly a challenge."

"Well, know-it-all," I began self-importantly as I stepped into my closet and began riffling through my ten thousand outfit selections. "Turns out you're wrong. I *didn't* call him. I bumped into him at the Range Rover dealership."

"And you decided to finally listen to the universe," Zoë pointed out.

I bit my tongue in defeat. "Okay, so you *were* right about that."

Zoë plopped down on the bed with a bounce and smiled proudly. Sophie, slightly more dejected and feeling very out of the loop, settled with less celebration into the seat next to her.

"Soph," I said, sensing her feeling of exclusion. "I'm so useless with these things. Will you *please* just pick out something for me to wear? Or I could be in here all night."

Sophie's face immediately brightened as she eagerly rose to her feet and waltzed into the closet to perform her civic duty as the fashion-adept friend.

When Jamie called my personal cell phone to let me know he was just pulling up in front of my building, I quickly interrupted him. "I'll come down," I blurted out before he could even finish his sentence, most likely leaving him with the suspicion of dead bodies that I had yet to clean up after, or a variety of illegal drugs laid out on the coffee table awaiting proper measuring and packaging, or possibly even an estranged husband who thought I was going out with the girls this evening. But truth be told, I wasn't quite ready to let him into my house yet. Giving him my address had been hard enough. But the thought of having him walk around inside my home made me just the slightest bit nauseous.

I began to pack my Marc Jacobs clutch with all the essentials: breath mints, keys, lip gloss, credit cards, cash, ID . . . and, finally, my personal cell phone. I stopped and stared down at my Treo, lying lifelessly on the kitchen table. I reached out to grab it and then slowly recoiled, as if the small, metallic device was threatening to scorch my skin upon contact. For some reason this moment, this seemingly insignificant decision, seemed like a major turning point in my life. I took one last glance at the phone and then triumphantly zipped up my bag and slung it over my shoulder.

It was amazing how much lighter I felt. Like I had not just left behind a six-ounce communication device but a two-hundred-pound burden.

As I rode the elevator down to the ground floor, I started to get butterflies in my stomach. This was by no means my first first date. Technically, I go on "first dates" three or four times a week. True, they weren't exactly honest in their intentions, but I was supposed to be a pro at this . . . dealing with men. Getting them to like me. Playing their game. Reading their minds. But then again, that had always been Ashlyn's forte . . . not mine. And as the elevator doors opened menacingly, as if in slow motion, I felt like I was entering very uncharted territory.

I checked my reflection in the mirrored walls of the lobby. Sophie had done an amazing job navigating through the treacherous jungle of my closet. After only a few minutes of sifting through rows and rows of hangers, ruling out selections at record-breaking speed, she finally arrived at a pink lace camisole with a cream cardigan and a pair of skinny jeans.

Sophie had then moved into my bathroom, where she proceeded to make a complete mess of my accessories drawer and had finally topped off the ensemble with a ceramic bangle bracelet and dangling dark pink-and-nickel chandelier earrings.

I exited and immediately spotted Jamie's white Jaguar XK convertible waiting in front of my building with the top up, lights on, and the engine still running. I approached it.

The driver's-side door opened and Jamie stepped out to greet me. He looked amazing. Better than I remembered, actually. He was wearing a pair of light khaki slacks, a fitted black-knit shirt, and a black collarless jacket over it.

He kissed me tenderly on the cheek and I felt a small chill rush up my body. I cleared my throat. "So this is the Jag?"

"This is it. It's supposed to impress you. Is it working?"

I laughed and shook my head. "Not really."

"Damn. I'll have to ask for my money back," he said, walking around to the passenger side and opening the door for me. "The guy who sold it to me said it was supposed to impress all the ladies."

Jamie got in the driver's seat and pressed a button on the console. The top of the car slowly started to come down, and I felt the cool night air hit my face.

"What about now? Impressed?"

I considered. "Getting there."

"I'm five years away from forty. I figured I'd start the midlife crisis thing early with a convertible."

"Wow!" I exclaimed. "Almost forty! You're so . . ."

He shot me a warning glance.

". . . young-looking for your age," I said with a grin.

Jamie nodded his head in gratitude. "I'll keep the windows up so it doesn't mess up your hair."

"That's very considerate of you," I joked. But in all actuality, it was a concern that had crossed my mind when the top started coming down.

"So," Jamie began while buckling his seat belt. "I figured that a girl like you probably goes on a lot of dates."

"Oh, really? And what does that mean? A girl like me?"

He adjusted the radio. "I mean, a girl as pretty as you."

I swallowed hard and looked out the window to hide the warmth I felt come over my face. "Oh. Thank you."

"So I thought tonight I should probably come up with a way to distinguish myself."

I laughed nervously, thinking about how distinguished this night had become already, and we had barely left Brentwood. "And what did you come up with?"

"Golf."

I looked at him incredulously. "Golf?"

He nodded. "Yes. Golf."

"You came up with golf?"

He smiled proudly. "Mmm-hmm. Have you ever played?"

I turned my head again. In fact, I had played golf . . . several times. And after a handful of lessons to get me up to "par" with the husbands I inspected *on* the golf course, I was actually fairly good at the game.

"Yeah, a few times," I said modestly. "But I didn't bring my clubs."

"That's okay, we can rent some."

"So we're going to play golf?" I asked again, still wondering when the "joke's on you" was coming.

"You like saying the word *golf,* don't you? I mean, we can do something else if you—"

"No, no! That's fine. I like . . . *golf*."

"Good," he said with a laugh. "Now, what's the quickest way to get back to Wilshire Boulevard from here?"

Without thinking I directed Jamie to make a right at the stop sign, then a left at the next street, a right at the next. Another left, then right, until we finally arrived on Wilshire.

Jamie waited at the stoplight and shot me a strange look.

"What?" I said, feeling self-conscious and instinctively smoothing my hair down.

"I know this isn't my 'hood' and all, but wasn't that, like, the longest possible route to Wilshire?"

I felt my stomach lurch. So much for appearing like a "normal" girl who dates all the time. I hadn't even realized that I had just taken Jamie through my six-turn safety route. Although now that my face was plastered all over the Internet, I had a hard time considering it very safe. I attempted to cover with a weak laugh. "Scenic route."

Jamie looked in the rearview mirror at the rows of apartment buildings and condos that looked pretty much exactly the same. "Well, thank you for that," he offered sincerely, with just the smallest trace of friendly sarcasm.

Ten minutes later we arrived at a popular nine-hole course in Rancho Park. I recognized it immediately. It had been the site of the Oliver Hender assignment. A high-up business executive who was in town from New York and wanted to fit in a quick round before his very important meeting with a group of Japanese investors.

His wife had contacted me by phone a few weeks in advance and I agreed to take on the assignment. I paid the course attendant a hefty tip to be paired-up alone with Mr. Hender. Two lonely golfers just trying to take advantage of the beautiful L.A. weather before heading off to their respective meetings. One of these golfers just happened to be a sexy young lawyer named Ashlyn who was apparently just as good on the golf course as she was in the courtroom. Oliver was extremely impressed. And with those flirtatious looks she was tossing him in between practice swings, and that tiny golfing skirt barely covering her perfectly tanned legs, how could he not take her right there? After all, it *was* a fairly slow day on the course.

I stepped out of Jamie's car and breathed in the night air. It was a beautiful evening, just around seventy degrees, barely any wind. The perfect night for a round of golf, although had I expected to be playing tonight, I might have chosen a different outfit. I could only imagine what golfing in my wedge-heeled espadrilles would be like.

Jamie popped open his trunk and began to remove a set of golf clubs.

"Wait a minute." I stopped him. "You mean I have to rent clubs and *you* get to use your own? Now that seems to put you at a very unfair advantage, doesn't it?"

He considered that, and then placed the clubs gently back into the trunk. "You're right. I should rent clubs, too. That way we'll be on an even playing field."

No such thing, I thought.

We started walking toward the clubhouse, and Jamie glanced down at my feet. "Maybe we should rent you some shoes, too."

After the fourth hole it was pretty clear who the better golfer was between us.

"So," Jamie began as he placed the pin back into the hole on the green. "I actually chose this specific activity because I was supposed to impress you with my extraordinary golfing skills. But it doesn't seem to be quite working out the way I planned. Does it?"

I shook my head. "Not so much."

"You know," he continued as we walked back toward our awaiting cart. "I don't think you've been properly educated on the *purpose* of a first date."

"Well, then, I guess you better enlighten me."

"I'll do that," he asserted. "See, the purpose of the first date is for the *guy* . . . that would be me . . ."

"Right . . ."

". . . to *impress* the girl." He emphasized the word *impress* as if I were a foreigner hearing the English word for the first time and he wanted to make sure I could properly pronounce it later. "You know, like show off his colorful feathers, bob his head up and down, play golf really well. It's all part of the ancient dating ritual."

I pretended to be extremely intrigued by his lecture as we approached the golf cart, and I sat down in the passenger seat. "I see."

Jamie got in behind the wheel and quickly marked down our strokes on the scorecard. "And the *girl* . . . that would be you . . . is supposed to be so taken by these impressive displays that you just can't help but . . ."

"But what?" I interrupted him with a playful smirk.

He shot me a knowing glance. "But swoon, of course. Fall all over yourself. Fail to find the ability to stand upright without losing your balance from all the swooning."

I laughed. "Wow, you've really thought this through, haven't you?"

Jamie pulled the cart onto the cement path. "There's nothing to think through. This is just how it works. It's the natural order of all things that you, Miss Jennifer H., are severely disturbing with your three pars and a birdie."

"Hey, I let you drive the cart, didn't I?"

He nodded. "That you did."

I grabbed the bar on the outside of the cart as Jamie made a sharp turn. "Sorry," I said. "I guess I just come from a completely different school of thought."

"And what school would that be? Please enlighten *me.*"

Well, technically, it was my own school of thought. Something along the lines of not letting yourself be *swooned* by any guy no matter how good their golf game or how bright their tail feathers. But at that moment, I suddenly couldn't remember where those rules had even come from. And I kind of liked it that way.

"Well, basically it goes something like this: Old-fashioned dating rituals are completely outdated. Girls can be better at anything . . . even golf."

Jamie nodded. "Well, it looks like I'll just have to rely on my charm, then. Since golf doesn't seem to be working."

I smiled. "I guess so."

He parked the golf cart in front of a small snack stand that stood off to the side of the cart path.

"What are we doing here? The fifth hole is that way," I said, pointing back the way we came. "Maybe I *should* be driving."

"Well, I *did* promise you dinner," he reminded me, motioning to the snack stand.

I laughed. "Are you serious?"

He straightened his face. "Extremely. I take my golf hot-dog breaks very seriously. As you probably know, it's customary to visit the snack stand after nine holes. But since we're on only a nine-hole course, I figure the fourth hole is probably the best place to break."

"Well, in theory, it would be after four-point-*five* holes," I pointed out.

"And here we go again with the human calculator."

I laughed. The truth was, I'd actually never made it to the ninth-hole snack stand. None of my "golfing" partners had lasted that long.

I glanced skeptically at the shack in front of me. "So . . . hot dogs?"

"Do you have anything against hot dogs? Like a personal vendetta or something? Because I bet I could get them to whip you up a grilled cheese instead."

"No. I love hot dogs."

Jamie pantomimed a notch on an invisible scoreboard. "Jamie, one . . . all other dates, zero."

I giggled, wishing I could ease his mind and tell him that there were no other dates to compare himself to. This was, for all intents and purposes, my first one. Although I was pretty confident that, had there been others, the scoreboard would have looked pretty much the same.

We approached the counter and ordered two hot dogs and two Cokes. Jamie paid for the food and, in return, the cashier handed over our food and drinks.

"How's that for fast service?" Jamie asked with a wink.

I headed over to the toppings bar and started to spread ketchup on my hot dog. Jamie came up beside me and pumped mustard out of the dispenser. "I'm more of a mustard kind of guy."

I made a face. "Just ketchup for me."

Jamie took a bite out of his freshly topped hot dog. "So we could essentially buy one of those twin packs of ketchup and mustard from the supermarket and never fight over who gets what."

"Unlike those Fun Packs of cereal. My half sister and I always used to fight over those."

We sat down on a nearby bench and I placed my white paper plate on my lap.

"I have to have the Apple Jacks," Jamie said, popping the top of his Coke.

"No! I get the Apple Jacks!" I insisted before taking a bite out of my hot dog, and then with a mouthful of beef and bread mumbled, "They're my favorite!"

"Well, then, this is never going to work. We might as well end it right now."

I nodded solemnly as I chewed and swallowed. "You're probably right. It's better off this way. We won't ever have to deal with the problem of who's going to eat the Smacks. They're always the last box to go."

"You're right. Well, thank God we solved that problem. You know how many uneaten boxes of Smacks we just saved ourselves?"

"Hundreds," I replied quickly.

He nodded, and we both stared out across the darkened golf course. The overhead lamps were just bright enough to light the outline of the fairway.

Jamie glanced down at my new, blindingly white golf shoes. "Those shoes look good with your outfit."

"You think?" I asked, sticking my feet out in front of me and twisting my ankles to show off my new footwear.

"Definitely. I just don't understand why they don't rent shoes here. I mean, bowling alleys do it."

"I know. What's up with that? Because bowling alleys and golf courses certainly have a very similar clientele," I noted as I popped the last of my hot dog into my mouth.

"How am I doing on that whole distinguishing thing?" he asked.

I sipped my Coke. "Pretty good, actually. You're the first person to ever buy me shoes on a date."

"Good. So are we really going to let this whole cereal discrepancy keep us from finishing our game?" Jamie crumpled up his napkin and tossed it in a nearby trash can.

I considered. "It *would* be a shame to let my new shoes go to waste."

An hour later we returned our rented clubs to the pro shop and headed back to the parking lot. Jamie walked close to me and I could feel his body heat through the cloth of my cardigan. I once read that everyone is made up of energy, and if you allow yourself to be in tune with that energy, you can literally feel it pulsating from anyone around you. The more receptive you are to the presence of other human beings, the farther away you can sense the energy radiating off of them.

At that moment I was fairly certain I would have been able to feel Jamie from halfway across the golf course.

As we stepped in unison, his hand brushed against mine and he immediately grabbed it and interlaced our fingers. I had felt so many hands before. I had felt so many fingers intertwine with mine. I had pretended to get chills from so many casual touches like this one. But the heat rushing from his skin onto mine was something I had never felt before, and it was rendering me nearly powerless. I carefully watched the ground in front of me, afraid that the slightest piece of unevenness in the pavement might cause me to trip.

Just as Jamie had predicted: I suddenly felt incapable of standing upright without losing my balance.

He walked me to the passenger door and paused just before opening it. "Did I tell you that you look really amazing?"

I opened my mouth to speak but nothing came out, so I shook my head instead.

"Well, you do."

I smiled and swallowed hard, immediately wondering if he'd kiss me. And then wondering when the last time I'd ever wondered something like that was. Certainly not recently. I always knew when the kiss would come. I'd made a living out of clocking it to the second.

But not tonight. Not with Jamie.

I could almost feel his lips less than a foot away from mine, and suddenly a sense of urgency rushed over me. It was as if I simply *had* to kiss him or I might implode.

But he kept his distance.

"I thought the same thing when I saw you on the airplane," he admitted.

I finally managed to speak. "Really?"

He reached out and ran his fingers lightly across the surface of my lips. I could smell the remnants of leather from his golfing glove. I fought the burning desire to close my eyes.

"Amazing," he repeated softly.

"Thank you" was all I could think to say.

"So what does *your* school of thought say about kissing?" he whispered softly, his warm breath taking mere moments to reach my face.

I bit my lip. "Um . . . what about it?"

He brought his face even closer, and for the first time in the evening I could smell the faint scent of his aftershave. "Well, technically, according to your more *modern* rulebook, the girl should initiate any lip-to-lip action."

I smiled. "I never said that."

"I was just speculating." He reached up and gently brushed a strand of hair from my forehead.

"Don't," I whispered.

He came even closer, the tips of our noses only millimeters apart. "Don't what?"

"Speculate."

Then he kissed me. It was soft and delicate. He tasted like hot dogs and Coke and I couldn't get enough of it. Even the faint lingering taste of mustard was like heaven in my mouth. His hand rested softly on my cheek and then slowly made its way to the back of my head. He pressed me closer to him and the kiss intensified . . . but only slightly . . . nothing more.

There were no kissing calculations floating through my mind. No ratios to compute. The connection was flawless and completely spontaneous.

My whole body felt like it was on fire. I wanted nothing more than to take off all my clothes and make love to him right there—in the golf course parking lot. I wasn't sure if it was Jamie or the fact that I hadn't had sex in such a long time. But I wanted him so badly it was driving me crazy.

Maybe it was both.

Fortunately, he had much more restraint than I did. He eventually pulled away and allowed his mouth to linger close to mine.

With his hand still on the back of my head he rested his forehead against mine, as if surrendering himself to me. I closed my eyes again.

"Where did you come from?" he whispered with a half laugh, and then, before I could respond, kissed me on the forehead and reached around me to open the car door.

When we pulled up in front of my building, Jamie asked me if he could see me again on Saturday night. Without even thinking, I agreed. Because at that perfect moment, there was nothing to think about. There was nothing to consider.

But as I unlocked my front door I was unsure of how I would deal with what was waiting on the other side.

Silence.

Deafening silence.

The kind that makes you think. The kind that forces you to face realities. The kind that begs for answers and clarification and decisions.

And I knew for sure that I didn't want to make any.

I didn't want to define anything.

I didn't want to answer the questions that would certainly start pouring in from every corner of my brain the minute that door closed behind me.

I had always lived alone, but tonight my house felt emptier than it had ever felt before.

I quickly made my way to my bedroom, without even bothering to illuminate my path with any of the hallway lights. I plopped down on the bed, laid back, and allowed my eyes to shut. But only for a moment, while I took a long, deep, purposeful breath. Attempting with all my strength to regain my composure. Steady my heartbeat. Recover control.

My thoughts were a blur. I couldn't stop thinking about the events of the evening. Every word that had come out of his mouth was replaying in my head. I could still feel the soft touch of his lips as if they had become a permanent part of me.

And then a disturbing image started to swirl around in my head, refusing to disappear. It was a picture of Jamie waking up tomorrow morning, the sun shining brightly through his windows, the thought of our kiss still lingering in his mind, a piece of paper with my phone number written on it sitting on his desk next to the computer. He'd sit down with his coffee, and while his laptop booted up, he'd glance down at my phone number and smile, looking forward to Saturday night. Looking forward to another night just like last night. *Better* than last night.

And then he would open his e-mail application and wait as the server downloaded the million and a half messages he had accumulated since he left the office the night before. He would slowly sift through them, deleting the junk, saving the ones that required follow-up, and smiling at the funny jokes sent by friends.

Then he would arrive at a very special e-mail. One from a close acquaintance or friend, or maybe even a former colleague. And what would make this particular e-mail special was that there would be no text inside . . . only a mysterious link. Intrigued, he would click on that link, and after an innocent sip of his coffee, he would casually glance over the content of the Web page that had magically appeared on his screen at the click of a button. And just as he was about to dismiss the information as yet another useless forward, his fingers would stop. His hand on the mouse would freeze. His eyes would be glued to the screen. He would blink. Once, twice, then again. *Is that really her?* he would think. It can't possibly be her! But it looks so much like her. And what does this say? That she's hired by wives to seduce husbands?

And then he would think, *What kind of girl even does that?*

And it would all be over.

Tonight wouldn't exist anymore. Except in my mind. And then, even the memory of it would soon become jumbled up in the pollution of dishonesty and lies, where the lines between dark and light are blurred. The memories of good and bad slowly merge into one.

And the saddest part was, there was nothing I could do about it.

Except pray that Jamie never opens forwards.

19

engaging the enemy

The next morning I woke up feeling inspired.

My near perfect first date with Jamie had motivated me to do something about Raymond Jacobs.

Although it was probably less of an inspiration and more of a life-threatening fear that any minute now Jamie might be forwarded that doomsday Web site link, and I would become just a distant and rather unpleasant memory in his mind.

I found the address for Kelen Industries' headquarters on their Web site, and after e-mailing it to my Treo, I picked out the most respectable-looking outfit I could find in my closet. No cleavage-bearing tops this time, no eye-popping miniskirts, no cropped T-shirts—none of it. Today I would be the very epitome of refinement and class. Today I would play the role of the pissed-off entrepreneur who meant business.

After I picked up my Range Rover from the dealership, I entered the address into my navigation system and I vowed to stay focused on the situation at hand. No time would be wasted thinking or reminiscing about Jamie or our amazing kiss last night, because nothing beneficial ever comes from obsessing (unless you're dieting). And the more I kept my mind off of him the better.

But the more I tried not to think about it, the harder the task became. Plus, the unbearable stress of everything else that was haunting me was coming at me from all directions. And I wasn't sure how to prioritize the influx.

Was I supposed to worry about how I was going to keep my career a secret from Jamie? Or was I supposed to worry about keeping my career a secret period? Which seemed like the logical avenue, since without the secretive nature of my career, I would cease to have the career in the first place.

On top of that, this afternoon I had a meeting with another suspicious wife to discuss her husband's possible infidelity. The motivation for taking this meeting was, of course, the very reason I had my secretive career to begin with. Not to mention the fact that that so-called motivation was dimming in its intensity on a daily basis.

What had started out as a mission to save the world was feeling less and less like a noble quest and more and more like a noble pain in the ass.

Case in point: Next week's dreaded assignment with Eric, Sophie's fiancé, which I still wasn't sure I was ever going to find the nerve to go through with.

The whole situation was pretty much a huge mess, and the only thing I was certain about at this point was that I didn't feel like dealing with any of it. My life was quickly turning into a confusing roundabout of motivations, and I wasn't quite sure which exit to take. But the best thing about roundabouts: You can just circle around and around forever, until you figure out where you're supposed to get off.

And that's exactly what I intended to do.

As I drifted from lane to lane on the uncharacteristically empty 405 freeway, I couldn't help but agonize over the fact that I was about to go into battle completely unarmed. I still had no action plan as to how I would deal with Raymond Jacobs in just a few minutes except to march in there without any semblance of an appointment and simply demand that he take down that god-awful Web site.

Yeah, that plan sounded like a real winner.

I was kind of hoping that just my showing up would count for something, and he would magically reveal the hidden soft side that had been buried away for his entire life, and possibly cut me some slack. But the realism gauge in my brain was definitely pointing toward empty for that idea.

Would I be able to reason with him? Threaten him? With what, though? I had absolutely no leverage; he was already exposed. It wasn't like I could walk into his office and say, "Take down the ridiculous Web site or I'm telling your wife what you did to me."

The point was, I wasn't used to being so unprepared. I'd built my life around always being ready for anything. Always one step ahead of the prey. One level up in the game. But today I would certainly be the underdog. It was no secret who had the upper hand in this situation. And for the first time, it wasn't me.

I would have to do what I did best . . . fake it.

I stepped out of the elevator on the ninth floor of the Kelen Industries headquarters building in Long Beach. I pulled my dark purple suit jacket taut around me, and with my head held high, marched in the direction of the receptionist's desk. "I need to speak with Raymond Jacobs, please," I said in my sternest yet politest voice.

I half expected the receptionist to be a buxom twenty-something with red lipstick, bleached blond hair, and a low-cut sweater top—something out of the *Playboy* Bunny Casting Rejection File. But I was greeted curtly by a plump older woman in her early fifties who had probably worked there longer than Raymond himself and, judging by her less-than-bedside manner, was just as happy about being there as I was.

"Do you have an appointment?" The words were chewed out of her mouth as she sat flipping pages of a *Redbook* magazine and attending to a persistent series of high-pitched *dings* coming from her computer screen.

I stood up straighter. "No, but you can just tell Mr. Jacobs that Ashlyn is here to see him. I'm sure he'll know what this is regarding."

"I'm sorry," the woman said to me, without even a hint of sincerity. "But Mr. Jacobs does not see anyone without an appointment."

I decided I would have to play to her strengths. Or, better said, her obvious weaknesses. I flashed a phony smile and leaned over the high receptionist counter. She instinctively retracted, as if half expecting me to grow fangs and start gnawing on her face.

I lowered my voice to a near whisper. "I hate to bring you into this whole, uncivilized mess. But your, um, boss is attempting to ruin my life because his wife, whom I'm now assuming is probably in the process of becoming his ex-wife, found out he tried to seduce me in a hotel bar in Denver. And now I'm here to deal with him."

I casually stood back up and sucked in a relaxed breath. As if I had simply leaned over to thoughtfully tell her she had food in her teeth. But judging by the sinfully delighted grin on her face, I knew I had played the right card. The disgruntled employee whose only joy in life comes directly from bearing witness to any even remotely unpleasant occurrence brought upon the evil and ungrateful boss man. That, and really good office gossip.

I suspected my news counted as both. She picked up her phone and held it to her ear. "Ashlyn was it?" she asked graciously.

I nodded with a satisfied smile and waited as she spoke softly into the receiver. After a quick eyebrow raise she hung up the phone and said, "You can go right on in."

Wow. Quicker than I thought. I took a deep breath and stepped around the reception desk.

"Straight down the hall, last door on the left," she informed me.

"Thanks."

"Good luck!" she whispered loudly.

I smiled and gave her a thumbs-up sign before starting down the long, looming corridor ahead of me.

My nemesis was seated in a large executive chair facing out the window, bellowing into a wireless earpiece. "I told you I wanted those figures yesterday!" he yelled at what seemed like thin air. "I don't care what time it is over there! Here it's ten A.M., and that makes you more than twelve hours late!"

Ah, yes. Raymond Jacobs. I remembered him well. That deep voice. That large, ominous presence. The attempted bribe in his moment of defeat. Throwing money at any unfortunate situation might not have been the only thing that got him to where he is today, but it was certainly helping him stay there.

I knew from the moment I saw him in that hotel bar in Denver that he was definitely *not* a man you wanted to mess with.

But I had.

Because I was being paid to.

And now, I was definitely being paid back for it.

I quietly closed the door behind me and waited for the scary man in the big chair to turn around and reveal his hideous face.

And when he did, a knowing smile crept across it. It was almost creepy. As if he had been waiting for me to walk into that office. Any day now. Waiting for his rematch in chess. Because he knew just as well as I did that this time . . . he was *several* moves ahead of me.

"I was hoping you'd stop by," he said, leaning back in his chair, not bothering to stand up and greet me, for which I was grateful. I preferred to keep as much distance between us as possible.

I reminded myself to stay calm. Emotionless and, above all else, ruthless.

This man couldn't be given any idea how much he'd upset me. And he had to understand that I was not going to back down, even though I felt like crawling under his desk—and never coming out.

My goal was to get as much information as possible and get out. I was in no position to win at this point; I needed more data, more insight into the game itself. Then I could go home and strategize my next move.

He studied me from behind the desk, his perverted little eyes running up and down the length of my body. "Ashlyn, I believe it was."

I smiled callously as I sat down on the couch across from him. "Good memory."

"But of course that's not your *real* name," he ventured.

"Let's just cut to the chase," I said, marveling at how much I sounded like I belonged in one of those old black-and-white PI movies.

He smiled at me, almost as if he felt sorry for me. "I'm afraid there is no chase, honey. I'm not taking down the Web site."

I returned his patronizing grin. "Of course you're not. Why would you?"

Raymond chuckled, highly amused by the situation.

"And I wouldn't dream of asking you to take it down. I'm quite honored that you spent so much time and resources outing me. And such flattering pictures of me as well. You simply have to give me the name of your photographer. Maybe I can hire him to take some publicity shots."

Raymond smiled again and pointed his finger at me. "You're a sassy one, aren't you?"

"You tell me. You're the one with all the inside information these days."

Raymond tried to stare me down. I held my ground. Never blinking, never faltering. Never exposing that, in the end, I had nothing. And everything to lose.

"It's a bitch, isn't it?" he asked.

I pretended to ponder his question in all seriousness, as if it contained an answer to one of life's most unsolvable puzzles. All the while I was actually racking my brain for my next course of action. I had to get answers to my questions. How did he find me? Who took those pictures? How much did he really know about me? "Actually, I'm quite impressed," I began. "I'm a pretty difficult person to track down. I'm surprised that your spies were even able to find me at all."

Raymond scoffed at my remark. "You're not that difficult to track down. Granted, I'm sure you've made significant efforts to cover your tracks in order to avoid any unpleasant run-ins with people like me. And I may not have known exactly where you'd be buying your weekly groceries or which store you frequent to stock up on all those cute little outfits of yours. But after you so rudely left my hotel room that night, I knew one place that you'd undoubtedly be visiting."

As my ears followed his sinister series of words, my mind was coming to the most horrifying conclusion. I couldn't believe I hadn't thought of it before. After all the precautions I take on a daily basis—unlisted phone numbers, indirect routes to and from my house, fake jobs that I tell my family about—I had never even considered this one. He had been tracking me from the moment I stepped onto his property. At his very own house! While I was inside consoling Anne Jacobs with hugs and Kleenexes and kind words about moving on and knowing the truth, Raymond's wretched little spy had been outside taking down my license plate number and doing God knows what else. It was almost too brilliant for me to be angry. *Almost.*

"Clever," I managed to get out, despite the deafening pounding of my heart inside my ears. "So what's your corruption of choice? DMV or FBI?"

Raymond shook his head. "A magician never reveals his secrets."

My mind raced. If he had access to files like driving records and license plate databases, there was no end to the possible extent of his knowledge. That wasn't public information. You can't just enter a license plate number into a Google search and out pops a nice and neat little personal biography. As far as I could tell, he had some type of government hookup. Not that I was surprised. The businessmen I dealt with in my line of work were rarely ever squeaky clean.

I needed leverage. And I needed it now. Something to throw back in his face. But I had nothing!

So I took a gamble.

"What about your new girlfriend? I'm sure she'd be delighted to know about your 'past.' "

To which he chuckled again. This time it was loud and dripping with disdain. "There is no new girlfriend, sweetie," he began. "There's just an ex-wife, some very expensive attorneys' bills, and a large divorce settlement. Thanks to you."

I swallowed hard. I knew I was trapped. There was nothing else I could do at this point. I would have to leave and regroup. Given enough time, I would surely be able to think of something. This evil man *had* to be stopped!

"Well," I said, gathering up my things, "sounds like you've got a lot on your plate. I'll leave you be."

That's when Raymond stood up and walked over to the couch. I suddenly felt very small under his towering six-foot-three frame. He sat down next to me—dangerously close, his proximity making me painfully uncomfortable.

But his ominous facade seemed to soften somewhat as he brought his face close to mine. I could feel his breath on my skin, and it made me want to squirm. But I struggled to remain poised and controlled, not flinching, even for a second. Because I couldn't give him that satisfaction. I couldn't let him know what kind of effect he was having on me.

But the truth was, I had no idea what was coming next. I hadn't a clue what he was about to say or what other surprises he had hidden up his sleeve.

Then he placed his hand gently on my thigh, leaned in closer, and whispered, "We never got to finish what we started. Back at the hotel."

I tried hard to suppress the gasp that was building up in my throat. I couldn't believe what I was hearing. Was he really implying what I thought he was implying?

I suddenly felt small and lost, sitting on that red leather couch, in that dauntingly large office. I closed my eyes, pulling the strength from the very depths of my soul.

"I'm a reasonable man. I'd probably be willing to work something out." His tone was soft, almost amicable. But I could sense the rage buried deep within. It poured out of his eyes and burned into my skin. Lingering aggravation and promises of revenge. He moved his hand farther up my leg. "You know, call off my spies."

I looked down at his hand, resting dangerously close to the hemline of my skirt. It felt like a thousand tiny spiders crawling on my skin, making me want to jump up and scream and brush them away with swift, merciless motions.

I knew exactly what I needed to do.

And it was exactly the right time to do it.

I stood up, pushing Raymond's grubby hand violently from my leg.

"You're disgusting," I said vehemently, before storming to the door, purse in hand, self-respect in tow.

But just as I laid my hand on the doorknob and pulled the large, wooden door toward me, revealing a small inch of space between me and the salvation of the outside world, he opened his mouth once again. And this time, the words that found their way out were surprisingly much worse. "I wonder how your mother would react when she learns what you really do for a living."

I paused, my hand still on the doorknob, my heart in my throat, the realization of the unexpected, deeper complexity of the situation immediately appearing across my face.

"Especially after the *very* similar way her own marriage crumbled," he continued, leaning back on the couch, relaxed in the safety of his upper-hand position.

I closed my eyes again. This time, much tighter. I could feel the weight of the world slowly come down upon my shoulders.

It wasn't supposed to happen this way. This was supposed to be the part where I stormed out, victorious in my resolve. Warning him to "beware" because I, too, had a couple of tricks up my sleeve. And he would soon experience firsthand what I was capable of. Then I slam the door on my way out, leaving him to wallow in his palpable defeat.

But I was far from victorious.

And he was clearly far from defeat.

"How do you think she would react . . . *Jennifer Hunter*?" Hearing his voice uttering the syllables of my name was like nails on a chalkboard. I could feel my whole body shudder with repulsion

And then all of a sudden, it became painfully clear just how deep his corruption went. Just how much he knew. And just how far he would go to make sure I suffered just as much as he had. To make sure my life was ruined just as his had been. And I realized, I had even more to lose than I'd originally thought.

With my hand on the doorknob and my heart in my throat, I slowly closed the door—once again trapped in the dark, morally depraved confines of Raymond Jacobs's corner office.

Later that afternoon, as I drove to my next destination, I added yet another item to my seemingly ever-expanding list of things *not* to think about today:

what happened in Raymond Jacobs's office. I would have to fully digest that turn of events at another time. Lately I seemed to be getting really good at storing things away to be dealt with at a later date. This would have to be no different.

There was work to be done. More women needed my help. And I would give it to them. Because I had promised to. Despite the existence of creepy, power-hungry businessmen and the shadowy offices that hide their sins.

After pulling into a random Jiffy Lube and persuading the highly skeptical mechanic to inspect my Range Rover for any bugs or suspicious tracking devices that Raymond Jacobs's spies could have attached to my car, I convinced myself that I was thankfully not under any permanent surveillance.

Feeling more at ease, I followed the navigation lady's detailed directions to the tucked-away neighborhood of Topanga Canyon, in the Santa Monica Mountains just inland from Malibu Beach. Ninety minutes later I pulled into a long, winding driveway and followed it for nearly a quarter of a mile, until I reached a secluded mansion carefully hidden amid a forest of pine trees. This was the home of Sarah and Daniel Miller, possible future beneficiaries of my one-of-a-kind service.

"Ashlyn, I presume?" A tall, elegant woman wearing a pink, Jackie O–style suit answered the door. I almost had to laugh at her overly theatrical presence. It was as if she'd been hired to play the part of a self-important prim and proper wife of a well-known political figure. And she certainly looked the part with her perfectly coiffed, bobbed hairdo.

I forced myself to keep a straight face. "Yes, that would be me."

"Please, come in," she said pleasantly, holding the door open so that I could enter. "Can I offer you some tea or coffee?"

My eyes darted back and forth, searching for a hidden camera. This had to be a joke. One of those *Candid Camera*–type TV shows. Did women like this really still exist after 1962? I mean, I'd seen my share of housewives before, but this was almost too much. I felt like I had just walked into Stepford, Connecticut. Although after reading the book and seeing *both* films, I knew that the Stepford wives *never* would have hired a fidelity inspector. It would be against their better programming.

"No, I'm fine. Thanks."

"How about a muffin? I just baked them."

I stifled a laugh. "No, thank you."

"All right then," she said softly. "Let's take a seat in the living room, shall we?"

I followed her petite frame as we walked through the immaculate house and into the adjoining living room. It was an eerie place. Empty and lifeless. Almost as if no one even lived there. Where were all the photographs? Cat hair? Dirty socks and toys that the kids forgot to put away. Not even a single vacuum mark on the carpet.

"It's a beautiful house," I remarked, hoping her response would offer me a much desired clue about its mysterious perfection.

"Thank you," she replied without looking back. "We really like it here."

No such luck.

"How long have you lived here?" I inquired. *Two weeks? Two hours? We haven't actually moved in yet?*

"About three years," she said mechanically, almost as if she were reading from a script.

She motioned for me to take a seat on the couch and then took the seat across from me, keeping her legs tightly together and her hands folded properly in her lap.

She smiled amicably at me and I did my best to return the smile. This woman did not strike me as someone who was about to hire a fidelity inspector. But then again, you just never know these days. People are weird. Married people are weirder.

"I'm terribly worried about my husband," she began, with little emotion in her voice. "We've been married for ten years and we've always been happy. But lately I've sensed a change in him. He's become distant. Far away. In his own world. We don't even make love anymore."

I swallowed down another inappropriate giggle and bit my lip to hide my expression. I knew this woman's predicament was no laughing matter. No client who hires me is ever in the mood for comedy, and I would certainly lose all credibility if I were to suddenly break out in a laughing fit as a client was explaining her marital concerns to me. But this one was difficult.

I silently scolded myself for being so insensitive and prudently chalked it up to the unusual amount of stress I had been under lately. "Well, I can certainly understand your concern."

"I was told by a friend of mine that you conduct something called a 'fidelity inspection.' Can you explain that to me?"

I went into my usual explanation of the test: the popular locations that people choose, my fees, the expenses, etc. Mrs. Miller listened intently, very interested in the details.

"So there is no actual intercourse, then?"

"No," I confirmed. "It's an intention-based business only."

"And do you make exceptions to that rule?" she asked, almost eagerly.

The question caught me off guard. Especially coming from her. No woman had ever actually *wanted* me to go through with sleeping with her husband. They were all perfectly satisfied with stopping at "intention."

I cleared my throat. "No," I said, not really sure what else I could say to that.

"Oh, all right," she replied. "I just thought I'd ask. I would really like to know for sure if my husband would cheat on me."

I forced a smile. "I understand, Mrs. Miller. But it's extremely safe to assume that with the intimate level of my inspection there leaves very little room for doubt."

She nodded. "Yes. Yes, of course. Well, I'd like to take care of this right away. I'll pay you extra if you'll conduct the test tomorrow night."

And suddenly I thought of Jamie for the first time since leaving Raymond Jacobs's office. Tomorrow night was our second date. And I couldn't think of any better reason to turn this offer down. "I'm sorry, Mrs. Miller. But I have prior engagements tomorrow."

"Monday night, then?" she asked hastily. This woman certainly was anxious to get this over with. "Daniel has drinks scheduled at the W that night; it's perfect timing."

I hesitated. I normally like to have at least a week between the initial meeting and the assignment. "Well . . ." I began.

"I'll triple your fee," she offered.

I looked at her strangely. What was up with this woman? She was clearly one sandwich short of a picnic basket, and in serious need of a firm dose of present-day reality. But still I felt a strong desire to take her offer. I probably could use the extra money. After my previous meeting I wasn't sure how much longer I'd be in business.

I agreed.

"Excellent," she said. "He'll be having drinks with business associates, but he almost always stays afterward for another drink. It's his way of unwinding and processing all the details of his meeting before coming home."

I jotted the information down in my notebook. "Okay. I'll just need to borrow a picture of Mr. Miller."

"Of course," she replied, standing and walking over to a small end table next to the couch. She delicately opened the drawer and removed a wallet-sized photograph from inside. As I watched her I couldn't help but notice that it was the only thing in the drawer. It was completely empty; not one other item was inside. I stared at the open drawer curiously until she closed it and handed me the picture.

The man in the photograph looked vaguely familiar, although I was fairly certain I had never met him.

"Is something wrong?"

I shook my head. "No, no. Your husband just looks like someone I know."

She smiled, as if she'd heard that many times. "Ah."

"And what does Mr. Miller do for a living?"

Mrs. Miller seemed to fidget slightly in her seat, as if the question made her uncomfortable. I found it terribly out of character for her impenetrable facade.

"Well, actually," she began, tugging gently at her earlobe, which also seemed out of character. As if this of all questions had been the one that made her nervous. "My husband is between jobs right now."

I nodded and made a note in my book.

"He was just laid off from his previous company and he's searching for new work. I believe that's what his Monday night meeting is about."

"Understood," I said as I continued writing.

"But don't bring that up!" she practically shouted.

Her unexpected outburst caused my hand to jerk upright, leaving an unsightly black line across the open page of my notebook. "Okay," I answered warily. "That's fine."

This woman was a freak. So seemingly concerned about hurting her husband's jobless feelings that she had decided to hire a fidelity inspector? Not exactly the best timing on her part, was it?

I went over all the final details with Mrs. Miller, and then finally arrived at the part about the expenses retainer that I require for all of my assignments.

She nodded pleasantly as she stood up and walked over to a dark wooden secretary in the corner of the room. From another empty drawer she pulled out a large white envelope from which she produced a thick stack of one-hundred-dollar bills. "I assume cash is fine?" she asked, counting out the correct number of bills.

I felt my eyes scrunch up in stunned bewilderment as I watched her from across the room.

She looked over to me. "Is it?"

I nodded, unable to speak. This woman had just offered to pay me *triple* my fee, and on top of that she was paying me in cash! Cash that came out of an otherwise empty drawer in the middle of an otherwise empty house.

I only offered two payment options for my services: cash or a check made out to "cash." Most clients chose the safer, cleaner, less drug dealer–like method of payment. But judging by the amount of money that was still left in the envelope after she removed my portion, this woman had clearly been prepared to pay me more than three times what I normally charge. Who keeps that much cash lying around?

I was starting to wonder if this so-called job of his that I wasn't supposed to mention happened to involve taking off articles of clothing or smuggling illegal immigrants into the country.

As I held the money in my hand, something about it felt almost dirty and immoral. Like I had just been paid off for knowing and *keeping* a very destructive secret. And I didn't like it.

I tried to shake the feeling, convincing myself that Sarah Miller, given her obvious peculiarity, simply felt more comfortable paying me in cash, and I had to respect that.

But as I gathered my things a few minutes later, I felt extremely relieved to finally be leaving the twisted Stepfordville/Twilight Zone home of Sarah and Daniel Miller. I got into my car and leaned my head back against the headrest. I was grateful that my long day was officially over. But as I drove down the winding canyon road, back toward the familiar, straight-lined streets of Westside Los Angeles, I knew that my day might have been over but my problems were far from resolved.

I didn't drive home. I couldn't stand the thought of entering that empty house all alone and coming face-to-face with the judgmental silence. There was only one person I wanted to see right now.

Sophie answered the door wearing her lounging jeans and a T-shirt. "Hey, honey. What a nice surprise." And then after seeing the distressed look on my face, she asked me what was wrong.

"How long have you got?" I asked, suddenly very thankful that my best friend was now in the know. Because for the first time in my life, I could actually talk about everything I'd never been able to talk about before.

She shrugged and looked at the clock. "However long you want."

I stepped inside, dropped my stuff on the coffee table, and fell onto the couch with an exasperated sigh. "Good. 'Cause it's finally my turn for a session. And I don't think you're going to find this problem in any textbook."

20

leaving . . . and a few jet planes

"Oh my God!" Sophie sat motionless on the couch after I had relayed to her the horrid details of my visit to Raymond Jacobs's office today.

"Well, what did you say?" she asked, her eyes wide, as if she were watching the season finale of *24*. Although given the recent drama in my life, I didn't feel far from it.

I looked down at the floor where Sophie's cat, Pollo, was playing with a string attached to a stick. "I didn't know what to say. I was speechless. Sophie, he knows who my mother is, he knows where she lives, what she does. If I don't do what he asks, he'll make sure she finds out about . . ." I paused and gulped, barely able to stand the thought of it. "All of it," I finished softly.

"So, you didn't do it," she confirmed apprehensively.

"No! Of course not." I took a deep breath. "At least not yet."

"Jen!"

"What? What else am I supposed to do?"

"And he gave you a deadline or something?"

I stared straight ahead of me, a defeated look on my face. "Sort of. He told me to take some time to think about it." I shivered. "The whole thing is just so creepy."

"Is he going to take down the Web site while you're 'thinking about it'?"

I shook my head. "I don't think so."

"Well, when do you have to decide by?"

"Two weeks." I closed my eyes.

"And then what? You self-destruct?" Sophie attempted a joke.

"Then I guess I need a bigger boat," I said, referring to Richard Dreyfus's line when he first saw the shark in *Jaws.*

Sophie nodded her agreement.

"But I have to resolve this sooner than that or someone is going to see it. Someone is going to find out. And I'm afraid it might be Jamie. Or worse . . . my mother! If he knows where she lives, I'm sure he'll have no trouble getting his little minions to track down her e-mail address."

"Your mom has e-mail?"

"She's learning," I explained. "Ever since the divorce she's been on some kind of mission to become more techno-savvy."

"Wow, my mom can barely turn on the DVD player."

I sighed and dropped my head in my hands. "This is hopeless!"

"Shhh," Sophie cooed as she rubbed my back. "It'll be fine. We'll figure something out."

Despite the grim outlook of my current situation, I quietly remarked to myself how nice it was to have Sophie in the loop about everything. I had missed her natural ability to comfort me.

"What if," Sophie began thoughtfully, "you just *told* your mother?"

I picked my head up and looked at her as if she were crazy.

"That way," she continued, ignoring my skepticism, "it wouldn't matter what e-mail she got, or who managed to sneak notes into her mailbox. She'd already know."

"I don't think so." I shook my head.

"Just think about it," Sophie went on. "You didn't want *me* to find out, right? You probably would have gone through just as much agony figuring out a way to keep me in the dark. And now that I know, it's totally fine. And aren't you relieved?"

I considered. "Yeah, but . . ."

"Maybe it'll work the same way with your mom. Maybe if you just—"

"No," I interrupted, attempting to chase the disturbing thought from my mind *and* Sophie's lips. "She's finally started to get over the divorce and get back to normal . . . after *three* years. And then to find out that her daughter is breaking up marriages all over the country? She'll never see it clearly. She can't see anything clearly right now."

Sophie nodded, silently forfeiting her argument. "Okay, well, most people don't even *open* random e-mail forwards anyway. I know I don't. I usually just delete them right away out of sheer annoyance."

"Are you kidding? My mom *lives* for e-mail forwards. She'll take e-mails any way she can get them. She even subscribes to those stupid retail newsletters just so she can hear the AOL man tell her she has mail."

I leaned down and picked up the cat's toy stick from the floor. I waved it through the air, causing the attached string to dance spastically around my feet. Pollo batted it curiously with his paw. "Not to mention, I'll soon be out of a job if that thing continues to circle the globe."

Sophie leaned back against the couch. "Well, I could say the thing that both of us are refusing to say, or I can just shut up and let you contemplate it yourself."

I sat back up and looked at her. "Which is what?"

"Quit."

And there it was, dangling in front of me just like the string tied to the stick, just begging to be batted around in my head. The word I had been refusing to acknowledge for almost a month now. "Quit."

Quit, quit, quit.

Start over. Leave it all behind. I'd thought about it casually on rare occasions, as someone offhandedly talks about wanting to write a novel or take up ballroom dancing. Everybody close to them *knows* they'll never actually go through with it, just as I'd always known I was nowhere near quitting.

Until now.

"What would I do?" I asked softly.

Sophie's eyes widened as she looked at me. She couldn't believe I was actually taking the suggestion seriously. "Well," she said, after seeing the true pain of my dilemma settling into my face, "how much money do you have saved up?"

I shrugged. "Some. Maybe enough to get me by for a few months. But I wouldn't be able to stay in my condo. I'd have to move."

Sophie nodded. "Yeah, probably."

"Besides, I don't even know what I would *want* to do. I don't even know who I am without this job. It's been my life for two years now. And it's made me a completely different person. I wouldn't even know where to start. It's not like there's a guidebook out there: *Career Options for Former Fidelity Inspectors: Find the One That's Right for You.*"

Sophie chuckled. "You could always go back to investment banking."

"Yeah, wouldn't that tie up a lot of loose ends."

"Well, if you do quit," she began lightly, "just make sure you complete my assignment first!"

I laughed . . . even though I felt like crying. "Right." I stood up and gazed desolately in the direction of the front door. "Well, I guess I'll go home and try to get some sleep."

"Okay."

I reached out and pulled Sophie into my arms, squeezing her tightly. "Thanks," I whispered in her ear.

She pulled back and looked at me. "For what? I didn't even do anything."

"No, you did," I assured her. "Trust me."

The next night Jamie Richards arrived at my front door. I half expected him to call me again so I could meet him downstairs like I did last time. I hadn't exactly had time to think about whether or not I was ready to let him into my house yet. But apparently I didn't have a choice. It's not like I could crack the door open, stick out my head, and say, "Hold on a sec, I'll be right out," and then slam it in his face while I finished gathering up my stuff.

I hid my reluctance with a warm smile and swung the door open for him. "Hi. Come on in." The words practically caught in my throat.

He gave me a quick kiss on the cheek and told me that I looked beautiful.

I thanked him, as I once again felt my cheeks flush.

"So this is your place?" he asked, stepping inside and surveying the living room. He gave an appreciative nod. "Not bad. You've done well for yourself. It's very . . . white."

I let out a nervous giggle. "Yeah, I . . . um . . . like white."

"I think the PC term is 'Decorationally Colorless.' "

"Hey, I'll be just a second. Um . . ." I could feel a panic bubble rise up in my throat, but I managed to get out, "Make yourself at home."

I ducked into my bedroom and picked out a white Chanel knitted clutch from my closet. I took one last look in the bathroom mirror. I had put together an outfit consisting of a black A-line skirt that ended right above the knee and a fitted three-quarter-sleeve boat-neck shirt with horizontal black and white stripes. My hair was up in a tight ponytail, and I had selected a pair of small silver hoop earrings. Finally, I had matched up the entire ensemble with my black Michael Kors pumps that had dull silver hardware and a rounded toe. I had to admit, for someone who generally found it difficult to dress herself, I was rather proud of my selections.

Upon returning to the living room, I found Jamie meandering around, casually observing his surroundings. I watched him closely from the hallway as his eyes surveyed the small details of my living room. He walked to the TV and nodded approvingly. Then he made his way to the dining room and ran his fingertips across the tops of the wood chairs. At first watching him made me extremely nervous. I felt the sudden desire to remove him immediately from my room, to make this uneasiness subside in any way I could. But it wasn't until he stopped at the fireplace in the living room and paid particular attention to the framed photographs lining the mantel that I felt something else.

An entirely new and unfamiliar feeling.

I noticed a smile appear across his lips as he studied the photograph of me and my mom taken on a cruise a few years back, and then the picture of me, Sophie, Zoë, and John, taken at Jayes Martini Lounge. And that's when I realized:

Jamie was the first man to enter this house (besides John). I had obviously never brought any clients back here. And since I hadn't been on a real date in years, there had been no other man *to* bring back here.

Jamie was the first.

And suddenly, watching him inside my home, observing my life, it somehow no longer felt nerve-racking.

It felt . . . right.

It was a feeling I'd never quite experienced before. A pang of some sort. Warm and peaceful yet completely terrifying all at the same time.

And it didn't disappear the moment we stepped out the front door.

It didn't even disappear after we drove away in Jamie's car and turned onto Wilshire Boulevard.

In fact, that pang inside me, that small twinge of something unknown, it kept growing. Stronger and stronger. On the way to dinner, while sitting in the gourmet French restaurant he insisted on taking me to in order to prove that he doesn't only eat hot dogs and Coke for dinner, and by the time our dessert was delivered I wasn't sure what the hell was going on inside me. It felt like someone had unleashed a flock of hummingbirds inside my stomach and they wouldn't stop buzzing around.

Thirty minutes later Jamie and I lay on the front hood of his car outside of the Santa Monica Airport and watched small jets and propeller planes land on the runway in front of us.

His hand was firmly wrapped around mine and his leg was resting so close to mine that every time one of us moved, even the slightest bit, our legs would touch. There was a faint chill in the air, but I could hardly feel it. I felt warmer than ever.

"So, airplanes, huh?" I asked him with amusement.

"I figured it could be kind of like a theme for us," Jamie replied, squeezing my hand.

I smiled at the sky. "Makes sense."

"Tell me about your job," he said, turning to face me.

I continued to stare straight up into the sky. I couldn't look at him. Not when answering a question like this. Not when I was about to lie to someone I suddenly felt the strongest desire to never lie to.

I wanted desperately to tell him the truth. To be as honest with him as I just *knew* he had been with me from the moment we met. I wanted to tell him about everything. Raymond Jacobs and his atrocious blackmail, Andrew Thompson and his weakness for beer-guzzling flight attendants, Parker Colman and his attempted "intervention" in the elevator, Sarah Miller and her robot facade, even Sophie—my best friend and her unthinkable request—all the way back to Miranda Keyton, my first, accidental, inspection.

Something about him, something about lying next to him, holding his hand, and watching private jets zoom over our heads, made it impossible to lie to him.

Well, nearly impossible.

"What do you want to know?" I asked casually.

"Well, you told me you're an investment banker. What kind of deals do you work on?"

I shrugged. "All kinds."

"Too much detail. Stop! I've heard enough."

I laughed. "You know, mergers and acquisitions, hostile takeovers, private equity, risk management."

"Wow, you're quite the Jill of all trades."

"Uh-huh," I said, eager to change the subject. "What about you? Tell me more about your job."

I wanted nothing more than to just be myself, and I felt an unbearable frustration in knowing that I couldn't.

Jamie gave me a puzzled look, most likely sensing my uneasiness, and I'm sure it confused the hell out of him. *Why doesn't this girl like to talk about her job? What's her problem?* But fortunately he didn't press the issue.

"Companies hire us to help them develop marketing strategies, redesign logos, research new ways of reaching out to customers. That kind of stuff."

I turned and smiled at him. "That sounds interesting."

He nodded. "It is . . . most of the time."

We sat in silence for a moment as a loud plane passed overhead. "Think they sat here on a Palm Springs runway for four hours before landing?" I asked, looking at the sky.

He nodded. "No way. That runway's reserved for us."

I smiled. "Have you ever heard of an airplane bag?"

"You mean like the one they give you onboard to throw up in?"

I laughed and playfully slapped his leg with the back of my hand. "No! Like a bag with lots of stuff in it. You know, stuff for airplanes."

Jamie turned his head. "Airplane stuff?" he asked with a puzzled look on his face.

"Yeah, like food and Mad Libs and playing cards, Silly Putty. Stuff like that. I used to make them for me and my parents before we'd go on trips. I always had the best time picking out the contents. As soon as my parents announced a vacation, I would start planning each person's airplane bag."

"Oh, so they were personalized?"

I nodded proudly. "Of course. I was no amateur bag maker. I was like the master airplane bag maker."

"Is it weird that I've been thinking about you?" he asked after a beat.

I couldn't help but smile. "Well, that depends on *how* you've been thinking about me. If it was like, me riding an elephant through the desert with a clown and a cheerleader . . . then yeah, maybe that'd be weird."

Jamie jokingly nodded his agreement, and then his expression turned serious again. "No, I mean . . . a lot. I've been thinking about you a lot."

I looked into his eyes as I tried to reciprocate the sweet sentiment. I tried so hard to open my mouth and tell him I had thought about him, too. But with that would come so many other truths. Like, "I thought about you because I don't want you to know what I do." "I thought about you because I'm deathly afraid that you'll find out and never want to see me again." And of course the new one: "I thought about you because every two minutes I think about leaving it all behind . . . the job, the money, the cheaters, the quest, the skepticism . . . all of it . . . for you."

But all I managed to say was, "No, it's not weird."

And it wasn't weird. It was exactly what I wanted to hear. And at the same time, exactly what I didn't want to hear. How much easier would my life be if Jamie didn't even exist? If I hadn't met him? Or if he simply had decided that there could be no future with a girl who ate all the Apple Jacks?

He leaned in and kissed me. It was just as amazing as I remembered. Maybe even more. The sound of his radio playing from the open convertible mixed with the sound of the next jet plane a few miles out. It felt like we were kissing forever, yet when it was over, I only wanted more.

"I thought about you, too," I heard myself say as he pulled away and laid his head back down on the hood of the car. I didn't know where it came from or if anything remotely like it would ever come out again. But it felt good to say it, regardless.

He looked at me and smiled. Then he kissed me again. This time he pressed his body close to mine, and I felt as though the incredible warmth radiating off of it and passing effortlessly through his clothes could melt me in an instant.

There were no stars out that night, not that there ever are in this city. Too much smog, too many bright lights. But for some reason, tonight, I didn't really miss them.

At the end of the night, Jamie walked me back to my front door.

"Thanks for hanging out with me again tonight," he said softly, brushing his lips against mine.

I closed my eyes and allowed the numbness to invade my entire body once again.

"I like you," he whispered as he pulled his face away just enough to look into my eyes.

I swallowed hard. "You shouldn't," I heard myself say softly aloud. I had hoped the thought was only in my head, but evidently it had escaped.

"And why is that?" he asked, delicately kissing my neck.

Because I'm not who you think I am, I thought. *Because I'm a fraud.*

Thankfully those thoughts stayed in my head.

And then I said the only thing I could think of, the only thing that came to mind. "Do you want to come in?"

I saw him hesitate, and out of sheer panic I added, "Like for a drink or something." It was funny. I suddenly realized I never say the words "Do you want to come in?" On all my assignments I make it a strict rule that the subject has to initiate. He has to invite. I only follow. I don't lead.

And now I was on the other end. Dying for him to come inside. No longer nervous or apprehensive about letting him walk into my house, into my life, but instead wanting nothing more than to entrap him inside and never let him leave.

"I don't think I should," he said, almost pained. As if he obviously wanted to but something was holding him back. "Unless you have some Macallan twenty-five-year-old Scotch."

I laughed, relieved that he had made a joke and successfully managed to cover up his blatant rejection of me.

"Do you honestly think a twenty-eight-year-old girl would have aged Scotch in her apartment?"

"Ah! So *that's* how old you are," Jamie said with a bright smile that lit up his whole face. "You're way too young for me."

"I know," I said playfully. "I'm practically paying your social security."

"Ooh, that's hot." He kissed me again, and then buried his head in my neck.

I reached around and rested my hand on the back of his head. His dark brown hair felt soft on my skin as I gently ran my fingers through it.

Was he going to say anything else? Or was he just going to leave it at "I don't think I should"? Obviously a response like that warranted an explanation. But I didn't want to bring it up again. Why should I? I was the one who just got rejected, a feeling I certainly wasn't all that familiar with. And not sure I liked very much.

He pulled his head up. "I really like you, Jen. I just think we should take this slow."

Slow? I repeated the word in my head, although I hadn't the faintest idea what it meant. When had any guy ever wanted to take things slow? In my world, men had sex (or thought they would have sex) after two hours of flirting . . . maybe three. Some of them only waited thirty minutes. My version of taking things slow was making out for twenty minutes before he tries to remove my pants.

But I knew that my world was far from the norm. So I said, "Yeah, that sounds like a good idea."

Jamie nodded and smiled, seemingly relieved. "I don't want to rush into anything. And honestly?" He touched my face again. "Not to sound presumptuous, but I kind of have the feeling that I might be around awhile."

I couldn't resist a girlish grin. "Really?" I asked him, amused. "Is that what you think?"

Jamie raised his eyebrows. "Yes." He kissed me on the lips again. "I'm going to New York for business next week, but I want to see you as soon as I get back."

I shrugged my shoulders callously. "I don't know. I'm getting pretty bored of you."

Jamie's eyes pleaded with me.

"Fine. What night?"

He pretended to search his pockets. "Damn, I forgot my Palm Pilot. I'm gonna have to get back to you on that one."

I laughed and pushed him in the direction of the elevator as I started to fish through my bag for my house keys. "Get out of here."

"I'll consult my secretary and have my people call your people," he said, stumbling across the hallway. "You do have people, don't you?"

I put my key in the lock. "Yeah, sure. We'll do lunch."

Jamie ran back over for one final kiss before I stepped inside. "Bye," he said as he watched my face disappear behind the slowly closing door.

Once I was on the inside, I silently leaned my forehead against the back of the door. *This is insane,* I thought. Nobody is supposed to fall this fast. *I'm* not supposed to fall at all. Especially when it's become my job to remain unattached—no matter what.

I couldn't understand what was happening to me. I couldn't understand why I was feeling things I swore I would never feel. That I *promised* myself I would never feel.

Because I had become so certain that there was no point in feeling them.

God, was I ever wrong.

21

celebrity status

I'd had little time to prepare for tonight's assignment.

And the only reason I'd had little time to prepare was because Sarah Miller had *given* me little time to prepare when she insisted that this inspection take place tonight, a mere three days after our initial meeting. The fast-track approach was extremely unorthodox in my line of work, and I didn't really like the ad hoc feeling of it all. Given that I knew very little about Daniel Miller, I opted for a fairly generic wardrobe selection. A pair of black dress pants with a tan sleeveless turtleneck sweater and my red backless Manolo mules. One of the biggest mistakes you can make is to overdress. Since this inspection would take place at a regular, upscale bar in Westwood, I had to look the part. Showing up in this bar wearing an over-the-top designer dress that drew the attention of every man and woman in the place would not do the trick. Then I would just come off looking like a gold digger, hitting on older men who appear to have money. It was the last image I wanted to put forth. Men don't want to cheat with gold diggers because they're not trustworthy. Well, most men anyway. Raymond Jacobs would probably cheat with anything with two legs and a pair of boobs, the disgusting, classless asshole.

I checked my reflection in the mirror and decided that the ensemble was perfect for the occasion. Sexy enough to draw attention but classy enough to make it look like that's not all I was after. Tonight the key was to be just another girl in a bar. Not looking for anything in particular. But also not ruling anything out.

I hurried into my office while I attempted to put my second diamond-stud earring into my ear. The folder labeled *Daniel Miller* was sitting on my desk. I had put together a few pages of his biography based on some of the information shared by his wife, but I hadn't had time to do a lot of additional research. And the fact that my Google search for Daniel Miller had yielded 261,000 results and more than four thousand images, none of the first two hundred of which even remotely resembled the photograph that Sarah Miller had given me, didn't help much, either. This was going to require some serious mind-reading, superpower "wingage." I flipped through the pages casually, reminding myself of some of the smaller details, and then retrieved the key hidden in my office closet to open the bottom locked drawer of my desk. I pulled out one of my black business cards, running my fingertips over the slightly raised surface of the crimson *A* on the front. Then I flipped the card over and studied the toll-free number on the back. The number that Daniel Miller would call at the end of the night should he *choose* to fail his inspection. The same number that everyone calls.

And yet every time I pull one of these identical black business cards out of my locked bottom drawer, I silently pray that I won't have to use it.

Every time I place that card in my bag at the beginning of the night, I fantasize about ceremoniously tossing it into a nearby trash can on the way out of the bar or the hotel, or wherever I have just been rejected.

Sadly, though, those cards, more often than not, end up in someone else's hands by the end of the night . . . and not in my fantasy trash can.

I dashed into the living room and stuffed my red Louis Vuitton leather pochette with all the necessary items: keys, credit card, cash, ID, phones, failed fidelity inspection card. Then I was out the door.

When I arrived at the bar I spotted Daniel Miller in a back booth, nursing a drink and gazing off into space. His half-empty glass on the tabletop was clenched tightly in his hands. He looked concerned, lonely, contemplative. The glass itself was not quite as lonely as the man holding it, however. Surrounding it were several other empty glasses, once belonging to Mr. Miller's former company.

To anyone else it might have looked like he'd recently said something offensive, causing everyone at the table to abruptly depart, leaving him there alone. But to me it looked just as Mrs. Miller had described it. *He most always stays afterward for another drink.* The business associates she mentioned appeared to have already left, and from the look on his face, the meeting hadn't gone quite as well as he had hoped. I remembered what she'd said about his recent layoff and made a mental note not to bring up the topic of employment.

I walked in the direction of his table, exuding confidence, my failed-inspection card burning a hole in my Louis Vuitton handbag. All I had to do was get him to ask me upstairs. According to his wife, it wasn't unusual for him to drink too much and just rent a room here in the W Hotel instead of making that long, dangerous drive through the canyon.

Overdrinking husband and frequent hotel stays in the same city he inhabits? No wonder she hired me. That would sound fishy to anyone.

Walking into an assignment location is a lot like walking onto a brightly lit stage. Poised and ready to perform in a play in which the main character's name is Ashlyn. But to the outsider, and soon to Daniel Miller as well, Ashlyn would not be a character in a play. She would be real. Just another girl in a bar.

I took a deep breath, reminded myself of the exact role I was to play tonight, and stepped onto the stage, walking slowly as I passed Daniel's table in my usual attempt to capture the attention of my chosen audience.

But tonight my audience was distracted. And despite my slow, purposeful stride and my carefully selected outfit, Daniel Miller barely even blinked as I walked by.

So I stopped about a foot in front of his table and looked down into my purse, feeling the sudden urge to check for something that might be missing, and as a result, buying more time in front of my distracted audience. And after verifying that everything seemed to be in place I continued walking. Daniel Miller, however, still did not look up.

That's when I knew that I had to pull a shameless maneuver, one that I rarely ever have to resort to. But I conceded that tonight would just have to be one of those rare times. After all, it's not like I could go back to my car, change into a miniskirt, and walk by his table again, hoping his preference for legs would cause him to finally turn his head.

No, I would have to trip.

So I did.

And not surprisingly, I fell right into the man sitting alone in the back booth. And he caught me.

"Oh!" I exclaimed as I used the top of the booth to steady myself. "I'm so sorry!"

"Are you all right?" the man asked, helping me regain my balance.

"Yes," I replied, obviously embarrassed at the incident. "Thank you." Then I pointed down at my shoes. "They're new."

Daniel nodded his understanding and laughed politely. "It's no problem at all."

I was *just* about to walk away when suddenly a small trace of recognition happened to wash over my face. "Hey . . . haven't I seen you down at the marina?" I asked.

Reference: Section 2a of the Daniel Miller biography. He has a boat docked at the marina.

Daniel's distressed mood seemed to change slightly with the mention of the marina, and his lips curled into a humble smile. If he didn't know any better, he might have thought that this beautiful young stranger somehow knew *exactly* what would cheer him up and get his mind off of less fortunate things.

But that, of course, would be impossible.

"Probably," he replied. "I'm there a lot. I have a boat docked there."

I scrunched up my forehead and bit my perfectly glossed, bottom lip as if attempting to solve a very difficult logic problem, when suddenly the name of a sailboat hit me. As if it had been swirling around in the back of my foggy memory and I was just able to grasp it as it flew by. "*The Five Winds,*" I said, nodding my head proudly.

Reference: Section 2b of the Daniel Miller biography. His boat's name is The Five Winds.

These words cheered him up even more. "Yes! You know my boat?"

I smiled brightly. "Oh, of course! It's one of the nicest boats down there, a 2000 Morgan Classic sloop, forty-one feet with a thirteen-foot, ten-inch beam, cutaway forefront, fin keel, skeg-hung rudder. I bet that thing can be sailed at 35 degrees off the wind."

Reference: Page 3 of the 2000 Morgan Classic sloop electronic sales brochure available on most sailboat Web sites.

Daniel nodded, thoroughly impressed. "Wow, you certainly know your sailboats."

I shrugged modestly. "My dad taught me all about boats. I go down to the marina a lot with my family. I knew you looked familiar."

He stretched out his hand. "I'm Daniel."

I shook it eagerly. "Ashlyn."

"Nice to meet you,"

"Thanks. You, too," I said, standing awkwardly and glancing off in the direction of the bar, apparently wondering if I should go up and order myself a drink or continue standing there, talking about boats.

At this point I had to make it appear that I truly *wanted* him to ask me to sit down but that I was too much of a lady to ask myself. So I decided to look bored.

And to my surprise, he did, too.

Daniel checked his watch. "Well, I better be getting home. It's late and I have quite a drive in front of me." He scooted out to the end of the booth and offered me his hand again. "It was nice meeting you, Amy."

"Ashlyn," I corrected as I stood quite dumbfounded in front of him and slowly shook his hand.

"Right, sorry. Well, maybe I'll see you down at the docks," he said, pulling a large bill out of his wallet and dropping it on the table.

"Yeah, maybe you will," I replied softly.

I stood speechless at the back of the bar as my eyes followed Daniel Miller making his way toward the archway that led into the main hotel lobby. As soon as he disappeared from sight, I followed a safe distance behind and watched him with great curiosity, like an animal researcher who has just witnessed a dolphin walking on dry land. He exited out the front door of the hotel and never came back.

He was really gone.

He had actually *left*.

To everyone else in the bar it probably looked as though I had just bumped into a celebrity, and like any star-struck American obsessively continued to stare at him as he walked out. In fact, upon following my unwavering gaze, some of the other bar clientele turned curiously and watched Daniel leave as well, wondering why they hadn't recognized him as someone famous when he walked in.

But I knew quite well that Daniel Miller was nobody famous. You wouldn't see him on the front page of *Us Weekly* magazine, or even on some random page in the middle. You wouldn't catch a thirty-second blurb about him on the next edition of *Access Hollywood,* and you certainly wouldn't hear him plugging his latest album or blockbuster movie on one of L.A.'s top radio stations.

But after tonight, Daniel Miller would now and forever be a celebrity in *my* mind.

When I got home the first thing I did was run to my nightstand. And when I say "run," I mean it. I literally threw my bag down on the sofa and raced across the living room and into the bedroom like a child running outside to catch the ice cream truck. I knelt down beside my nightstand, and with the same anticipation and excitement normally reserved for Christmas morning, I opened the bottom drawer and removed the box.

I held it in my hands, stroking the soft wood with my fingertips.

This was my timeless moment. The equivalent of hearing the song that's been stuck in your head all day suddenly come on the radio, your favorite food listed on the specials board of a restaurant, the accomplishment of fitting the last puzzle piece, the exhilaration of the first kiss, the smell and touch of hot laundry, fresh from the dryer, the quiet peacefulness of three A.M. . . . all wrapped up into this one little, seemingly insignificant box.

The only thing I held sacred.

I removed the key from the velvet lining in the drawer and turned the lock.

This time, I didn't just look. Because this time would be one of those rare moments when I would actually be able to do more than look.

When I would be able to contribute.

I reached inside the box and pulled out a small piece of paper and a black fountain pen.

This was my list.

It had exactly nine names on it. I read them aloud slowly one by one as I ran my fingertips over each. And then I rested the piece of paper against the top of the box, pulled the cap off the pen, and delicately wrote the name Daniel Miller at the bottom of the list.

Daniel was my number 10.

The tenth reason to believe that love is possible, despite everything else that goes on in the world.

Despite the thousands upon thousands of reasons not to.

And I had a feeling . . . it was exactly what I needed right now.

The pen had cost me five hundred dollars. I bought it in one of those fancy stores that sells pens to business executives who would later gift them to special clients and employees. I had never in a million years thought I would ever spend five hundred dollars on a pen. Or even step into a store like that. But I felt that it was appropriate, given the nature of this ceremony.

Needless to say, there was still a lot of ink left in it.

After taking a few moments to bask in the initial glory of the newest name that would now run through my head at least five times a day during my internal battle of good versus evil, I strolled back into the living room, giddy as a lovesick schoolgirl, and picked up my bag from the sofa where I had hastily flung it on my way in. I fished out my *unused* black inspection card and stared at it. If I *were* a lovesick schoolgirl, then this would be the forbidden love letter passed to me during second period.

I opened the trash compactor in the kitchen, took one last glance at the card, and silently ripped it into as many pieces as I physically could. And then I watched them fall gracefully into the garbage, like a rainstorm of broken doubt.

And in slow motion they came to rest on top of an empty cereal box and a banana peel.

Exactly where they belonged.

I slid the trash compactor closed and flipped the switch. It came to life with a soft hum as it started on its only quest in life—to compress all trash into one unrecognizable lump of waste.

I returned to my bedroom and changed out of my work attire and into the comfort of my Victoria's Secret pink silky pajamas. I liked the way they felt on my skin. And deep down inside, beneath the fear, beneath the anxiety, beneath all the other garbage I had compacted over the years, I suddenly felt very good about the world around me.

22

do over

In my adult life I could only recall a handful of times when I would actually go as far as to define my current state as one of "exhilaration." For me, that kind of euphoria was usually observed in others and not normally experienced firsthand.

This morning was one of those rare moments when I was . . . dare I say it . . . happy.

Daniel Miller was my first "pass" in over two months, and that was cause for celebration. Well, not a *real* celebration. Like with champagne and those little paper coil things that expand when you blow into them. A little personal celebration, in my head.

I poured myself a large bowl of Honey Nut Cheerios and plopped down on the couch to enjoy my carb-o-licious breakfast. As I crunched on a spoonful of honey-sweetened Os, my feet on the coffee table, the bright, warm sunshine seeping in through my white satin curtains, I felt like I was in a cereal commercial.

With the help of this nutritious breakfast, I was ready to take on the world.

All that was missing was the little Honey Nut Cheerios bee buzzing into my living room to graciously pour the milk into my bowl and giggle when I poked him in the stomach. Or was that the Pillsbury Doughboy? I get all of those cartoon spokespeople confused.

It was a beautiful day. And it was about to get even better. Because in only a few short hours I would be making the long, winding drive to Sarah Miller's house to deliver the good news personally. If there was anything better than a proven faithful husband, it was informing the dubious wife of the fact.

And to be honest, unfortunately, it's not news I've been able to deliver very often in the past.

Only nine times, to be exact.

And I know that doesn't sound like a lot. It may even seem downright depressing. But here's the way I see it (or at least the theory that I've invented to keep myself from jumping in front of an eighteen-wheeler on the 405): Nine men out of around two hundred is 4.5 percent. And yes, *that* is a depressing statistic. But you have to figure that the pool of two hundred men I'm dealing with is not an accurate sampling of *all* men. These are not the husbands, boyfriends, and fiancés of normal, trusting women. These are not the husbands, boyfriends, and fiancés of women in healthy, trusting relationships. These are the husbands, boyfriends, and fiancés of women with reasonable cause for suspicion. And if you give women's intuition the benefit of the doubt, then these two hundred men were pretty much doomed to fail from the start.

It's not to say that 95.5 percent of all men will cheat given the opportunity. I look at it as 95.5 percent of all women are correct when they get the "feeling" that their men are capable of adultery.

And that's why I do this. Or at least, that's how it started out. To give these women the opportunity to confirm or deny their suspicions.

But today was a different day. If there was ever a suspicion that you'd want to be wrong about, I suspect this would be it. And I was more than certain that bringing this good news to Sarah Miller, no matter how strange a person she was, would be the highlight of my week. And hopefully, the highlight of *her* century.

Not even the thought of my upcoming fidelity inspection of Sophie's fiancé could get me down right now. In fact, I don't even know why I was so reluctant to agree to it in the first place. He would obviously pass.

Friday night would be a breeze. Eric would barely even look at me twice. Why should he? He has an amazing, sexy, sweet, intelligent fiancée waiting for him at home. What the hell would he want with me?

And then a disturbing thought hit me. My chewing slowed from a crunchy chomp to a soggy, cowlike gnaw.

What if he didn't?

What if he took the bait, flirted, bought me drinks, stared at my cleavage, kissed me, unzipped the back of my dress, touched my . . .

I suddenly felt nauseous. I placed the bowl of cereal down on the coffee table with a loud *clank*.

This was the love of Sophie's life. And I was about to throw myself in front of him with a low-cut top and a face full of sultry eye makeup?

Had I lost my mind?

What kind of a friend even does something like that?

I picked up the phone and dialed Sophie's number from memory. Her number was stored in my speed dial, but somehow, punching in all the digits felt more dramatic. More proactive.

She answered after one ring. "What's up?"

"Are you sure you want to go through with this?" I kept my tone light and casual, as if this was a common courtesy call I placed to all my clients on the Tuesday before their scheduled inspection. Just part of the proper fidelity inspector protocol—make sure your clients are fully onboard before you throw yourself into the wolf's playground dressed as a sheep.

Sophie sighed loudly into the phone. It came through sounding like a muffled Darth Vader breath. "Yes, Jen. We've been over this. I *need* to know."

"I can tell you right now what you need to know." I could feel desperation seeping into my voice. I tried to filter it out. "He's going to turn me down. He's going to pass. So there's really no point in putting yourself through this."

Or me, I thought.

"Well, if you're so sure," she began sensibly, "then it should be no big deal for you to go down there and get it over with."

Damn it. She was using logic. I hate it when she does that.

"But after he passes, don't you think it will be a little weird when he finally meets me for real and suddenly realizes that his fiancée's best friend had just *happened* to be at the same bar as him before the wedding and pretended not to know who he was?"

I could almost hear Sophie's gears turning as she thought about this for a few seconds. "Well, I guess we'll just have to deal with that when the time comes, won't we? It's more important that I know the truth. And besides, you *owe* me."

"For what?" I asked insistently.

"For keeping your entire life a secret for the past two years," Sophie said matter-of-factly.

I fell silent. "Oh, that."

She laughed. "Yes, that. And now is your chance to repay me. And I must admit, the punishment fits the crime pretty damn well, don't ya think?"

I muttered some type of agreement and hung up the phone.

So much for getting out of that one.

Let's just hope I'm right and my cheater radar isn't giving off false hopes.

Later that morning I pulled into the Millers' driveway and stepped out of the car. Just as I placed my finger on the doorbell, the front door swung open. Sarah Miller stood in the entryway, smiling ear to ear with an unnatural look about her. But this time it was something I had prepared myself for.

"Fresh-baked cookies?" she offered me as I sat down on the couch.

What kind of wife offers a fresh-baked cookie to the woman who might have successfully seduced her husband into bed? True, he hadn't, but she couldn't have possibly known that for sure. Because if she had, what was I even doing here in the first place? I thought this lady had spent a little too much time in front of an open oven.

"No, thank you," I declined politely. I vowed to remain completely professional and curb my own enthusiasm about the assignment's positive outcome.

Sarah smiled and took the seat across from me. "My husband got home fairly early last night. You're quite efficient," she said with a creepy wink.

"Well, Mrs. Miller," I began, ignoring her unsettling attitude. "This is how it works." I launched into my usual preresults speech about giving her the opportunity to hear as little or as many details as she feels comfortable with.

She nodded eagerly. "Yes, yes. I understand. What happened?"

I took a deep breath. "I'm happy to inform you that your husband passed the fidelity inspection."

Wow, it sounded even better out loud than it did in my head. I watched her anxiously, anticipating the sigh of relief. The tears of joy. The deep breath that she had been waiting to exhale for nearly five days. And maybe even an appreciative hug to go with it.

But it never came.

Sarah Miller looked at me with a baffled and somewhat discouraged expression. "What do you mean, he *passed*?"

I assumed she simply didn't understand the terminology, and was fairly confident that once it was explained, I would get the response I was looking for.

"I mean," I began willingly, "your husband did not engage in any actions that would imply his propensity toward unfaithful behavior."

Her face remained a blank page, with perhaps one of those confused emoticons that people use in their instant message conversations. The one that looked like: :s. Pasted smack dab in the middle of the blank page.

"I don't understand," she said. It almost sounded like she was arguing with me. Like she was questioning my results. "How could he have *passed*?"

I wasn't quite sure how to proceed from here. I never thought that a "passed" inspection would get this kind of scrutiny. Apparently, when describing an assignment's outcome, the word *positive* is a subjective term.

"Well," I stated warily. "He, um—"

But she didn't let me finish. "You must have caught him on a bad day," she speculated accusingly.

My mouth dropped open. She couldn't possibly be serious.

"I mean, did he seem distracted?" she continued. "There has to be a reason. I'm very convinced that my husband is a cheater. I kindly ask that you retest him."

She didn't even flinch. It was as if she were standing at the counter of McDonald's simply saying, "I ordered this Quarter Pounder with *no* mustard. I kindly ask that you remake it."

"Um, Mrs. Miller," I attempted. "I don't think retesting your husband will change the results. I stand by my assessment wholeheartedly. He was clearly uninterested in any type of extramarital activity."

But she wasn't satisfied with this response. She clasped her hands tightly together in her lap, and I could have sworn I saw her knuckles go white. "Yes, well, if I recall, he came home that night very tired and preoccupied. He wasn't himself. I think, given the circumstances, a retest is in order. He'll be down at the docks on Saturday afternoon. You can bump into him there."

"But . . ." I protested.

"I'm sure he'll be more than willing to invite you onto that boat of his. You being as pretty as you are."

I couldn't believe what was happening. I bring this woman the best news you can bring a suspicious wife, and instead of being overjoyed and breaking open champagne, or running out to buy some new, sexy lingerie at

Victoria's Secret to reward her faithful husband, she simply demands a recount?

I tried to get myself out of it. "I honestly don't think that will do any good, Mrs. Miller," I said as gently as possible.

"I will pay you for a second inspection if that's what you're worried about," she said immediately. "Same fee as before." And with that she was up, off her seat, and back in front of the wooden secretary in the corner. I watched again with fascination as she counted out large bills from the same white envelope, and then walked over to me and shoved them into my hand. "For Saturday afternoon," she clarified.

I studied the equally large, second stack I was now holding. The amount was staggering. I could barely fathom what was going through this woman's head. And before I could say another word, or give it another thought, she was literally hustling me to the door.

"Well, I have tons of housework to do, so I guess I'll speak with you next week."

And that was that. The next thing I knew, I was standing outside the house, wondering what the hell had just happened inside.

"You absolutely *have* to let me come!" John gushed the moment I told him about my mysterious "do over" of Daniel Miller's inspection. We were sitting on the floor of my living room, sharing a take-out dinner from the Indian restaurant down the street while half-watching *Talk Soup.*

I suddenly wished I had chosen Zoë to vent to instead of John. "Are you insane? Of course you can't come. Why would you even want to?"

"Because I've been dying to watch one of these things ever since I saw your face on that Web site."

"Ugh," I said, taking a bite out of a piece of naan. "Don't remind me. Yesterday the link was forwarded to me in an e-mail from someone I went to *high school* with, asking if this was really me. I was mortified. I've literally become *afraid* of e-mail now. And trust me, this is not the day and age to be afraid of e-mail. Every time my Treo beeps with an incoming message, I instantly start to panic. I'm convinced that this is the one, the one that's going to break me. From my mom, or Jamie . . . or my fifth-grade teacher maybe."

"Gotta love viral marketing."

I shook my head. "Well, I guess that answers my question of whether or not I'm going to go to my ten-year high-school reunion."

John laughed. "Jennifer Hunter, voted most likely to sleep with married men for a living."

"For the last time, John, I don't *sleep* with them!"

"C'mon. Just let me come. I want to learn the biz."

"What do you think this is, Take Your Gay Friend to Work Day?"

"I'm serious!" he whined. "I love going down to the docks."

"You just like saying 'the docks.'" I licked the last of the chicken tikka masala sauce from my fork and stood up to bring the plate into the kitchen.

"Pleeeeeease." He pulled himself onto his knees in front of me and pleaded with his eyes.

I rolled my eyes at him. "Fine."

"Yes!" John jumped up and celebrated with an over-the-top victory dance in the middle of my living room.

"But you have to be inconspicuous. I can't have my cover blown. Especially since this will already seem suspicious enough . . . bumping into him for the *second* time."

He rubbed his hands together eagerly. "Oh, don't you worry, little missy. My disguise will be so good, even *you* won't recognize me."

I shot him a warning look. "John, do not go *overboard*."

He gazed at me innocently. "What? When do I ever go overboard?"

The clock hadn't moved in what felt like two hours. But that didn't stop me from staring at it.

9:13 P.M.

I silently willed it to fast-forward to midnight, like a Cinderella hopeful in reverse, knowing full well that at midnight it would all be over: the coach would turn back into a pumpkin, the dress would disintegrate into rags, and I would be once again alone, in my bedroom.

Unlike me, Cinderella actually wanted to go to the ball. She wanted it so badly that a fairy godmother magically materialized to grant her wish with the wave of a wand.

And if I knew there would be a Prince Charming waiting for me at *my* destination this evening, I would have wanted to go, too.

But tonight wasn't about Prince Charmings. Not for me, anyway. For me it was about charming somebody else's prince.

Somebody I cared dearly for and would have done anything in the world to keep her safe and happy—even this, apparently.

The clock flipped to 9:14.

Exactly fourteen minutes ago Eric Fornell, the love of Sophie's life, should have entered a local bar merely minutes from my house with a group of friends he hadn't seen since college.

In exactly forty-six minutes, Ashlyn would be, coincidentally, entering the same bar. Or at least that was the plan. Leave the house at 9:45 P.M. so I could arrive at the bar at ten o'clock, which would give me ample time to determine whether or not Eric was the cheating type and then get the hell out of there. After that I would call Sophie at midnight with the long-awaited results.

Until then she would be waiting by the phone.

Nine-fifteen P.M.

I sighed loudly and pulled my eyes away from the digital clock on my nightstand. I stood up and walked into my bathroom to start on my makeup.

"Nothing too dramatic," Sophie had instructed me yesterday. "Eric likes girls with natural beauty. But be sure to show cleavage. He's a textbook boob man. Although he'd never admit that to me, but a girl can just sense these kinds of things."

I stared at myself in the mirror and adjusted my cleavage-maximizing bra until my breasts pressed against each other to form a perfect crease down the middle of my chest. I opened my makeup drawer and fished around for my earth-toned shades.

"And don't play dumb with him," she continued earnestly. "Eric likes well-read women who have something to contribute to the conversation, not just pretty faces."

Part of me wanted to do and say the exact opposite of whatever Sophie had instructed me: dramatic eye makeup, the flattest-chested shirt hanging in my closet, and a conversation filled with comments that made me look like a complete airhead. Such as, "If this is a German beer, why is the label in English?"

But I knew that would be dishonest.

If I were really going to go through with this, I would do it right. No shortcuts, no skipping ahead in line, no *cheating* the potential cheaters. I would give Sophie the same dedicated focus and work ethic that I offered to every other client.

9:34 P.M.

God, I hate that clock.

I sat back down on my bed and refocused my eyes on it.

This is ridiculous, I thought to myself. *Just get up and walk out the door. It's very simple. You open the door, you walk through it, you close it behind you. What's so freaking complicated about that?*

9:40 P.M.

But my body wouldn't move. The backs of my legs were cemented to the white down comforter. My feet were melded to the floor. My eyes were fixated on the clock.

9:42 P.M.

Get up!

I tried to tell myself this would be an easy night. Quick and simple. I'd probably be out the door in a matter of minutes. I'd walk in, order a drink at the bar, and upon locating the subject in question, I'd flash my flirty eyelashes, keep my breasts in his eye line, and then do my best to cram witty and intelligent quips into what was sure to be a short, five-minute conversation—if that.

Sophie could finally rest easy tonight—and every night for the rest of her life. And I would once again feel the rush of adrenaline and satisfaction that had inspired me to start this job in the first place. Knowing that I had just helped someone.

9:45 P.M.

Okay, it's time, I told myself. *This is what you do. If you can't do this for Sophie, then what's the point in doing it at all?*

Maybe it was the padding in my push-up bra, maybe it was the gold chain necklaces wrapped around my neck, or maybe it was the weight of something far heavier, and much less tangible, but my body felt like it weighed a zillion and a half pounds.

And once again, I couldn't bring myself to move.

I didn't move at 9:46 P.M., and I didn't move at 10:30 P.M.

I didn't even move when the clock struck eleven.

I was paralyzed. Completely and utterly paralyzed.

As in no movement whatsoever. I could barely even feel myself breathe. I wondered if this was what an out-of-body experience felt like. But I didn't exactly have the sensation of looking *down* on my body; more like my body was keeping me glued down.

When midnight finally fell upon my lonely, white room, my arms broke free from their invisible straitjacket and I reached over and picked up the phone—just as we had planned.

I dialed Sophie's number and I waited.

It seemed like forever before the phone rang. And, just as I suspected, it only rang once.

"Hi." Her voice sounded breathless and I was almost positive it wasn't from running to the phone, but more from not being able to take a decent breath until now.

And, regrettably, I knew exactly how she felt.

"Hi," I said cautiously, careful not to let my voice give anything away. But I knew, no matter how cautiously I spoke, no matter how carefully I chose my words, the fact still remained: What was about to come out of my mouth was a lie. Despite all the efforts I'd made to come clean to my friends.

"Well, what happened?" she asked without any delay.

I felt like I had just gone in a complete circle. Three weeks ago I would have given anything to tell Sophie the truth. To put an end to my deceitful world. And for a brief moment, I did.

But now things were different.

Now would be a time to lie again.

Because the truth was much too complicated for even me to hear aloud. And somehow the lie was easier—it always had been.

"He passed," I whispered.

23

sail on through to the other side

There was silence on the other end of the phone.

"Sophie?" I asked, immediately petrified that we had been disconnected and I would have to find a way to force the lie out a second time.

And then her quiet, shaken voice came through. "He passed?"

I nodded, knowing full well she couldn't see me but still somehow wishing the thought would permeate through the phone so I could avoid having any further deceit leave my lips.

"Yes," I finally said aloud.

"Oh, thank God!" Sophie let out a huge breath. "Thank *God*!"

"Yes," I said again, failing to think of anything else to say.

"So what happened? What did you do? What did he say? How did it happen?"

I cringed. *No details! I can't come up with details! It's too painful.*

"Well," I began, "he um . . ." And then I stopped and paused. "You know, it really doesn't matter *how* it happened. Why dwell on it? He passed and it's done. Time to move on and leave it in the 'past.' " I forced out a weak chuckle.

She ignored my attempt at humor. "But was it immediate? Or did he chat with you for a while and *then* turn you down. I mean, geez, Jen, I want some details, for Pete's sake. I've been dying over here!"

I grimaced, knowing full well that I wasn't going to be able to get out of this without giving her at least some specifics. So I decided to go with the simplest, most gratifying story. If I was going to whip up the whole thing from scratch, there was no reason to complicate it or leave any room for doubt. "Nope," I said. "Turned me down flat. Didn't want *anything* to do with me."

"Really?" she squealed with delight. "What'd he say?"

"Well," I began, "I recognized him from the picture you gave me, walked up to him, tried to spark up a conversation, and he said, 'Sorry, I'm just here with some old buddies of mine, trying to catch up. Plus, I'm engaged.' "

Then there was silence on the other end. "That's weird," Sophie remarked warily.

I was immediately defensive. "Why?"

"Um, it's just that, why would he tell you he had a fiancée right off the bat like that? He didn't even know why you were talking to him. Doesn't that strike you as a bit odd?"

Shit.

"No," I said frantically. "Not odd at all. Well, okay, I'm paraphrasing a little. I mean, there were a few lines of dialogue going back and forth before he came out with the engaged line. It's not like that was the first thing out of his mouth."

"Oh," she said, and then fell silent again.

"Trust me." I filled in the pause. "I know odd situations. And this was definitely not one of them. A textbook case of being madly in love with the person he's with and not interested in meeting, talking to, flirting with, kissing, or going home with anyone else. Plain and simple."

I heard another sigh come through the phone, and I was fairly confident I had managed to dodge that bullet successfully.

But then she asked, "So now I guess we have to figure out what I should tell Eric." As if it were the most obvious next step in the world.

"Nothing!" I blurted out quickly . . . maybe too quickly. This was one of those tiny details I hadn't completely thought through yet. It's like what they say about committing murder: Everyone makes at least three mistakes. Three details that never even cross your mind as the adrenaline of committing a crime is pulsing through your veins.

This would be one of those details.

In my adrenaline high of not following through on the promise I had made to my best friend and then lying to her about it, I hadn't even thought that she might suddenly decide she wants to tell Eric about the successful inspection.

"What do you mean, I *shouldn't*?" she asked doubtfully. "Why shouldn't I? He deserves to know. I want us to be honest with each other. Plus, I want to commend him for passing. Positive reinforcement."

"He's not a dog, Soph." I tried to release a mocking chuckle, but it came out more like a snort.

"I know, but . . . I just think . . ."

"There's no reason he has to know," I interjected.

"But why?"

My mind raced. I had to come up with something good—and fast. "Well, Sophie," I said, "think about it. You can't tell your fiancé—the man who asked you to marry him, to be with him for the rest of your lives—that you had absolutely no trust in him at all. So much so that you actually hired someone to hit on him in a bar! And not just anyone . . . your best friend! He'll think you're crazy."

Silence ensued on the other end. She was considering this. "I guess you're right," she said with hesitation.

"Of course I'm right! I mean, as of right now, to him I'm just some lame-ass random chick at a bar. It doesn't have to be any more than that."

"Yes, but what about what you said the other day? About when he meets you again?"

I swallowed hard.

Good question.

Overlooked Murder Detail #2.

"Well . . ." I paused, pulling bullshit right out of my ass. "That's easy. I doubt he'll even recognize me. He barely saw me for a minute. Plus he was drunk."

Oh, my God . . . Please buy it, PLEASE BUY IT.

"You really think he wouldn't recognize you?"

She wasn't buying it.

I swallowed again, refusing to give up. "Sophie, be reasonable," I began with a tone that unmistakably implied she was being ridiculous. There's nothing worse than lying to someone and then making *them* feel stupid for questioning your cover-up. "The bar was dark, he'd had a few drinks. I'm sure my face just blended in with all the other random girls in the crowd."

I held my breath and waited for her response.

"That's true," she admitted thoughtfully.

I released the breath.

"But you said the other day that if he *does* recognize you, it will be really weird. And I just don't want him to figure out what we did and then get mad that I didn't tell him about it. Maybe I should just tell him. I mean, honesty is the best policy, right?"

"No, it's not!" I shot back.

Spoken like a true professional.

"It's not?" Sophie questioned. "Jen, you're acting weird. If anyone should be an advocate for honesty in relationships, it's you."

"I know, I know. I just think that sometimes there are things that people don't need to know. Especially people you care about. I don't think he *needs* to know about this. Telling him will just cause more problems than the honesty is worth."

She contemplated again. "Maybe you're right."

"And trust me. He most definitely will not recognize me."

And this time, I didn't need my special mind-reading superpowers to know with 100 percent certainty that I was right.

After I hung up the phone the silence of my bedroom overwhelmed me. I lay in the dark, thinking about what I had just done. What it would mean tomorrow when I woke up. And the day after that.

Would I ever be able to look Sophie in the eye again?

I mean, sure I've lied to her plenty of times in the past. The last two years had been one huge lie. But those were virtually harmless, right? They didn't even affect her . . . directly. This was something much bigger. This was a very important piece of information that I'd promised to deliver to her and then failed to do so.

And now she'd be making a decision based on the possibly false information I *had* supplied her with and it could affect the rest of her life!

I felt sick to my stomach.

I thought about calling her back and telling her the truth. But then she'd most definitely ask me to try again. "That's okay," she would say. "He's in town tomorrow night, too; you can just go through with it then."

And if I couldn't go through with it a few hours ago, why in God's name would that change overnight? It wouldn't.

So there went that idea.

I continued to lay in the darkness, trying to talk myself out of the nauseating feeling that was filling my stomach and inching its way up to my throat.

And just then, my phone beeped.

Without moving my upper body, I turned my head and looked over at the nightstand. The backlight had illuminated and the message on the screen was informing me that I had a new e-mail in my in-box.

I stared at it for a good thirty seconds before I finally surrendered and reached for the phone.

I clicked on the e-mail program and my entire face went white with horror.

Staring back at me was an e-mail from Jamie.

And the subject simply read: *Fwd:*

I bolted upright to a sitting position. *This is it,* I thought. The e-mail I'd been dreading since our first date. Since he first asked me for my e-mail address so that he could e-mail me during his business trip. The notorious forward that exposed me to the world as the true home wrecker I supposedly was had finally found its way to Jamie's doorstep. Or rather, his in-box.

My heart clenched in my chest as I took a deep breath and clicked on the e-mail. I braced myself for what was sure to come: that familiar link followed by that inevitable "Is this really you?" question, paraphrased depending on my relationship with the sender and their level of doubt that the Jennifer Hunter they knew could ever be mixed up in such a charade.

My Treo seemed to be functioning abnormally slow tonight. "C'mon!" I urged the two-inch screen. But it remained blank. I shook it violently, as if trying to actually jolt the gears into action. Then the screen went black. With a frustrated sigh I tossed it down on the bed and jumped to my feet.

My phone sure picked a hell of a time to freeze, I thought as I sprinted down the hallway to my office.

I opened my laptop and quickly found the same e-mail staring back at me. I clicked on it, secretly hoping that maybe my computer would crash as well or my Internet would go out. Then I wouldn't have to deal with it.

I wouldn't have to come face-to-face with what I knew deep down was coming all along.

But it did open. And as soon as it did, my eyes were immediately drawn to the distinctive, underlined blue text that has come to be recognized in all countries as an invitation to click and read more. A link. A signpost leading to a Web address that would be forever known as the Web site that had ruined my life.

My eyes suddenly started to blur and my vision clouded over. I could barely see the link clear enough to actually click on it. Not that I needed to see anything. I knew what was there. I knew what information my eyes would report back to me had they been functioning properly.

Through my hazy vision I managed to place the cursor over the blue, underlined text and press down on the mouse button. My mind immediately began to search for possible stories. Cover-ups. A believable excuse. Something to get me out of this. An evil twin sister. A mad scientist cloning people all over the city and I just happened to be one of them.

Or I could just tell him it was a joke. A prank. People put up fake Web sites all the time to be funny, don't they? April Fools'! . . . in October.

Yes, I would just sit Jamie down, and with a straight face explain to him that the whole thing was just a . . .

"Panda cam?" I said aloud, as my eyes refocused on the screen. "What the hell is a panda cam?"

I blinked and looked at it again. On my laptop was a streaming live video of a baby panda walking around his habitat at the San Diego Zoo. Dazedly, I flipped back to the original e-mail.

Underneath the link Jamie had typed in:

Thought you might find this cute.
Can't wait to see you again.
Jamie

I sighed dramatically and fell back against my chair, suddenly feeling like a counterterrorism agent who had just stopped a nuclear bomb from exploding over the city of Los Angeles. He had sent me a link to a freaking camera that's pointed at an infant Asian bear. That was it! Nothing more.

I breathed a heavy sigh of relief as I slowly made my way back to my bed.

I laid down and reached under the sea of sheets and blankets until I found Snuffles and tucked him under my chin.

After one more wary glance over at my frozen phone, I drifted off to sleep.

When I woke up in the morning, I knew what I had to do.

I had to cancel my third date with Jamie.

There was no other choice. I couldn't spend the rest of my life running to my computer to see if my life was over every time I heard an e-mail *ding*. What was next? A heart attack over a link that turns out to be a koala bear mating video? It was obvious that my life was just far too complicated to try to start up a relationship. I had just lied to my best friend about something that could easily affect the rest of her life. Who was I kidding, attempting to date right now?

I sifted through my top nightstand drawer until I located Jamie's business card. I picked it up and stared at the number that was labeled "cell phone" as I unplugged my pink Razr from its charger. Without lifting my eyes from the card, I started dialing.

"Miss Hunter," Marta's voice came hurtling through the room, startling me so much that I dropped the phone on the carpeted floor with a muted thud. I looked up and saw her heavyset frame in the doorway of my bedroom.

"Marta, you scared me," I said, catching my breath and bending down to pick up the cell phone. When I checked the screen the number had been erased.

"So sorry, Miss Hunter. I come while you sleep. I start the laundry."

"Very good," I said, picking up the business card again and preparing to punch in the numbers for the second time.

"Problem is," Marta continued, "you no have more laundry detergent."

"Don't I?" I asked curiously, placing the cell phone and the business card on my dresser and walking toward the doorway. "I thought I just picked up some at the supermarket last week."

Marta followed me down the hallway into the laundry room, where I discovered that she was right. The room was completely devoid of any fabric-cleaning substances. "Well, that's weird," I said, studying the room. "I guess I just *thought* about buying it but never actually did it. I'm sorry, I've had a lot on my mind lately."

Marta nodded understandingly. "So you go buy some now?"

I looked down at my pajamas. I really didn't want to leave the house just yet. In a few hours I would have to get dressed to meet John down at the docks for Daniel Miller's take-two assignment. "Nah," I said, waving my hand in the air. "I'll just pick some up on my way home today."

Marta shrugged. "Okay. I do the laundry next week when I come back."

I followed her gaze until I came face-to-face with the pile of dirty clothes on the floor. I squinted at it, just barely able to make out the shirt I had worn on the day I went to Raymond Jacobs's office. When he propositioned me for sex. And below that, I could see the outfit I had worn to Sarah Miller's house, when she handed me a wad of cash and told me to test her husband for the second time. And at the very top of the pile was the shirt I had picked out for Eric's assignment last night . . . the one that I never went through with.

If I stared at the pile long enough, I could almost "see" the bad vibes and creepy germs pouring off the clothes, onto my laundry room linoleum floor, and crawling toward the doorway where I stood.

I backed up slightly.

"Next week?" I asked, slightly tense.

"Yes," she replied. "I come back on Tuesday."

As stupid as it sounded, part of my ability to reset and start fresh every morning was because of laundry. Well, actually, because of Marta's expert laundering skills. It was like she had a special touch, a special decontamination superpower of her own that allowed me to wear an item of clothing to dinner with my friends even though it had been removed by a cheating husband only days before. Marta got rid of all the dirt and grime I picked up during the course of the day. She cleansed my life of all things relating to betrayal and other negative forces.

I had come to depend on that decontamination as a means of survival.

And the thought of that laundry piling up and sitting there for another three days made me not want to sleep in my own bed at night.

"No, no," I responded quickly. "I'll go to the store right now and get some."

Marta simply flashed a satisfied smile and went into the kitchen to start doing dishes.

I pulled on a pair of sweatpants and a long-sleeve T-shirt and ran out to my car. In addition to laundry detergent, I picked up some breakfast and coffee at the Coral Tree Café. After that I stopped at the bank to deposit what was left of the cash that Sarah Miller had given me. I had decided to deposit the sum in unequal installments over the past five days to avoid any unwanted attention or questioning from the bank. And finally I dropped in at the Apple store to buy a new charger for my iPod.

By the time I got back to the house, it was time to start getting ready for today's assignment. I hadn't completely forgotten about my almost phone call to Jamie to cancel our date. I had just *chosen* to overlook it.

Besides, I had things to do. Laundry detergent needed purchasing, iPods needed charging, and ridiculously large amounts of cash lying around needed depositing. And after that I had to go to work. John would be meeting me at the docks in less than an hour. I certainly wasn't about to change around my whole schedule just for a guy.

When I reached our previously agreed-upon meeting point at the marina, I found John pacing anxiously in front of a large yacht, dressed in white pants and a white collared shirt, with a blue handkerchief tied meticulously around his neck. He tilted his head back to salvage the last drop from his Coffee Bean paper cup.

"What are you wearing?" I asked, trying to stifle a laugh as I approached and stared incredulously at his outfit.

John looked down at his clothes and carefully pressed his finger against a piece of red lint on his pants, and then flicked it into the warm sea air. "Hello! It's sailor chic," he informed me condescendingly, as if he were trying to explain a Renoir painting to a culture-deprived teenage girl.

I smiled. "Ah . . ."

"So what's the plan? Where is he? What should I do?" he asked anxiously.

I looked around the dock and tried to match up the photo of Daniel Miller's sailboat that his wife had given me with the real thing. It was going to be difficult, since they all kind of looked alike. I now wished that she had given me some type of parking space number. Is that even what they call them? Parking spaces? Designated boating spots? Docking zones? What the hell did I know about being down at the "dock of the bay" except for that one song about wasting time there. Although Ashlyn was supposed to be quite the dock rat, according to her last meeting with Daniel Miller.

"Well . . ." I began.

"See, here's what I was thinking," he quickly interrupted, tossing his empty coffee cup into the nearest waste bin.

I laughed. "Go ahead."

"Okay. So here's you and me, just casually strolling the docks. Ashlyn with her good friend *Wallace*. And then suddenly . . . 'Well, well, who do we have here?' A friend of Ashlyn's. 'Hey, you're the guy from that something or other bar,' etc., etc. You introduce us and I say something brilliant like 'It's chilly out here. I'm just gonna grab my sweater from the boat,' and then you make your move . . . or do whatever it is you do. Seal the deal. Sink the bait. You know."

John stood back with his arms folded across his chest, patiently awaiting my praise.

I bit my lip, holding back a smile that almost refused to be stifled. "First of all," I said, "Wallace?"

"I needed an alias. And I think it sounds very 'Saturday afternoon at the docks,' don't you?"

"Fine," I replied, choosing my battles. "And second of all . . . it's almost eighty degrees out here. I don't think your little brilliant, sly sweater escape story is gonna fly."

John waved my objection away with his hand. "Well, whatever, two nickels or a dime. I'll go get coffee or something."

I looked at him strangely. "Don't you mean 'six of one, half dozen of another'?"

John frowned. "Details, Jen. Useless details. We're wasting precious inspection time."

I shook my head. "Fine, let's go." I had a feeling this was going to be a disaster, but at this point, I hardly cared. Sarah Miller was in denial. Sure, it was some sort of peculiar, reverse-psychology denial. But denial all the same. Her husband had already passed my test. As far as I was concerned, he was not the cheating type. I didn't even make up another inspection card. The fact that she wanted to pay me an exorbitant amount of money on top of the triple fee she already had paid me the first time around to come down here and confirm what I already knew to be true was, I guess, her problem.

John self-importantly cocked his elbow at his side and nudged me with it until I slipped my hand through it, and we walked arm in arm along the dock, keeping an eye out for the boat in the picture.

"You look ridiculous," I commented quietly, out of the corner of my mouth.

"*I* look like I belong down here among the rich and famous," he insisted. "*You* look like you should be drinking a diet Coke out of the can in the Valley somewhere."

"John, it's not the Governors Ball. It's Marina Del Rey. I saw a bum sleeping with a stuffed Pooh doll on a bench about three minutes ago."

John loudly cleared his throat. "Don't you mean '*Wallace,* it's not the Governors Ball'?"

I shot him a look. He ignored it. "And yes, you're right, Miss Ashlyn. They really do need to do something about the dreadful homeless problem down here. Where do they think this is? Venice Beach?" He pronounced the location as if the words themselves were somehow dirty and full of beach trash.

I stifled a giggle and we continued walking. A few yards ahead I saw a man hanging over the side of a boat, diligently scrubbing off dirt with a white rag. I slowed my step. "That's him," I whispered to John—pardon me . . . to *Wallace*.

John stopped dead in his tracks, as if we were stalking a deer in the woods and the smallest sound or movement might scare away the prey. I could feel his body tense up next to mine.

"Relax," I reassured him, finding his hesitation somewhat endearing. "This will be an easy one."

John took a deep breath and we approached the boat.

"Daniel?" I said with great surprise in my tone as I shielded my eyes from the sun and looked up at the man aboard the boat in front of us.

He looked down at me and smiled. "Yes?" I could tell I was familiar to him but that he embarrassedly couldn't remember my name or who the hell I was. I was suddenly further reassured that this was going to be just as I suspected . . . an easy confirmation of what I already knew to be true.

"It's Ashlyn. We met the other day at the W Hotel bar."

His brain spun around like the reels of a slot machine, searching for the right combination of name, face, location. I could see it in his eyes. And then suddenly . . . . *ding, ding, ding*. Jackpot.

"Ah, yes. The sailboat lover," he ventured, hoping desperately that he had gotten his facts right.

"So you *do* remember me," I said with a fabricated sigh of relief. As if his recollection of our previous night together meant the world to me.

"Of course." He stepped down from his boat onto the dock and offered me his hand.

I shook it, and then turned to John. "And this is my friend . . ." I forced a straight face. "Wallace. Wallace, Daniel."

"Pleasure to meet you," John said, shaking his hand eagerly.

"Pleasure is mine," Daniel said.

I stood to the side and watched the two of them shake hands. I looked from John to Daniel, and for a second I could have sworn their handshake went on for just a touch too long. But before I could even contemplate it, Daniel had turned back to me.

"So what brings you down to the marina today?"

"Oh, well," John began, not even allowing me the opportunity to open my mouth, "Ashlyn and I often walk the docks in the afternoon when the weather's nice. She loves coming down to see the boats . . . and I like coming to see the . . . well, you know, people on the boats."

I subtly elbowed John in the side to warn him about flirting and overly sexual innuendos. "Yes," I said, attempting to cover his tracks. "It's such a nice day, we just couldn't resist."

Daniel looked around and took in the Saturday afternoon sunlight. His gaze circled back in our direction and seemed to linger on John, although it was hard to tell behind his dark sunglasses.

John watched him intently, as if trying to get a lifetime's worth of gossip on the man in only a short glance. The situation was beginning to feel awkward, and I knew I had to speed the process along.

"Hey, Wallace, weren't you talking about getting some coffee? I think I would really love a latté if you're still going to go."

John looked at me with begging eyes. Eyes that said "*Please, Mommy, can't I stay and watch just a little bit longer?*"

I shook my head discreetly at him, but the disappointment that filled his face was much less subtle. "Yes," he finally replied, sulking. "I was going to go get some coffee. Would you like any, Daniel?"

Daniel smiled kindly. "Yes, I would love an iced coffee, please. Thank you."

"You got it." He then turned to me and, with his back to Daniel, sneered mockingly. I smiled politely back.

John walked quickly toward the boathouse at the end of the dock and I turned my attention back to Daniel. It was time to get down to business and get this over with.

But as soon as I turned my head back, I noticed that Daniel's attention certainly was *not* back on me. As I followed his gaze this time, it was undisputable. Sunglasses or not, there was no doubt that his eyes were aimed directly at John, aka Wallace, as he merrily trotted down the wooden planks of the dock, his blue handkerchief blowing in the ocean breeze.

And like a gush of hot air, everything hit me at once. It suddenly all made sense. The reason that Daniel Miller seemingly wanted nothing to do with me. The reason Sarah Miller insisted that I try again—and try harder. Because cheating with another *woman* was better than the alternative, the one she had really been suspecting all along.

And just as quickly as it hit me, an idea came rushing to me as well.

"Can you hold on a minute?" I asked Daniel politely. "I forgot to tell Wallace that I wanted soy milk in my latté." And with that I spun on my heels and practically ran to catch up with John.

"Wait up!" I called after him.

He turned around with a confused look on his face. "What? Did he turn your sorry ass down already?"

I shook my head as I caught my breath. I patted John on the shoulder and smiled. "It's a good thing you came along after all."

He furrowed his eyebrows. "Why's that?"

I smiled at him, knowing that what I was about to ask would surely make his day—and possibly his year. "Because I have a better idea."

I sipped my coffee and glanced at my watch for the third time in the past forty-five minutes. The wooden park bench I was sitting on was starting to get rather uncomfortable. And it didn't help that I had to perch on the very edge of the bench to avoid getting splinters in my bare legs. The white sailor-style miniskirt had been my last attempt to get Daniel Miller's attention. But as it would seem, no amount of *female* skin was going to cut it.

I immediately felt sorry for his wife. There she was, sitting in her empty Stepford house in the canyon, wanting so much to believe that maybe he was just bored with *their* sex life, not with sex with women in general. Because if that were the case, I'm sure she would blame herself, thinking that she had literally pushed him away from the female species altogether. What a terrible thing to have to live with. And why hadn't she seen it before? As in, fifteen years before, when they first met? Or thirteen years before, when they exchanged wedding vows? How can someone hide something like that for this long?

Just as I stood up to stretch my legs I saw John walking toward my bench.

I quickly hurried over to him, and the first thing I noticed was that his blue handkerchief was tied on the *opposite* side of his neck and his hair was slightly out of place. Or as out of place as John would ever allow it to get.

"So?" I asked eagerly.

His expression turned serious and he shot me a glance that said, *This isn't the time nor the place.* Then he grabbed hold of my elbow and roughly steered me back toward the parking lot. "Let's talk somewhere private," he said in his best 1940s detective voice.

"Oh, c'mon, John. Tell me what happened!"

He nudged his head warningly toward the entrance of the dock and I decided to just play along and let John bask in his artificial moment of glory.

He walked me up the stairs, through the parking lot of cars all valued at fifty thousand dollars and up, and then over to a large oak tree, rooted purposefully at the corner of the lot to create ambience.

John turned and faced me. He closed his eyes as if attempting to muster up the courage to break bad news. I let out an impatient sigh.

He took a deep breath. "Um, yeah . . . he's gay," he said matter-of-factly.

I let out a laugh. "That whole charade was just for *that*?"

"Hey, I'm a professional. I couldn't risk any of the elite dock crowd overhearing and possibly ruining his reputation. He's obviously not out of the closet yet." He paused for a moment and then added, "Although he should be. I mean, anyone who kisses like that shouldn't be locked up in no closet!"

I laughed again. "You kissed him?"

"He kissed me!" John corrected. "Just like you told me. I didn't initiate anything! It was all him."

"Really?" Even I was enjoying a small portion of this TV-worthy drama.

John nodded proudly. "Yes. I told him *you* were going to get the coffee because you thought I would screw up your order. So he invited me to see his boat. We talked, flirted, et cetera. And then he leaned in and just went for it."

I shook my head in disbelief. "I can't believe this."

"Yeah. Me neither." John cocked his head to the side. "I mean, how did he even know I was gay?"

I stared at him in disbelief. "You can't be serious."

He looked down at his outfit again. "What? Is it really that obvious?"

I decided not to even go there. Besides, I had bigger things to worry about than whether or not John thought he *looked* gay.

"So I guess now the only problem is: How on earth do I report something like this back to his wife?"

John shook his head and offered me a sympathetic smile. "Yeah, you're on your own for that one, honey."

24

the two-date itch

I sat across from Sarah Miller, and for the first time in a long time, I was actually fidgeting. I couldn't sit still. I had to literally hold my hands together in my lap to keep them from wandering up into my hair, to the back sides of my earrings, into my mouth. This kind of post-assignment review was definitely a first for me.

"Snickerdoodle?" Mrs. Miller offered, pushing a small plate of unidentifiable chocolate lumps toward me. I would have normally said no, but I suddenly felt bad for her: cooking up a storm, trying desperately to win back her husband's attention by becoming the next Betty Crocker, when, in the end, all he wanted to do was find a Bobby Cocker.

So I grabbed a lump off the plate and took a small nibble. "Thank you. This is delicious."

"You're welcome." Sarah sat upright in her seat and folded her hands neatly in her lap.

"I don't know how to tell you this, Mrs. Miller, so I'm just going to come right out and say it."

"He cheated, right?" she asked, with hope in her voice.

I tilted my head to the side. "Well, actually . . . not in the way you would think."

This seemed to throw her off. She delicately scratched an itch at the base of her hairline and looked to me for further explanation.

"As it would turn out, your husband really wanted nothing to do with me . . . in an intimate sense."

She nodded, unsure of where this was going, and motioned for me to continue.

"He was actually more interested in my friend . . . my *male* friend."

Mrs. Miller pressed her lips together tightly, and I could see a puzzled expression come over her face. "How do you mean? As in a business sense?"

I shook my head. "No, as in . . . my friend is . . . um . . . gay."

It took her a few moments, but she eventually got it. "Oh dear," she said, her eyes narrowing, her lips curling into a solemn frown.

I felt a wave of sympathy suddenly wash over me. This poor woman. I couldn't even imagine what she must be feeling right now. But as I studied her face, for some reason, I got the sense that her reaction to the news wasn't exactly sincere. She didn't at all resemble a person who had been dreading this kind of truth, trying to prove it wrong, trying to ignore it until she just couldn't ignore it any longer. She more resembled someone trying to hide some kind of self-indulgent amusement with a mask of surprise. Which confused me even more. Just when I thought I had figured her out, figured out exactly what was going on behind the closed doors, I suddenly felt like I was right back where I had started: sitting across from a robot wife who likes to wear aprons and hum while she does dishes.

"I'm sorry I have to be the one to tell you this," I offered, almost as if I was poking at the wound, trying to see if I could rouse any predictable responses.

"Yes, yes," she repeated softly. But it was as if she had something else on her mind. Something quite far from the topic at hand.

And as she ushered me politely out the door less than five minutes later I tried to remind myself that all people grieve in different ways. And I was in no place to judge the way Mrs. Miller reacts to shocking news. After all, I wasn't being paid to contemplate the various emotions that every person must feel on their own. I was being paid to deliver my findings and leave. Which is exactly what I did.

But it still didn't stop me from wondering what the hell was going on in that house after she closed the door.

When I got home and changed out of my slacks and cardigan sweater set, I noticed Jamie's business card, still sitting on my dresser where I had left it the day before.

Oh, that's right, I reminded myself, as if I hadn't tenaciously stuck it at the back of my mind for the last twenty-four hours. *I was going to cancel our date.*

I picked up the card again and stared at the phone number. I reached for my phone and held it tightly in my hand.

Just do it, I repeated to myself. *You know it's for the best.*

I started dialing the area code but my fingers felt heavy and almost numb. I was having trouble pressing the right buttons. As I went to press the number 4, my finger slipped over to the 5. When did the buttons on this cell phone get so goddamn close together? I hit *Clear* and started again.

After entering the last digit, I studied the completed number on the screen of my phone, my finger poised and ready to press the green *Send* button like a finger on a trigger.

It's easy, I told myself.

I would just press *Send,* he would answer, and I would simply say something like, "I'm sorry, my mother is sick . . . in Guam, and I'll be moving there for God knows how long . . ."

"No!" I said aloud. "No more lies."

"I'm sorry, my life is just too complicated right now. I feel that I shouldn't drag you into it."

Perfect.

Honest, truthful, painless . . . in theory.

I took a deep breath and began to apply pressure on the green button.

And that's when the doorbell rang.

I released my finger and looked curiously in the direction of the hallway. As I made my way to the front door, I checked my watch, and then remembered that my mom, Julia, and Hannah were coming over today to take me out to lunch.

I quickly put my phone and Jamie's business card down on the dining room table and went to the door.

"Hi, all!" I said, trying to sound excited and well rested. After all, that's how normal people sound on Sunday afternoons, right? Relaxed, calm, enjoying the weekend, reading the paper, maybe even watching a TV movie.

Hannah hugged me briefly and then rushed passed me to do what she always does when she comes to my house: explore my closet.

"Oh my God," I heard her yell from my bedroom a few seconds later as I hugged my mom and Julia. "I love this skirt!"

"Great," Julia said, rolling her eyes. "Now, that's all we're going to hear about on the way back home."

I smiled politely back at her.

Julia stepped inside and took a look around, silently judging everything with her eyes. "Hmm . . . It's amazing. I always manage to forget how *white* this place is."

I bit my lip to keep myself from throwing back a snide retort, knowing it would get me nowhere.

"Who's Jamie Richards?" I heard my mom's voice ask in a very interested tone.

I immediately swung my head around to find my mother holding Jamie's business card in her hand and examining it with great interest.

"Calloway Consulting," she read aloud from the card, and then picked her head up. "A business associate?"

I shrugged and tried to downplay it. "No. Just a guy I'm dating."

Her face instantly lit up. I could almost see the silhouettes of unborn children appear in my mother's pupils. I suddenly wished I had just lied and told her he was a business associate.

I tried to cover. "It's no big deal, really. I don't think it's going anywhere. Where do you want to go to lunch?"

"How many times have you gone out?" Hannah asked, returning to the living room and plopping down on the couch. She shifted to get comfortable, as if getting ready to watch a movie she'd wanted to see for months. All she was missing was a large bucket of popcorn.

"You know, I don't really want to talk about it," I replied, walking over to my mom and gently removing the white card from her tightly clasped fingers and placing it back on the table. Her fingers had instinctively clenched around what had become a small token of hope.

I didn't see any good in telling them about Jamie since I was undoubtedly going to end it anyway. What was the point in getting them all excited? My life had no room for a man. In fact, I don't even know why I agreed to go out with him in the first place. A cute distraction from my hectic existence? What a pathetically lame thing to do. But I knew my family would never understand my reasoning. "What's so complicated about your life?" Julia would sneer. "You can't avoid your issues with your father forever," my mom would warn in a maternal tone. "He's ugly, isn't he? That's the real reason, right?"

Hannah would naively speculate, extremely proud that she had unraveled the truth behind the great mystery that was my love life.

They all stared at me. A woman on trial for her life. Would she please the jury with her agreeable response? Or would she be sent to the gas chamber?

I sighed and threw my hands up in the air. "Twice, okay? We've gone out twice. And I'm afraid it's not working out. Now can we go to lunch?"

"You know," Julia began thoughtfully. The look on her face implied that she was conjuring up something that in her mind would be as significant as the latest scientific breakthrough in cancer research. "Two dates sound like a very familiar number."

"What do you mean?" I asked, genuinely curious.

"Well, don't all of your so-called relationships last about two dates?"

The members of the jury looked to me with eyes that said, *She does have a point, Jen.*

Busted! Julia had hit the nail right on the head. All of my so-called relationships *did* last two dates. But what I couldn't tell them was that those "relationships" never actually existed. The fictitious men of my past were usually given two dates before I came up with a reason to scratch them from the lineup. Because I always figured two dates was just long enough that no one could argue I hadn't given them enough time to make an impression, and just short enough that no one got their feelings hurt.

As I contemplated Julia's observation, I suddenly felt very bad for wanting to cancel my third date with Jamie. He was the first "real" guy they'd ever known about. And it was appearing that my artificial "two-date" stigma had actually manifested itself in my real dating life. That couldn't be healthy.

But then again, it was starting to become obvious that *healthy* was definitely not the best word to describe any aspect of my life.

"I don't know what she's talking about," I fought back shamelessly. "Jamie's different. He's not like any of the others."

Meaning he's real.

"For starters," I continued, on the verge of rambling, "he took me golfing for our first date. And we ate hot dogs. I just don't think that I . . ."

"That's cute!" Hannah interrupted. "Isn't that cute?" she surveyed the rest of the group.

I smiled to myself. It really *was* cute, actually. I had an instant flashback of the two us sitting on that bench outside the snack stand, eating our hot dogs and making jokes about his golfing skills. Or lack thereof. I almost let out a small, reminiscent giggle.

"He sounds delightful," my mom pointed out contentedly.

"Yeah," I admitted softly, sitting down on the couch next to Hannah. "He's really funny, too." A rush of enthusiasm unexpectedly filled my voice as I continued, "He does this thing where he calls me Jennifer H. like they used to in elementary school, because when I first met him I wouldn't tell him what my last name was."

I laughed to myself, as if no one else was in the room. And for a moment . . . no one else was. I don't know how long I sat there talking about Jamie to seemingly nobody, but I repeated everything. His age, his job, how we met, our extended "stay" on the airport runway, how cute it was that he teased me about having a Palm Pilot . . . everything. And when I finally stopped, I suddenly realized that everyone's eyes were on me. They waited for more. They longed for it.

I blushed as I became inundated with a strange, unfamiliar feeling.

It was what honesty felt like. It had to be. There was nothing else it could be.

I had talked to my family for a good ten minutes straight without one, single lie coming out of my mouth.

It felt amazing. To talk to the people I love. And to tell them everything. No stories, no made-up details, no alibis. Just me.

It was liberating.

I took a deep breath and ventured a look at their smitten faces. I knew my mom was thinking about the wedding, Hannah was thinking about our first kiss and what it must feel like to have someone's tongue in your mouth, and Julia was still silently gloating over correctly pointing out one of my inherent flaws.

But it didn't matter what any of them were thinking.

All that mattered was that I finally had told them the truth. Well, at least a small portion of it. And now all I wanted to do was tell them more.

But I couldn't.

Not yet.

Maybe not ever.

I couldn't let myself get carried away. They say anything can be addicting. I believed it now. The truth was the most addictive drug I had ever tried. But a few dates my family could handle. A career of fidelity inspections . . . not so much. So I kept that part inside and tried to enjoy my moment of pure honesty . . . while it lasted.

"So tell me again why it's not working out?" my mom asked, completely confused. After hearing me go on nonstop for as long as I had, I'm sure things weren't adding up.

In fact, they weren't really adding up for me, either. When I thought about Jamie I wanted to be with him all the time. But when I thought about everything else, my job, the lies, the blackmailing, the dishonesty, I knew I shouldn't ever see him again.

Right now the only way to avoid a long and eventually heated discussion about the future of my love life was to dodge the question completely. "I don't know," I replied. "I guess we'll have to see."

That seemed to satisfy the lot of them. The hope in their hearts winning out over all the cynicism in mine.

Just then my business line rang. Everyone turned and stared at the ringing phone as if they'd never seen such a futuristic gadget before. "Work," I said, feigning annoyance as I picked it up and quickly stepped into the other room.

Like I said . . . while it lasted.

"Hello?" I said as quietly as I could into the phone without sounding like I was trying to whisper.

"Yes, hello, Ashlyn?" It was a female voice. Kind and compassionate, with just the slightest trace of sorrow in it.

"Who's calling, please?"

There was a pause on the other end. "Um, my name is Karen . . . Howard," she said, her voice wavering slightly. It wasn't an uncommon voice characteristic among the females who call this number. "I got your name from a friend."

"Yes, Mrs. Howard. What can I do for you?"

"Well, as you can probably guess, it's about my husband. Although I would really rather discuss it in person. Telephones make me nervous. Would you be able to meet with me?"

"Well, I usually like to get more details over the phone before I agree to meet in person."

"Right," she said, with an air of disappointment. "Of course." Then, after a deep breath, she said, "I guess he's just different. Distant. Always coming home late. Sometimes not at all. And I just thought . . ." Her voice trailed off, as if she was either too distraught to continue or just wasn't ready to actually hear herself say it aloud. Because that would mean she would be admitting defeat.

"Of course I can meet with you," I compassionately filled in the uncomfortable gap in the conversation.

She let out a loud sigh, relieved that I hadn't forced her to complete that horrific thought. "Thank you."

"When is good for you?"

There was a moment of silence on the other end, and I assumed she was checking her calendar. "Well, my husband has a business trip coming up in a few weeks, so sometime before that I would imagine."

"I have an opening at the end of the week. How would Friday work?"

"Oh, that would be perfect," she replied. "Can we say eight o'clock?"

"At night? Won't your husband be home?"

"Um, no," she said quickly. "He'll be working late." She sighed into the phone. "Again."

"I see. That's fine. Eight it is, then."

I took down Karen Howard's contact information and home address and hung up the phone. I returned to the living room to find the conversation had gone on fine without me. Julia, of course, was in control, and she was passionately discussing how reality TV was corrupting America's youth. Hannah looked bored to tears.

I quietly entered my appointment with Mrs. Howard into my phone and slipped it into my bag.

"So, should we go to lunch?" I asked, clapping my hands to get everyone's attention.

Hannah jumped up enthusiastically, as if I had just saved her from a trip to the dentist. My mom and Julia stood up as well and stretched their legs.

"Yes," my mom replied, coming over and putting her arm around my shoulders. "Where shall we go, Jen? This is, after all, your . . .'hood."

"Reality TV corrupting our youth?" I said sarcastically to Julia. "More like our parents. No more *MTV Cribs* for you, Mom."

I locked the door behind me and herded everyone into the elevator. "How about Mexican?"

As Julia started to tell us a story about the last time she ate bad Mexican food, Hannah motioned me close to her. I smiled and bent down next to her ear so she could tell me whatever juicy secret she had stored up during the week.

"I have a question," she said timidly.

The elevator doors opened and my mom and Julia walked on ahead as I slowed my pace to stay behind with Hannah. "What is it?" I whispered, half expecting a question about sex in general and half expecting a question about *my* sex life specifically. Those are usually what Hannah's "secret" questions are about.

She cautiously glanced at our two mothers up ahead, making sure they were a safe distance away, and then whispered back, "Who's *Ashlyn*?"

25

raw fish . . . dead meat

I froze in my tracks.

My mom and Julia continued ahead unsuspectingly, but Hannah and I stayed behind as I struggled to come up with something to say. She must have heard part of my phone conversation. I had to create a lie. And quickly. You would have thought I would be good at it by now. But I'm rarely put on the spot so unexpectedly, especially by my niece, whom I loved dearly and hated lying to more than anyone.

"Um . . ." I stalled. "Ashlyn is . . . my boss at work. She went on vacation this weekend, but she doesn't want any of her clients to know, so she asked me to answer her calls as if I were her."

I exhaled loudly. Not bad. Not bad at all. I looked up, past the top of Hannah's head, and saw Julia and my mom approaching Julia's Chrysler parked on the street. I began to walk toward them until I saw the look on Hannah's face. She now appeared more confused than ever. As if my solution hadn't shed *any* light on the subject but rather had made things even more unclear.

What was wrong with her? That was a perfectly believable explanation for why I would be calling myself Ashlyn on the phone . . . and then I stopped again. A chill ran through my entire body. My legs and arms were like dead weight.

I never say the name Ashlyn on the phone. In fact, I make it a point *not* to.

In a silent panic, I quickly rewound the conversation with Karen Howard in my head. "Yes, hello, Ashlyn?" is what she said. And then I replied, "Who's calling, please?" The name Ashlyn never came out of *my* mouth.

I looked down at Hannah, who was obviously reviewing facts in her head as well. Trying to make sense of my bogus explanation and fit it together with whatever unknown pieces she had swimming around in there. She knew my explanation had to fit somehow. Because why would I ever lie to her?

My hand was shaking as I tenderly rested it on her shoulder and pretended that nothing was wrong. "Um, Hannah. Where did you hear that name?" I asked, fearful of what answer would come back.

She bit her lip and looked up at me, squinting from the sun glaring in through the windows of my building's lobby. "From the letter."

I suddenly felt like I might throw up. The hand that I had gently placed on her shoulder for reassurance was now being used as support to keep myself from falling over. I breathed in deeply and tried to regain my composure.

"What letter?" I managed to ask with feigned nonchalance.

"I got a letter the other day. Like a real one. In the mail."

"From who?" I blurted out desperately. So much for my calm, composed self.

She shrugged indifferently, surely not understanding the complete horror of this situation. "Don't know," she said. But she was starting to sense something was wrong. She looked up at me again. "What's the matter?"

"What did the letter say?" I insisted with dire urgency.

She scrunched up her mouth as she thought back to the mysterious piece of mail. "Um, it was a picture. Like a copied picture. You know, with a copy machine."

I nodded. "Of who?"

"Of you," she said, as if it were obvious.

I nodded again and listened, trying to keep my breathing steady and even. Now wasn't the time or place to start hyperventilating.

"You were like talking to a guy or something . . . it looked like you were in a restaurant or a bar," she added, pleased with her first-rate recollection skills.

"Uh-huh," I said, my throat getting drier by the second.

"And on the back it said 'This girl's name is Ashlyn. She looks a lot like your aunt Jennifer, doesn't she?' "

I ran my fingers through my hair and closed my eyes.

"Ashlyn's a pretty name," Hannah offered, as if it might help cheer me up.

"Did you show that to your mom?" I asked frantically.

"No," Hannah replied, offended at the mere suggestion that she would share her private mail with her *mother*.

"Good," I said, patting her arm. "Let's not show her or tell her or mention this to anyone, okay?" My voice was shrill, as if I might lose it at any moment.

"Okay," Hannah agreed as we exited the building and started walking toward the car. "But how can she be your boss?" she asked.

I stopped and looked down at her. "She's not. She's . . . no one. I just like using that name sometimes," I said with a shrug, hoping this rationalization would be enough but knowing full well that it would never suffice.

Hannah looked at me as if she was meeting me for the first time. Her eyes begged for more of an explanation. An explanation that would bring back the Jennifer Hunter she knew and loved. "But why would someone send a—"

"You know what?" I began, my voice cracking slightly. I knew I needed more time in order to fabricate a believable story that would tie up all the loose ends in Hannah's head—and mine. And that's exactly what I bought myself when I said, "I'll explain this all to you later. It's a big, juicy secret that I don't want my mom or yours to know about or even overhear."

This apparently made her happy. A huge smile appeared across her lips and she gladly sealed them tight, pantomiming a long zipper being fastened across them and locked at the end with a key. Then she placed the "key" in her pocket for safekeeping.

I tried to act like I was truly sharing in the fun of this juvenile secret-sharing time by nodding approvingly at her charade, but my mind was racing.

Apparently Raymond Jacobs had already started the next phase of his "plan." It had barely been a week! I thought I was supposed to get more time than this. But I guess that's the number one rule of blackmail: There are no rules.

We all piled into the car and headed off to my favorite dive Mexican restaurant for lunch.

Hannah looked content in her seat, staring out at the passing streets of Brentwood and probably fantasizing about what my big secret could possibly be. Maybe a clandestine affair with the gardener like she'd seen when we watched *Desperate Housewives* together at my house because her mom would never let her watch it at her own house. Or maybe I was leading a double life with a husband and two kids who lived in Oregon whom I only saw twice a month. Whatever it was, she knew it would be good.

As I stared out *my* window, my thoughts were far from gardeners and desperate housewives. All I could ponder was whether or not Raymond Jacobs knew about Jamie. And if he didn't, it certainly wouldn't take him long to find out.

"So we still on for Tuesday?" Jamie asked when he called later that night.

I thought about his business card lying on my dining-room table. About my unsuccessful attempts to cancel our date because I knew my life was too complicated to add him to it. And about my fear that Raymond Jacobs would discover there was yet another Kryptonite and exploit it as well.

But I knew there was only one answer to his question.

And that answer was yes.

Because Jamie was my escape.

It was becoming more and more clear with every moment I spent with him, and when I saw his face on the other side of my front door on Tuesday night, it was confirmed.

I had never really had an escape before. For the past two years I had been held captive in a prison of my own thoughts and fears, knowing full well that there was a key to unlock the door, but so afraid of what was on the other side that I just simply had chosen to remain locked inside. And just as soon as I realized what this strange feeling of release was, I knew I wanted more of it. I knew I wanted it all the time. The pieces were all adding up. The street signs were all leading to one thing, and one thing only.

I wanted out.

There's a name for the condition I was in. It's called cloud nine. I imagine it's called that because you feel as if you're floating. And I was. I was floating, high above my everyday life. And it looked so small from up here. I felt so peaceful. So serene.

For a moment, I actually believed that it was.

But that's the problem with cloud nine: It can be deceiving. The sheer state of ultimate bliss can cause you to ignore things you wouldn't normally ignore. Like the several curious stares I got as Jamie and I entered the sushi restaurant that night. I barely noticed them. And the scattered whispers that spread throughout the room as we sat down? I barely heard them.

I should have been asking myself why they were staring. What are they whispering about? Do I have something on the front of my dress? But like I said, everything is benign when you're looking down from a cloud. And as far as I was concerned, they were all simply commenting on what a cute couple Jamie and I made, and how happy we looked together, just as I was doing every minute of the evening.

So I merely noted their existence and then quickly forgot all about them as soon as Jamie looked across the table at me and smiled.

"You like sushi, right?"

"I don't trust anyone who doesn't," I replied.

"That's my girl."

My heart flipped. *My* girl? As in possession? Ownership? Exclusivity?

Two weeks ago a comment like that would have probably made me run for the hills. But tonight the sound of his words made me want to jump into his arms, wrap my legs around him, and never come down.

Of course I wouldn't. How stupid would that look?

With Jamie I didn't have to be anyone else but myself. Because, let's face it, I never got the guys. That was Ashlyn's forte. I stayed home on Saturday nights and watched whatever lame-ass TV show the networks had programmed for lonely girls who stay in on Saturday nights. Ashlyn was the one who got all the looks, while I was hardly noticed. Ashlyn had all the interesting things to talk about, all the amazing stories to tell. I used to crunch numbers for a living.

But Jamie liked me, anyway. He laughed at my jokes, complimented my outfits, and made my knees weak when he kissed me. In his mind that other person, the one who had gotten me into so much trouble over the past few weeks, didn't even exist.

"Okay, so what do you like?" Jamie asked me, glancing over the sushi list.

"Um, let's see. Tall men, fast cars, loud music, and hallucinogenic drugs," I replied, counting out the list on my fingers.

He glanced up over the top of his menu. "Damn," he said with a mocking trace of disappointment in his voice. "And I left my mushrooms in my other pants."

I sighed loudly. "I guess I'll have a spicy tuna roll, then." I set my menu down on the table and looked up at him. But for some reason my eyes went right past him and landed on the two men at the next table. They were staring at us and exchanging remarks. Then one man took out his BlackBerry, clicked a few buttons, showed the screen to the second man, and they both looked over at me and nodded to each other.

My heart started to pound.

How could I have missed it before? The looks? The whispers? It was so obvious. All those people had seen the fucking Web site! They'd all been forwarded that dreadful link, and now they recognized me. From my pictures. And they watched me walk into the restaurant, all smitten and googly-eyed, looking like I was in love and they . . .

Oh my God! A sobering realization settled in. *They think I'm on an assignment . . . with Jamie!*

"What's wrong?" Jamie asked, sensing my mood alteration and turning around to follow my glance. "Is there a celebrity here?"

But I barely heard him. I sat motionless in my chair. Frozen. Panicked. I couldn't believe what was actually happening. How would I ever get myself out of this one? And even if I did, what did I expect to do? Eat in for the rest of my life? Wear a wig whenever I was in public with Jamie so that no one would be able to corner him and tell him the truth?

And then my eyes widened even farther. One of the men was actually standing up and walking toward our table!

I blinked, hoping—no, more like praying—someone might have slipped a hallucinogenic drug into my green tea. This could *not* be happening.

I knew I had two choices. Hide behind my menu all night and pray that I wouldn't be noticed . . . or run. And I figured that since waitresses usually come and take your menus away anyway, I really didn't have a choice.

"You know, speaking of celebrities," Jamie continued, obliviously, "I was having lunch with a colleague once and Jennifer Garner was sitting at the next table—"

"You know, I really don't feel very good," I interrupted suddenly, throwing in a clichéd cough for credibility.

"Oh, really?" Jamie asked, concerned. "Is there something going around again?"

I clutched my stomach. "Maybe. I think I should go. Raw fish probably won't help much."

"Sure, of course. If that's what you want." He was being extremely accommodating.

And before he could finish his sentence I was up, out of my seat, pushing my chair back with a loud scrape against the floor. "Good, let's go," I said in a voice that I hoped sounded calm and composed but more than likely was on the verge of cracking.

Jamie quickly removed his napkin from his lap and stood up. "Are you sure you're all right? Do I need to take you to the hospital?"

"No! I'll be fine. I just need to lie down for a minute." I grabbed his arm and literally pulled him toward the back door of the restaurant, the opposite direction of the menacing man making his way to our table.

"But the front door is this way," Jamie pointed out, placing a tender hand on my arm and gently leading me in the other direction.

My breathing sped up as I saw the man get closer. I needed to come up with a reason to leave through the back door or even through a window in the bathroom, but there just wasn't any. At least none that would sound logical and convincing. There was no way out of it. We were going to come face-to-face.

The man's eyes locked with mine and a knowing smile crept across his face. He knew who I was. And he knew why I was trying to escape.

"Excuse me." He stepped in front of us. "You look awfully familiar," he said, looking straight at me.

"Really?" I said casually, attempting to step around him, with Jamie in tow. "I get that all the time." I pointed haphazardly at my face. "One of those faces."

But he stepped in front of us again. He eyed Jamie warily, as if to warn him with a look. *Beware, this girl isn't who she says she is.*

"Ashlyn, isn't it?" the man asked.

Oh, holy shit.

Jamie looked from me to the man and then back at me again. The curiosity on his face was hard to miss.

I tried to take deep, steady breaths as I plastered a look of unfamiliarity on my face. As if the name Ashlyn was as foreign to me as the name of an unknown Russian ballerina listed in the program for *Swan Lake.*

"Sorry," I said with an apologetic smile. "You must have me confused with someone else."

I took another step toward the safety of the front door. Jamie followed quickly behind, clearly a little thrown off by the whole situation and probably eager to get the hell out of there so he could question me about it.

"I don't think so," the man said, taking hold of my arm.

I closed my eyes in silent defeat. This was it. The end was here. Haku Sushi on Main Street would forever be known as my Waterloo.

He looked toward Jamie. "I'm sorry to be the one who has to tell you this, but—"

And then, unexpectedly, Jamie's hand landed directly on top of his and he proceeded to "gently" remove it from my arm. "I think you have the wrong person," Jamie repeated, looking the man sternly in the eyes. "Why don't you leave her alone."

The man took a step back and threw his arms up in the air. "All right, man. It's your funeral. But don't say no one tried to warn ya."

And with that he turned around, shoved his hands in his pockets, and walked back to his table.

"Wow, the fresh air feels nice. I feel better already," I said to Jamie, after we exited the restaurant and strolled through the parking lot. I was kind of hoping there might be a small, tiny, minuscule chance that he might not ask . . .

"So what was that about back there?"

Yeah, I knew it was a long shot.

I looked into his eyes, so filled with innocent curiosity. So longing to know everything and anything about me. Especially the things that explained why someone would mistake me for a girl named Ashlyn, and then try to deliver some type of warning about me. I felt a pang of guilt, followed by a very unavoidable realization.

I had to tell him.

If this were going to continue, if I were really going to give this thing a chance, he would have to know. I would have to be 100 percent honest with him.

I swallowed hard and leaned against the side of his car. "Jamie . . ." I began. I could feel the truth welling up inside of me. It was time. Time to come clean. Time to reveal everything and finally begin the truthful and trusting relationship I knew we could have if we were only given the chance.

"I honestly have no idea who that was," I finished with a sigh.

Okay, so maybe not quite *yet.*

"It's true. I do have one of those faces. People confuse me for other people *all* the time." I looked to him for a sign that he was buying it.

Jamie was either satisfied with my shameless lie or he didn't feel like pressing the issue. "Hmm," he responded. "Interesting. So how are you feeling? Do you want me to take you home?"

As much as I hated thinking about ending my night with Jamie early, I decided it would be smart to continue with the "coming down with something" charade, so as not to give him any other reasons to be suspicious of me. I nodded weakly and said, "I think that would be a good idea."

He gave me a quick kiss on the cheek and touched my face. "Okay, cutie. But I have something to ask you first."

Oh, great, I thought. *He's not going to let it go. He's going to keep drilling me until I crack. Until I crumble under the pressure and spill everything right here and now.*

"What's that?" I asked casually.

"Well, my company's sending me to Paris in a couple of weeks and . . ."

"And you want me to water your plants?" I asked with a mocking smirk.

He laughed. "No. But wouldn't it be awkward if I did?"

I smiled, suddenly feeling very comforted by the light change in topic.

"Actually . . . I want you to come with me."

These are the moments in life when you would expect the expression on your face to be something along the lines of enthusiasm, excitement, exhilaration, one of those *E* words. But not for me. No, for me it was actually more of a muted stun. One of those jaw-dropping, not-quite-sure-if-it's-really-a-joke, waiting-for-the-punchline-to-come moments.

"C-c-come with you to Paris?" I finally got out.

He smiled and nodded his head with excitement. "*Oui.*"

"You're serious?" My tone was overflowing with doubt.

"Yes, I'm serious. Will you come?"

"Um, yeah!" I immediately responded, without thinking. Without reflecting. Without doing anything, really. And suddenly, my *maladie imaginaire* was nowhere to be found. I jumped up and down ecstatically like a little girl just told she was going to Disney World for the first time. And frankly, I couldn't remember the last time I had actually jumped up and down . . . well, without an aerobic jump rope in my hands.

"I can't believe this! Paris?"

"I'm glad you're so excited," Jamie mused.

"Are you kidding? It's Paris! I love Paris!"

Translation: *I love Paris when I'm not there with someone else's husband.*

Jamie reached down and grabbed my hand. "Good." He stared into my eyes for a long moment, and then added, "Honestly, as soon as they told me I was going, I thought of you. For some reason, I just couldn't imagine being there without you. Is that crazy?"

I quietly shook my head. That was the craziest part of all: It wasn't crazy. And trust me, I know crazy.

"C'mon," he said, giving my hand a quick squeeze. "Let's get you home and into bed."

I beamed as I sat down in Jamie's car and he closed the door behind me. It was the smile of someone who didn't have all the evil spirits of Pandora's box chasing after her. The smile of someone who could just smile, knowing that the man she was falling in love with was taking her to Paris.

And right then, at that moment, in the parking lot of a trendy sushi restaurant in Santa Monica, the world slowed down, the door to my prison cell unlocked, and my heart finally opened.

26

last tango before paris

The timing couldn't have been more perfect.

I had a secret to tell Jamie and he had invited me to the most romantic city in the world. There wasn't a better time and place to tell him. Because strolling down the banks of the Seine in the city of love, with the moon overhead and the water down below, makes any dark and dirty secret sound like poetry.

Even mine.

Or so I prayed.

Besides, he couldn't be mad at me. Not when I would follow the shocking and unsettling story of my questionable past with the even more shocking and unsettling decision I had just made about my future.

The one I was now proud to share with all three of my friends.

"It's over," I said to an impatient John, an eager Sophie, and a seemingly bored Zoë, as we sat at the Urth Café and ate overpriced sandwiches and salads for lunch.

"You mean Jamie?" Zoë asked in a panic, suddenly no longer bored. "But I thought you were going to Paris with him!"

I shook my head. "No, we're still going." And then for a brief moment I got lost in another one of my daydreams about me and Jamie in Paris having wine and cheese picnics on the Eiffel Tower lawn. I had been having daydreams like this ever since he asked me to go. Although, I must admit, most of them were much more titillating than wine and cheese.

"What's over, then?" Sophie asked, concerned, snapping me back to the present.

"I'm quitting," I proclaimed. The sound of my own voice, announcing it aloud, sent a surge of vibrant energy through my body. It was the first time I had actually heard myself say it. Although I had made the decision a few nights ago, I'm not sure it had really sunk in yet.

I sat patiently, waiting for the anticipated round of "What?" or "Huh?" or "Are you serious?"

But surprisingly, it never came.

The three of them just sat there, staring at me, completely confused. Then they kind of looked at one another, hoping one member of the group might shed some light on this seemingly out-of-the-blue decision. But they all shook their heads and shrugged their shoulders to imply *This is news to me.*

Sophie was the first to speak. "You're *quitting* quitting? As in . . ."

I nodded. "As in no more assignments. No more cheating husbands or fiancés or boyfriends. I'm done with it. All of it."

"But what about your quest? Your life mission? All that wannabe superhero stuff you told me about?" Sophie, seeing herself now as a direct beneficiary of my battle against evil, had recently become an avid supporter.

Of course her question had crossed my mind before. In fact, it had been the biggest thing holding me back during my decision-making process. Actually, it had been the *only* thing holding me back. I shook my head. "It's just gotten to be too much. I can't handle it anymore. Even Superman has to retire sooner or later and just say, 'well, I did my best. I hope I made an impact.' "

"I'm sure you made a huge impact!" Sophie offered supportively.

I smiled. "Thanks. I just realized that spending my entire life surrounded by cheating men wasn't giving me the opportunity to focus on the fact that there *are* men out there who *don't* cheat. It's like you manifest what you focus on, you know?"

"Like Eric." Sophie beamed.

I took a sip of ice water and swallowed hard, the cold water stinging my throat. "Right," I croaked. "Like Eric."

"So this is because of Jamie?" Zoë asked anxiously. I could tell she was trying to round up all the details before she let herself get excited. She probably would have made an excellent lawyer. Evidence first, then move for an emotional verdict.

"Not entirely," I said, taking a bite of my portabella mushroom sandwich.

"Not entirely?" John begged for clarification.

I shrugged, as if all of this came straight from *yesterday's* headlines and therefore it was no longer gossip-worthy news. "Well, I mean, there's a lot of stuff that's been going on lately. And then with all the stress and the secrets . . ."

"What secrets?" Sophie asked. "I thought you told us all your secrets."

The guilt instantly washed over me, knowing there were still some secrets that I would never have a chance to reveal. There was no way I could ever tell Sophie that I didn't go through with Eric's inspection.

I looked down at my plate, avoiding her glance. "I did. I mean, like secrets from my mom . . . from Jamie . . . from everyone else."

"So you're gonna come clean to everyone then?" Zoë confirmed with a doubtful inflection.

I balked slightly. I wasn't really planning on it. I had made a promise to myself to tell Jamie everything while we were in Paris, but as for the rest of them, I kind of hoped that if I could just from now on tell the truth, all the lies from the past would sort of be absolved. I didn't really want to start coming clean to *everyone* in my life. Well, because honestly, I wanted to *keep* them in my life.

"I'm not sure. I don't think so," I replied hesitantly. "It'll just be nice not to have to tell any more lies . . . you know, from now on."

"Well, what will you do?" Sophie asked. "Like for money and stuff?"

Ah, there it was. The million-dollar question . . . literally. I still had no clue. I sighed and took another bite of my overpriced sandwich, wondering how long I would be able to actually continue biting into overpriced sandwiches. "I don't know. I have enough money saved up to last me about six months. I guess I'll take that time to figure it out."

The three of them nodded—almost simultaneously. I could tell this was uncharted territory for all of them. My *real* problems were still fairly new and unfamiliar. They were used to being summoned for the typical "this person in my office drives me crazy" *fake* pep talk, but this was different. And they had no idea what to say.

So I spoke again. Listing all the things I had been sorting out since the other night. "I'm going to take one last assignment, and then after that I'm . . ." I paused, letting the anxiety, the ecstasy, and the sheer terror of my next word fully wash over me. "Done."

Sophie took a sip of her Diet Coke. "What happens when people call?"

Ah, yes . . . another detail I had already gone over in my mind. "I guess I'm just throwing away the cell phone. Disconnecting the service. Whatever. I have to keep it long enough to tie up loose ends, but then . . . it's going in my trash compactor. Along with so many other things."

I was proud of how on top of everything I was. I doubted there was a question they could ask that I hadn't already thought of and made an informed decision about.

"What about that Raymond Jacobs guy?" Zoë asked. "Have you figured out what you'll do about him?"

Okay . . . well, that was the *one* issue I hadn't quite yet resolved. I lowered my head. "I still don't know what to do about him. I mean, I'm quitting, so it's not like he can ruin any of my future assignments, but he knows where my family lives. Hell, he's already contacted Hannah."

"You could just come clean to your family," Sophie suggested again, still holding on to her idea that honesty is the best policy.

I shook my head. "No. No way. They would disown me. And I could never explain that to Hannah. She's so naive and just starting to get into boys. Besides, one of the biggest reasons for getting out of this is to avoid them ever finding out. So essentially, it would be counterproductive to tell them."

Sophie nodded reluctantly, still not entirely convinced.

I blew out a loud gust of air. "Well, I'm sure something will come to me. It has to." And just as the words were uttered, I felt discouraged. Would I actually have to sleep with that slimeball just to save my family from the truth? And what's to say he would even keep his end of the bargain? There had to be another way. And I was determined to find it.

"So what's this last assignment, then?" Zoë asked.

The words "last assignment" rang in my ears like church bells on a Sunday morning. Was it really happening? Was this really the *last* one? The whole idea just seemed so surreal.

"I don't know yet," I replied. "I'm meeting with her tomorrow. Some woman named Karen Howard or something. She was very vague on the phone. So I guess I'll find out."

The next day I got a call from my mom as I was on my way to Karen Howard's house for our pre-assignment meeting.

"Are you busy?" she asked sweetly.

I looked at the navigation screen. It read: *Time to Destination: approx.* 7 *minutes.*

"I have a few minutes," I replied into my headset.

"Well, I've been thinking," she began.

As soon as the words came out of her mouth, I knew it wasn't going to be good. Recently, whenever my mom spent time "thinking," she almost always ended up in hysterics at the end of it. Blaming herself for my father's multiple affairs, questioning her ability to ever love again, doubting the likelihood that anyone will ever love *her.* It was never a joyful thing when my mom called me up to think. And I feared today would be no different.

"About what?" I asked breezily, praying that she'd simply been thinking about joining a gym and wanted to get my opinion of which one was better. Today was supposed to be a happy day. A celebrated affair . . . so to speak. I was on my way to my *very* last client meeting, and I selfishly didn't want to take any of my mother's baggage with me.

"About your father," she said uneasily.

And here it goes.

I took a deep breath. "Mom, I'm sorry. I'm running into a meeting, I don't really think it's the best time to get into this. I'm going to have to—"

"I think you should call him," she calmly interrupted.

I swore I must have misunderstood her. "Huh?"

"Your dad. You should call him. Talk to him again. Try to rebuild a relationship with him."

My mind kind of zoned out just then, and I had to slam on my brakes to avoid hitting the car in front of me. "Why would I do that?" I asked her.

"Because you've been angry long enough. And I believe it's having an adverse effect on you. Now it's time to forgive."

"Forgive? After everything he did?"

My mom exhaled loudly. "He didn't do anything to *you,* sweetie. He loves you. He misses you. It was unfair of you to cut him out of your life like you did. No matter how bad of a husband he was to *me,* he's still your father. And he was always very good at being that."

I couldn't believe what I was hearing. From my mother of all people! She was actually taking *his* side. What was the matter with her? Did she have no self-respect at all?

"Mom," I began, determined to convince her of my motivations—obviously without revealing *all* of my motivations. "He hurt you. And by hurting you, he hurt me. And that's reason enough to keep him from my life."

"Jen," my mom said warningly, "I don't think that's a healthy attitude. You have to let go of your anger. You don't want to end up like Julia, do you?"

"What?" I immediately responded. Since when did Julia find her way into this conversation? This was a discussion about me, my mother, and my father. Not about my father's first wife's daughter. How did she even factor in? "What does Julia have to do with it?" I asked in a snotty voice.

"Well, you know how she is," my mom explained gently. "She's bitter, and overprotective of her daughter, and, well, for the most part . . . angry and unhappy because she never learned to let go. Do you really want to end up like that? Because that's what happens when you hang on to resentment."

Wait a minute, I thought. Julia is angry and unhappy? About what? And who does she have to resent? I mean, I know she's never really liked *me,* but I always assumed it was because I was the half sister. The unwanted sibling from her father's new wife. I couldn't really blame her for that. If my dad had a child with this next wife of his, I would probably have a hard time taking a liking to him or her, too. And it would be even worse in this case, because his *new* wife is the last woman he cheated with when he was still married to my mother. And . . .

Oh . . . my . . . God.

My foot suddenly slammed on the brakes, and I pulled the car over to the side of the road. I struggled to take deep breaths. How could I have missed it all this time? How could I have not put all the pieces together? Especially when they had been there all along, lying right in front of me.

"Jen?" my mom's voice came through the line. "Are you all right?"

I ignored her question. My mind was stuck on a completely different path. "Mom," I began in a wobbly voice.

"Yes?"

"Did Dad cheat on Julia's mom, too?"

"Yes," she said, as if it were obvious. "I thought you knew that."

"No!" I nearly cried. "How could I have known that? No one ever told me. How would I know?"

My mom laughed weakly at my delayed realization. "Why else do you think Julia was so mean to you as a child? And she really never liked me either until after the divorce."

"You mean he cheated on her . . . *with you*?" I shrieked.

I took my mom's silence as a yes. And actually, I much preferred the silent response. I was speechless. It felt like a curtain had just been lifted, revealing a room in my house that I didn't even know was there to begin with. And it was full of new and interesting things to explore and play with . . . and analyze!

"But if you were the one he cheated with, why would she want anything to do with us now? She hangs out with you all the time!"

My mom chuckled softly to herself. "Ever heard the phrase 'Misery loves company'? She clung to me after my divorce was final. I think she felt like we were finally on the same page. She's a very wounded little girl under all her thick layers. I'm glad I could be there for her."

"So *that's* why she hangs out with you instead of Dad?" I asked skeptically.

"Honey," my mom began in a gentle tone, "Julia hasn't spoken to Dad in ten years."

"What?" My voice strained as I tried to condense ten years of memories into one fleeting moment of thought.

"I assumed you knew. I just don't want your relationship with Dad to turn out the same way."

I nodded weakly and stared at the license plate of the car parked in front of me. "Okay," I surrendered softly. "Maybe I'll give him a call."

After all, I had already let go of so many things this week. What was one more?

I hung up the phone and pulled my SUV back onto the road. Everything was becoming clearer now. The reason Julia was so overprotective of her own daughter suddenly made perfect sense. She was trying to shield Hannah from a world that she had never learned to forgive . . . just like me.

And suddenly I realized that Julia and I had more in common than I thought. But I was desperate for the decisions I had made in the past week, and even the past two minutes, to be what finally set me apart from her.

The biggest of which was about to start right now.

As I pulled up in front of Karen Howard's house, I could feel the butterflies start to multiply in my stomach. This was it. The very last one. The last million-dollar mansion that I would step into. The last suspicious wife I would attempt to console. And, in a few days, the last cheating husband I would allow to kiss me.

To my great relief, and now my mom's as well, I was finally starting to let go.

I went into this thinking I could help people. And I know I did. Lots of people. Even if I never got the satisfaction of knowing for sure they ended up better off, I believed in my heart that they were. Because I had seen what happens when you don't know. I had experienced firsthand what happens to a family that lives in denial.

And yes, I had fully contemplated the consequences of quitting. It would mean that more women would have to go through what my mom had gone through. And apparently Julia's mom, as well. But there comes a point, when the bad guy is after you, when the good guy can't break through to you, when a world of cover-ups and lies feels like it's going to come crashing down on top of you, when you realize: Sometimes you have to stop, take a step back, relieve your tired shoulders of the rest of the world's burdens, and take the time to help yourself.

Because truth be told, I *wasn't* a superhero. I couldn't fly. I couldn't spin intricate webs and cling to the sides of walls. I couldn't leap tall buildings in a single bound. I was just an ordinary girl trying to make a difference.

And I believed I had.

Now it was time to make *me* different. And that's exactly what I would do.

After this one, last, final, closing assignment.

I was about to step out of the car and walk to the front door when my personal cell phone rang. I fished it from my bag, and upon seeing Jamie's now stored name and number on the caller ID, I flipped it open with excitement.

Speak of the angel.

"Hey, you," I said.

He cleared his throat and spoke in a deep, self-important voice. "Yes, um . . . Mr. Jamie Richards for a Ms. Jennifer H., please."

I played along, lowering my voice to a sultry but professional tone. "I'm sorry. Ms. Jennifer H. doesn't know any Mr. Jamie Richards."

"Hmm . . . There must be an error here on my paperwork. I was calling to confirm a plane ticket to Paris and, well, I guess I dialed the wrong number. I'm sorry about the confusion, miss. Have a good—"

"No, wait!" I stopped him.

He laughed at my franticness, and then in his normal voice asked, "So have you started packing yet?"

"We're not leaving until *next* Saturday!"

"But you've thought about it."

"Maybe a little," I admitted nonchalantly, not wanting to confess that I had pretty much the entire contents of my suitcase planned out in my head. Not to mention the fact that every minute I was in my house I had to hold myself back from pulling out my large, non-carry-on, non-assignment suitcase from my hall closet and filling it to the brim with cute, *non*-assignment outfits. It was hidden behind all of Marta's brooms and mops and things. I imagined I would have to start using them myself soon. There was no way I would be able to afford her on my unemployed, still-don't-know-what-to-do-with-my-life-but-very-happy-to-be-doing-it-nonetheless salary.

"Are you home?" he asked.

I looked through the windshield at Karen Howard's large, two-story house looming in front of me. "Actually, I'm working right now."

I was *dying* to tell Jamie about the conclusive nature of my so-called work tonight. To allow my elatedness to spill forth through the phone and give him all the credit he deserved. *"You made me believe again. You gave me faith, something I haven't known since I was twelve years old!"* But I knew that (1) It was pretty heavy stuff for a relationship that hadn't even passed the four-date mark, and (2) It would require a *lot* more explanation. And given the fact that I was now running ten minutes late to my meeting, it would have to wait. And so I bit my tongue and said nothing.

"Ooh, working hard, huh? Burning the midnight oil on a Friday night, are we? Miss Important?"

I looked up at the beautiful home in front of me. Burning the midnight oil? Not exactly.

Possibly burning a dishonest man's metaphoric castle of deception to the ground?

More like it.

"That's right," I replied. "And what are you doing?"

He sighed loudly. "I'm afraid I'm burning the oil as well. Gonna be here for at least another couple of hours. We're getting ready for the Paris trip."

My stomach did a small flip and I smiled into the phone. "Oh, yeah?"

"Yeah. But I just wanted to check in and say hi."

My stomach flipped again, and my body seemed to melt right into the car seat. "That's so sweet." I checked my watch. It was already 8:12 P.M. "Well, I should probably get back to work," I added.

"Me, too. Talk to you tomorrow?"

"Definitely."

I ended the call and rested the phone against my lips as if trying to suck the conversation right out of the pink metal and into a safe, photographic memory bank in the back of my mind.

I put the phone back in my bag, opened the car door, and stepped out into the crisp October evening air. I took a ceremonial walk up the front steps, pausing frequently so I'd remember the feeling I had with each step, as they were about to become my last.

Karen Howard's house was almost as beautiful as she was. Both well groomed, well polished, and furnished with expensive accessories.

She welcomed me nervously into the living room, and I tried to focus on the task at hand. I just had to get through this meeting, the assignment, and then I was home free.

Off to Paris.

I quickly stopped myself before slipping into another daydream.

"Thanks so much for meeting me," Karen said warmly as we sat down in the living room.

"It's no problem. Why don't you tell me why you called," I replied, gently attempting to push the process forward and eliminate all small talk.

"Right," she began cautiously. "Well, my husband . . ."

"Mr. Howard?" I said assumingly, jotting down the name in my notes.

"Actually, no. Howard is my maiden name. I gave it to you over the phone because I . . . I don't know, I guess I was just nervous about the whole process and I didn't want to give out my real name, just in case—"

"I understand," I said quickly, striking a line through the name I had just written on the page. "Many women do that. It's quite normal. I've seen it several times."

I fought to keep my tone calm and steady. The worst thing I could do to this woman was make her think I was trying to rush her. She certainly didn't need to know that I was in a hurry to get through this meeting, especially in the state she was in. I've learned over the years that women in her condition need all the patience and attention you can give them. It's that lack of attention that probably drove them here in the first place.

"So what *is* your husband's name, then?" I asked.

Karen swallowed hard and fidgeted with her hands. It was as if saying his name aloud to me was making this whole process even more real. A bit too real.

"It's okay," I offered sympathetically. "We can come back to that part if you'd like."

"No, no," she insisted. "I'm fine." She clasped her hands together tightly and held them in her lap. "My husband's name is Jamie . . . Jamie Richards."

27

battle scars

I absentmindedly started to write down the name Karen Howard had just given me until I got to the letter *R* of his last name. I stopped cold. "Jamie Richards?" I clarified, certain I had heard it wrong.

"Yes," she repeated.

My heart started to pound. I struggled to keep my breathing steady. Surely there were several Jamie Richards in the city of Los Angeles. Surely.

I mean, there *had* to be.

I attempted a smile. It came out more like a possessed lip spasm. "What does Mr. Richards do?" I asked professionally. "Construction? Medicine? Law?" The speculations were spewing uncontrollably from my mouth like water coming out of a hose that someone had dropped on the ground and suddenly appeared to have taken on a life of its own.

"Oh, God no," Karen said, with a meek smile. "Jamie hates lawyers."

I nodded slowly, practically engaging in a staring contest with her mouth, as I desperately anticipated the next words to leave it.

"Jamie's a marketing consultant," she said, leaning back in her chair, her eyes wandering toward the ceiling. "For Calloway Consulting."

And that's when I threw up.

Not then and there, on Jamie Richards's plush, Burberry *married* carpeting. Although I really would have liked to have left that little present for him.

Rather, I excused myself quickly, asking—no, more like *demanding*—to know where the bathroom was, and ran from the room.

I vomited twice in the toilet, flushed, and then rinsed my mouth out with water. I stared into the mirror. All the color had completely vanished from my face. Even my eyes, normally a sharp shade of green, seemed to have turned gray and lifeless. My lips, despite the double application of gloss I had applied before leaving the house earlier, were dull and pale.

I swallowed hard.

This was not happening.

This was not real.

It was all in my head.

I would march out there, double-check all the details, and then reassuringly hear Karen's lighthearted laugh resonate through the room as she said, "You thought I said *Jamie Richards*? Hahahaha. No, no, no. I said Maley Pichards!"

Yes, that's exactly what would happen.

I wiped a bead of sweat from my brow and another one from my upper lip, flipped off the light switch, and with my head held high in the air made my way back to the living room to put an end to this silly little confusion.

But as I quietly took my seat again, it was evident that carefree laughter was nowhere to be seen—or heard. Instead she looked at me curiously, wondering if this whole running from the room at the mention of her husband's name was all a normal part of the process. After all, this fidelity inspection business was completely new to her.

"Is everything all right?" she asked warily.

I attempted a smile. "Yes, I believe so. Sorry about that."

Karen let out a sigh. "Good, good. Well, anyway. Jamie works a *lot*." Her emphasis on the word left no doubt that his work schedule must have been a problem area in their marriage.

In their *marriage*! So it really *was* happening! I couldn't believe this. Jamie Richards . . . the perfect, adorable, charming, "Come to Paris with me" Jamie Richards was married! As in "I do," as in "Till death do us part"—or more like, "Till I meet some chick on an airplane who's stupid enough to believe that I would be single!"

Every conversation we had had, every single movement that he had made was swirling around in my head. I tried desperately to slow the images down and look for clues. A wedding ring tan, a mention of a "we," nervousness around the topic of marriage. Something I might have missed. But there was nothing. Absolutely nothing!

Except . . .

I suddenly thought back to that moment outside my front door after our second date: *"I really like you, Jen. I just think we should take this slow . . . I don't want to rush into anything."*

That was the reason he didn't want to have sex with me? Because he was *married*? And this whole time I thought he was just being sweet. Considerate. Genuine. But in reality, it was just code for "I'm actually married and I don't want to do the whole full-blown sex cheating thing? I'm perfectly happy with just the half-ass, making-out, cheating thing."

For God's sake, he invited me to Paris!

But why even bother with the half-ass thing? If you're going to cheat, why not just cheat and get it over with! Why drag it out?

"Are you *sure* you're all right?" Karen's voice snapped me back into the moment, and it was then I realized that my mouth was half open and my head was cocked to one side.

I quickly jerked my body upright and shut my mouth. "Yeah, sorry. What were you saying?"

She shot me a strange look but then appeared to brush it off. "I was just saying that my husband works a lot. He's always traveling for business. I just have no idea what he does when he's away. I'm worried he might . . . you know . . ." Her voice trailed off.

Oh, I *knew*! Did I ever! I wanted to pipe in right then and there and inform her of just how much I actually did know about her husband's little business trips. But instead I just nodded.

"He's going to Paris next week," she continued. "And I don't know how far you normally travel for this sort of thing, but I thought maybe that would be a good time to . . ." She swallowed. "Test him . . . or whatever it is you do."

"Yes!" I exclaimed loudly. Karen jumped at my unexpected enthusiasm. I cleared my throat and played it off. "I mean, yes . . . that would be a *very* good opportunity to test your husband."

Well, if this wasn't the mother of all last assignments. In fact, this wasn't even *just* an assignment anymore. This was personal. In one swift, unexpected motion, this had suddenly turned from just another day's work into just um . . . *my life*!

"Of course, I'll pay for all of your travel expenses," she offered. "I just really want to know . . . I *need* to know."

That makes two of us, I thought.

"I understand," I said calmly. I could feel the heat rising in my stomach. I knew that after a few more seconds in that chair the anger would probably boil over and come spilling out of my mouth in the form of many profanities and inappropriate gestures. I had to get out of there.

So I listened impatiently as Karen ran over all the details of the trip. I pretended to write down every one of them, although, in reality, I'd had them memorized since the day Jamie e-mailed me our itinerary. The lovesick idiot that I was.

As Karen walked me to the front door, she finished listing all of Jamie's hobbies and interests, his background, and his likes and dislikes. And upon hearing all the familiar things I had only just started to learn about the man I had been so very wrong about, the anger slowly started to dissolve into a flood of tears. I fought to keep them back. I just had to get out of that house.

As the door closed behind me, the first tear fell.

And as soon as I sat down in my car, the floodgates opened. I lowered my head onto the steering wheel and sobbed uncontrollably. I couldn't even remember the last time I had cried that hard.

I hated myself right then. I hated myself for believing. For trusting. For feeling. I never wanted to feel anything again. Nothing had to be better than this. *It's better to have loved and lost than never to have loved at all?* Fuck Shakespeare! That's a load of crap.

I wiped away some of my tears, started the engine, and drove away.

Normally I would have driven to Sophie's apartment . . . or even to Zoë's. But for some reason I didn't think that a normal "session" was quite going to cut it this time.

I didn't want to see anybody. I didn't want to talk to anybody. I just wanted to drive home, fall onto my bed, and cry.

So I did.

I didn't answer my phone for a full twenty-four hours. I watched it ring. In the span of a day I had three "concerned" calls from Sophie, two from Zoë, in which she proceeded to call either me or the person who dared share the road with her both a "whore" and a "dumb ass," one from John, two from blocked numbers, and two from Jamie.

Sophie eventually came knocking at my door. And when I didn't answer, she used her key.

She found me lying on my bed in the same clothes I had been wearing the day before when I met with Karen Richards, wife of the cheating bastard, also known as Jamie Richards.

"What happened?" she asked, running to the bed and sitting down on the edge. She tenderly stroked my hair.

I looked at her with tired, sleepless eyes. I hadn't eaten in over a day and my energy level was at an all-time low. "Jamie's married," I said lifelessly.

"What?" Her hand stopped cold in the middle of my forehead.

My voice was monotone and drained. "My last assignment. Karen Howard. Actually, Karen *Richards*."

Sophie stared at me in utter shock. "Maybe it wasn't the same Jamie."

I looked her directly in the eye. "She's sending me to Paris, because he's going there for business next week."

"Oh."

I rolled onto my side so I was facing away from her and tucked my hands under my cheek.

Sophie was silent. I knew she didn't have a clue what to say. And I was almost more grateful for her silence. At least it was honest.

We sat there for a long time. A few minutes even. Then finally she asked, "So are you going to go?"

Without even turning back to face her I replied, "Yes. I want this cheating bastard caught and brought to justice."

Sophie cracked a smile. "You sound like a district attorney."

"Well, now I know what it feels like to be one."

"But why even go? Why put yourself through it? You know he's a cheater. Cancel on him and tell his wife that he failed."

"Because *I* have to know," I insisted.

"Know what?" Sophie asked, puzzled.

"If he'd really do it. Really *cheat*."

Sophie reflected momentarily. "You mean sex?"

I twisted my neck and turned my head toward her, struggling to give her an obvious nod. "Um, yeah! We still haven't had sex! He said he wanted to wait . . . no reason to rush into anything, let's take it slow . . . blah, blah, blah . . . asshole."

"And you think he did that because he's married?" Sophie asked.

"Can you think of any other reason?"

She took a deep breath. "But sex or no sex . . . he still cheated."

"Did he?"

She looked at me and our eyes locked. She knew what I was getting at. It was the question that all of us women ask ourselves. It was the age-old question of relationships. The question as old as the institution of marriage itself.

What constitutes cheating?

Is it the removal of the wedding ring? Is it the failure to mention a wife? Is it kissing? Flirting? Touching? Talking?

Where's the line? And when do they cross it?

When do you consider your husband to have cheating tendencies? When is it confirmed that he has an "intention" to be unfaithful? And is an intention even enough?

But these were questions I left up to my clients. Questions I never had to answer myself.

Until now.

Because now it was *me* who needed to know.

It was me who had to define the act of cheating.

And it was suddenly a whole different ball game.

"So you're going to have sex with him?"

I closed my eyes tightly. "I can't now!" I practically yelled. "I wanted to. I mean, what's more perfect than making love for the first time with someone in Paris? It's like a movie."

Sophie nodded. "Yeah."

"But now, if I have sex with him to prove a point . . . to myself, or to anyone . . . then *I'm* just as bad as he is! I'm having sex with a married man. A man I *know* is married. That's just plain wrong."

"So what then?" Sophie asked. "What are you going to do?"

I rolled onto my back and stared at the ceiling. "I guess the same thing I always do."

"Intention?"

The tears began to form again. "The very highest level of it."

"But you guys are sharing a hotel room, right? Isn't that pretty much proof of an intention right there? I mean, he didn't book you separate rooms, did he?"

I shook my head. "No. But a hotel room is not enough. I have to be absolutely sure. I have to know if he'd really go through with it. If not for his"—I paused and fought back a break in my voice—"wife . . . then for me."

Sophie looked at me and gently reached over to wipe away a stray tear that had rolled down the side of my face. "But Jen," she began. "What if he doesn't? What if he doesn't go through with it?"

I let out a frustrated laugh. "I've thought of that," I admitted. "And I think that's the scariest outcome of them all."

What *if* he didn't go through with it? Would that make him honest? Faithful? What? Would I be able to actually add him to the sacred list in my secret, wooden box and say "Yea!" for all the faithful couples in the universe? I hope they're all very happy. Maybe they can form a club and celebrate together. All ten of them. Or nine, or whatever the real number was. I didn't have a clue anymore.

Hell, I didn't even know if my best friend's future husband was the cheating type. I didn't know anything these days. And the things I thought I knew, the things I thought I could be sure of, turns out they're a bunch of crap, too.

It just wasn't fair. The first time—the *only* time—I let my guard down, I get stuck with a complete jerk-off who parades around as a decent guy, asking me to go to Paris and take things slow. And after I'd been so careful for two years not to fall for anyone because, as I'd just proven, they call it "falling" for a reason. If I remember correctly from age five: You fall, you hurt yourself. You scrape your knee or your elbow and you have to wear an obnoxious, brightly colored, *Sesame Street* bandage to show off your wound to everyone. Look at me! I got hurt. I was running around the pool even though I was told not to and look how well that turned out.

After Sophie left, promising she would be back in a few hours to check on me, Jamie called for the third time, and after the fourth ring I decided I had to answer it. For *work* purposes. If I were going to pull off a flawless act of "nothing's wrong and I still have no idea you're married" while we were in Paris, I would eventually have to answer his calls. Otherwise he'd start to suspect. And I couldn't allow anything to interfere with my very important, top-secret, under-the-covers assignment.

So I tried not to let any of the bitterness seep into my voice when I answered, but it certainly wasn't an easy feat.

And I must admit I wasn't doing the greatest job.

"Are you all right?" Jamie asked less than a minute into our conversation.

"Yeah, fine," I replied shortly. "Just a rough day at work."

"Ah," he replied, "the bank running you around?"

I rolled my eyes. "Yep, definitely getting the runaround."

"I'm sorry, baby," he said with such genuine compassion that I almost wanted to throw up . . . . again.

This guy was quite the actor. D in drama? Yeah, right! I was surprised he wasn't acting for a living. Who needs marketing consulting when you can pull off Academy Award–winning performances like that?

"Yeah, well . . . I guess that's the nature of the job," I responded.

"But they're still letting you off for Paris, right?" he asked with concern.

"Yeah," I said. "I'll probably just end up having to bring a little work with me to make up for lost time."

"Okay, good."

I wanted to reach through the phone and strangle him. But the hardest part about it—even though my perspective had completely changed—was Jamie was exactly the same. He was the same sweet guy he always was. Caring, considerate, real. It baffled me. As much as I hated him right now, there really wasn't anything hateable about him . . . at all. (Well, minus the stashed-away wife part.) He was just the opposite. Nothing but lovable. And that made me hate him even more!

"So, do you want to have dinner this week? One last time before we leave the country."

"Well, it's not like we're not coming back," I said matter-of-factly. And then almost added, "Although you might be coming back in a body bag."

Jamie laughed. "I know. I just thought it might be fun."

Yeah, super fun! I thought. *Me staring at your wedding-ring finger all night as a phantom gold band fades in and out of my imagination, and then picturing you in bed with Karen Richards as soon as you drop me off at my door with your usual "let's take it slow" good-night kiss. That sounds like a total blast. Even better than getting my cervix poked at the gynecologist's office, if you can believe it.*

I took a deep breath and calmed my voice. "I don't think I'll be able to go . . . baby." I choked back a small amount of vomit rising up in my throat. "I have so much work to do to make up for the time I'll be gone."

"Ah, right. That makes sense," he conceded, and then an awkward silence followed. It was honestly the most awkward I'd ever felt with him. We always clicked. It had always been so easy between us.

"Are you sure everything is all right?" He finally broke the silence.

For a small moment I almost felt sorry for him. He had no idea why things were suddenly different. He had no idea why *I* was suddenly different. Because as hard as I tried to hide my anger, some things you can just *feel*. You didn't have to be a psychic to sense the obvious shift in energy between us. But that small moment passed quickly, when I reminded myself of *why* I was suddenly different.

"Yes, everything's fine," I replied, lying back on my bed. "I'm sorry. Work's just been crazy. What time are you picking me up for the airport on Saturday?"

Jamie cleared his throat. "Well, the flight is at one-thirty, and because it's international and all, we should be there two hours ahead of time, so I'll come by your house with the car around ten o'clock. How does that sound?"

"Sounds good to me," I said hastily.

"Great."

"Yeah. Well, I better run. Lots of stuff to do. I guess I'll see you then."

"Yeah, okay. See ya," he replied with uncertainty.

I shut off the phone and laid it across my stomach.

"I don't have a choice," I repeated softly to myself. "I have to know the truth. I deserve to know the truth. Don't I?"

I closed my eyes and tried to imagine what it would be like when I got into that car. And onto that plane. And into that hotel room. Suddenly, doubt clouded my mind. How was I ever going to get through this? I could barely even make it through a three-minute phone conversation. There was no way I was going to be able to keep up this unsuccessful charade for five days while gallivanting around Paris, remarking on Impressionist art and sipping overpriced café au laits. I was too hurt. Too affected. Too involved.

This bandage may not have been brightly colored with images of Elmo and Big Bird, but it would certainly be hard to miss.

There was really no other choice. If I wanted to get through these next few days without Jamie suspecting anything was wrong, I was going to have to bring in an expert. Someone who could get through this without becoming emotionally involved. Someone cold, detached, indifferent. Someone who could care less whether or not Jamie was married and failed to tell me about it. Because honestly, when has she cared about the marital status of any man before?

As much as I never wanted this moment to come, it was really the only option I had.

It was time for Jamie to finally meet Ashlyn.

28

from bags to baggage

The packing process for my trip to Paris turned out to be quite the emotional roller coaster. All the cute outfits and sexy underwear I had once mentally selected with excitement and giddiness, before the news of Jamie's marital status, were now being bitterly thrown into my bag even though I knew that they would be used not as fun props for our romantic Paris getaway but rather as pieces of a uniform for the challenging and nauseating assignment that awaited me in the city of ~~love~~ deceit.

Now they were all just costumes in a play that I would be performing practically against my will. It was a part that I once took pleasure in playing, because I knew that each and every member of that audience would walk out of the theater a changed person. Most of them for the better. A play that would have an impact on people. But now it was as if I was being shoved onto the stage to bring to life a production that no longer felt meaningful.

Because all I felt was pain.

And that performance was starting now. Curtains up.

Jamie was right on time.

I opened the door wide and smiled as if he were the only person in the world I wanted to see behind that door.

"Well," he began, his face quickly lighting up. "Someone's excited."

"It's Paris! Why wouldn't I be excited?"

He laughed and leaned in to hug me. As he pulled away he started to go for the kiss. I closed my eyes and tried to pretend I was kissing Josh Duhamel, not some cheating scum of a husband standing in my living room about to take his *girlfriend* to Paris.

But the moment his lips touched mine, I remembered again what it was like to kiss him. The smell, the taste, the softness of his lips, the heat that began to rise in the pit of my stomach.

I quickly pulled away, disturbed by my involuntary reaction. "C'mon. We're going to be late!" I said, pulling my large suitcase behind me, and at the same time, using my free hand to push Jamie back out the front door.

I turned and locked it behind me.

There was a long, black limo parked outside my building, and as soon as we emerged from the front door, a chauffeur appeared and took my luggage. I climbed into the backseat, and Jamie followed quickly after me. A few moments later we were off.

We drove in silence. I immediately wondered if I should start talking about something. Strike up a conversation. Kill the silence. That's what I would normally do if I were on any other assignment. Or at least that's what *Ashlyn,* the pro, would do. Never let the silence last for too long. Always keep the conversation light and flowing smoothly.

I started to open my mouth to spew out some insignificant little-known fact about the history of our destination city when Jamie said, "Oh, I almost forgot."

He opened the cabinet under the limo's bar and pulled out a small blue gift bag with red and white tissue paper sticking out of the top and handed it to me.

"Pour toi," he said in a thick American accent.

I looked at the bag with confusion. Of course I recognized the colors: blue, white, and red, the colors of the French flag. But I didn't have the slightest idea what might be inside of it.

"What is it?"

"It's your airplane bag," he replied with a knowing smile.

The hand that was holding up the bag suddenly seemed to lose all of its strength, and it dropped heavily into my lap, bringing the bag down with it.

"My what?"

"Your airplane bag. You know, 'like a bag with lots of stuff in it . . . stuff for airplanes.' I think that was the official description."

I stared at it quietly. Completely speechless. He had remembered the story about my airplane bags? That as a kid I used to make them for every trip I went on with my family? I had told him about that on our second date as we lay on the hood of his car and watched the planes land. And he had actually *remembered.*

"I had to visit the official Web site to get the exact protocol for building a professional airplane bag," Jamie said, sitting back in his seat and resting his hand innocently on my leg.

I looked down at his hand and forced out a weak laugh. He wasn't the only one who remembered that conversation. I remembered all of our conversations. Because they actually meant something to me. Because I thought one day I would look back at them and smile. Now I just looked back at them to try and figure out how on earth I could have been so blind to all the signs. That there was someone else in the picture. They had to be there . . . somewhere. I just hadn't found them yet. Like a Where's Waldo? picture. You know he's hidden in there somewhere. Behind the sailboat, next to the lion's den, under the traffic bridge. You just have to keep looking. So I would. For the sake of my own sanity.

"Well, aren't you going to open it?" he asked.

I wanted to shake my head determinedly. Like a child who refused to get into the bathtub. The truth was, I didn't want to open it. I was afraid of what might be inside, that the contents of the bag might actually be even more heartbreaking than the thought of the bag itself.

But I couldn't *not* open it, because that's what I was supposed to do. I was supposed to be so touched by his thoughtfulness that I couldn't keep myself from eagerly tearing out the red and white tissue paper and rummaging inside.

I slowly pulled out the tissue paper.

"I hope the contents are to your liking," Jamie said. "I'm really just a novice at the fine art of airplane-bag making."

The first thing I pulled out was a container of Silly Putty. I smiled and placed it on the seat next to me. "You even remembered the Silly Putty," I stated absently, my mind in a daze. "What did you do, tape-record our conversation?" I was only half joking.

"For training purposes only," Jamie said as my hand reached into the bag again.

Next out was a bag of Goldfish Crackers, followed by two packs of gum, one bubble and one spearmint.

"I didn't know what type of gum you liked. I figured you can't go wrong with one bubble and one mint."

"I like bubble," I said quietly as I placed the gum packs next to the growing collection of items on my seat.

"Good, 'cause I like mint," Jamie said with a wink.

I swallowed hard. "I guess it's perfect, then."

"There's more, there's more," he urged me, motioning toward the bag.

With every item that I removed, my hands grew shakier. Mad Libs, playing cards, candy bars, mini-bottles of alcohol.

"Yeah, I figured *those* were probably not part of the bags you made when you were a kid," Jamie said, pointing to the bottles. "But I decided that the bag-making ritual needed to grow up a bit."

Then I reached down into the bottom and pulled out a medium-sized, light blue, Tiffany jewelry box. My heart somersaulted.

"Well, *that* is not exactly for the plane. I mean, you could wear it on the plane, but I thought maybe it would be better suited for Paris itself."

A weak smile appeared across my face as I lifted the lid and braced myself for what was inside. It was a silver-chained necklace with a tiny, circular rose pendant hanging from the center.

A gasp escaped from my mouth when I saw it. I just couldn't help myself. Cheater or no, it was just so beautiful. It looked *just* like one of the rose windows in the Notre Dame Cathedral. And I had no doubt that he had selected it for that very reason.

"I guess that means you like it," Jamie ventured.

I couldn't speak. I tried, but nothing came out. I could barely even nod my head. My entire body was in shock. The airplane bag was the most thoughtful gift anyone had ever given me.

"Either that . . . or you already have two of them," he continued, after my period of silence had reached a few extra long seconds.

My head became free from my spell and I nodded it profusely. My lips followed. "Yes."

"Yes, you have two of them?" Jamie laughed.

I shook my head numbly. "No, I like it. I mean . . . I love it."

Jamie moved his hand from my leg and laced his fingers with mine. Then he brought my hand up to his lips and kissed it tenderly.

"Good. I thought of you as soon as I saw it."

His comment stung. My only consolation at that moment was the hope that maybe he had sent his assistant to pick something out. Or maybe Calloway Consultants had a special gift services department that they hired for this kind of stuff. I could only pray that he had placed a quick phone call saying, "I'm too busy balancing my wife, my new girlfriend, *and* my work so can you please put together a nice 'airplane bag' for my trip to Paris, which I still have to pack for." And then I assumed he had called the in-house packing service shortly after.

But deep down I knew it wasn't true. I knew he had picked it out himself. Meaning, he took *more* time away from his wife than he already had, just to go shopping for a stupid airplane bag for me. It didn't seem fair. And it definitely didn't seem right that I loved it this much.

It shouldn't have been this way. Why was he making it so hard? As much as I knew I should throw my arms around his neck, kiss him, and then thank him profusely for being such a sweetheart of a guy, I just couldn't do it. And the reason I couldn't do it was because I wanted to.

My head was spinning like a broken compass. I didn't know which way was up and which way my true feelings were pointing. As I looked at his face, lit up with the anticipation of my approval, and then over at the contents of my custom-made airplane bag sprawled out on the seat next to me, I wanted to love him. I wanted it to all be a mistake. I wanted to take the goddamn blue pill and erase everything that had happened in the last week.

But as the limo pulled up to the curbside check-in at LAX, I knew that I couldn't forget what had happened. I couldn't erase the fact that I was getting on a plane to Paris with another woman's husband.

And if Jamie continued to throw these unhittable curveballs at me, I knew it was going to be a very long trip.

As I stepped out of the limo onto the curb I wasn't sure what I was getting myself into. And we hadn't even gotten on the plane yet.

I SOON discovered that working for a consulting company that allows you to charge all travel relating to your multimillion-dollar client was not a bad gig at all. Everything was first class. First-class baggage check-in, drinks in the international first-class lounge, first-class seats on a nonstop flight from Los Angeles to Paris, and reservations at the Hotel Ritz in the First Arrondissement of Paris.

Even I, a frequent first-class traveler due to my former—or now *current*—job was impressed.

I could tell Jamie was trying to impress me. Each time we entered the new and exciting next stage of our trip, he would watch my reaction. I could feel his eyes on my face as we walked into the international first-class lounge and I glanced around at all the plasma TV screens, the three open bars, and the buffets lined with various food choices. I let myself nod a small indication of approval and turned to smile at him.

Then he watched me again as we stepped onto the plane and the flight attendant graciously guided us *through* the business class, up the stairs, and into the exclusive first-class cabin of the plane. Each seat was like its own little apartment, with a TV screen, a desk, a retractable table, a fully reclinable swivel seat, and even a small supplementary seating area across from the seat. Jamie and I sat side by side as he, like a child with a new toy he wanted to show off, demonstrated all the features of our airplane "apartments."

"See, if you push this button, the seat swivels, and you can turn it around toward this little desk area and, you know, do important desk things."

I laughed at him. "Like what?"

"You know, save the world, start a war, pay off the national debt, whatever you want!"

"Can I borrow your checkbook, then?"

He smiled. "And then, if you push this button and hold it down, the entire seat reclines into a bed."

I watched him demonstrate and again nodded my approval. "Yes, Mr. Richards, I *have* been in a first-class seat before."

He frowned for a moment, as the thrill of being able to take my first-class virginity suddenly vanished into thin air. "Ah, yes, the elusive investment bank treats you well, I would imagine."

I nodded as I remembered what really was happening on those international first-class trips.

"Would you like something to drink?" the flight attendant asked.

Did I ever?

I nodded sweetly. "Yes, please. A vodka tonic would be great. Thanks."

The flight attendant smiled and headed back toward the galley.

As Jamie rested his head back against the seat and closed his eyes, I quietly reached down to my Dior handbag and lifted it into my lap. I opened the main compartment and slipped my finger into the small, zippered pocket that was sewn against the inside of the bag.

My fingertips softly brushed against the cool, glossy surface of the black business card that lay inside. The one that represented the end of Jamie Richards's marriage. And the thought of that immediately brought mixed emotions.

I could feel the raised surface of the ornate letter *A* that decorated the front. It seemed like such a stretch to even start to compare Jamie with all the shameful adulterers of my past.

I looked over at him, his eyes still closed. A sudden wave of guilt washed over me like a tidal wave. He was different. He had to be. He was no Raymond Jacobs or Parker Colman, or even Andrew Thompson.

I used to think they were all the same. Just "cheaters" in my mind, and nothing more. But the man sitting next to me wasn't the same.

He was Jamie Richards, the first man to ever break through the iron gate around my heart, the one I'd barely even known was there until it came crashing down. And then I knew for sure that it had been there all along, keeping me safe. Keeping me sane. Keeping me alone.

And I desperately feared that Jamie wasn't only the first man to break through it . . . but would also be the last.

Because once your fortress is destroyed only a fool would rebuild it exactly the same way. The next time, you use concrete. You use steel. You use the most impenetrable substances known to man.

To make sure that the chink in your armor is long gone.

"On behalf of Air France, we would like to be the first to welcome you to Paris," the flight attendant announced in a thick French accent after we landed at Charles de Gaulle International Airport.

Jamie turned to me with tired eyes and smiled. "Welcome to Paris."

I looked up at him from over the top of my magazine. "I'm sorry, I've already been welcomed. You're too late."

He snapped his fingers. "Damn, and only by a few seconds, too."

"You have to work on your timing."

We made it through customs and immigration to find a tall French man, dressed all in black, waiting for us outside the inspection point.

"Monsieur Richards," he announced as we approached.

"Yes, that's me," Jamie replied.

"What? No dorky sign with your name on it?" I asked as the driver began to wheel Jamie's suitcase outside.

He shook his head. "They all know me here."

"Impressive."

The man came back inside the doors and bent down to grab the handle of my suitcase. "And you must be Mademoiselle Jennifer H.," he stated in all seriousness.

I let out a loud laugh, causing a few people around me to turn and stare. The man looked at me as if I were crazy.

Jamie waved his hand in the air. "Sorry. Stupid American joke."

"Ah, *oui*." The driver nodded understandingly, as if this one simple explanation could clear up any and all misunderstandings in the history and foreseeable future of French/American relations.

"And apparently they know *you* here, too," Jamie pointed out as we followed the man out the sliding doors to an awaiting car.

"Yes, they know my first name and last initial. I feel so special," I said sarcastically.

Jamie shrugged. "Well, until not so long ago, that's all *I* knew about you, too. You are quite the mysterious woman, Miss H."

"More than you know," I replied smugly.

We drove for at least thirty minutes through miles of Parisian suburbs, and then slowly, in the distance, I could make out the impeccable white dome of the Sacre Coeur peeking out above a blanket of dark clouds. I immediately got a small twinge of excitement in my stomach. I couldn't believe I was actually in Paris again. It was truly one of my favorite cities in the world. And even after all I'd seen in the past two years, the sight of this city stretched out before me was still enough to make me feel giddy.

The genuine excitement I felt certainly helped me keep up my innocence act. Just plain old Jennifer Hunter, happy to be in Paris with her boyfriend . . . or whatever Jamie was to me. I still hadn't mastered all the appropriate terminology. If I was his mistress, what did that make him? Besides a lying bastard?

"So what do you want to do first?" I asked, turning from my perma-stare out the window toward Jamie.

"Sleep," he responded immediately.

I slugged him with the back side of my hand. "No! You can't sleep. You'll never catch up to Paris time if you sleep now." I looked at my watch. "It's only eleven in the morning. You have to wait until at least eight before you can sleep."

He looked at me, unconvinced.

"It's a rule," I assured him.

"According to who?"

"Me."

"And who are you?"

I crossed my arms smugly. "As if you don't know."

Jamie smiled and played along. "I don't."

"Excusez-moi, monsieur," I said toward the front of the car.

"Oui, mademoiselle," the driver replied.

"Est-ce que vous pouvez me dire exactement qui je suis, s'il vous plaît?"

The driver looked at me in the rearview mirror, puzzled. These Americans were quite the conundrum.

"So I guess that answers the question of whether or not you speak French," Jamie said to me.

I nodded.

"*Qui vous êtes?*" the driver confirmed, quite certain that he had either misunderstood me or my effort to speak French was flawed.

"*Oui,*" I confirmed. *"S'il vous plaît."* Then I turned to Jamie. "I asked him who I was. Since you seemed to have forgotten."

Jamie was completely entertained by the exchange. He turned his head toward the front seat and waited for the answer.

"*Vous êtes* Mademoiselle Jennifer H.," the driver responded with hesitation, seemingly concerned that a failure to solve the mystery of this dynamic duo might cost him his job.

"*Merci beaucoup,*" I said to him, and then turned back to Jamie with a satisfied grin. "See, there you have it. Jennifer H., expert in international jet-lag saving tactics. Even *he* knows who I am."

Jamie laughed. "Fine, fine. We'll stay awake. We'll do whatever you want to do. But you better keep me entertained, otherwise I might fall asleep in a fountain or on the steps of a church somewhere."

I smiled. "Don't worry. I know just the place."

"To keep me entertained? Or with comfortable steps?"

29

guarding the prisoner

After a quick Parisian lunch consisting of salads and ham sandwiches by the Seine, Jamie and I spent the afternoon touring one of my favorite overlooked monuments in Paris.

"I think I might be the reincarnation of Marie Antoinette," I explained as we walked through the Conciergerie, the old French prison.

"This is really where she was held prisoner before she died?" Jamie asked, running his hands against the cold stone walls of the main corridor.

"Before she was executed," I corrected.

Jamie looked up at the dark, low-beamed ceilings. "Not a very happy place."

I nodded. "Not at all. Especially compared to the châteaux I was used to."

"And why do you think you're her reincarnation?"

I shrugged and continued down the corridor. "I don't know. Every time I've read anything about her, I've always felt a strange connection. An undeniable fascination with her life."

"Maybe you just like cake."

I laughed. "Ah, look who knows a little bit about the revolution française."

Jamie tried to appear blasé. "I paid attention in history class."

"You mean you paid attention during the *History of the World Part I*?"

He waved off my comment. "The novel," he replied defensively.

"Did that have Mel Brooks in it, too?"

He sneered.

"Well," I continued, happy to play tour guide to the amateur American tourist. "Marie Antoinette was captured and brought here to await her trial. Which I think is a complete joke. Like they were actually going to give her a fair trial. She was charged with treason just because she was royalty."

Jamie approached me stealthily and placed his finger against his lips. "Shhh. I don't think your monarchist convictions are going to be well received here." He pointed toward a wax figurine of a revolutionary guard who was positioned to watch over the entrance into the queen's cell.

I rolled my eyes. "Hey, it's a free country."

Jamie considered my comment. "Is it?"

I smiled and shook my head at him. "It is, actually."

He took my hand and pulled me close to him so that our bodies were touching. I could feel my heartbeat getting faster and I wondered if he felt it as well. "So should I call you Marie from now on?" he asked.

I swallowed and tried to force a smile. "Actually," I began softly, "most of her friends and family just called her Antoine."

Jamie leaned in closer to me. His lips were inches from mine. "Okay . . . Antoine." And then he kissed me. In the middle of the dark and dingy revolutionary prison, our lips met and our eyes closed. My body became warm and I tried to counteract the heat by filling my mind with cold, enraging images of Jamie's wife. But it was no use. Her face would disappear as soon as it entered my mind. I couldn't keep my focus on one negative thought to save my life.

So I pulled away. "Come here, I want to show you her cell," I said, reaching down for Jamie's hand and leading him past the motionless "guard."

Jamie mimed a tip of his hat as we walked by. "Monsieur," he saluted politely.

"As you can see," I said, laughing and motioning to the small stone room around us, "compared to the other prisoners' cells that we saw before, this was like a room at the Plaza."

The cell was about half the size of a typical motel room, with a small bed in the corner, low to the ground, and a modest wooden table sitting next to it. Behind a short, fabric-covered folding screen stood another wax figure of a guard, watching the room intently, as if at any minute the queen might pull out some kung fu fighting move and attempt to escape.

"What's his problem?" Jamie motioned toward the guard.

I looked up. "He's making sure she doesn't flee. She and the king tried it once before, you know."

Jamie eyed the statue incredulously. "No way. I don't buy that for a second. He's not waiting for her to try to escape. He's waiting for her to take her clothes off so he can get a glimpse at the queen's boobies."

I let out a stunned gasp. "He is not!"

Jamie nodded regretfully. "I'll bet this was the most coveted shift. All the guards would sit around and play cards or dice just to try to win the position of the queen's 'guard.' And the night shift? Forget about it! That was reserved for the warden himself."

The truth of the matter was, it wasn't just Marie Antoinette who fascinated me. All the kings and queens of the old French monarchy did. Their lives intrigued me. All the sex, the scandal, the drama. It amazed me how you can look back at the interwoven story lines of their relationships and clearly see that nothing has really changed since then. If you compare a basic plot line of an episode of *The O.C.* with a real-life story of a French aristocrat, his family, and all of his personal "dealings," you'd see it's basically the same story. People's obsession with drama and gossip is nothing new.

Back then people also gossiped about the rich and famous. Adulterous sex could also captivate an audience. And dishonesty was practically a spectator sport. The only difference between then and now is that these days the adulterers make more of an effort to keep their mistresses well hidden. Or so they'd like to think.

I watched Jamie as he examined some of the old relics of the French Revolution protected behind thick sheets of unbreakable glass casing, and I suddenly heard myself saying, "You know, the king, Louis XVI, had a mistress."

He turned his attention to me and my random comment, which seemed to come out of nowhere, and I quickly tried to cover it up with more arbitrary facts. "Actually, most of the kings had mistresses. At least one. Sometimes more than one. Sometimes like seven . . . one for every day of the week." I tried to force a chuckle.

I was rambling. There was no doubt about that. But Jamie simply nodded responsively, without any signs of remorse or discomfort. As if he were attentively listening to an interesting lecture but felt no connection with the subject matter whatsoever.

His silence pressured me to keep talking. "In fact," I pressed on shamefully,

"I wouldn't be surprised if Marie Antoinette kept a little lover on the side herself. You know, like a midnight snack. A box of Pop-Tarts, perhaps. I mean, *nobody* was faithful back then. It was practically out of style."

I was hoping that something would strike a chord, touch a nerve, evoke some type of reaction. I just had to keep searching until I found the right word, the right way to say it.

But all he did was laugh politely and say, "Well, you know how it was back then. Marriage was just a political arrangement. Particularly for kings and queens. They didn't marry for love."

I watched him intently as he spoke, searching for signs of hidden meaning. Hidden agendas. Subliminal messages trying to convert me to adulterer worship and trust in his evil cheating ways. But there were none. He simply knew his political history. And quite well, for that matter.

"You married the person who made the most sense," he continued. "Socially, economically, and politically. And *then* you fell in love with the person who made you the most happy."

I almost felt tears well up in my eyes right then. I wanted to run over to him, wrap myself in his arms, and tell him that I wanted to be the one who made *him* most happy. That the rest of it didn't matter. We could run away. Start over. Forget everything that had happened before this moment. But I could feel my feet getting heavy, gluing me to the spot I was in.

And against all my better judgment as an experienced fidelity inspector, trained to go nowhere near the topic of unfaithfulness while on an assignment, I couldn't stop myself from asking, "Do you think that still happens today?"

He walked over to me and rested his hand on the wooden railing that divided the tourists from the replica of the queen's cell. "You mean politically arranged marriages?" he asked incredulously, as if to say, "Have you been living under a rock or were you just hit over the head with one?"

"That," I said cautiously, "and mistresses." I pronounced the word carefully and watched for a reaction. None came. So I continued, "Do you think people still have them? Stashed away in places."

He laughed. "Like in Swiss bank accounts?"

I tried to laugh back, but I felt myself getting extremely irritated. Why was he joking about this? Why wasn't he taking my questions seriously? He damn well should! He'd been keeping me stashed away this entire time and I didn't see how that was so fucking funny.

"I'm serious," I insisted gently.

He cleared the smile from his face and looked me straight in the eye. "Yes, of course people still have mistresses. Where there are promises, there are broken promises. It's just the nature of being human."

I blinked in disbelief. What the hell did *that* mean? Rules are made to be broken, so we might as well just deal with it? What a load of bullshit!

But as we walked back over to the glass case and continued to study its various contents, like Marie Antoinette's water jug and a signed paper documenting her imprisonment, I wondered if maybe Jamie was making a statement about marriage itself. That maybe it's just a principle. A piece of paper, backed by the government. Endorsed by society rather than human behavior. Therefore, almost asking to be desecrated.

He looked up at me and smiled, completely unaware of the thoughts running rampant in my head.

No, I told myself. *That's not what's important here. It's not about a piece of paper or a societal behavior. It's about honesty.* One of the few aspects of humanity that can't be controlled by a society of rules and behavioral suggestions. He lied to me. And he lied to his wife. And that made him just as guilty as a French king with a bedroom full of forbidden lovers.

I took a deep breath and looked at my surroundings. And suddenly I was reminded, once again, that I had come here with a purpose. A job to do.

Maybe Jamie wasn't about to get a fair trial either, but if the French revolutionaries had taught us anything it was that, when you're fighting for a cause, there's no room for feelings. There's no space for doubt.

Treason is treason.

I stood in the old French prison and wondered if history was destined to repeat itself. More than two hundred years later, as the possible reincarnated Marie Antoinette, was I still just another prisoner of my own making?

But then I wondered if I was really the one being held captive here. This whole trip felt like one gigantic trap. And from the outside, I'm sure it appeared as though Jamie was the one about to walk right into it. But from the inside I knew that I was just as doomed as he was.

When dinnertime rolled around, Jamie and I sat down at a romantic outdoor bistro on the Avenue de L'Opera near our hotel. I looked out at the bustling street, and despite the reasons that had brought me here, I still felt a twinge of excitement. After all, it was Paris. The lights, the noise, even the smell brought back so many memories of my last visit.

I had come here on an assignment more than a year earlier. It was for a woman who had married a French native (one of those Paris summer romances turned serious) and relocated him to the United States. He was going back to France to visit family, and she was worried that those instinctive French womanizing tendencies might resurface once he was back in his homeland.

"Did you know that most French men don't even believe in monogamy?" she had said to me during our initial meeting.

And she was right. To Pierre LeFavre, monogamy was a word that didn't quite translate.

I was supposed to be a well-educated American businesswoman who was traveling to France to close an important transaction. My French was to be "passable." And my taste in wine and fine cuisine, impeccable.

The French I had studied in school wasn't quite going to cut it. I took three weeks of intensive French lessons to prepare for that assignment. And after it was finished, I didn't come home for another two weeks. I fell in love. Not *in* Paris, but *with* Paris. That's when my obsession with French history began.

And now, more than a year later, I was delighted to see that my French was still . . . well, passable.

"When do you have to start working?" I asked, folding my menu and placing it on the table next to my plate.

Jamie closed his as well and replied solemnly, "We have our first meeting tomorrow morning. So I'm afraid I'll have to leave you on your own for the day."

I smiled. "That's okay. I'll be fine."

"Do you really think you can handle this city by yourself?"

"I'm honestly more worried about you," I said with a tender smile.

Jamie bowed his head in shame. "Yeah, that makes two of us."

The waiter came and I ordered for both of us. Jamie's French was somewhere between pathetic and just plain embarrassing. His face seemed to reflect a mixture of relief and arousal as he watched the language of love float from my lips into the brisk Paris night air.

"Do you realize that we wouldn't be here if it weren't for our cars?" Jamie said after the waiter disappeared.

"What?"

"If you didn't drive a Range Rover and I didn't drive a Jag-yoo-ar, we wouldn't be here. I doubt you would have ever called me. So bumping into you at the dealer that day is essentially the reason we're in Paris together. It's funny how fate works like that, isn't it?"

I squirmed in my seat. *Goddamn, useless, meddling fate! Look how well that turned out!* "Yeah, it is kind of funny," I managed to mumble.

He lifted his wineglass in the air. "To gas-guzzling SUVs?"

I smiled and lifted mine as well. *Why didn't I just get that freaking hybrid?* "Yes," I said, clinking my glass against his. "To the cars. That brought us together in Paris for the next five days."

As I took a sip of my Bordeaux, I noticed Jamie fidgeting awkwardly in his seat. I watched him intently as he suddenly appeared extremely uncomfortable.

"Is everything all right?" I asked.

"I need to tell you something," Jamie replied immediately, as if he hadn't even heard my question.

I could feel my breathing get very shallow. The seriousness in his voice alarmed me. Actually, it scared the shit out of me.

"What's that?"

Jamie fidgeted again, shifting his weight around as if he were trying to get comfortable before the start of a three-hour *Lord of the Rings* installment.

"I've debated telling you for a while."

I swallowed hard. "Why's that?"

"Because I think it might upset you."

"Okay," I replied softly, preparing myself for what I already knew he was going to say. I knew it immediately. He was coming clean. He was going to tell me the truth. No more lies. No more deceit. No more pretending that he didn't have a wife back home. This was it. The one thing you wouldn't find in the story of a famous French king and his mistress . . . honesty.

But the question that spun through my mind at nearly a mile a minute was: Did I want to hear it?

At this point, would telling the truth really set him free? Could he be forgiven? Would it make everything all right?

Or was it already too late for that?

It would certainly destroy the assignment.

But then again, on any other assignment, when the subject stops the course of action to admit that he has a wife, and then politely excuses himself, it's considered a pass. It's a reason to rip up his failed inspection card. Frankly, that's only happened a few times. Most of them admit they have a wife, and then upon seeing the look on my face that says "Yeah . . . so?" they proceed, anyway.

But like I said before, I couldn't compare Jamie to any of the others. He wasn't like any of them. And I certainly wasn't the same girl I had been with any of them.

Ashlyn had been invited along on this trip because I had so desperately wanted her to help me through it, but she had barely made an appearance. She just didn't seem to fit into the equation.

Jamie took a deep breath and then scratched the side of his face. His mind was searching for words. I could tell.

He finally looked me straight in the eye and said, "There's a chance I might have to cut the trip short."

I stared at him blankly. What did he just say? I didn't hear any mention of a wife in that sentence. Maybe the wife part was coming next. As in, "I have to cut the trip short because my *wife* is expecting me." Or "Because my *wife* needs me to go to some dinner party with her." Maybe even "Because my *wife* asked me to pick up some stuff at the dry cleaner and I forgot."

So I painted on a disappointed expression and took the bait. "Oh, no! Why's that?" I asked.

He tugged nervously on his ear.

Here it comes, I thought.

"Because the client is having second thoughts about hiring our firm. Apparently, there's been a last-minute counteroffer by another company that came in far below our bid. They might pull the plug and go with someone else. And there's really no reason for me to be here if they're not going to hire us."

My mouth dropped open as I listened to him continue to ramble incessantly about the odds and ends of signing on new clients and requests for proposals and other crap that I managed to tune out.

"And they're right. I mean, there are at least three other clients back in L.A. that need my attention. You know how people can be. Completely fickle. Especially when they're spending this much money on something. One minute you're the hottest firm in the industry and the next minute you're colder than a corpse on *CSI*."

"What?" I was finally able to get out.

Jamie tilted his head to the side, seemingly confused as to what part of this whole thing was still unclear to me.

"That's what you wanted to tell me?"

He frowned. "Yes. Why?"

I tried to wipe the bewildered expression from my face, but it was like trying to clear your windshield with a broken wiper. "So we're going home early?"

Jamie sighed. "See, I knew you'd be upset. I'm really sorry. I should know for sure tomorrow. I would say we could stay. Just the two of us. But if they pull the plug, my firm is gonna need me back in the office right away."

I nodded numbly. "Right."

"Nothing's for certain yet. I'm just giving you a heads-up. I didn't want to mention it earlier because I thought at least we could spend a nice day together."

I managed to close my mouth and begin to gather my thoughts. "When would we have to leave?" I asked, trying to sound understanding.

"The day after tomorrow," he replied ruefully. "Of course, you're welcome to stay if you want. I just have to go back. I don't have a choice."

I was quiet. Not really sure what to say. And not really sure if it would even come out the way I wanted it to if I *did* have something important to contribute.

As much as I've made a living off of being able to read men's minds and predict certain behaviors, I've always said that people are never 100 percent predictable. And Jamie had proven that to me—numerous times. I had been wrong about nearly every aspect of him. And every time I had tried to predict his behavior, I was left with the same feelings I felt brewing inside of me at this very moment.

Surprise. Confusion. Disillusionment. And then, eventually, a total loss of control.

That's why you remain unemotional. Indifferent to the outcome. Completely neutral as to whether your mind-reading capabilities are accurate or not.

Because if you never anticipate, if you never feel hope, you'll never be caught unaware. It was a lesson I'd prided myself on learning, committing to memory, and following like a commandment.

But somehow tonight, and with every minute I'd spent with Jamie since that fateful trip back from Vegas, I'd managed to forget it. I'd managed to forget a lot of things lately. And I wasn't happy with the results.

I'd never been a big fan of uncertainty, and I thought I had figured out how to avoid it. Now it was chasing me down a dark hallway with no doors, no windows, no light switches.

Jamie reached out and patted my hand. I flinched. Something I've never done on an assignment. I attempted to play it off by flipping my hand over so that we were palm in palm.

"Sorry to bring it up," he said, interlacing his fingers with mine. "But let's not worry about it until it's certain. Okay?"

I smiled pleasantly. "Okay."

Jamie leaned across the table and kissed me tenderly on the cheek. "So tell me, how do you know how to speak French so well, anyway?"

I looked away, refusing to meet his glance. Instead I pretended to be distracted by all the Paris nightlife starting to fill up the street. I had always hated lying to him. But tonight, right now, something was different. A voice deep inside was telling me not to care. It was the voice of hostility. Bitterness. And even resentment. He had already lied to me. He'd been lying to me from day one. Every moment that we were together and the subject of his wife didn't come up was a lie. The trust had already been smashed to pieces. And he was holding the sledgehammer.

So what did it matter anymore?

"I studied it in school," I replied casually.

"Wow," he replied. "That's amazing. Most people who learn it in school don't retain any of it. But you seem to have a really good handle on the language. I've heard it's extremely hard when you have no practical application for it."

"Well, I *do* use it, okay? What's with the twenty questions?" I snapped violently.

My sudden outburst surprised us both. I shrank back in my seat with embarrassment. Jamie blinked and stared at me, waiting for the punch line.

Because that's what we do. We joke. We banter. We go back and forth, for hours. Playing off each other. Inspiring each other.

But the punch line never came. I simply sat back in my seat and surrendered my hands into my lap.

"I'm sorry, I didn't—" he began cautiously.

"No," I quickly interrupted him, frustrated with myself that I had let my emotions escape. Especially when they never do. Especially when they were always so well contained. Always guarded, twenty-four hours a day. Seven days a week. Because evidently, like members of the French monarchy, they couldn't be left unattended.

"It was me," I insisted gently. "I apologize. I guess I'm just feeling a bit jet-lagged."

Jamie looked at me with uncertainty. "Okay. Are you sure?"

I waved my hand in the air. "Yes. Completely."

"Is this about . . . ?"

"It's not about anything," I said hastily. And then covered it up with an agreeable smile.

Jamie nodded slowly and looked at me with tender eyes. They were filled with so much genuine compassion that it almost made me want to throw my napkin down and storm away from the table, yelling something like, "You're a cheater, so start fucking acting like one!"

The waiter brought our entrées and I quietly picked up my fork and began to shovel small pieces of steak tartare into my mouth.

"Well, I guess we're both tired," he admitted, watching me frantically stuff my face with raw beef.

"Mmm-hmm," I said with a mouthful of red meat. I swallowed. "I'm exhausted."

I guess deep down I always thought Jamie would save us. That he would tell me the truth before it was too late. And then maybe, just maybe, there would be room for forgiveness. After all, it seemed to be the word of the week. But it was obvious to me now that there was only one way out of this trip: for Jamie to fail his fidelity inspection. Honesty was no longer an option, as he seemed to have no idea what the word actually meant.

Jamie was right that the trip would be cut short. Because tonight it was show time. The black-and-pink lace bra and matching panties I was wearing under my skirt and sweater would certainly do the trick. If all went according to plan, I would be sleeping in my own hotel room tonight and on the next flight home in the morning.

"Well, we'll just eat fast and head straight back to the hotel," Jamie offered sympathetically.

I grabbed a piece of bread from the basket on the table and took an oversized bite as I replied to his comment with an empty smile. "Perfect," I said sweetly.

30

the naked truth

Jamie kissed me as soon as we entered the hotel room. It was a much-needed relief from the relatively quiet taxi ride home. I suppose we each had a lot on our minds. I was thinking about getting back to the hotel, stripping down to my sexy bra and matching underwear, and getting this damn inspection over with. He was, ironically, probably thinking about bras and panties as well. Or the lack of them.

I'm sure he took my silence as a sign that I was upset about the possible shortening of our trip. If he only knew how a shortened trip to Paris was the *last* item on my list of things to be upset about today.

His kiss was passionate and purposeful. As he pressed his body into mine and we fell onto the bed, it wasn't hard to speculate about what that purpose was. And my mind was immediately set at ease.

See, I told myself. *He* is *a cheater.* All this time worrying about how I would feel if he refused to have sex with me. It was pretty obvious from the hard bulge forming in his pants that he was far from refusing.

He eagerly reached down for the bottom of my sweater and began to pull it upward. Our kissing stopped only long enough for the sweater to slide over my head, and then his lips desperately lunged back for mine as if we hadn't kissed each other for a year—or longer.

I began to unbutton his shirt from the top. *His* fingers started at the bottom, and when our hands met at the middle button, I quickly slid the shirt off his shoulders. He twisted his body to help remove it faster.

Every action, every removal, every touch couldn't be done with more impatience. We had both been waiting so long to get to this very moment . . . but for different reasons. And now that it was finally here, there was no doubt that neither of us wanted to wait any longer than we had to. Clothing was only an aggravating obstacle at this point.

When I was finally down to my bra and underwear, he slowed down. *Way* down. He pulled his mouth away from me and looked admiringly at my body, sprawled out before him. I could feel his eyes on me as strongly as I could feel his hands. When he looked at me, it was as if they, too, were caressing my skin. And as much as I hated to admit it, his eyes felt almost as good.

I lay on my back with Jamie resting closely at my side, his head propped up with his hand, one leg between mine. He carefully traced the tops of my breasts with his fingertips, and then he lowered his head to kiss them. They were perfectly rounded by the push-up wires of my bra and I tilted my chin up and moaned with pleasure.

The scary part was . . . the moan was real.

It wasn't fake.

Where the hell was Ashlyn?

She had left me here to fend for myself, and I clearly wasn't doing a very good job at it.

Everything felt amazing. The incredibleness of this moment was undeniable.

He kissed me again, and delicately pulled himself on top of me. The kiss grew deeper, and I could feel him getting harder. His body sunk into mine, and we slowly rocked together as our lips touched, parted, separated, and then touched again.

My eyes were closed yet I felt like I could see everything. As if I no longer needed them to open . . . ever again. The sensation of Jamie's body on top of mine was all I needed to feel for the rest of my life.

And then all of a sudden, panic set in.

What are you doing? I asked myself.

We were about to have sex and I was about to let it happen. I wanted nothing more than for it to happen. But it *couldn't* happen. That was not in the agenda. The rules are and always have been very simple: I test for an "intention to cheat" only. There is no sex involved. There never has been and there never *can* be. Otherwise, it's just plain prostitution. Yes, *prostitution.* I had to keep one very important and sobering fact in mind: I was being *paid* to be here.

Not to mention that I would *knowingly* be having sex with another woman's husband.

I again felt the incredible longing for the bliss of ignorance. The mind-eraser drug. Something to wipe out all memories from the past week so that I could go back to that perfect day when she didn't exist. *Mrs.* Jamie Richards.

How wonderful would this moment be if I could?

Jamie stopped kissing me and reached up to touch my face with the back of his hand. "Hey," he said gently.

I opened my eyes and smiled at him. A genuine, real, authentic smile. "Yeah?"

He continued to stroke my cheek and then tucked a strand of my hair behind my ear. "I can't believe what I'm about to say, but maybe we shouldn't be doing this right now."

My eyes opened wide and I stared at him in disbelief. "Why? What's wrong?"

"Nothing," he said hurriedly. "I just . . ." His voice trailed off and he rolled onto his back. "I just don't know if we're ready for this yet."

I didn't know how to respond to that. It was definitely a new kind of rejection. One I hadn't heard before. And most of the time, unlike other girls, I'm all for the rejections. But this one brought a mixed bag of emotions. Why didn't he want to? Was it me? Was the underwear not sexy enough? Was the push-up bra not pushing up enough? What the hell was it?

"Well, you certainly *felt* ready," I half joked, trying to hide my wounded ego.

He laughed. "Yeah, well, that's only natural. I mean, you *are* unbelievably sexy."

"But you don't want to have sex with me," I reminded him bluntly.

He reached out and grabbed my hand tightly. "I do. Believe me, I do. Please, don't be offended. I'm just not sure we should . . . *yet*."

I nodded apprehensively. "Okay."

"How gay am I?" he asked, rolling onto his back and staring up at the ceiling.

I chuckled. "You're not *gay.* Trust me, one of my best friends is gay . . . and you are definitely nowhere near anything like him."

He laughed. "Thanks. I'll keep reminding myself of that."

I watched him as he watched the ceiling. He looked . . . troubled.

"Is everything all right?" I ventured.

He turned toward me and offered me an apologetic sigh. "Yes. Everything's fine. I'm sorry, baby. I'm just . . . preoccupied."

I grabbed his hand and kissed it. "I understand."

I sat up and slid off the bed. "I guess I'm going to get ready for bed, then." I walked through the large expanse of the suite into the bathroom and closed the door behind me. For a minute I stood in the darkness, afraid to turn on the light. Afraid of what it might reveal to me. And what that revelation would mean.

I slowly reached out and flipped the switch. I took a long, hard look at myself in the mirror. My reflection said it all.

I was beaming.

I know most girls would be confused. Hurt. Rejected. But not me. Jamie's rejection was the best gift he could have ever given me. Because I knew exactly where it came from. The reasons behind it. And they were good reasons.

But then a thought came to me. He said, *"I'm just not sure we should . . . yet."*

What exactly did "yet" mean?

Did it mean tomorrow we should? Or the next day we should? When did it end? When *should* we? And would this assignment have to go on for the next week? Month? Year? Until he finally felt ready to cheat on his wife?

At first I thought the rejection was a good thing. But on second thought, could it be just a prolonging of this god-awful assignment?

Could it possibly just mean that my work here was "yet" to be complete?

"Hey, Jen," Jamie's voice called through the door.

"Yeah?" I replied, my eyes still glued to my befuddled reflection.

"I think I left my Amex at the front desk. I'm just going to run down to the lobby and check. Do you need anything while I'm down there?"

"No, thanks. I'm fine!"

I ran the hot water and kept my finger under the faucet, waiting for the flow to get warm. I quickly splashed my face, squeezed out a dollop of face wash, and saturated my skin in it.

"Hey, I can't find my key," I heard Jamie's voice through the door again. "Do you have yours?"

"Sure," I called back, my eyes closed and my face covered in white cream. "It's in my purse."

"Okay, thanks!"

I rinsed my face off, patted it dry with the soft, fluffy white Ritz Paris towel, and then rummaged through my toiletries bag to find my toothbrush. I did an abbreviated version of my usual three-minute brushing routine, and then with a heavy sigh I shut off the light and opened the door.

The first thing I saw when I came back into the bedroom was the gold-trimmed, white satin bed frame and the rumpled sheets from our *almost* French love affair. The thought of his words of refusal, once again, filled me with confusion. Confusion that I desperately wished to resolve but, quite frankly, didn't know how.

The second thing I saw was Jamie. Standing motionless in the middle of the suite. In one hand, he held his cell phone up to his ear, listening intently, his eyes strangely filled with what could only be described as painful disappointment. Whatever he was listening to on the other end of that call was bad news. Very bad news.

And that's when I saw what he was holding in his *other* hand.

My failed fidelity inspection card. The one I had tucked ever-so-safely into the inside pocket of my purse. The one he was only supposed to see if and *when* he actually did fail.

From where I stood, at least twenty feet away, I could just make out the red letter *A* on the black surface, shining fiercely from across the room, illuminating the shadowy, moonlit suite like a red spotlight.

The sight of it burned a hole in my irises. The same effect, I imagine, that the letter was intended to have when sewed into the fabric of Hester Prynne's clothing.

I stopped in my tracks. Our eyes met and locked. He looked at me with such sadness and betrayal that my heart shattered into a million tiny pieces.

Without moving his eye line even an inch, he pulled the phone away from his ear and closed it with a snap that reverberated in the empty room like a gunshot.

We stood still for what seemed like an eternity, staring into each other's eyes, silent questions and accusations bouncing back and forth between us like invisible sound waves.

Jamie was the first to speak.

"It's a setup?" he asked quietly, with, thankfully, no trace of anger in his voice. Just pain. Deep, confused pain. "It's *all* been a setup?"

I closed my eyes and struggled to come up with the right words. Until I realized that they didn't exist. They don't write speeches for moments like this. "Jamie, I—"

"From the beginning!" he said, his tone raised, the anger finally creeping in. "From the fucking beginning!?"

"No!" I cried desperately. "Not from the beginning. Not until a few days ago!"

"And *this* is what you do? You set people up? To fail?"

I shook my head, the tears stinging my eyes. "Not with you! It didn't start out that way. I wanted to tell you about it. I had decided to tell you about it, and then—"

"That man in the sushi restaurant. He was trying to warn me about you. And I, like a fucking fool, stood up for you!" He dropped both items from his hands. The phone fell with a loud thud while the card danced and twirled gracefully to the ground, landing, most appropriately, A-side up. "You lied to me!"

"Me?" I shouted, feeling the passion rise up inside me. "*You're* the liar here! Do I have to remind you that you have a fucking wife? I guess I do, because you seemed to have forgotten. It *seemed* to have slipped your mind. Because you 'conveniently' forgot to mention her this *whole* time!"

"Yeah, a wife who *hired* you! To act like you were falling for me just as hard as I was falling for you!"

"Jamie, I *did* fall for you," I practically begged.

But he refused to listen. He believed what he wanted to believe. I guess the same way I did.

"So do you get to go to Paris with all these guys?" he prodded sadistically. "Or was I the only one foolish enough to invite you along? You've probably gone on a *lot* of nice trips in your line of work! That's quite an employee benefits package, Jen. And I'll bet every single one of them has made you an airplane bag, too."

The tears streamed down my face, but I didn't care. I didn't even bother to wipe them away. I simply charged toward him, as if I might try to take him down with one of my self-defense maneuvers. But instead I reached around behind him and grabbed my bag up off the nightstand and shoved my arm through the strap. Then I bent down to his feet and picked up the black card.

I stood up and held it out to him. "I think this belongs to you."

Jamie threw his hands in the air. "I'm not touching that thing."

"Fine!" I yelled as I slammed it down on the nightstand. "I'll just leave it where I always leave it." I stormed in the direction of the door. "Because you're *exactly* like all the rest of the cheating scum I meet!"

I opened the door and stepped into the hallway. I knew I should have just kept walking and never looked back. But something made me turn around, just to see what was written on his face.

Jamie's head was down, staring at the ground. The battle was over. Now all that was left was the aftermath. And he could feel it. It enveloped him. He backed up slowly until the back of his knees softly collided with one of the antique Louis XV armchairs, and he allowed himself to collapse into the seat.

"I'm not the one who cheated," he said softly, just in case anyone was listening.

But I wasn't.

I was too busy slamming the door.

It wasn't until I stepped off the elevator into the hotel lobby that I realized I was still in my underwear. Yes, I happened to have my very fashionable Dior purse around my shoulder, but in my underwear nonetheless. There were a few stares from some of the patrons and a few hotel employees trying *not* to stare. I looked down at my ensemble, and instead of trying to cover myself up like they always do in the movies when a woman finds herself minus a few necessary items of clothing, I decided my virtual nakedness was the least of my problems right now. So I held my head up high and marched purposefully toward the front desk. I guess I could at least be thankful that I was wearing a matching set.

"I need another room," I announced decisively to the front-desk clerk.

The man didn't even blink. I suppose that as an employee of the Hotel Ritz in Paris he had probably seen it all. And most likely much worse than a woman in her underwear with dried tears on her cheeks, demanding a second room.

"I'm so sorry, mademoiselle. But we are fresh out of rooms this evening."

I groaned loudly. *That* was something I certainly hadn't planned for. And *that* was also the reason I always booked in advance. But with Jamie I hadn't. I guess it was faith, blind, idiotic faith that he just might pass the test and I would never find myself in the situation of having to book another room in the middle of the night. Obviously I didn't exactly count on this particular scenario.

"No, you *have* to have a room. A suite, a closet, anything! I will take whatever you have. I'm leaving in the morning anyway, so it's just for one night."

The clerk looked at his watch and then shot me a sympathetic glance. "Well, we are holding a room for a guest that has yet to arrive."

"I'll take it!" I said anxiously.

He smiled politely at me, as if to say, *And if you'll just let me finish . . .*

"Sorry," I apologized.

"But hotel policy says we cannot rent that room out until eleven P.M."

I anxiously looked around me for a time-telling device of some sort. "Well, what time is it now?"

"Ten, mademoiselle."

I gave him a look of incredulity. "You expect me to wait in the lobby like *this* for the next hour?"

It was at that moment that the clerk first acknowledged my obvious disregard for the hotel's dress code. He cracked a small smile and then quickly covered it up with a loud clearing of his throat. "Of course not, mademoiselle . . ."

I let out a sigh of relief and began to dig through my purse in search of my wallet so I could offer him my credit card.

". . . you are welcome to wait in the bar," he offered in all seriousness.

I froze and looked up at him. The expression on his face revealed nothing but complete sincerity.

"You're kidding?"

"I cannot give out the room until eleven. I am terribly sorry. If you would like to kindly wait in the lounge, I can come look for you when the room becomes available."

I grunted as I shoved my wallet back into my purse. "Very well, then," I responded as graciously as possible through gritted teeth. "I'll be in the bar."

I turned defiantly on the bare skin of my heels and stomped through the lobby.

No one in the Hemingway Bar (the Ritz's celebrated hotel lounge) seemed to take notice of me when I walked in. I quietly took a seat in a back booth, thankful that I had chosen to wear the underwear set with the *bikini* bottom as opposed to the alternative thong variety.

I ordered a vodka on the rocks from the cocktail waitress, and just as she was leaving, I stopped her and said, "Actually, can you just bring me two? It'll save us both time."

"Two?" a man's voice said in an American accent. I looked up anxiously in hopes that it might be Jamie.

I saw a tall stranger standing in front of me, holding a half-empty glass of ice and brown liquid. He smiled at me and suavely started swirling the drink around in his glass.

I quickly looked away and rolled my eyes.

"May I sit down?" he asked, hardly waiting for my response and sliding into the booth next to me.

"Now's *really* not the time," I warned him.

"A fellow American," he ventured, ignoring my comment and placing his glass on the table in front of us.

"Yeah, that's right," I said coldly.

"Bad night?" he asked with such obvious feigned concern that it made me want to break out in a loud, sadistic laugh.

"Look, I am in no mood for company, so if you could just—"

"I can make it better," he offered quickly.

I stared at him skeptically. "And how on earth could you possibly do that?"

His eyes swept the room cautiously and then leaned in closer to me. I could smell the alcohol on his breath. It smelled like whiskey. "I can make up for your lost time, I mean."

I pulled my head away to avoid catching another whiff of his breath and threw my hands up in the air, exasperated. "What the fuck are you talking about?"

The man flashed a patient smile. "I mean, I can pay you double. Triple, even."

I looked down again at my outfit and immediately knew what he was getting at. I rolled my eyes. It certainly wasn't the first time someone had confused me for a prostitute. "I am *not* a hooker!" I shouted loudly with frustration, causing the entire bar to turn and stare.

But I didn't care. Not in the slightest. Nothing really seemed to matter anymore. Not even sitting in one of the classiest, most elegant hotel bars in Paris in my black lace underwear, announcing to anyone and everyone that the man next to me thought I was a hooker (and probably with good reason). I just wanted eleven o'clock to arrive so I could climb into the fluffy white hotel sheets and cry myself to sleep.

Was that so much to ask for?

The man turned to me, horrified and speechless, and then quickly stood up and bolted from the room.

I sat back against the booth and crossed my arms over my chest. This was turning out to be quite the night.

"I thought this might make you more comfortable, mademoiselle."

I looked up to see the front-desk clerk standing over me with a white hotel robe hanging from the tip of his index finger.

I smiled and thanked him graciously. Both with my words and my eyes. He seemed to understand my appreciation explicitly as he bowed his head. "You are quite welcome."

I slid on the robe and immediately felt more comfortable. I allowed my head to drop back onto the top of the booth and I spread my arms out to my sides.

The waitress soon came with both of my drinks and I reached into my bag and handed her a fifty-euro bill. She took it and disappeared. I downed the first drink like a shot and then sat back and held the second one in my hands, staring at it. Waiting for it to turn into the salvation I needed.

By the time eleven o'clock rolled around and the clerk reentered the lounge, I was still holding my untouched drink, steady as a rock. There wasn't even the slightest ripple in the surface of the clear liquid.

"Mademoiselle?" the clerk's voice woke me from a trance, causing my hand to jerk up suddenly, spilling a small amount of alcohol on my fingers and some on the hotel robe.

I popped my fingertip in my mouth and sucked off the vodka. "Yes?" I asked anxiously.

"As you requested, your room is ready."

"Thank God!" I exclaimed, jumping up and quickly downing the drink in my hand. I grabbed my bag and headed out of the bar, purposely ignoring the clerk's somewhat appalled reaction toward my blatant disrespect for France's finest vodka.

As soon as I was alone in my room, I ransacked the minibar. I had sent the bellhop to Jamie's room to gather my belongings, and by the time the long-awaited knock came at the door, I was already surrounded by three empty mini-bottles of Grey Goose. The best French-made export, as far as I was concerned at the moment.

I opened the door for him and watched as he carried in my luggage and placed it near the closet.

"Was there a message?" I asked hopefully.

He clearly did not understand what I was requesting. "A message, Madame?" he repeated in a thick accent.

"From the man in the room. Did he tell you to tell me anything?"

He shook his head, confused. "No, madame, za room waz empty."

"Empty?" I asked in disbelief, and stepped closer to him. "You mean no one was in there?"

I could tell the desperate, half-intoxicated look on my face was making him uncomfortable. Not to mention my proximity to his body.

"Nobody. And no . . . zing," he said cautiously, shaking his head.

"What do you mean?" My voice cracked with fear.

"Uh, empty?" he repeated again, apparently concerned that maybe he wasn't translating his thought into the correct English word. "*Vide,*" he reaffirmed in French.

There it was. I knew what both words meant. In both languages. Because they meant the same thing: Jamie had left. He had taken everything but my things. And God knows where he had gone.

I felt more tears welling up in my eyes as I backed away from the frightened bellhop and he began to close the door. "*Merci beaucoup,*" I said softly.

"*Je vous en prie,*" the man replied, noticeably relieved that I was letting him go. He bowed slightly as he backed out through the closing door.

I pushed the empty bottles off the bed and collapsed into it, letting my tears fall freely down the sides of my face. I reached up and pulled down the comforter. The brilliantly white satin sheets were inviting me in. *Come to us, Jen,* they were saying. *We will give you the same safety we always have.*

I climbed under the covers, grabbed the spare pillow, and held it tightly to my body. I squeezed my eyes shut and tried to meditate. I thought of happy places. Far-off places. Green meadows and blue skies.

But as I let myself be engulfed in a world of warm, heavenly white, I felt nothing but the cold, merciless darkness.

31

home is where the broken heart is

I can think of several famous people who, at one time or another, were trying to get to Paris. Charles Lindbergh, Lance Armstrong, Audrey Hepburn, Ernest Hemingway, even Hitler. But I, however, staying true to my Marie Antoinette–reincarnated self, was trying to escape.

"I don't think you understand what I'm telling you!" I practically screamed into the phone as I paced the floor of my hotel room. "I already *have* a ticket back to L.A., but it doesn't leave until Friday."

I had been on the phone with the Air France customer "service" department for the past hour, trying to get on an earlier flight home. And because it was still one o'clock in the morning in L.A., I knew I would never be able to reach my travel agent.

Unlike the last time I was in Paris, when I chose to sightsee for three weeks following my assignment, this time I wasn't really in the mood to stay any longer than I had to.

I had seen enough sights.

"Yes, but what I have been trying to tell you, Miss Hunter, is that all of our flights are already full." The customer service rep spoke with only the slightest trace of an accent.

"Well, what about standby? Or don't you have that here?"

Her patience was waning almost as fast as mine. "We do have standby, Miss Hunter, and you're welcome to put your name on the list, but I cannot guarantee that we will be able to honor your first-class status."

I sighed. "I don't care if I have to sit in the cargo section with the suitcases and the dogs. *I have to get out of here!*"

"Very good, Miss Hunter. Please just let me put you on hold and I'll—"

"No, no . . . please don't put me on hold again!"

But she was already gone. And I was once again stuck listening to the supposedly soothing sounds of classic French songs converted to elevator music.

I sighed and looked around in search of the television remote. I flipped through the channels until I finally found one in English. It was CNN. I tossed the remote down on the bed and attempted to drown myself in other people's problems while I waited for Air France to resolve mine. I was selfishly hoping that the war in Iraq, suicide bombers in Israel, and the complete disregard for international child labor laws in Mexico would make my life look like a dream world.

Unfortunately, CNN was airing some type of special report on American political scandals, which did nothing at all to alleviate my current pain.

"Hello?" A male voice came on the line.

"Yes?"

"How can I help you today?"

"Was I transferred again?"

"I'm afraid so," the man replied. "How can I help you?"

I groaned loudly into the phone and began my story for the tenth time. "I'm trying to get on a flight to Los Angeles today. I am already booked on a flight on Friday, but I need to change my reservation."

I heard typing through the phone. "I'm sorry, but all of our flights into Los Angeles are booked solid today. I can get you on a flight on Wednesday morning."

But I barely heard what he was saying. My eyes were suddenly glued to the screen. "Oh my God!"

"I'm terribly sorry for the inconvenience, Miss Hunter."

I grappled for the remote and turned up the volume full blast.

"This Republican senator from the California State Senate had just recently announced his candidacy for the U.S. House of Representatives," the reporter was saying.

"Hello? Miss Hunter? Are you still there?"

"Um . . ." I stammered, trying to make sense of the images on my screen while at the same time trying to guarantee myself a way out of this city. "I'll just go standby," I said hastily into the phone and then absently placed it back on the cradle.

I gawked at the TV screen and listened intently as the voice-over commentator continued speaking.

"But shock and astonishment reached the Austin family when it was revealed by his political adversaries that Daniel Austin was, in fact, hiding his homosexuality."

"I don't believe this," I said aloud as the segment then cut to a news conference where none other than *Daniel Miller,* the lonely man John and I had "bumped into" at the docks only a few weeks back, stood in front of a large podium with an unfamiliar woman in a blue-skirted suit by his side. At least I *thought* his name was Daniel Miller. That was certainly the name I had been given. But according to this commentator, apparently his name is not Daniel Miller, but rather Daniel *Austin,* a California State Senator running for a seat in the U.S. House of Representatives.

"I am neither ashamed nor embarrassed by the news that was brought forth by my political opponents. And although I don't believe it should have any effect on my ability to do my job as a representative of the California State Senate, I have decided to withdraw my name from this election's ballot for U.S. representative and focus first and foremost on my family."

"I knew he looked familiar!" I shouted to the empty hotel room.

The man at the podium looked over at the woman standing next to him and smiled adoringly before continuing. "My wife, Sarah, has been very supportive during this somewhat turbulent period of our marriage. . . ."

Wait a minute, I thought, studying the woman in the blue suit. *That's not Sarah Miller.* Or Austin, or whatever her name is supposed to be.

At least it wasn't the Sarah I had met. And I think I would remember. That strange robotlike woman invited me into her stark, desolate mansion in Topanga Canyon three times! I'm pretty sure I remembered what she looked like. And she didn't look like . . .

But then I stopped. Suddenly everything was becoming very clear to me. The clouds were parting and the sun was beating down on my head.

That wasn't Daniel's wife that I met.

She was some kind of poser. Or decoy. Possibly a real robot!

And that house! It was fake. I mean, not a fake house, like with cardboard walls that fell down when you leaned on them. But I mean, not really Daniel Austin's house. It was probably just some furnished rental. No wonder it looked like no one lived there. Nobody did!

But then if that wasn't Sarah Austin . . . *Who* was it?

I looked back up at the TV, searching for more clues. And then suddenly I remembered something that Daniel had said only a few seconds ago.

"I am neither ashamed nor embarrassed by the news that was brought forth by my political opponents."

"Brought forth by my political opponents"? I repeated aloud, and then gasped.

Oh my God! I'd been used as a political spy! Daniel Austin's enemies must have rented that house, hired that woman, and then paid her to pose as his wife, contact me, and then pay me (in cash!) to prove his unfaithfulness. So my first impression had actually been right on the money. She was hired to play the part of a self-important prim and proper wife of a well-known politician. He just wasn't well-known to *me.*

Whoever his enemies were, they had obviously been trying to catch him in a cheating scandal. No wonder she insisted I go back out there and try again. No wonder she appeared disappointed with my first round of results. *And!* No wonder she looked oddly amused when I came back with the news that Daniel was gay.

They must have had a field day with that!

A Republican politician with a dark and dirty gay secret in the closet. Um, hello . . . can anyone say "jackpot"?

I had heard about stuff like this going on in our "honest" system of government, but I had never thought I would be involved in any way. And although I felt like maybe I should have been outraged, thinking, *How dare they use me like that? How dare they involve me unknowingly in their petty little sex scandal?*

But there was just no way I could possibly be mad. It was way too cool!

And I couldn't wait to get home and tell John. He would be even more excited. Hell, he'd probably already seen the news and told everyone that he had personally outed a right-wing Republican politician.

In fact, the news had probably already spread across Los Angeles's entire gay network, and half of San Diego's. I watched the screen as the segment came to an end. ". . . Democratic candidate, Paulson, is still refusing to comment on his sources."

After four standby flights, two middle seats, and three layovers in London, Chicago, and Denver, I finally landed on an LAX runway early Tuesday morning.

And I'd never been more happy to do so in my entire life.

I had called Sophie from the Chicago airport the night before, and after hearing about the series of events, she had insisted on picking me up and taking me home.

"Let's just look on the bright side," Sophie suggested cheerfully after ten minutes of silence in the car on the way home from the airport.

I picked my head up from the headrest and looked at her. "What bright side? I'll give you a million dollars if you can tell me what the bright side is."

Sophie pursed her lips and stared at the road. "Well, there's . . . um . . ."

I plopped my head back again. "Exactly."

"There's *always* a bright side," she insisted. "You just have to look hard enough until you find it."

"You mean you just have to delude yourself long enough until you start to believe it?"

Sophie glanced at me from the corner of her eye. "Haven't we gotten cynical in the last twenty-four hours?"

I closed my eyes. "I've always been cynical. I just hid it well."

Even from myself, I thought.

"So what do you think you'll do now? Are you going to go back to doing the fidelity inspector thing?"

"Don't know," I said vaguely.

And the truth was, I didn't. I had certainly thought about it during my nearly twenty hours of travel time. But I had yet to come up with any solid conclusions. I hadn't quit *entirely* because of Jamie. Sure, he had been a big part of it. But it was more about what he had made me realize.

That there was more to life than just cheaters.

But now I wasn't so sure.

Sophie pulled up to my curb and put her car in park. She turned and looked at me, almost as if she could read my mind. And right at that moment, I would have bet money that she could.

"Eric's coming into town this weekend. We have our first meeting with the wedding planner."

I offered her a weak smile. "Fun."

"I'd love for us to all have brunch together on Sunday. If you're feeling up to it."

"You, me, and the wedding planner?" I attempted my first bit of humor.

Sophie rewarded my efforts with a genuine laugh. "No, silly. You, me, and Eric. I want you to meet him . . . for real this time."

I turned and gazed out the window. "Okay."

Sophie struggled to come up with something to say. "I just thought that . . . you know, maybe it would cheer you up to be around someone who's *not* a cheater for a change."

And after that I was *convinced* she was able to read my mind. But also thankful that she most likely wouldn't be able to read all of it. Because all my cynical mind could come up with at that very moment was *I wouldn't be so sure.*

"I'm sure it will," I said blankly as I reached down and unbuckled my seat belt.

"Sorry," she quickly added. "Maybe that was too harsh. I'm not usually the one doling out these kinds of pep talks. That's always been your department."

I flashed a feeble yet affectionate smile and reached over to touch her shoulder. "You're doing fine."

We both stepped out of the car, and Sophie helped me unload my bags. "Do you want me to come up? I can sit with you for a while. Maybe make you some tea?"

"Sophie, I'm not going to slit my wrists. I'm going to go to sleep. I've just flown back and forth to Europe in less than seventy-two hours." I pulled up on the handle of my suitcase.

"I know! I didn't think you were going to—"

"I'll call you when I wake up."

"He didn't *actually* cheat," Sophie reminded me.

Although she technically didn't have to. It was the same mental Rubik's Cube that I had been twisting and turning around in my head for two days. And no matter how many combinations of left, right, up, down, backward, and forward I tried, none of the colors seemed to be lining up. There were no concrete conclusions drawn.

Where was the solid wall of red that meant he was a cheater just for *being* in Paris with me? Or the nine solid green squares, forming an impenetrable argument for his innocence?

But no matter how many times I rotated those cubes around, nothing matched up. Every side remained an ambiguous mélange of colorfully incomplete rationalizations.

"Didn't he?" I asked her skeptically.

I could see Sophie's mind start to drift away into the endless sea of possible answers as well. It was a dangerous sea to drift on. If you weren't careful, you might never come back. "Did he?" she finally asked back.

To which I simply chuckled hopelessly and said, "Welcome to my world."

And then, with suitcase in tow, I walked into my building and said a bittersweet good-bye to the sunlight. I had no intention of seeing it for the next two years.

I entered my condo to find it just as clean and white as it always was. Marta had apparently stopped by either during the time that I was flying *to* Paris, breaking up *in* Paris, or trying to get the hell *out* of Paris. I dropped my bags by the front door and stumbled into the bedroom, like a drunk person stumbles home after a night of boozing.

Although, I had to admit, flying for twenty hours in coach class wasn't far from it.

I collapsed onto my bed and turned my head to see the blinking red light on my answering machine. As much as I wanted to reach over and toss the entire thing into the garbage, instead I got it into my head that whatever was on that message might distract me from my utter agony. Maybe it was good news.

I flung my hand over the nightstand, knocking off a few books and a bottle of lotion in the process, and pressed the *Play* button.

Hannah's young, carefree voice came through the speaker. "Hey, Jen! It's me," the message began. "So, next week is Halloween and I just wanted to let you know that this will officially be my last year of trick-or-treating because, you know, next year I'll be thirteen, and Olivia said that thirteen is way too old to be going door-to-door asking for free candy."

See, I reassured myself, *it's your adorable little niece, whose untainted innocence and trivial little concerns about trick-or-treating always manage to make you feel better when you're down.*

"Oh," Hannah's voice continued, "and I also called to tell you that I got another letter from that person. You know, the one who thinks your name is Ashlyn, and—"

I quickly reached over and shut off the answering machine. So much for that idea. I should have known. When did *anyone* I know *ever* call with good news? Oh, no. I was like a bad news magnet. And not just one of those wimpy little refrigerator magnets in the shape of a hot dog or a teapot. I'm talking one of those high-power, superconducting, propulsion magnets that NASA is developing as a way to launch objects into outer space.

I wanted to forget all of it. I wanted to make it all disappear. And the only way I knew how to do that was to sleep.

When I woke up I looked at the clock. It read 2:45. And I seriously wasn't sure if it was 2:45 in the morning or 2:45 in the afternoon. My body clock was completely out of whack. But to be honest, I didn't really care. What did I have to be late for? Another assignment? Nope, no more of those. A date with Jamie? Nope . . . definitely no more of those.

Time was an illusion, anyway. Pacific Time, Eastern Time, Central Time, Daylight Savings Time. Those were all just man-made words used to keep us all in line. And, of course, *on time*.

Because without time, how would we be able to set appointments? Make dates? Measure driving distances in Southern California?

Well, screw that. All of it. I reached down and violently yanked the clock plug from the socket.

I would be the first person to live entirely without time. I would revolt against the very institution of time. I would rage against the machine. Defy the system.

According to Einstein, time didn't even exist.

So why should I change my whole life around just to adhere to something that doesn't even exist?

I would sleep when I felt tired, eat when I felt hungry, and watch whatever TiVo had recorded when I felt bored. It was the Zen routine of the twenty-first century.

Although at this point all I felt like doing was the sleeping part.

The thought of fishing my cell phones out of my bag and listening to all the messages from people trying to get ahold of me with more bad news made me feel tired.

The thought of getting up and getting some food out of the refrigerator made me want to close my eyes and go to sleep again.

So I did.

But I woke up to the sound of my home line ringing.

"Hello?" I said groggily into the phone.

"Good morning, Jenny." My mom's cheerful voice vibrated into my ear.

"Hi, Mom."

"Were you still sleeping?"

I looked at the clock on my nightstand. It was blank. Then I remembered unplugging it after my whole time-doesn't-exist phase a few hours ago. Or was that days ago? I fell onto my back and rested my palm on my forehead. "What time is it?"

"It's eleven-thirty," my mom replied.

"Oh."

"Have you called your father yet?"

I pulled the pillow over my face. "No. And I'm not going to."

"I thought you said you would!"

I threw the pillow to the floor. "Well, I changed my mind. I'm allowed to do that, Mom."

There was a long, meaningful pause on the other end, and I could almost hear my mother's disappointment come through the phone. "Honestly, Jenny, I think it's about time you grew up and started acting like an adult."

Her words stung me. "I've been acting like an adult for the past sixteen years, Mother. If anyone should be allowed to act like a child and wallow in her misery, it's me!"

My mom sighed. "I don't know what you're talking about, but you're going to have to learn how to forgive your father or else . . ."

"Or else what?" I shot up in bed. "What, Mom? This I would love to hear. What if I don't forgive him? Ever? What if I stay mad at him for the rest of my life? Would that be so terrible? I'll tell you one thing, it certainly wouldn't be as terrible as what he did to us. To our family. And he kept it a secret for over a decade . . . maybe longer. Who knows? As far as I'm concerned, I have at least eight more years of feeling bitter and angry before my dad and I are even. The only thing I've ever learned from my father is that men can't be trusted. And if they can't be trusted, then they certainly don't deserve our forgiveness!"

My mom was silent, and I immediately worried that I had gone too far, said too much. I was about to open my mouth to apologize when she replied, "You're obviously not ready yet, honey. But don't worry, you'll be ready someday."

I wasn't quite sure what to make of that response. It was as if overnight my mom had transformed into a Buddhist monk. Had she been taking meditation lessons at the local community center or something? Where was the sudden need to forgive and the "you're not ready" speech coming from? It was like something straight out of the *Spiritual Guide to Raising Children* book.

"You're right, Mom. I'm not ready to forgive yet. And I'm not sure I'll ever be."

I hung up the phone feeling worse than I had when I picked it up. I'm sure my mom was just trying to help. That was, after all, what moms did. But I wasn't used to getting help from her. Sure, she was always around to help me with homework, or raise hell when a teacher gave me an unfair grade, or help me pick out decorations for my first college dorm room. But I never went to her with the big stuff.

In fact, I never went to anyone.

I had always felt alone when it came to dealing with my personal problems. And so I had always managed to solve them myself. Or at least I thought so.

But given the state I was in now, I couldn't help but come to the conclusion that maybe you can't do *everything* alone.

I eventually pulled myself out of bed long enough to walk to the living room and plop myself right back down on the couch.

I turned on the TV and started an episode of *Extreme Makeover: Home Edition*. That always used to cheer me up. But it was slowly becoming obvious that my old tactics weren't going to cut it anymore. All my problems weren't going to just vanish into thin air, no matter how many episodes of *Extreme Makeover* I had stored up on my TiVo and no matter how many sets of white satin sheets I had folded up in my linen closet. And this time, no amount of staring into a wooden box with a list of names inside was going to change anything that had happened in the past few weeks.

I suddenly longed for the days when everything in my life fell nicely and neatly into two independent categories: Ashlyn and Jen. The cheating, the infidelity, the sinful touch of a married man could always be successfully tucked away inside an alias that I could turn on and off with the touch of a button.

And it was worlds away from Jen's world.

It wasn't even real.

But now the line, once as stable and sturdy as the Berlin Wall, had officially crumbled.

And it was real.

And it was personal.

And it was all happening right in front of me.

The doorbell rang a few hours later. But I must have fallen into some kind of trance because it felt like only a few minutes had passed.

"Get out of bed," Zoë said as soon as I opened the door.

I looked down at my feet. "I am."

"Physically yes, but mentally, you're still in bed."

I considered this. She was probably right. "Sophie told you what happened, huh?"

"Every painstaking detail. Sophie doesn't miss a word, does she?" She stepped by me and plopped down on my couch. "What are we watching?"

I closed the door and sat down next to her. "I don't remember," I said with a despondent sigh.

"Oh, no," Zoë groaned. "You're not turning into one of *those* girls, are you? Please don't turn into one of those girls. Once you're gone, I'll be the only normal one left!"

"Which girls?" I mumbled.

"You know *exactly* what girls I'm talking about. The kind that bury themselves in their bedroom for two weeks because of some stupid guy."

"Clearly, I'm not buried in my bedroom."

"But you would be if your TiVo was in there."

Damn, she knew me too well. And all along I thought I was so unpredictable. "I knew I should have bought a second TiVo for the bedroom."

Zoë grabbed the remote control from the coffee table and clicked on the "Now Playing" list. She started scrolling through my recorded programs. "Some brilliant lunatic with a wannabe license almost killed me on the way over here. So I literally risked my *life* to come here. Which means I'm eventually getting you out of this house."

I curled up into the fetal position in the corner of the couch and pulled the white cotton throw around my legs. "Leave me alone," I whimpered. "You know my problems run much deeper than just a stupid guy."

"I don't care if your problems run all the way to the freaking center of the earth! They're not just going to magically disappear while you're lying in bed all day. You need to get up and deal with them!" She continued browsing with the remote.

I knew she was right.

Raymond Jacobs wasn't going to just all of a sudden, for no good reason, decide to stop sending obnoxious letters to my niece. The server that held all the information for www.dontfallforthetrap.com wasn't going to just spontaneously combust. Jamie Richards's wife wasn't going to just evaporate into thin air so I didn't have to face her with an answer. And Sophie's fiancé wasn't going to just test himself and then send me the results via FedEx.

Yes, I knew all that. But it's not like I knew what to do about any of it. Or else I'd be out there doing it!

"Um, why do you have an episode of *Desperate Housewives* in Spanish?" Zoë said, stopping at the most recent recording on the list.

Still curled up in my ball, I turned my chin toward the screen. "I don't know, when was it recorded?"

Zoë clicked to display the program's details. "Yesterday," she read aloud. "While you were traveling."

I tucked my hands under my chin and closed my eyes. "I guess Marta must have been watching it while I was gone."

I heard rapid dialogue in Spanish and I opened my eyes to see Zoë had started playing the recording. "What? You're actually going to watch it? You don't understand a word of Spanish."

She shrugged and set the remote down next to her. "Nothing else on this thing but *Extreme Makeover.*"

I closed my eyes again.

"Ooh," I heard Zoë cry out. "This is a good one. I saw this one. It's when Gabrielle turns all that stuff over to the FBI that leads to her husband's conviction."

It took a moment for me to register Zoë's brief episode synopsis, but once I did, I opened my eyes again and sat up. "What do you mean? She turned in her own husband?"

She nodded. "Don't you remember? She found all those documents in the safe that implicated him in the crime he was pleading not guilty to. And she was so pissed off that he had been hiding them from her, she handed the information over to the feds. Then he was found guilty for laundering money or whatever and they sent him to jail."

I racked my brain. The story line was definitely familiar. I had seen every episode of the show, so it had to have at least rung a bell. But at this moment, I couldn't believe the idea hadn't crossed my mind before.

I reached over and grabbed the remote. "Let me see that scene."

I fast-forwarded through three quarters of the episode until I found the event Zoë was referring to. And sure enough, there it was. Of course, it was in Spanish, and I really only understood about every other word that was being said. But the intention was pretty clear, no matter what language was being spoken.

She betrayed her own husband—in a selfish act of revenge.

All because he had betrayed her first.

"¡Es tan simple!" I cried out, jumping off the couch in my first burst of energy since I had left Jamie's hotel room.

Zoë looked at me like I had suddenly become possessed by some type of Spanish-speaking, *Desperate Housewives*–watching demon, and she feared she might have to start looking through the yellow pages for an exorcist. "What's simple?"

"And positively genius!" I hurried into the office like a crazy mathematician off to chart out his next thirty-page equation on an old dusty chalkboard.

Zoë warily pulled herself off the couch and followed after me. Most likely just to make sure I hadn't completely lost it and retreated into my office to fetch my book of magic spells.

Instead she found me kneeling on the floor in front of the closet. The mirrored doors were slid all the way open, and inside was a metal file cabinet, one that I used to keep locked up with a hidden key so that anyone who was inside my house wouldn't accidentally happen upon it and come face-to-face with the truth about my life that I had carefully concealed for more than two years. But now there was really no point in hiding it anymore. It seemed like these days just about everyone knew my secrets.

I pulled out the bottom drawer, and immediately began thumbing through the maroon-colored hanging file folders. "I can't believe I didn't think of this before," I said, mostly to myself, but Zoë just happened to be there to hear it.

"What are you talking about, Jen? Have you eaten anything today?"

I ignored her question as I continued rummaging through the drawer, mumbling incoherently to myself.

"Jen?" Zoë demanded an explanation.

I stopped my mad file search long enough to look up, and with sheer excitement in my eyes replied, "I think I just figured out how to take down Raymond Jacobs."

32

all but erased

I never contact a client once the assignment is complete, mostly because there's just no point. It's awkward enough telling a woman her husband tried to have sex with me; I didn't see any reason to attempt to build a relationship on that.

I gave them what I promised to give them. And after that, my part was done.

Divorce, custody battles, uncomfortable nights on the couch, therapy sessions—those all fall under the category of things I just didn't need to know about. And in all honesty, I don't think I even *wanted* to know.

But then again, I suppose there are always exceptions. And I think I had just encountered my first one.

Zoë stood behind me and watched curiously as I flipped through hundreds of folders in my file cabinet. All appearing essentially identical—except for the printed name on the top.

A graveyard of the betrayed.

I pulled out the file folder labeled "Anne Jacobs" and began to flip through it. As much as I always attempt to distance myself from my clients and their lives, flipping back through the pages of Anne's file was like flipping through the pages of a diary.

These weren't just pages in a locked archive somewhere; these were pages of my life. And stories like hers—like those of all of the clients in this cabinet—were my memories from the last two years.

That was the choice I had made. And this file cabinet was the very proof that my choice had produced results . . . many of them.

Anne's file was laid out in the same way all my client files were. Stapled to the inside front cover is the photograph of the subject, supplied by the client during our initial meeting. The first page of the file is a client bio for the person who hired me, followed by a subject bio for the man in question. I always prepare a one-page overview for every person I evaluate. It includes the basic information: name, age, occupation, hobbies, school affiliations, a summarized background of the relationship with my client, and then a section that describes the client's reason for suspicion. I also note the date, time, and location that the assignment will take place. Then, at the end, I leave a small space for any additional notes or comments that pertain to the case.

These bios are always prepared *before* the assignment . . . or pre-facto. The next page of each client file is the post-assignment review. This is basically just a summary of exactly what happened during the assignment (or as well as I can remember). I try to be as precise as possible, throwing in times and exact locations or room numbers if I can recall them. After all, this was a business like any other. And in order to keep it as professional as possible, I had to treat it as such.

Plus, you just never know when the information might prove useful.

Case in point . . . right now.

"Is that him?" Zoë asked, peering over my shoulder at the photograph stapled to the inside front cover of the file. "Is that the Raymond Jacobs guy?"

I followed her eye line to the haunting picture staring back at me. I shuddered as I allowed his eyes to pierce through me. All I could think about as I glared at the picture was the look on his face when I sat across from him in his office. That look of pure satisfaction, knowing that he had all the power. And I had nothing.

That is . . . until now.

Or at least I hoped.

I casually flipped past all the articles I had collected and committed to memory on Kelen Industries, Raymond himself, and the automobile industry in general, until I finally arrived at what I was looking for.

At the back of every file are the handwritten pages of notes from the client meetings themselves. These are the things I write down in my portfolio as the client is telling me their all-too-familiar story. The raw data, before it is skimmed through and filtered for all information deemed important enough to include in the bio.

And the reason I was so anxious to reach that particular page of nearly illegible scribbles was because of a very small, very tiny detail that, taken out of context, might seem fairly insignificant. But put *into* context (especially the context of my current situation) was exactly the opposite.

I could just faintly remember something that had come out of Anne Jacobs's mouth as we began to wrap up our initial meeting. As she was walking me to the door she stopped long enough to ask me a question about confidentiality:

"Just one more thing," she had said. *"I just want to make sure that this whole thing is kept between us. Raymond's reputation in the industry is almost as important as the reputation of his engines themselves."*

And at that moment I had stopped in the middle of her hallway, reopened my portfolio, and jotted down one final thought before walking out her front door.

"Of course," I had said, snapping my portfolio shut again. *"I've made a special note of it. But please rest assured that* all *of my assignments are done on a confidential basis. Just as I would expect my clients to keep* my *information confidential, I offer the same courtesy to them."*

"What the hell does that say?" Zoë said, leaning over my shoulder and attempting to decipher my handwriting. I looked down at the folder in my hands, and there it was. Just as I had remembered. In my own, indecipherable handwriting: *Confidential. Reputation of subject is high priority.*

I snapped the folder shut and looked up at Zoë with a confident smile. "It says he's got a lot to lose."

"Ah," Zoë said, sounding somewhat disappointed. I could tell that this little episode in my closet wasn't quite living up to the *Da Vinci Code*–esque fantasy she had been hoping for. I pulled myself to my feet and shut the file cabinet with the heel of my foot. "And this woman knows exactly how much that is."

After Zoë left I stood in my dining room and reopened the file to the client bio page in the front. I carefully dialed the printed phone number, praying that after not having spoken for over a month, and God knows what kind of repercussions, she would still take my call.

"Hello?" Anne Jacobs answered, in a cheerful, airy tone.

My tone, on the other hand, was high and squeaky. "Hi!" I cleared my throat. "Hi. Um, Mrs. Jacobs?"

"Speaking."

"Hello. This is . . . uh . . . this is Ashlyn?" My voice rose at the end of the sentence, as if I were actually *asking* her who I was. Or more like asking her to accept who I was.

There was a long pause, and for a moment I was more than convinced that she was going to hang up on me. At least she was contemplating it—seriously. I glanced at the clock on my oven. The silence was making me nervous and extremely uneasy.

So I spoke again. "I hope you remember me. We, um . . . Well, I, um . . ." Holy crap, this was difficult. "You hired me to . . ."

"I remember you," she quickly interrupted, clearly preferring that I didn't complete that particular sentence. "What can I do for you?" It was obvious that I was no longer deemed worthy of receiving the cheerful, airy telephone greeting that she reserved for her more welcomed callers.

I sucked in a hopeful breath. *Here it goes.* "Oh, good. You *do* remember!" I said, trying to duplicate her initial cheerfulness.

"Kind of hard to forget."

"Right." I scratched the tip of my nose. "Well, Mrs. Jacobs, I don't normally—"

"Actually, it's Lappelle now. Anne Lappelle. I went back to my *maiden* name."

I swallowed. "Of course."

Damn, that was fast.

"You were saying?"

As she spoke, I couldn't help but detect traces of blame in her voice. *My last name is Lappelle now . . . whose fault is that?* But I quickly told myself it was just my imagination.

"Yes, I was saying," I began timidly. "I don't normally contact clients after the . . . I mean, once the assignment is complete, but I kind of, well, I ran into a little . . . actually . . ." I stopped. The words weren't coming out right. I felt like a babbling fool. I paused and tried to collect myself.

"Look," Anne began impatiently, "I don't have a lot of time. I'm late for a—"

"I need your help," I blurted out desperately.

There was another long pause on her end, and for a moment I thought that she might have just set the phone down on the table and continued about her day. "Hello?" I asked cautiously.

"I can give you five minutes," she offered in a sharp, unforgiving tone.

"I'll take it."

Anne hung up after she agreed to meet with me in her home the following morning. She was by no means the warmest person on the phone. And, in fact, it came as somewhat of a surprise after the kind hospitality she had shown me the last time we met face-to-face. But given enough time to let reality truly sink in, to let divorce lawyers start working their black magic, and to let the bruises really start to take shape, I guess anyone can turn cold on you.

Not that I blamed her. I'd come to expect every woman I met under these circumstances to be cold and distant. More often than not, it's probably a defense mechanism. And I knew I was the last person on earth they'd want to be cordial to.

Yes, Anne was the one who had hired me. She had reached out to *me.* But sometimes that was just how it went. It's part of the job . . . or at least it *was* part of the job. When it actually *was* my job. Being hated, even by the person you supposedly saved, was always in the description. I suppose that was the one big difference between me and Superman. When Superman rescues you from a collapsing building or a plummeting airplane, you're eternally grateful. Unfortunately, the women I "rescued" from collapsing marriages and plummeting relationships didn't always see it that way. And I feared the person I was about to encounter at eleven o'clock the next morning would be no exception.

"Ashlyn," Anne said impersonally as she opened the door. It sounded more like an obvious statement of my existence than an actual greeting. I followed her into the living room and she motioned toward the same seat I had occupied under completely different circumstances less than two months earlier. When this all started. When Raymond Jacobs's spies were outside taking down my license plate.

I sat down and glanced around me. The room was, of course, familiar. And for the most part everything *looked* the same. Some of the plants were facing opposite directions to maximize or minimize sun exposure, the framed artwork had clearly been moved from wall to wall in search of a happier ambience, but it was, all in all, the same living room. The same house. And the woman sitting in the all-too-memorable seat across from me on the couch was the same woman I had spoken with only a short time ago.

But in sitting there, across from her granite face that revealed nothing, it certainly didn't *feel* the same.

And it wasn't just the obvious shift of power: Me now sitting in the figurative seat she had once occupied, asking *her* for help, pleading for *her* compassion . . . instead of the other way around.

There was a void in the room. An emptiness that was palpable.

That's when I noticed the photographs on the table.

The same photographs that I'm sure I once tried desperately to ignore, because they said too much. Because they divulged details that I didn't want to know, details that I didn't *need* to know.

A month ago the framed pictures showed five people. Five seemingly happy faces. Now there were only four. Anne and her three sons—who all appeared to be under the age of ten. It was as if someone had taken a plain, old-fashioned rubber eraser and painfully eliminated one particular face, wiping out all evidence of *him*.

That's also when I noticed the empty ring finger on Anne's left hand.

If I had tried to ignore it up until now, there was no use trying anymore.

It was the answer I never wanted to know—to the question I never dared ask. And now it was staring me straight in the face, refusing to be ignored.

I remembered when I was in grade school and my teachers always required that we write in pencil. We were never allowed to use a pen. Because it wasn't erasable. It wasn't fixable. If you made a mistake in pen, misspelled a word, accidentally wrote a backward *R*, you had to scratch it out, leaving behind a messy and very unsightly blob of black ink on your page. Proof. Evidence that you had erred. And everyone would know—everyone would see it.

Pencil, on the other hand, was so impermanent. So, changeable . . . so forgiving. Or at least that's what they told us. You make a mistake, you erase, and you rewrite, and no one knows the difference. No one sees the ink stain. Your steps are essentially untraceable.

But that argument never seemed to make a whole lot of sense to me. Because as I soon came to notice, sitting at my wooden desk, frantically trying to purge my errors with my brick-shaped Pearl eraser, they never completely vanished. No matter how hard I tried to rub out that flawed lettering, that misused word, that backward *R*, no matter how furiously I ran that rubber eraser back and forth across my page, leaving behind mountains of pink, confetti-like dust, the mistake never fully disappeared. I could always see traces of it.

It was always there.

Peeking out from behind the forward-facing *R*'s and the replaced words.

And even at such a young age, all I could think was, *At least the unsightly pen blotch was honest.*

Sitting in the former Mrs. Jacobs's living room that day, I saw the traces. The ones the magic eraser just couldn't seem to fully remove. They were there, in the faces of her three children, in the rotated ficus plants, in the rearrangement of the art on her walls—and especially in the lightness of her left hand, the one that not so long ago had borne a ring of diamonds so heavy that sometimes her fingers cramped at the end of the day—but she never complained.

In that moment I understood why I never stayed in contact with any of my clients. It was self-preservation. Because the weight of all those diamonds, all those photographs, all those faces—somehow, in the process, I unconsciously transferred it over to myself. And it was far too heavy for me to bear.

Even if reasonable logic told me I had no responsibility for these outcomes, and even if I knew that I had once offered this woman a gift that many women never have the opportunity to receive, as I looked into Anne's eyes I knew I wasn't the *right* person to blame, but for her, I certainly was the easiest. And I would continue to be for the next several years . . . maybe more.

"What was it that you needed to talk to me about?" Her question was polite but unfeeling.

I did my best to ignore her cold demeanor and accusing stare. This woman was the only person I knew who could help me. I had to at least ask.

I reached down and opened the black leather briefcase I had brought with me and removed my laptop. I turned it on and waited as it awakened from hibernation.

"I take it you remember what my occupation is." I smiled warmly.

She nodded. "If memory serves."

But as I launched a new Web browser on my laptop and navigated to the last page viewed, I had to wonder if *I* even knew what my occupation was. Part of me wanted to continue doing exactly what I had been doing. Reinitiate my quest. Pick up exactly where I had left off and pretend that I never left. Encountering someone like Jamie Richards was certainly enough to make it feel like more than just a viable *option*. And the less-than-subtle, *very* personal reminder that those types of men are still out there made me want to continue my fight against them even more.

But then there were all those other factors.

The secrets I would have to continue to keep from the people I love and everyone I meet on the street. The lies I would have to keep telling them.

"Well, my family doesn't know anything about it," I continued to Anne.

She studied me with distrust. "I would assume as much."

I turned the laptop around so the screen faced her. And then I gave her ample time to take in the entire essence of what was now sitting in front of her before I blankly added, "Your husband put it up. About a week after he failed his assignment. And he refuses to take it down."

I watched as her eyes quietly scanned the page, and then a sly smile appeared across her lips.

In that moment my hope sank. I knew immediately that she was mocking me. Quietly triumphing in my misfortune. And even though I knew she blamed me for all the wrong reasons, I couldn't blame *her.*

The heart heals in different ways. But I guess the most important thing is that it heals at all.

I nodded knowingly and slowly shut the lid of my laptop, placing it back in my briefcase. "Well, sorry to take up your time. I'll let you get back to your day."

I slid my handbag strap over my shoulder and rose from my seat in a quiet surrender. I should have known it was a long shot.

"Wait." Anne stopped me.

I turned back around. "Yes?"

"You still haven't told me what you want me to do." Her tone revealed nothing. It remained blank, detached, and completely void of compassion.

But my spirits lifted in spite of it. "Well," I began, standing awkwardly in the center of the living room. "I don't have any sort of leverage. I have nothing to bargain with. I know you said that Mr. Jacobs's reputation is very important to him, and so I thought that maybe . . ." I let my voice trail off, hoping that I had said enough. That the implication was there and I wouldn't ever have to say the very words that I wanted to say: *I need some dirt on your husband.*

And then, as if our earlier conversation had never even taken place, Anne tossed me a vacant glance and said, "I'm sorry. I'm really not sure what you're referring to."

I uncomfortably shifted my weight, standing in the middle of the living room—halfway to her, and halfway to the door, wondering if I had just received my cue to exit.

I opened my mouth to speak, not quite sure what was supposed to come out—or if anything even would. But before my scattered thoughts could begin to form into a sentence that, for once in the last two days, didn't begin with the word "Um," Anne's lips slowly curled up into a cunning and deliciously wicked smile. The kind you would only see on the faces of witches and evil sorceresses in your favorite childhood movie.

"But I do have something you might find interesting," she said at last.

33

beware of the ides of march

"I see you've decided to come back and pay me a little visit," Raymond Jacobs said smugly, as I stepped into his large corner office once again and took a seat on the all-too-familiar couch across from his desk.

I nodded, keeping my head low.

"And to what do I owe the honor of this visit? Reconsidered my offer, I hope."

I lifted my head slowly, looking demure, unsure of myself, and completely defeated. "I . . . um," I began timidly. "I can't take it anymore. The Web site, the e-mail forwards, the letters to my niece . . ." My voice trailed off, the painful memory of Hannah's questioning face too much for me to handle.

He smiled and rose to his feet. "I agree," he said, nodding his head sympathetically. "It's too much. Maybe I went a little overboard."

My eyebrows raised hopefully as I watched him walk over to the small bar tucked in the corner and pour himself a glass of clear, syrupy liquid. "Drink?" he asked.

I shook my head. "No, thank you."

He nodded, and with drink in hand walked around his desk and leaned assuredly against the edge of it. "So what do you propose we do about it, then?" Raymond asked, seemingly delighted to finally be on *my* side. To finally have us both on the same page.

"You *could* just take the Web site down and leave me alone?" I suggested softly.

He considered this option as he took a sip of his drink. "Yes, I suppose I could do that," he offered thoughtfully. "But honestly I don't know if that's the *best* option. I mean, it certainly is *an* option. But it feels somewhat incomplete to me."

He was enjoying this. That much was clear. He knew he still had the upper hand in this negotiation and that made him happy. After all, it was a hand he had grown accustomed to having. Raymond Jacobs did not become the multimillionaire he was today by settling for low hands.

"Why's that?" I asked quizzically.

He took another sip of his drink, and from behind the rim of the glass, his eyes flashed me a creepy smile. His face gave away the bitter taste of his cocktail as he willfully swallowed it down. Then, with his hand still wrapped around the glass, he stretched out his index finger and pointed at me. "I'm glad you asked that."

He pushed himself off the edge of his desk and began walking toward me. This time his steps weren't menacing or filled with wicked amusement. They were gentle and purposeful, as if he were walking toward a small child who had gotten lost in a large shopping mall and needed an adult to help her find her way.

He approached the couch and I tilted my head to look up at him. He motioned to the seat next to me. "Mind?"

I nodded reluctantly, and then scooted all the way to the edge, my body practically wrapping around the armrest. He took a seat on the other end.

"So," he began, settling with his drink in one hand and his other hand resting on the opposite armrest. "Your question was: Why does your proposed solution feel somewhat incomplete?"

He was clearly playing games with me. And even though I hated him for it and it made me want to stand up, knee him in the crotch, and then pour his stupid little afternoon cocktail over his head, I played along.

Because this was the game.

And Raymond Jacobs was 100 percent certain that he would once again be victorious.

But what was so unbelievable to me was how a successful businessman, who had obviously created his wealth and power by making wise choices and playing off of people's strengths and weaknesses, had so blatantly forgotten the history of our relationship.

The story of Raymond Jacobs and the elusive Ashlyn had begun not with a victory on his part but with a defeat. And, therefore, he should have remembered that one of Ashlyn's strong suits is knowing *exactly* how to play along.

"Yes," I replied anxiously.

"Well," he stated, turning to look at me from the far opposite corner of his office couch. "The answer is quite simple. In order for a solution to be complete, it has to satisfy *both* interested parties. And your solution, unfortunately, fails to do that."

I stared at him, mouth open, exuding a sensation of absolute bemusement, as if to say, *I have no idea what you're getting at.*

He smiled condescendingly at me and even allowed a low guttural laugh to escape his lips. "In other words . . ." He transferred his drink to his other hand and then leaned deeply toward my side of the couch turned battlefield. "There's nothing in it for *me.*"

The physically and emotionally exhausted woman had returned to the living room with a large manila envelope. She stood before me, clutching it tightly, as if parting from it would mean parting from the only thing that had ever made her feel safe.

I looked at her, longing to ask what was inside. Longing to rip it from her hands, dump the contents out on the coffee table, and riffle through it like a child searching desperately for the best pieces of candy from the recently busted piñata.

But I knew this process would have to go at her pace. And so I would wait.

"I don't know why I've kept this," she said softly, still holding the envelope close to her body like a shield. "My husband doesn't even know I have it."

I nodded, trying to look sympathetic and understanding, while all the while trying to keep my lips as tightly closed as they would go. Because I knew that one tiny crack would leave enough space for those persistently inquisitive words to pry my mouth open and escape.

She moved back to her seat on the couch, clutching the envelope in her hands. "I guess it always made me feel like I had something. Something that would protect me. Doesn't that sound silly?"

I shook my head insistently. "Not at all!"

She shrugged and eventually surrendered a nod. "Yeah. I guess it doesn't seem so silly now."

I smiled, the impatience boiling up inside of me. This had to be it! This had to be my key. The key that fit the rusty lock that kept me chained to the evil man's maliciously destructive schemes.

And then I watched as the woman's tightly clasped fingers slowly started to loosen. And her firm, securely wrapped arms slowly started to relax. Until I could see the mysterious manila envelope held close to her body slowly starting to be pulled away.

She looked at it as if she were saying good-bye to an old friend. Throwing away the security blanket that used to keep her warm at night, the only thing that promised her a way out from under a pile of rubble that had hung threateningly over her head for what felt like a lifetime.

Then she began to laugh at her own foolishness, mocking her childish desire to grasp on to something that had promised to keep her out of harm's way. When all along, as it would turn out . . . she had never been safe. "Well," she said, extending the envelope across the coffee table in my direction. "Looks like *you* have something now."

Raymond Jacobs was quite pleased with himself.

He had successfully managed to lure this helpless little girl into his clever web of trickery and illusion. And I had without a doubt fallen into it.

And the reason he *knew* I had fallen for it was because I now sat on his red leather couch, feeling overpowered and lost and ready to give in. To lie down and simply accept my defeat . . . literally.

This time . . . *he* had won the game of chess.

This time . . . *he* had conquered the conqueror.

This time . . . he had made *me* feel small and helpless. Just as I had done to him. And he took every ounce of satisfaction from the triumph that he knew he deserved.

Raymond shifted his weight onto one hip so he could dig into his pocket and pull out a mangled piece of paper. From the inside of his suit jacket he carefully removed a shiny, silver ballpoint pen that he clicked to life with great fervor and pride. He then began scribbling words onto the piece of paper and handed it to me.

"Here's my address. Shall we say ten-thirty? I have an early meeting tomorrow morning, so I don't want to be up too late."

He winked at me as I hesitantly reached out and took the death sentence from his large grimy hands and attempted to read the illegible black handwriting

He smiled and stood up, offering his hand for me to shake as if we had just completed a successful business transaction and I could now happily go forth and produce, or build, or invest, or whatever it was we had just agreed upon.

But I didn't shake it. I simply stared at it. Then at him. "I think you're wrong," I said modestly.

He flashed an amused grin. "Oh yeah? About what?"

I swallowed hard. As if what I was about to say was the hardest thing I'd ever had to force out of my mouth in all my life. But in all actuality, I had been eagerly, breathlessly, impatiently waiting to say it from the moment I walked in the door. "I think you're wrong about there being nothing in it for you."

His grin never faltered. He was clearly entertained by my last-minute attempt to negotiate a better deal. "And what would that be, my dear?"

"Silence," I replied matter-of-factly.

A hint of confusion spread across his eyes, but he immediately shook it away. "Silence, huh? What kind of silence?"

"*My* silence."

His smug grin faded into a slightly irritated roll of his eyes. He was now starting to lose his patience. "Silence about what?" he grumbled.

But I had plenty of patience left. I had a whole lifetime's worth of patience in my vault. "About March 15, 1989," I stated simply.

March 15, 1989, is what I read off the document that I had hastily pulled out of Anne Jacobs's enchanting manila envelope. And the reason I read that particular line of text first was because it was highlighted. Along with the ten lines below it. All offering the same seemingly useless piece of information—March 15, 1989.

"What is it?" I asked, my anticipation no longer kept inside, rather now written all over my face.

"Look at the highlighted lines," she instructed me.

I felt an overwhelming sense of frustration. I *had* been looking at the highlighted lines for what felt like an hour. And they still made no sense to me. I read through them once more, and then looked up desperately at Anne. "They all just list stock trades that took place on March 15, 1989." I studied the paper again. "Each for ten thousand shares of 'KII.' "

Anne nodded. "Kelen Industries Incorporated."

I held the paper up in front of my face. *Of course! Kelen Industries! Raymond's car-engine manufacturing corporation.* Honestly, I don't know why I didn't recognize the stock symbol when I first looked at it. I had seen it listed on several reports that I had read while doing my research for his assignment. But what was so significant about that date? And what did it matter if Raymond Jacobs had trade confirmations for buying stocks of his own company?

Then I noticed something at the top of the document. My eyes had been so attracted to the bright yellow highlights radiating off the middle of the page like rays of sunlight that I hadn't even noticed *who* the stock trade confirmation belonged to. *Kenneth Pauley.* That name certainly didn't sound familiar.

"Who's Kenneth Pauley?" I asked.

Anne sat back in her seat and folded her hands in her lap. She looked so at peace now. As if she had just eliminated a gigantic burden she had been carrying around for years. And now that it was no longer in her hands, literally, she could finally relax. "He's an old college friend of Raymond's. They got their MBAs together. Supposedly they stopped talking soon after graduation. But apparently"—she motioned to the document in my hands—"that wasn't the case."

I looked at her curiously. *That's it?* That's the only explanation I was going to get? That still didn't make any fucking sense. That still wasn't enough to march into Raymond Jacobs's office with and wave in his face. *"Ha-ha, I know who Kenneth Pauley is. You're a dead man!"* I still had nothing!

"There's more," Anne urged me, gesturing toward the envelope I had tossed down beside me.

I frantically snatched it up and reopened it, pulling out three more documents that looked surprisingly similar to the one already in my hand. Stock trade confirmation pages. All dated March 15, 1989. And all with several highlighted lines of purchase activity for stocks of Kelen Industries Incorporated.

But as I looked closer at the second page, and then the third page, I noticed one very distinct difference among them. They all had different names listed at the top. *Lawrence Wilson, Gary Morningstar, Weston Davidson*. "More MBA buddies?" I speculated.

She shrugged. "Some."

Why was she being so damn elusive? Why couldn't she just spit it out and tell me what these stupid documents meant. *Why?*

"Do you know what March 15, 1989, is?" she asked, possibly sensing my growing aggravation.

I shook my head adamantly.

"I'm sure you must have come across it in your research," she prompted, as if this were a final exam. My whole career, life, and happiness came down to this one moment. This *one* question. And out of the kindness of her heart, she was offering me a clue. Tipping me off to the exact page of my textbook from which this answer would have come.

I thought back to all the articles and annual reports and financial statements I had read about Raymond Jacobs. But honestly, they were blurring together in my mind with all the other articles and annual reports and financial statements I had read about every other man I had ever tested.

Car engines. I remembered car engines. I remembered that he took over his father's small engine-manufacturing company right out of grad school. I remembered one particular article that told the story of Raymond's path to success, and how he had managed to take the small manufacturing outfit and turn it into the huge corporation it was today. And how his big break finally came when he . . .

"Oh my God," I suddenly said aloud, my stomach doing a small flip.

Anne smiled. She knew I had stumbled upon it. She knew I had sourced the right page in my memory and had finally come up with the correct answer.

And like any proud teacher, she knew I would pass the test . . . with flying colors.

Raymond Jacobs staggered backward. I watched him intently, my eyes never blinking, my face never revealing a thing.

"What about March 15, 1989?" he said, desperately trying to hide the obvious terror that was filling his eyes. "I don't know what you're talking about," he said dismissively.

"Hmm," I continued, staying true to my mastered game of coyness and modesty. "That's funny. I would think you would remember that day quite well, given your obvious success and all." I nodded, indicating his spacious corner office.

He closed his eyes tightly, feeling the humiliation of an unforeseen, surprise attack. One he had never seen coming in a million years, but one that he would inevitably never forget for the next million.

"I mean, March 15, 1989, was a *huge* day for you, wasn't it, Ray?" I continued, basking in my glory yet refusing to outwardly gloat. It was much more fun this way. Playing the unassuming detective who would have *never* guessed that this man was anything more than just an honest, hardworking businessman.

Raymond shook his head, refusing to speak.

So I continued. After all, I still had *plenty* to say. "Because, as I recall, if I'm not mistaken, March 15, 1989, was the day before March *16,* 1989, a *very* important day in the history of this company." I brought my finger up to my chin and pretended to rack my brain for all the important details. "Yes, I believe March 15 was the day before you announced to the world that Kelen Industries, once a small, humble, tiny little manufacturing plant, was now teaming up with Ford Motor Company to supply engines for their newest line of midsized cars. Wow!" I took a deep breath and feigned an impressed nod of appreciation.

"You know," I said, thinking long and hard about my next seemingly puzzling statement. "I would have thought that you'd be out celebrating on March 15, 1989—the day before such a *huge,* important announcement. But no, you were probably too busy for that, huh?" I speculated. "I can imagine. I mean, rounding up all your long-lost, grad school buddies and telling each of them to buy tens of thousands of shares in your company before this big exciting news hit the public would certainly tie up a *lot* of time. Not to mention all those stressful negotiations of who gets what percent of who and what and where and . . ."

"What do you want?" Raymond said, infuriated.

"Some people call me a human calculator," I continued, ignoring his question. "And it's true. I *have* been known to do the occasional computation in my head. But this one was actually quite staggering: two hundred thousands shares total at five dollars a share is impressive enough. But then to have the stock price rise from five dollars to fifty dollars in less than a year? Now that's some serious cash." I paused and pretended to punch the corresponding numbers into my mental calculator until I had come up with the final tally. "That's like ten *million dollars* made on insider trading alone! Not to mention what you must have made legally on the deal itself."

"What do you want?" he repeated, seemingly fed up with my ongoing rant, and no longer willing to suffer through it quietly.

I stood up and looked him directly in the eye. No longer afraid. No longer the one with the lower hand in this game. "I believe we've already established what I want," I said firmly. And after that there was really nothing more to be said.

So I walked out the door, careful not to let it slam behind me. After all, I had probably disturbed his peaceful world enough for one day. And no one appreciates a slammed door.

34

the puppet master

I knew it was only a matter of time before the phone rang and Karen Richards was on the other end, demanding to know why her husband had unexpectedly returned early from his business trip a few days earlier, and she had yet to hear from me regarding the outcome of his inspection.

So when the phone *did* ring on Friday morning while I was still basking in the triumphant glow of my battle against Raymond Jacobs, I assumed it would be her.

I unplugged the Treo from its charger on my nightstand and answered the call. "Hello?" I said, my voice still overflowing with traces of sweet victory.

"Yes, hello, Ashlyn?" It was a female voice. Kind and compassionate, with just a small hint of something familiar about it. But after having Karen Richards's voice burned involuntarily into my memory, I was certain this wasn't her.

"May I ask what this is in regards to?"

There was a pause on the other end. "Um . . ." the voice began hesitantly. "This is Lauren Ireland. Do you remember me?"

I grimaced. Of course I remembered her. She'd practically bit my head off. Not that I blamed her. I mean, I'm sure the fact that her father hired me behind her back came as quite a shock. But the question wasn't, did I remember her, but why the hell was her voice coming through my phone?

"Yes, I remember you," I said cautiously, worried that she might be calling to give me another earful, or worse yet, a guilt trip about her canceled wedding or nonrefundable plane tickets to Fiji. I placed my finger, poised and ready, on the hang-up button, as a precaution.

"I hope you don't mind me contacting you. I found your number on my father's desk. He doesn't know that I'm calling."

"I don't mind," I replied, unsure of whether or not I meant it.

She took a deep breath. "First off, I want to apologize for my behavior a few weeks ago . . . in my father's office. I assure you, that's not how I normally behave. It's just that with your news and the whole thing . . . well, I was definitely taken by surprise."

"No need to apologize, Miss Ireland."

"Please, call me Lauren."

"It's fine, Lauren. I assure you, I've heard much worse."

She laughed nervously. "I can only imagine."

There was an awkward silence on the phone, and I wasn't sure who was supposed to speak next. I still had no idea why she was calling. Was it just to apologize? Or was there something else?

"Actually, the reason I'm calling . . ." she began.

Okay, so there was something else.

". . . is because I was kind of hoping we could meet. For coffee or something."

I shifted uncomfortably and finally took a seat on the edge of my bed. This was definitely not something I did often. Why did she even feel the need to meet me, anyway? Did she suddenly want us to become friends? Best buddies with the woman who destroyed her engagement? That seemed a little far-fetched.

"Honestly, Lauren. If you just want to apologize, there's no need. I completely understand why you reacted the way you did. And I don't hold it against you."

"No," she replied. "It's not that. Actually, it's regarding a different subject altogether."

She had certainly piqued my curiosity. "And what would that be, exactly?" I asked as politely as possible. Given my recent track record, I wasn't really in the mood for any more surprises.

"I'd actually rather discuss it with you in person, if you don't mind. I promise I won't take up more than an hour of your time."

My first reaction was that it was a setup. An ambush. Lauren and ten of her biggest friends would be waiting for me at whatever tunnel or deserted playground she suggested for our rendezvous. But I could hear something deep in her voice that immediately ruled out that possibility. She sounded humbled. Despairing. Looking for guidance. Well, I certainly wasn't one to be writing an advice column right about now, but I supposed it couldn't hurt to meet with her. Besides, what else did I have to do these days? Take up knitting?

So I agreed.

To my relief, she didn't suggest an abandoned playground or back alley somewhere. She asked if we could meet at a simple coffee shop in Santa Monica.

"The 18th Street Café, do you know it?"

I smiled. "Yes, it's a nice place."

Lauren and I agreed to meet the following evening, and as I hung up the phone I immediately wondered if I would regret it. But I convinced myself that I should be welcoming any distraction at this point. Because as much as I hated to admit it, it was nearly impossible not to think about Jamie with every passing minute. A small, tiny, insignificant part of me wondered why I hadn't heard from him. Especially when he was clearly the one in the wrong about this whole thing.

I mean, sure, I had the card in my purse. I know how it must have looked to him when he found it. Especially given the odd encounter we had had with the man at Haku Sushi who almost spilled everything.

But wouldn't he at least call or e-mail to make sure I had gotten home all right?

He had basically deserted me in a foreign country.

Okay, I had deserted myself. But nonetheless, despite my better judgment, despite my better self telling me not to, I still caught myself staring longingly at the phone from time to time. I still couldn't help but check my voice mail *even* when there was no voice-mail indicator on my screen.

And I hated that I did that.

I hated that he had made me care. The lying, cheating scumball had me wondering whether or not he would ever pick up the phone to call me again.

And then there was the next question: Was he a lying, cheating scumball to begin with?

And then there was the question after that: What was I going to tell his wife?

My services had always been very clear: intention to cheat. Displaying unfaithful tendencies. Almost sex. That's what they were, and that's what they'd always been.

Everyone got the same treatment. Every man got the same, up-to-the-last-minute thrill ride. And if this were any other assignment, Jamie technically would have passed.

So is that what I should tell Karen Howard Richards? That he's innocent?

Or would I tell her the truth? All of it. The plane trip from Vegas, the round of golf, sushi, airplane bags, Paris. And then let her decide. Let her try to answer the question I still hadn't been able to answer.

And what about the reverse scenario? The one where Karen doesn't call at all. The one where I never hear from her again—for whatever reason. Maybe Jamie flew home from Paris all full of remorse and regret, and spilled his heart out to her, confessed everything, and they had a passionate night full of honest communication and incredible make-up sex.

Good for them.

I hope they're *very* happy together.

At least I'd never have to deal with either one of them again. As unlikely as I believed that scenario was, I did find it strange that I still had yet to hear from her since I got back. Jamie would have obviously taken a flight home right away, wouldn't he?

His trip was more than likely cut short. He told me he had to come back to Los Angeles to work on other accounts. So why wouldn't she know he was here? And if she knew he was here, why wouldn't she call me for the results?

The whole thing was just very strange. It always had been. It had never *quite* added up entirely. And I was in no mood to start trying to dig to the bottom of it with a teaspoon. It would undoubtedly take forever and the metal would probably give out halfway through.

So I vowed not to even try.

Not to even think about it.

But I knew that was easier said than done.

I wasn't exactly looking forward to my meeting with Lauren Ireland, but I wasn't exactly dreading it, either. I was certainly intrigued by her request to meet, not having a clue about what she might possibly want to talk to *me* about.

Her phone call had come about a month after I informed her and her father about Parker Colman's failure in the hotel room—and at the poker table, for that matter. And she had been completely blindsided by the information. So not only did she have to digest the fact that she and her soon-to-be husband had differing opinions on what was "appropriate" bachelor party behavior, but she also had to come to grips with the fact that her *father* had hired someone called a "fidelity inspector" to prove it. Most people don't even know that someone like that exists to begin with.

That's why I initially suspected an attack. A way to get me alone so she could give me another piece of her mind. A more well-thought-out, well-taped-together piece. I mean, her previous outburst was entirely impromptu, no preplanned speech or carefully premeditated insults. I could only imagine what the girl would be able to come up with had she been given adequate time to prepare.

But something inside me was telling me it wasn't a trap. That Lauren had another agenda, a much less violent or verbally abusive one. And that something inside me was the very reason I was now stepping into the coffee shop on the corner of 18th Street and Santa Monica Boulevard.

Well . . . that and just plain old curiosity.

"Ashlyn!" I heard someone call out.

I turned to see Lauren seated at a small table with one empty chair. She appeared well rested, peaceful, not at all what I imagined my clients (or daughters of clients in this case) to look like only a month after an assignment. I immediately remembered how attractive she was. Conservatively dressed once again, but without a doubt, a very pretty girl.

She waved amicably and I made my way over. As I approached she put away a small, wireless device that she had been toying with and stood up to greet me with a handshake.

"Thanks again for coming." Her face was pleasant and relaxed. And she looked extremely grateful to see me show up.

If this was a surprise attack, she certainly took the word *surprise* very seriously.

"It's no problem," I replied, and took the empty seat across from her.

"Can I get you something to drink?" she asked. "Coffee, tea . . . they have amazing chai lattés here."

"Chai would be fine."

I watched her hurry to the counter, order the drinks, and then return to the table. "They'll bring them over," she said as she pulled her calf-length A-line skirt close to her legs and sat down.

I smiled politely. "Great."

"So," she began, fidgeting with the sugar holder, "you're probably wondering why I asked to meet you."

I nodded. "Yes, I am a bit curious. Your phone call definitely wasn't expected."

"Do you get a lot of nasty phone calls?" she asked with genuine interest.

I shrugged. "Some," I said, cautiously opting *not* to share the privileged information about my recent retirement until I knew a little bit more about her reasons for bringing me here. "I can usually tell by the person's tone of voice within the first five seconds of the call, and I simply hang up," I continued. "Then I store their number under the word *screen*."

She listened to me speak, her eyes devouring my words, thirsty for more. I started to feel a bit uneasy. And then a strange thought crossed my mind. Maybe she had a crush on me.

I immediately dismissed it. *That's ridiculous!*

"So what do you charge for something like this?" she asked next.

I looked at her peculiarly. What was with all the interest in my job? I'd never had a former client be this probing before. "Wait a minute," I said apprehensively. "Are you writing an article or something? What is this about?" I demanded, my tone instantly changing from patient to borderline aggravation. I eyed my bag on the floor and wondered if I should make a mad dash for the door before some hidden photographer busted out to take my picture (again!) and plaster it all over the front of *The LA Times:* THE LEGENDARY "FIDELITY INSPECTOR" CAUGHT ON FILM!

All I needed right now was another dose of national exposure.

Her eyes shot open. "No! Oh, no! I'm sorry. I should have told you why I was here before I started in with all the questions."

I raised my eyebrows suspiciously. "Okay, then, why don't you tell me now?"

She lowered her eyes slightly, as if embarrassed about the topic of discussion. After a brief moment she lifted her head and focused on me. "Actually, I asked you here because—"

"Two chai lattés," a voice announced.

We both looked up at the teenage boy in a green apron hovering above us holding two ceramic cups filled to the brim with steaming hot liquid.

"Yes," Lauren said anxiously, taking one of the cups from his hand. He set the other mug down in front of me.

"Thanks," I said with a half smile before immediately turning back to Lauren. "You were saying . . ."

She took a deep breath and blew on the surface of her tea, causing small ripples to form and dissipate over the short distance to the other side of the mug. "Yes. Well, the truth is, I asked you here because I'm interested in your job."

I shot her a confused look. "Well, that much was obvious with all the questions. But *why* are you so interested in my . . . *job*?"

In all honesty, I could certainly see how this job *would* be fairly interesting to people on the outside. It was different, a bit scandalous. I could see how the curiosity factor would set in upon mentioning it. But the fact was, I was *so* very over it at this point that I could hardly relate to her level of fascination.

"Well," Lauren continued, "I'm interested in it because . . ." She bit her lip. I could tell whatever she was about to say was difficult.

I started to take a sip of my chai latté. I could feel the heat of the tea underneath my lips, so I cautiously tried to regulate the amount entering my mouth.

"Because I want to do what you do," she finished.

So much for a small sip. It was like a floodgate had opened and half of the mug of hot chai flowed into my mouth, scorching my tongue and the back of my throat. I coughed violently. "You what?" I managed to get out as I rubbed my charred tongue against the roof of my mouth.

"I want to do exactly what you do. You know, test people for infidelity."

I stared at her in disbelief, and then spun my head around the coffeehouse. Was this a joke? Was I being set up by Zoë or Sophie, or somebody?

When my eyes returned to hers I could see absolute sincerity in her face. She was 100 percent serious, and was now waiting for my response. My advice.

I leaned forward. "You want to be a fidelity inspector?" I confirmed in a low whisper.

She nodded her head firmly.

"Why?" I asked, leaving my mouth disturbingly agape as if I were asking someone why they would want to be dunked under water three times and only brought up twice.

She looked down at the table and rubbed her temples. At that moment, for the first time since I had walked through that door, I saw the same pain on her face as I had seen a month ago in her father's office.

She swallowed hard and looked up again. "Because I want to devote the rest of my life to making sure the cheating scum of this world are brought to justice."

I continued to massage my burned tongue against the inside of my cheek. I opened my mouth warily and said, "Lauren, I think you're overreacting here. I understand that you're feeling hurt and betrayed. But I doubt you're thinking rationally right now. You should probably let this whole event settle and clear your head before you start thinking of ways to get revenge on the male species."

She shook her head stubbornly. "No, I *am* thinking rationally. For the first time in my life. Ashlyn—" She stopped abruptly. "Wait, that's not your real name, is it?"

I folded my arms across my chest. "No," I said with a definitiveness that implied she would not be learning my real name any time soon.

She nodded her understanding, not pressing the issue. "Well, whoever you are, you opened my eyes. You showed me something that probably would have taken me years to see on my own . . . if I even ended up seeing it at all. And that's an amazing gift to give someone. I want to give it back to as many people as I can."

I considered her argument. It was a good one. After all, it was the same one I used to use. "Well," I began admitting, "the truth is most people don't exactly see it the way you do . . . at least not right away. I mean, gratitude is hard to come by in this job. It's an assumption you have to make on your own. So if you're looking for instant gratification, this isn't the place to find it."

I paused. "Plus, it's a *very* difficult thing to go through with."

"I realize that," Lauren said. "But I can do it. I know I can. I mean, if I can fix outsourced programming code for a customized app without ever learning the business process, I can certainly handle this."

I shot her a puzzled look.

She continued. "Sometimes at night, when I'm lying alone in my bed, I think about how if it weren't for you I would have married that guy. And God knows how many times he would have done exactly what he did. While I stood by, faithful, loyal, and completely naive. I can't *not* do this."

She looked at me with a determination that I hadn't seen in anyone in a long time. A determination I used to see in myself. Every time I looked in the mirror. Give people the gift my mother never got.

It was what had kept me going every day. What had gotten me out of bed every morning.

And then suddenly, as I listened to her familiar words and sympathetic quest for purpose, I came face-to-face with a cold, hard realization.

What was going to get me out of bed now?

What would be my purpose . . . now?

"The truth is," I began, "I retired a week ago."

Her ears perked up. "You did? Why?"

I should have told her everything. All the ugly aspects of this business: the lies you have to maintain, the secrets you have to keep, the double life you have to lead, and even the revenge that some people will seek. Because believe it or not, not everyone thinks of this as a service to humanity. A lot of people—people like Raymond Jacobs—think of it as grounds for retribution.

But I didn't tell her any of these things, because I felt it wasn't my place. And I knew that when I was in her shoes, when I had come face-to-face with the decision to sink or swim in my sea of regrettable mistakes, I had chosen to swim. I had chosen to find purpose in those mistakes. And if someone had warned me of what was to come, I doubt I would have listened. I doubt it would have put me off my mission for even a second.

I saw that willpower in Lauren's eyes, and I wouldn't have done anything in the world to try to take that away from her.

"It was just time to stop," I said simply, in response to her question.

"So, do you have any advice for me? A place to start? Where to begin?"

I almost had to laugh. It was as if she were seeking business advice from a tax attorney. Should she set up an LLC or a corporation? And in that case should she opt for an S corp or a C corp? And what the hell did I know about C corps?

I had stumbled into this job . . . and in all honesty, I had stumbled out as well.

I shook my head. "Not really. I don't really know what to tell you. I can refer all my future business to you, if you'd like."

Lauren's eyes lit up like a car's headlights illuminating a dark country highway. "That would be perfect. Thank you!"

I smiled back at her, but frankly, the whole thing just felt very odd. Like I was being asked to pass on my legacy key to the next lucky recipient. Although I honestly wouldn't use the word *lucky* to describe her.

But I suppose *legacy* was accurate enough.

Ashlyn had certainly left her mark on the world. And I suppose it would be difficult to follow in her shoes. But as I left the café that night, I felt a pang of emptiness. Like a part of me was missing. A part of me that I had gotten very used to over the years. And I supposed I truly would miss Ashlyn from time to time.

She did have some really nice shoes.

When your entire house is decorated in white, you would think that one, tiny out-of-place object would stick out like a sore thumb. A red stain on a white sofa. A piece of black lint buried inside the white Burberry carpeting. An unsightly blue pen mark stretched across a whitewashed wall.

So the fact that I hadn't noticed the small, mysteriously misplaced object under my dining-room table until that night, when I came home from the coffee shop, was somewhat surprising to me.

I tilted my head in bemusement as it caught my eye all the way from across the living room. When you live in a place as immaculate as mine, strange, unfamiliar articles don't go unnoticed for long. So I immediately wondered why I hadn't seen it earlier, like when I was leaving. Or the other day when I came home from Raymond Jacobs's office. Or the morning I arrived home from Paris. (Although that day should be omitted given the nature of my condition at the time—I probably wouldn't have noticed a herd of elephants sitting around my table smoking cigars and playing poker. Or rather, I probably wouldn't have cared.)

But I certainly noticed it now.

Granted, it was mostly white itself, thus lending an obvious rationalization to its extended oversight. But as I drew closer, crouching slightly to get a better look at the peculiar trespasser, I noticed that it wasn't *completely* white. It was speckled with some type of black markings. And upon even closer inspection, I concluded that the markings consisted of handwriting in black ink.

As I approached the dining room, I stuck my foot far beneath the glass table in an attempt to trap the item under my shoe and drag it out into the open.

But my foot couldn't quite reach it.

So I reluctantly got down on all fours, crawled underneath the table, and retrieved the object by hand.

As I pulled myself to my feet and casually flipped the item over in my hand, I immediately felt a strong wave of nausea flow over me.

It was Jamie Richards's business card, showing up once again at the most inopportune time. Evidently (and appropriately) knocked from its coveted place atop my glass table and landing facedown on the white carpet.

I fought back the queasiness in my stomach, and with a deep, surrendering sigh, I walked into the kitchen, opened the trash compactor, and held the card dangerously over the top. Then, with one last look at the name I'd read and touched a thousand times, I released the card, and watched it float aimlessly into the bin.

And just as I was about to close the trash compactor drawer once again, flip the switch, and bring it to life, I stopped and thought back to all the times I'd picked up that card. Some had been to call Jamie for a confirmation, some had been to attempt to cancel a date, and some had just been for the sake of staring at his name on a piece of a paper.

But there was one thing *all* of those times had in common: never once had I noticed writing on the back.

As I reached into the trash and picked up the card again, I thought back to the day I had first received it:

"I think it's my last one. I've been saving it for you," Jamie had said, handing it over. *"Look, it's even got some of my random scribbles on the back from when I ran out of scratch paper."*

I flipped over the card and read the so-called random scribbles.

September 26th. 11:00 a.m. 1118 Wilshire Blvd.

I scrunched up my face in confusion. Why did that date and address sound so familiar?

September 26, 1118 Wilshire. September 26, 1118 Wilshire.

I quickly fished my Treo out of my bag and navigated to last month's calendar page. September 26: Recall on Range Rover. Eleven A.M. Location: 1118 Wilshire.

I scratched my head and looked again at the back of the card.

That was weird. Jamie and I had the exact same car appointment time. At the exact same location. But I guess I already knew that because that's when and where I bumped into him. My surrender to the universe.

Well, the universe certainly had had its fun with me, hadn't it?

I shrugged and turned back toward the trash compactor, ready to flick the now slightly grimy card right back where it belonged. But then I caught sight of the oven in front of me. And my mind flashed back—just for a moment—to the day I was *told* about the recall appointment.

Marta had been cleaning the oven when she informed me that the Range Rover dealership had called to schedule an appointment. And oddly enough, I wasn't even *in* the appointment book. And come to think of it—even more oddly enough—my car model wasn't even marked for a recall.

I suddenly froze: the card in one hand, my phone in the other, as everything slowly started to make sense.

That business card had made its way from the back pocket of my jeans where I had placed it the minute Jamie had handed it to me to the top of my kitchen counter, where Zoë later picked it up and interrogated me on it. And there was only *one* person who'd had access to it in the meantime.

Marta.

She had found the card in my jeans pocket, noticed the handwriting, told me about a bogus recall appointment, all so I could bump into Jamie again?

It was almost too orchestrated to fathom.

I sounded like I was reading what I hoped to be the winning combination during a game of Clue. Marta Hernandez, in the kitchen, with the business card.

And I didn't even know she *knew* the word *recall.*

And what interest did she have in whether or not I bumped into Jamie again?

Then suddenly another idea hit me. I sprinted into the laundry room and started searching frantically through the cupboards and cabinets. I felt like I was on a wild-goose chase, hunting for clues to lead me to my next destination. And God knows what I would find there.

But what I found in *here* was exactly what I thought I might.

In the cabinet under the sink, carefully hidden behind the Drano, the Windex, and the roll of spare paper towels, was the laundry detergent I thought I had never bought. The laundry detergent that Marta interrupted me for while I was in the middle of trying to place a very important phone call, one that would have put an end to my third date with Jamie before it even began.

The laundry detergent she convinced me I didn't have.

There it was. Way, way in the back. And *I* certainly hadn't put it there.

Marta Hernandez, in the laundry room, with the detergent!

This whole thing was mind-boggling. How did she even know who Jamie was? Had she tapped my phones? Bugged my house? Implanted some type of mind-reading device in my brain while I was asleep?

Here I was tiptoeing around big words and complex English phrases so I could be sure that she would understand me when I spoke to her about how to wash my favorite pair of jeans. But all along she'd been devising complicated masterminded plots to intervene in my love life.

And all I could think was, *What else?*

What else had she been intervening in all this time?

I stood in the middle of the living room and walked slowly in a complete circle, surveying every inch of my immaculately clean house. And just when I'd almost made a full rotation, my eyes stopped at the TV.

The TiVo!

Desperate Housewives in Spanish?

Or more important, the *one Desperate Housewives* episode that *happened* to feature a plot to expose and incriminate one very dishonest husband?

Oh, this was just too much!

And I couldn't decide if it was comforting or just plain creepy, but Marta had single-handedly been responsible for not only initiating and later preserving my relationship with Jamie, but also for leading me to my victory against Raymond Jacobs.

"She saved me," I said aloud.

This whole time, she knew everything. And she saved me from it.

She was like my guardian angel. Watching over me. Protecting me from afar. Not just from the city's dirt and grime that I dragged in on my heels every day, but from the city itself.

Batman may have had Alfred.

But I had Marta.

I sunk into the couch in a stunned silence, Jamie's business card still clenched between my fingers. I felt like a hurricane had just swept through my life and all I had been left with was this little white card.

And I wondered if she had been right all along.

If she could save me from someone like Raymond Jacobs, maybe she had her reasons for making sure Jamie stayed in my life. And maybe the reasons were good ones.

A knock came at the door and I turned my head slowly toward it.

I didn't really have to open it to know who would be standing on the other side. Sometimes, in life, you just *know*.

"Hi," I said softly as I opened the door. "Do you want to come in?"

The visitor didn't respond. The visitor didn't have to. I knew that he would have plenty to say when the door closed behind him. And I knew that I had a few things to confess, myself. So I held the door open wide and watched as Jamie slowly made his way back into my house.

35

gray skies ahead

There are some things in this world you can't read about in books. They won't teach you about them in school. Your parents won't even include them in one of their many speeches that are supposedly meant to prepare you for the real world.

You can't research them on the Internet. You can't interrogate them out of a close friend. And you certainly can't draw them out of a love song or a painting hanging in a museum.

And the reason you can't find these things through your normal sources of inspiration and enlightenment is because you don't know to look for them. Because you don't even know they exist until they walk through your door and sit down on your couch.

Jamie and I stared at each other for centuries. Our eyes spoke words to each other that our thirty-six years of combined education had never taught us how to say.

I didn't know who was supposed to speak first.

So I started. "It wasn't from the beginning," I said softly. It was the only thing I could say. The only thing I desperately wanted him to know. Because it was the truth. And I never expected the truth to be so *hard* to believe.

"I know," he replied. "Karen told me."

The sound of her name coming from his lips sent cold chills down my spine. I wanted to cover my ears with my hands and hum loudly until his lips had stopped moving.

"So it's true?" I asked, a part of me still wanting to believe that it was all just a big mistake. A terrifying nightmare. And that Jamie had arrived to wake me up and take me back to Paris.

He nodded solemnly. "But not in the way you think."

I looked at him, and without saying a word I offered him my undivided attention. I wanted to hear what he had to say. A few days ago I may not have been able to give him the same consideration. But now, after all that had happened, I was finally ready to hear it.

Jamie took a deep breath and launched into the story that I prayed would change my life. "We got married five years ago. It was good for the first three. Then things started to go downhill. We became distant from each other. We started to go to counseling, but it didn't seem to be working. I wanted to make things work. I thought that's what you were supposed to do. Fight for it. Sacrifice everything to save it. But I guess she didn't feel the same way, because about eight months ago she cheated on me with a guy from my work. And we separated shortly after.

"I filed for divorce, and it didn't take long for her lawyers to remind her that she would get nothing from me in the settlement except what the prenup had promised her. Which apparently wasn't enough, because she insisted her lawyers find a loophole."

"Infidelity," I said softly. Finishing the thought as if the answer had been inside me all along. The last puzzle piece, hiding behind the couch. Even though the picture had *looked* complete without it, it wasn't until you slid it into place that the entire image magically transformed before your very eyes.

"Exactly," Jamie said, bowing his head and rubbing his temples. "My lawyers made me aware of the loophole as well. Warned me not to engage in any sexual activity until the divorce was final. And it was supposed to be final months ago. But she kept dragging it out. Pushing back legal appointments, skipping settlement meetings. Anything to buy herself more time. I was sure the papers would have been signed before we went to Paris. But she pulled another one of her stunts at the last minute."

"And that's why you wouldn't have sex with me?"

"Believe me, it was the hardest thing I've ever had to do!"

I bit my lip and felt myself blush. "Really?"

"Look at you! You're irresistible! I thought about canceling the whole trip just so I wouldn't have to put myself through that kind of torture, but I wanted to go to Paris with you so badly that I thought it would be worth the sacrifice."

I giggled girlishly. "Thank you."

"I even thought about just forgetting all about her and making love to you, anyway. Let her have whatever she wanted. I didn't care, as long as I had you. But I knew I had come too far to give up at the last minute. And I knew that was exactly what she wanted me to do."

I nodded my understanding.

"And trust me," he continued, "I checked my messages *every* five minutes while we were there. Waiting for a call from my lawyers to tell me that they had the signed papers in hand so I could throw you down right then and there, in the middle of the French prison, and make love to you until those plastic guards threw us out."

I giggled again. "I wanted you, too. I wanted you so badly. I probably would have broken every rule in the book just to have been with you that night."

He smiled and reached out to touch my face. "God, I've missed you."

I lowered my head and fought back a small tear. "But why didn't you just tell me the truth from the beginning? So I wouldn't have had to find out that way."

Jamie gently touched my chin and lifted up my face. "Why didn't *you*?" he asked with a compassionate smile.

And there it was. The million-dollar answer to the million-dollar question. What constitutes cheating? The answer was, there is no *one* answer. There is no picture-perfect, clean, and simple solution wrapped up with a bow. There's only the answer that best fits the person asking the question. There's only the definition that makes someone feel loved, betrayed, guilty, innocent, deceitful, or deceived.

And Jamie and I had *both* felt every single one of them.

As hard as I'd tried to define it for the past two years, and probably even longer than that, the truth was infidelity *wasn't* black or white. It was a million shades of gray. And among those million varieties there was only one that filled the space between us now.

And, I had to admit, our particular shade of gray looked pretty good amid my world of white.

"I wanted to tell you," I insisted, begging him with my eyes to believe me. "I really did. But for so long you were the only thing in my life that didn't have anything to do with this tangled-up mess I had gotten myself into. I could think about you and it was like escaping from everything else. My blank page in a notebook full of illegible scribbles. I didn't want to bring you into that. I didn't want to taint that perfect feeling I had when I was with you. Plus, I was pretty sure if you knew, you'd leave anyway. So I had nothing to lose by keeping it a secret—and everything to gain."

He reached out to grab my hand, and he squeezed it in his own. "I wouldn't have."

"I was going to tell you in Paris. I swear. I had it all planned out. I had even decided to retire, and then . . ." I let my voice trail off, fairly confident that Jamie already knew the rest of that story.

He nodded. And then, after a moment of heavy silence, we both broke out into uncontrollable laughter. "How's that for crappy timing," he finally said, wiping his eyes.

"I know! Unbelievably crappy!"

"I can't even imagine what that must have been like for you when she hired you."

"She completely blindsided me!" I cried out. "I actually threw up!"

He laughed. "You threw up?"

"Twice! In *your* house!"

His hand slid down my arm and landed firmly on top of mine. "In my *ex*-house," he clarified.

"So . . ."

"It's over," he whispered. "Finally."

"Like really over?"

Jamie beamed. "She finally signed the papers this morning. Trust me, it's over."

I looked at him as a sly smile crept across my face. "So that means . . ."

He nodded slowly. "Yes, it does," he confirmed with a flirtatious grin.

The trail of clothes that led from our exact location on the couch in the living room all the way to my bedroom looked like a perverted reenactment of "Hansel and Gretel." Except with one important distinction:

The "bread crumb" pathway of my shirt, Jamie's belt, my bra, his jeans, my skirt, his polo, and so forth was not exactly left behind so we could find our way back. In fact, it was quite the opposite. We didn't want to go back to where we had come from. We only wanted to stay in the place that we were now. A place created by pure honesty, unconditional forgiveness . . . and truly mind-blowing sex.

Yes, it's true, I hadn't exactly *had* any sex in, well . . . let's just say, a very long time. But if memory served, I was quite certain that sex with Jamie was *amazing*.

"So," he said, rubbing my bare shoulder as I curled up close to his naked body.

"Yeah?" I asked, lifting my head up and staring adoringly into his eyes.

"Tell me. This *fidelity inspection* thing of yours. How does someone even get involved in something like that? It somehow doesn't strike me as something they offer in the career development office at college." He pulled his head up long enough to kiss me before plopping it back down on my white satin pillowcase.

I laughed and pressed myself closer to him. "Maybe we should save that story for another time."

He chuckled. "Always a mystery, Jennifer H. Always a mystery."

He kissed my forehead and squeezed me tighter as we drifted off to sleep.

My very first all-night slumber party.

36

woman full of wonder

I'm convinced that the concept of brunch was invented for three reasons: (1) to entertain in-laws; (2) for Saturday night club-goers who don't get up until one o'clock in the afternoon and still crave breakfast food to nurse their hang-overs; and (3) for meeting the future husband of your best friend who was supposed to have rejected you in a bar three weeks earlier.

As I walked into Chez Michel, a French/American fusion bistro in Bev-erly Hills, to meet Sophie and Eric for brunch, I could feel my heart start to pound.

This was either going to go *really* well . . . or *really* terribly. I had a feeling there was no in-between.

Sophie was either going to keep her mouth shut as we had agreed earlier or fish for small hints of details by saying things like, *"Hey, Eric. Does Jen look familiar to you at all? I think she has one of those faces."*

And then, of course, there was the possibility of total catastrophe. That I would show up, sit down across from them, and my radar would jump off the charts. My magic little men-reading device, which I had vowed to keep locked up in the closet for a long, long time to come, would start beeping fu-riously, alerting me to unmistakable cheating tendencies in the surrounding area. And the only man *in* the surrounding area would be Eric.

And *that* would not be good.

"Um, I think the reservation is under 'Sophie,'" I said to the hostess. She checked the book sprawled out in front of her. "Yes," she said with a charm-ing smile. "The rest of your party has already arrived. Right this way."

I followed her through the crowd of in-laws and recovering club-goers until I spotted Sophie sitting at a table against the far wall of the dining room with a tall, dark-haired man who I immediately recognized from the photograph Sophie had given me. The one I was *supposed* to use for Eric's inspection.

"Jen!" she said, scrambling over and giving me a hug. Then she turned eagerly behind her and said, "This is Eric. Eric, Jen." I reached out and shook his hand as I watched Sophie glance nervously back and forth between us, studying Eric's face for any flash of recognition.

And just as I had originally suspected, there was none.

"Nice to meet you . . . finally!" I said with an animated smile.

"Same here," he replied.

Satisfied with our initial encounter, Sophie sat back down at the table and gestured for me to take the seat across from them. "Isn't this fun?" she said, her face lit up like a halogen lightbulb. "My best friend and the love of my life meeting for the very *first* time." She tossed me a knowing look and winked playfully.

Eric and I both laughed at her endearing enthusiasm. "Yes, hon," he said, patting her leg affectionately. "It's nice to finally meet the famous Jennifer."

"You look better," Sophie pointed out.

I nodded, trying to keep the excitement from spreading over my face too fast.

Sophie was apparently oblivious to it, because she was too busy turning to Eric and explaining diligently, "Jen and her um . . . *boyfriend*. Or the guy she was dating, got into a fight a few days ago, and they broke up."

She then looked at me with sympathy, ready to receive my nod of approval at her flawless cover story, but instead she noticed something else. Sparkles dancing in my eyes. A glow radiating from my face. And she cocked her head to the side and asked, "Didn't you?"

"Well," I began, pulling my napkin onto my lap. "Actually . . ."

"Oh my God!" she nearly shouted. "You guys got back together, didn't you?"

I felt myself flush with exhilaration as my head fell into a humble nod. "Yes, we did. Last night."

Sophie clapped her hands ecstatically, as if she was a mother sitting in the front row at her child's first school play. "Oh my God. Tell me *everything*. What happened?"

I eyed her warningly. "It was just a misunderstanding."

She took the hint and nodded back at me. "Textbook case of Mars to Venus interplanetary communication failure," she confirmed, and then turned to Eric and kissed him on the cheek. "Well, no reason to bore *you* with all the juicy details, baby. Jen can fill me in later."

I smiled as I watched Eric turn to her, look adoringly into her eyes, and then kiss her on the lips. To my great satisfaction there were no bells going off. No warning lights. No radar beeps. He probably didn't have one unfaithful bone in his entire body.

But something inside of me refused to let it go. I no longer felt confident in my normal devices. Yes, I had essentially been right about Jamie all along. He wasn't the cheating type. But the whole experience had left me feeling unsure of myself. Uncertain of my abilities. Insecure, even.

And as I sat across from the loving couple, soon to be husband and wife, and listened to them take turns fondly rehashing the events of their very first wedding planning weekend, I knew I had to know for sure.

If there was even the slightest margin of error in my internal prediction software, it wouldn't be good enough for me.

Because seeing Sophie so happy, so in love, so hopeful for the future, I knew that "probably" wasn't going to cut it.

I needed a "definitely."

And for the first time, I also knew exactly how to get it.

October 31. Halloween. Time for goblins and ghouls and ghosts and monsters to come out of their dark hiding places into the open night air among the rest of us and beg for candy.

Hannah, having proclaimed this Halloween to be her very last one of trick-or-treating, had invited everyone to meet at my mom's house for her official "send-off."

Halloween was one of my favorite holidays. It always had been. And not just because it was a good excuse to eat bucket loads of candy without regret, but because I'd always loved the concept of dressing up. Pretending to be someone else, even for one night. Hell, I'd even managed to make a living out of it for a little while.

I pulled into the driveway at 1355 Mayfield Circle, my childhood home, and killed the engine. Before going inside I fished out my Treo and placed a very important phone call to someone who would hopefully prove to be a very important individual.

"Hello?" Lauren Ireland's voice came on the line.

"Lauren. Hi, it's . . . Ashlyn. What the hell, it's Jen. My real name is Jennifer. But most people call me Jen."

"Hi, Jen," she said respectfully.

"So, have you found your sanity and decided against becoming a fidelity inspector yet?"

She laughed. "No, not yet, unfortunately."

"Well, that's good to hear. Good for me, at least. Because I need your help."

"You do?"

"Yes. Truth of the matter is, I think I might have an assignment for you . . . should you choose to accept it."

"Definitely!" I could feel her excitement spilling through the phone. As if I had just told her I would be giving her the most rewarding, fulfilling, satisfying gift I could possibly give her.

But in all actuality, it was *she* who would be giving that gift to *me*.

"What's the assignment?" she asked eagerly.

I took a deep breath and started listing all the details I had once made a living collecting: occupation, hobbies, tastes, schools, fraternities, clubs, drinks of choice. But the first and foremost had always been a name. And today that name was "Eric."

"Can you guess who I am?" Hannah asked with excitement as soon as I walked in the front door. She leaped off the couch and came running over to greet me. I took a step back and examined her outfit carefully, taking in every stitch and every seam. She was wearing a short denim miniskirt, knee-high red boots, and an off-the-shoulder black sweater with a large red flower pinned to the front. Her curly blond hair was half up, secured by an entire box of bobby pins.

"Um . . ." I started to speculate. I knew from experience that incorrectly identifying a child's Halloween costume is about the worst insult you could possibly give them.

Thankfully, Hannah was too impatient to wait for my erroneous speculation. She leaned in close to me and whispered, "I'm Carrie from *Sex and the City*."

"Ah," I said, examining the outfit for the second time, with new eyes. "Very good."

She leaned in again. "Olivia is being Samantha. Rachel is being Charlotte, and our friend Michelle is being Miranda, 'cause she's the only one who has red hair."

"That sounds fun," I said.

"My mom doesn't know," she continued stealthily. "She thinks I'm dressed up as Hannah Montana." She rolled her eyes at me and let out a mocking giggle.

I stepped farther inside the house and briefly greeted my mom and Julia before plopping my stuff down on the dining room table and taking a seat on the couch. I was somewhat concerned that it might be awkward between me and my mom, given the way our last phone conversation had ended, but she seemed to be acting fairly normal.

"Wait!" Hannah shrieked just as my butt hit the sofa. "I have to show you something."

I reluctantly stood back up and followed her into the kitchen where, after checking that no one was behind me, she pulled out a folded-up piece of paper from the pocket of her denim skirt and handed it to me. "Here's that other letter I got," she whispered. "From that guy." She appeared very proud of her secret detective work, and I offered her a grateful smile.

But just as I was about to unfold the paper and take a look at whatever new situation Raymond Jacobs had managed to secretly photograph me in before my little surprise visit to his office, I suddenly realized that it really didn't matter. He was of zero importance to me now. So why give him the satisfaction of even looking?

So instead, I scrunched up the letter and tossed it into the garbage under the kitchen sink.

Hannah looked at me in astonishment, as if I had just destroyed the last piece of evidence that had any hope of convicting a known serial killer. "Why'd you do that?"

"Because it doesn't matter," I said matter-of-factly. "I've taken care of it."

"But who was that? And why'd he call you that other name?"

I'd spent the last three weeks trying to come up with a believable story to answer those very questions. One that would cover all my tracks and keep me safe from discovery, while at the same time protecting Hannah from the cold, hard truth that she wasn't ready to hear and the harsh, outside world that she wasn't ready to see.

But I suddenly realized that my essential problem didn't lie in coming up with a story that successfully answered all of her questions, but rather in the fact that a story like that didn't actually exist. Because it was based on a misconception, on a wrongful assumption that lies are better than cold, hard truths. When in all actuality they are just as destructive.

Unfortunately for Hannah, there *were* some things she was just too young to know. And if keeping them from her made me that much less "cool," then so be it.

I looked down at her with adoration and gently pushed a loose strand of hair out of her face. "I'll tell you when you're older. How about that?"

And then, just as I was expecting her to start grumbling and griping and tossing me disapproving looks that accused me of betraying her and turning into her mother, she shrugged her shoulders and wrote the whole thing off with a simple "Whatever." And then hurried back into the living room to start her night.

"You ready?" Julia asked, grabbing her keys and purse as Hannah and I reemerged from the kitchen.

"Mom," Hannah groaned, "for the last time, you *can't* come. We're all meeting at Rachel's house and then we're walking around *her* neighborhood."

"You know, Hannah," Julia began tactfully, "for someone who's nearly 'too old' for Halloween, you certainly are making a big deal about it."

Hannah turned to me and shot me a look. "She's driving me crazy," she said through gritted teeth.

I flashed her a warm smile and then leaned in and whispered, "Go easy on her. She cares a lot about you."

Hannah pulled her face into a frown and then reluctantly turned back to her mom. "Fine, you can *drive* me to Rachel's. But that's it."

Julia cracked a smile and shook her head as she started toward the front door. "All right. C'mon, Hannah Montana. Let's go."

The door closed behind them and my mom and I stood awkwardly together in the living room. I walked over to the couch, took a seat, and then began rummaging through the large candy bowl until I located a Butterfinger and snatched it up.

I sat in silence, avoiding her eyes; the only noise in the room was the crinkling of the plastic candy bar wrapper as I removed it and bit into the chocolate.

I chewed nervously as I glanced around the living room, the very place I'd witnessed my dad's infamous act of infidelity. Before I even knew what infidelity was. Before I even understood what it meant.

The couch was, thankfully, a new couch. My mom had replaced it years ago. The curtains had been selected to match it. The coffee table was purchased a few years after that. Even the carpet was new. But the guilt? The guilt was the same as it always was.

And despite the new decorations, new color scheme, new furnishings, the guilt still seemed to match everything.

"I'm sorry if I upset you on the phone, Jenny," my mom said, walking over and taking a seat next to me. She pulled a Milky Way bar from the bowl and unwrapped it.

"You didn't," I began softly. "I mean . . . you did, but it's not your fault. You were right. I need to learn how to forgive him. I just don't know how."

My mom reached out and tenderly stroked my hair. I fell into her, the tears slowly starting to make their way down my face as she held me close to her and kissed the top of my head.

Little did she know there was a lifetime of secrets trying to push their way out of my mouth. Secrets that could have changed everything. Secrets that might have given her happiness instead of stealing it away.

But just as I'd always done, I would keep them inside. Maybe for another few days. Maybe forever.

She rubbed the top of my head and cooed into my ear. "Shhh. It's okay. It's all right, sweetie."

"I'm sorry. I'm so sorry," I whimpered into her chest.

She laughed lovingly. "You have nothing to be sorry about."

I wanted to lift my head and cry out, "But I do! I have everything in the world to be sorry about! I ruined your life! Please just let me be sorry for it!"

But instead I simply laid in her arms and wiped the tears away from my cheeks.

"People are people," my mom said softly. "People make mistakes. In fact, life wouldn't be life without them. Your father made a mistake. And true, I would never be his wife again. I could never love him the way I used to love him. And I don't regret leaving. But leaving isn't what allows you to move on. Forgiving is."

I pulled my head up and looked at her. She smiled at me and reached out to wipe a patch of dampness from my cheek. I wasn't sure where all her strength was coming from. It didn't even sound like my mom. It sounded more like some spiritual Zen expert, leading a room full of lost souls seeking guidance and salvation. Not the wounded, brokenhearted victim I had comforted and nursed back to stability so many times in the past two years.

And now she was telling *me* to forgive? But it seemed so impossible. How can you forgive something that kept you chained to a life you didn't choose for so long?

You can't just flip a switch and absolve that kind of thing.

Can you?

"I can't," I said softly. "I can't let go of it. I can't forget what happened. And everything that became of it."

"Of course you can," my mom soothed. "If I can, you can."

I shook my head and felt the tidal waves of impossibility start to crash over me. I was overwhelmed by their salty taste and frightened by their threatening determination to knock me over. "I can't forgive something I've spent my whole life trying to make up for," I said softly to myself. But she heard it, anyway. I kind of hoped she would. And I kind of hoped she would tell me what to do.

And she did.

"But you have to if you want to find true happiness," she stated simply. As if it were the only truth in the world. And everything else around it was just there to purposefully cloud your vision. Distract you from it. Steal away your attention and refocus it on far more destructive thoughts. "You have to let go of your anger and resentment. You have to learn how to release it. Because if you continue to hold on to it, it will eat away at you until there's nothing left."

My mom may still have been referring to my father, but I knew there was someone else I had been struggling to make amends with—for years. And it would be far more difficult to do.

The doorbell rang and I jerked upright, snapping myself back into reality. Halloween, doorbell, trick-or-treaters, candy. I sniffled and wiped my nose with the back of my hand, chuckling slightly at my state of disarray.

"I'll get it," my mom said gently, placing her hand on top of mine and then reaching for the candy bowl.

"No," I insisted, standing up and taking it from her hands. "I want to do it."

I straightened my clothes and smoothed my hair back into my ponytail as I walked the ten paces to the front door, the door that once had offered me a daily escape from a prison I thought would never fully release me.

Telling my mother all the countless secrets of my past wasn't going to solve a thing. It would only generate more pain. And forgiving my father for creating those secrets in the first place might have allowed me to walk away and move forward, but it was a forgiveness much more profound, much harder to obtain, and much closer than I ever imagined that would eventually set me free.

I opened the front door to a group of three little girls. All roughly around the age of seven or eight. I smiled brightly, the mouthwatering bowl of chocolate sitting in my arms.

"Trick-or-treat!" the three of them recited in unison.

"Don't you all look great!" I exclaimed as I dropped a variety of chocolate pieces into their awaiting bags. "What are you dressed up as?"

The first little girl, wearing a gold, winged helmet on her head and a white-and-gold fitted dress on her body, proudly pointed to her cape and said, "I'm She-Ra, Princess of Power." And then motioned to her less articulate neighbor, who wore a gold headband and a red-and-blue leotard, and said, "She's Wonder Woman. Sometimes people get us confused. But we're totally different."

"I know," I said seriously.

"Wonder Woman can fly but She-Ra has superhuman strength," she continued knowledgeably.

"Really? I didn't even know that." I turned to the third girl, dressed adorably in a red tank top, red pleather pants, and a red handkerchief around her head. "And who are you?"

She smiled timidly and rocked back and forth on her heels. "I'm Electra."

"Cool!" I marveled. "What kind of special powers does Electra have?" I asked with extreme curiosity.

"Electra's a ninja assashin," She-Ra chimed in smartly. "She can move real fast and she's super flexible. I think she does yoga," she mused.

I stifled a small giggle. "Well, you guys look amazing!"

"Thanks!" chimed Electra, Wonder Woman, and the Princess of Power as they spun on their glitter-covered heels and took off for the next house.

I closed the door with a contented smile and leaned back against it. My mom had disappeared into the kitchen and I was left alone with my thoughts.

But interestingly enough, this time I only had one.

One that would probably shape the *next* two years of my life.

The world just doesn't have enough female superheroes.

epilogue

Six months later . . .

I pull up in front of a tall, thirty-story building in Santa Monica. As I step out of the car, I'm careful to smooth the front side of my Gucci suit. These days, it's all about appearances. Especially when you have a room full of people who look to you for direction and guidance. Wrinkles just won't do.

I hand the keys of my new Lexus hybrid SUV to the man in the valet uniform who greets me with a friendly smile.

This is the same man I see every day. Sometimes, if I have to come here on a Sunday, his weekend replacement completes the other half of the familiar exchange.

"Good morning, Pedro," I say warmly.

He takes the keys and disappears with the car into an underground parking structure reserved for tenants of 100 Ocean Avenue.

I walk briskly through the lobby of the building and into an awaiting elevator. In the past six months I've learned the difference between "walking briskly" and "rushing." Rushing is for amateurs. Brisk walking is for professionals. And as appearances go, it looks much more controlled.

I press the button that promises to drop me on the fifteenth floor, and I wait patiently for it to do so.

The elevator doors ding open, and I veer left down a long corridor and through a set of glass doors that lead into the office at the end of the hallway. The one with the best view of the ocean . . . naturally.

Why rent an office space in a building on Ocean Avenue if you can't have a view of the ocean?

Inside the glass doors sits a plump but attractive middle-aged woman whose workspace is appropriately situated directly under a large, silver-plated sign that reads "The Hawthorne Agency."

"Good morning, Ashlyn," the assistant greets me in her usual pleasant tone. Although she is actually Hispanic in race, her voice bears not even the slightest trace of an accent. Her English, as well as her Spanish, is flawless. And as I am clearly in the business of client relations, she is integral to the daily operation of this company.

"Good morning, Marta," I return, an equally pleasant salutation.

"Everyone is already inside the conference room," Marta informs me.

I shoot a short glance in the direction of the first door on the left and nod. I'm rarely what most would call on time to these meetings. But my timing is always intentional. Arriving just the slightest bit after the rest of the attendants gives off a certain air of importance.

Although I would never make them wait more than five minutes. After that it's no longer about appearances; it's just plain inconsiderate. And the people in that room are far too valuable to disrespect in any way.

"Thank you. You can tell them I'll be in shortly. Any messages?"

This is Marta's cue to rise to her feet, and she follows me as I glide down the office hallway to the last door on the right. My home away from home.

"Yes," Marta begins, handing me corresponding slips of yellow memo paper as she concisely verbalizes their content. "Your father called. He wants to know if it's all right to move your lunch from two o'clock to one-thirty because he has a conference call at three."

I smile to myself. The last six months certainly haven't been easy in respect to mending the severed relationship with my dad. Four years of silence doesn't automatically fix itself with one honesty-filled phone call. But the fact that we've agreed to get together at least twice a month regardless of our mutually busy schedules has helped things progress tremendously.

"Tell him that's fine," I reply to Marta with an authoritative nod. "But if he makes reservations at Valentino again, can you *please* ask him *not* to wear those dirty sneakers this time."

Marta releases a polite chuckle as she scribbles in her notebook, then returns her attention to the stack of yellow slips in her hand. She picks up the next one. "Zoë called. She said that she wanted to remind you to"—Marta cringes as she carefully reads word for word from the small piece of paper—"get a fucking brain or get your lame ass off the road."

I smile and nod. "Sounds about right."

"And Sophie called. She said to say, 'I'm having a breakdown. Eric's mother is insisting we have the wedding in Chicago because all of his relatives are there, but my parents are refusing to pay for it if we do. Help!' "

I laugh and reach out to take the message, taking the burden from the woman's shoulders. "I'll call her," I offer with an incredulous shake of my head.

I should have guessed that wiping out all of Sophie's doubt about the groom himself would only allow her to focus her obsessive behavior on new areas of relevant concern.

Marta and I arrive at the end of the hallway and I push open the door in front of me. I step inside the large corner office that I've chosen to decorate in white and soft grays, and take a seat behind the L-shaped glass desk. "Any others?"

Unlike the previous messages that Marta had simply breezed through without any trace of attachment and/or recognition, she takes particular care in relaying the next one in the stack. "Jamie called . . ." She allows her clear, accent-free voice to trail off and waits for the reaction she has come to anticipate every single morning when there is a message of this particular nature.

My eyes immediately light up and a smile flashes across my face. "What did he say?"

Marta, having now received the emotional response she was waiting for, continues with the message. "He said he left his black jacket at your house last night and wonders if you can bring it to dinner."

I allow the idyllic smile to linger on my face for just a mere moment longer before I return to my usual level of office professionalism. "Thank you, Marta. I'll return his call after the meeting."

Marta nods her head and begins to exit the office. "Oh," she says, turning back sharply. "And your friend John called . . . again."

I nod knowingly and ask, "About the same thing?"

"Yes. He wants to know if maybe *next* week there would be a good day for him to sit in on one of the staff meetings."

I roll my eyes with just the slightest trace of amusement and reply, "Please tell him I'm still considering it."

"Of course," says Marta as she backs out the door and shuts it behind her.

One would think that being the owner of a successful, thriving business, the first thing a woman in my shoes (and my size office) would do in the morning would be to sit down at my computer and sort through my in-box of e-mails.

I, however, don't have time for e-mails at the moment, for I have a conference room full of people waiting for me.

Nevertheless, I *always* manage to find time to squeeze in the most important step in my morning routine.

And that is exactly what I am in the process of doing at this very moment as I wait patiently for my laptop to boot up. I then navigate my mouse to the small icon in the corner of the screen that bears the Internet Explorer logo.

A browser window springs to life, and thanks to the high-speed wireless Internet installed throughout the office, I am instantly greeted by my home page, which I bypass by typing a very important Web address into the bar at the top of the window.

The fluency in my series of movements would certainly suggest that this is not a routine I do monthly or even weekly. This is a routine that I do *every* morning, as diligently as a stockbroker checks the opening NASDAQ price, a politician checks the morning polls, or a TV executive checks the latest Nielsen ratings.

The address that I type might, to anyone else, seem strange, odd, and bearing no relation to any aspect of my current day-to-day business. But then again, I know something they do not.

When I finish typing, the combination of letters on the screen spells out the following: www.dontfallforthetrap.com.

Upon pressing *Enter* and eventually receiving the same comforting page that appeared yesterday and the day before that, and the day before that, I smile with satisfaction, close the application, and begin to gather up the things I will need for the ten A.M. meeting that I am now exactly five minutes late for.

Right on schedule.

Each and every morning I marvel at how a simple line of text reading "Error 400: Web site not available. Bad Request" could so effortlessly put me at ease. And yet every morning I still crave that same reassurance, and still manage to chuckle quietly to myself upon reading the words "Bad Request."

After pulling a stack of glossy, crimson-colored folders from my briefcase and grabbing a yellow legal pad from my desk, I exit through the door from which I entered and make my way back down the long corridor, stopping in front of the awaiting conference room door.

Just before entering I reach up and delicately touch the silver Tiffany chain necklace with a rose pendant hanging from my neck. For some reason it seems to bring me more luck with every passing day. As soon as I enter, conversations around the room come to a halt. I can feel all eyes on me, and I smile politely and make my way to my regular seat at the head of the table.

"Sorry I'm late, everyone. I'll try to make this short."

In this conference room sits my five regular associates. Five vastly different individuals who I have come to trust wholeheartedly. These are the five people now responsible for carrying out my life's work.

Having always had a particular ability to analyze a situation and immediately decide how it should be best handled, I have brought together these unique personalities to form a very special and very talented team of experts.

Sitting to my immediate left is a young blond woman with soft, feminine features, a voluptuous figure, and a classic beauty that would turn the head of any *Playboy* magazine subscriber. And not coincidentally, those are exactly the kinds of heads she was brought in to turn.

The woman sitting next to her is also extraordinarily beautiful but in her own unique and self-defining way. She is petite and quirky, with a personality that is almost as captivating as her smile. Given that her genuine interests include football, poker, pool, Quentin Tarantino movies, and greasy fast food, this particular associate finds herself in many work-related situations where her non-work-related interests happen to come in handy.

The man directly across from me at the far end of the conference table looks remarkably like someone you'd find on the Abercrombie and Fitch shopping bag that holds your most recent in-store purchase. At six-foot-one and two hundred pounds, his purpose in this office varies with each given assignment, but more often than not requires the sporting of some type of uniform . . . military or otherwise.

Directly to his left sits a tall and strikingly exquisite Asian woman whose stone-cold exterior is nothing short of impenetrable. Not surprisingly, it is that very same enchanting indifference that helplessly seduces the people chosen to make her acquaintance.

And finally, to my right is an elegant and breathtakingly sexy young brunette who, with the just the right wardrobe selection, can effortlessly catch the eye of almost any man in any room. Although little of her free time is spent researching these wardrobe selections and more of it is spent rewiring portable computers and various electronic devices like the one she holds in her hand right now. She and I both know, however, that it is *this* specific skill, and not her fashion sense, that is most applicable to the conversations she has on a weekly basis.

And although every single one of my associates is important to this organization, the woman on my right is the only one in the room with whom I share a more personal connection.

Because not only did she have a direct influence on my decision to start this organization in the first place, she also conducted a very personal favor on my behalf.

Six months ago this woman walked into a crowded Chicago bar full of drunk male doctors celebrating their last day of a three-year residency and struck up a conversation with one of particular interest. After a short exchange, however, and to the blatant disapproval of his drinking companions, the man kindly excused himself from the conversation, stating that he was, in fact, engaged to someone else.

In other words, this woman is the reason my best friend is getting married to a doctor named Eric in six months.

And for that she will always be more than just an employee.

As I sit down in my chair, she takes the small silver-and-black device in her hands and slides it over to me. "I configured your new iPhone. You shouldn't have any problem accessing your e-mail. If you want me to show you how to use it later, I will."

I thank her, taking special care to address her by her code name, as no one uses their real name while in this room or while working in association with this room.

Lauren Ireland selected her own alias upon joining my staff, as did everyone else.

I open the glossy crimson folders in front of me, one by one, and begin to review their contents: an overly flirtatious real-estate agent in San Diego; a bored housewife in Dallas; a suspicious bachelor party celebration in Las Vegas. And countless more arriving every week. Almost too many to accommodate.

While unique in their origins, each of these folders contains a very familiar request for something universally acknowledged to be invaluable: the truth.

I distribute each of these fidelity files to the staff member most capable of handling the request inside.

Although I have experienced several changes in my life over the past six months, the most significant change came in the form of a discovery. A realization. That peace of mind can come in many forms. And more important, with the help of many different people.

And so now, with my conference room full of willing and capable associates, each in possession of at least one unique and distinguishing "power," one highly classified, secret identity, and a closet full of appropriate costume selections, I have finally discovered what it takes to change the world—without ever having to *personally* step foot in another strange hotel room.

Well . . . almost never.

acknowledgments

Last night while I was watching the Academy Awards and listening to all the Gucci- and Versace-clad winners thank their moms, dads, spouses, agents, makeup artists, and one-eyed cats, I was suddenly reminded (because of all the gratitude expressed, not because I also have a one-eyed cat) that I hadn't yet written the acknowledgments page for *The Fidelity Files*.

And yes, writing a novel is not exactly the same thing as winning an Academy Award. For one, I don't own a dress that wasn't made by H&M. And Ryan Seacrest has yet to show any interest in interviewing me. But as you'll see from the next few pages, there are still just as many people to thank. The only difference is I get to do it in my pajamas without the threat of the annoying music that plays when my time is up. Of course, you can always just close the book to shut me up, but that's a risk I'm willing to take. And since this is my first book, I pretty much have to thank everyone I know, because, honestly, there's a good chance that the people I leave out this time won't go out and buy the second book.

So this is the moment when those of you who don't know me and, frankly, don't care who I express my gratitude to can respectfully bow out, turn the page, and continue on with your lives.

First and foremost, I want to thank Laura and Michael Brody. My inspirations, my living heroes, my biggest supporters . . . oh, and they're also my parents. Without whom I wouldn't be here today . . . literally.

Thank you, Mom, for raising me with that "Free to Be You and Me" mentality and for letting me pour the milk into my cereal *all by myself*. I think we both know that little ounce of freedom is eventually what gave me the courage to become a writer.

And thank you, Dad, for bestowing upon me the "writer's bug" and for being my very first editor, for reading and rereading every single three-hundred-page draft (and we both know there were quite a few). I know how tired of this story you must be by now, and for that reason, I'm not going to let you read this page until the book comes out. How excited you'll be to have something new to read! The only downside is I won't be able to incorporate any of your one-liners.

Thanks to my very fashionable little sister, Terra, for being the official "fashion consultant" for the book. My main character's image would have suffered tremendously had you not stepped in and rescued it with your designer know-how.

Thank you to Charlie, my amazing boyfriend/domestic partner/best friend/soul mate. I am the balloon and you are the rock that I'm tied to. And I love you for that . . . more than you know.

To Walter Brody, for passing on your talented genes and for being the first person worthy of the title "the smartest man in the world." And to Roslyn Brody: I wish you were here to see me get published. But I already know exactly what you'd say: "Oy veh, I hope they're paying you good money!" Don't worry, Grandma, I paid off all my debt (almost).

To Steve and Cathy Brody for allowing me to follow in your published footsteps.

Thank you to my brilliant and supportive agent, Beth Fisher at Levine Greenberg, for believing in this concept from so early on and for being so patient with my endless influx of questions about the publishing process. And to Monika Verma, Stephanie Kip Rostan, and everyone who sits in those mysterious editorial meetings of yours.

Thank you to my wonderfully talented editors, Jennifer Weis and Hilary Rubin, for understanding Jennifer/Ashlyn's plight and for helping me make her story as strong as it could be. And thank you, Hilary, for saving this book with the perfect title!

To Anne Marie Tallberg, Ellis Trevor, John Karl, and all the marketing and publicity staff at St. Martin's for listening to all my ideas and not laughing at any of them (at least not to my face). Thanks to my elusive copy editor (you know who you are, even if I don't), who made me aware of my over-hyphenating-problem. Don't-worry-I-am-seeking-help. And to all the other amazing people at St. Martin's who helped take what used to be a four-hundred-page Word document and turn it into something you can actually pick up off the shelf.

Jerry Brunskill, you believed in this concept from the moment it came out of my mouth, and I am forever indebted to you for your support and encouragement. Thanks for your hours upon hours of work on the trailer. I owe you a really big and complicated spreadsheet! God loves spreadsheets.

Thanks to Megan Beatie, Kathleen Carter, and everyone at Goldberg McDuffie for all of your brilliant ideas, enthusiasm, and publicity know-how.

To all of my wonderful friends: Ella, for reading everything I ever wrote . . . and inspiring Zoë's road rage. Brad Gottfred, for being my producing soul mate. Katherine Carlson, my spiritual mentor and "Secret" adviser. Leslie, my "oldest" friend and the chick-lit queen! Shalini, for inspiring "Island Therapy" (even though it never made it into the final draft, I still think we're pretty hilarious). Allison, Kristin, and Alicia for being my very first target-demographic audience. Tina, for being my "marketing manager." Holly, for being the Internet "face" of Ashyln. Lindsay Wray, for giving voice to the hotline. Hilary and Jen, my New York and L.A. Bells. Megan, my fellow "Girl at Play." Angie, for your genuine excitement about everything I do. And Blair, for never getting annoyed by my continual annoyance and for being my inspiration for inner peace . . . . and a 99.99 percent alkaline diet.

Thanks to George, Vicki, and Jennifer, my Texas family. And Bob and Kitty for proving that target demographics were made to be broken.

To Sylvia Peck, my very first agent. Juliet will always be yours.

Brian Braff, thanks for the beautiful author photo and for keeping me humble with your transcriptions.

Thanks to all the talented actors who graced the scenes of the trailer with your beautiful faces (and feet): Deprise Brescia, Holly Karrol Clark, Katharine Horsman, Katie Hein, Chad Chiniquy, Elizabeth Weisbaum, Jeremy Pack, Kip Tribble, Sherry Zerwin, Keith Burke, Jason Rosell, Tye Nelson, Amy Warren, Lois Larimore, Nicholas Hosking, Rick Lundgren, Fabienne Mauer, and Cameron Daddo. And all the crew who dedicated their time and creativity to producing it: Ryan Rees (sound) Adam O'Connor (cinematography), Karen Stein (makeup), Chahn Chung (graphic design).

And last but not least, thanks to you, the person holding this book. I am so incredibly grateful. A writer without a reader is just a crazy person with a pen. And if you lasted through this entire acknowledgments section, you definitely deserve to be thanked.